D0098754

Ester's Child

A Novel
by
Jean Sasson

Windsor-Brooke Books

Also by Jean Sasson

The Rape of Kuwait

Princess: A True Story of Life Behind The Veil in Saudi Arabia

Princess Sultana's Daughters

Princess Sultana's Circle

Praise for Jean Sasson's books

"Absolutely riveting and profoundly sad..."
People

"Another page turner..."
Publisher's Weekly

"Consistently gripping...A fast-paced, enthralling drama, rich in detail..."
Salt Lake City Tribune

"One is compelled to read just one more page, one more chapter..."
Oxford Review

"Unforgetable in content, fascinating in detail...a book to move you to tears."
Fay Weldon

"Must reading..."
USA Today

"A chilling story..."
Entertainment Weekly

Windsor-Brooke Books
For Publisher contact information log on to:
Web site: www.Windsor-Brooke.com

SECOND EDITION

Library of Congress Cataloging-in-Publication Data

Sasson, Jean P.
Ester's Child : a novel / by Jean Sasson.
p. cm.
ISBN 0-9676737-3-9 (alk. paper)
1. Shåtålå (Lebanon : Refugee camp)–Fiction. 2. Palestinian Arabs–Lebanon–Fiction. 3. Holocaust survivors–Fiction. 4. Children of Nazis–Fiction. 5. Jews–Poland–Fiction. 6. Refugees–Fiction. 7. Lebanon–Fiction. 8. Israel–Fiction. 9. Poland–Fiction. I. Title.

PS3619.A27 E8 2001

2001017775

Cover Design by Lightbourne
Front Cover Painting by Robert Hunt
Interior Design by Rosamond Grupp
Interior Art Sketches by Janice Phelps

10 9 8 7 6 5 4 3 2

Published simultaneously in Canada by Windsor-Brooke Books

PRINTED IN THE UNITED STATES OF AMERICA

NOTE FROM THE PUBLISHER AND THE AUTHOR

Ester's Child is a work of historical fiction.
While the historical facts are accurate, the names
and characters, other than public figures, and
personal incidents are either the product of
the author's imagination or are used fictitiously.
Any resemblance to actual persons, living or dead, personal
events or business establishments is entirely coincidental.

Contact us at www.windsor-brooke.com

TO THE MANY READERS WHO HAVE WRITTEN
TO ME OVER THE YEARS:

Your thoughtful letters filled me with determination
to continue writing, despite many personal
and professional "bumps in the road."

I welcome your comments and can be contacted
through my Web site at www.jeansasson.com.

Jean Sasson

To Mike, the perfect friend...

"And in the sweetness of friendship let there be laughter,
and sharing of pleasures...
And let there be no purpose in friendship
Save the deepening of the spirit..."

Kahlil Gibran

In celebration of friendship, I dedicate this book
to my dear friend,
Michael B. Schnapp, D.O.

Jean Sasson

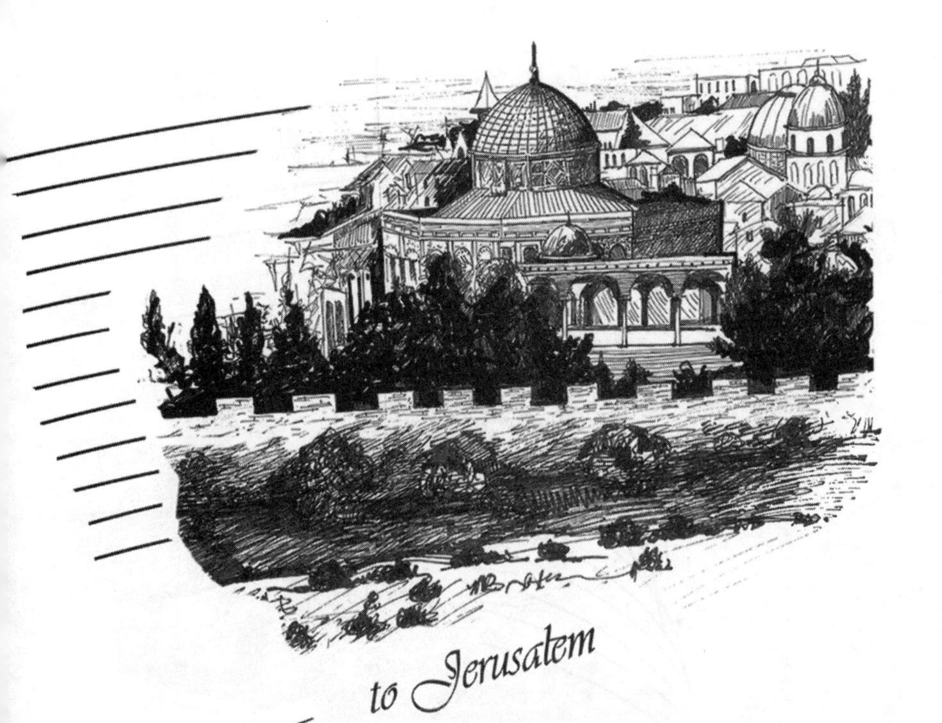

to Jerusalem

Ester's Child

Ester's Child

Prologue

On November 29, 1947, the future of 1.3 million Arabs and 700,000 Jews living in Palestine rested with the decision of fifty-six delegates of the General Assembly of the United Nations. Jewish celebration and Arab mourning commenced at the moment those delegates cast their votes in favor of partitioning the ancient land, thereby fulfilling the two-thousand-year-old Jewish dream of returning to their historic home.

From that day, Jerusalem became a war zone.

Jerusalem: Wednesday, January 7, 1948

Moving swiftly from side to side to avoid sniper fire, a tense Joseph Gale quickly approached the front door of his unpretentious block home. Once inside, he continued his fast pace, giving an alert glance at his sleeping son before rushing through the sitting room and into the cramped hallway that had been turned into a delivery room.

Ester Gale didn't notice her husband's return. She was rolling back and forth on the thin mattress, holding a damp cloth to her chest, making small, animal-like noises that broke the stillness of the room.

Joseph's sister, Rachel, and Anna Taylor, an American woman who had befriended the Gales upon their arrival in Palestine, were at Ester's side.

Joseph glanced at his sister and noticed that her eyes were fixed with a hopeful stare on the open doorway. Joseph shook his head and held out his arms in a gesture of defeat. He whispered, "I could find no one. Not even a nurse."

Rachel took a deep breath. She was relieved at Joseph's safe return, but dismayed that he had been unable to locate a physician. Rachel exchanged looks of apprehension with Anna before murmuring, "Well, we will do the best we can."

"Birthing is a natural act," Anna responded. "Ester will have a healthy baby."

Trying to hide her anxiety, Rachel agreed. "While being held at Drancy," she whispered, "I once assisted a woman in childbirth." Located on the outskirts of Paris, Drancy had been the most notorious of the holding camps for French Jews awaiting transport to the Auschwitz Death Camp in Poland. Remembering that terrible time, Rachel gazed into the distance, purposely not mentioning that the woman had died during childbirth.

Ester began to chew on the cloth, and the color of her face paled.

Rachel's thin lips grew thinner still as she spoke out of the side of her mouth, "Joseph, the time is near."

Joseph felt his stomach tighten as an inner voice whispered to him that their survival had been useless if he lost Ester. He bent over his wife's small form, brushing her cheek with his lips, and telling her, "Hold on, darling. Soon this will pass."

Ester grunted her disbelief, and spoke with a croaking sound, a hoarseness that hid the usual softness of her voice, "Never. *Never.* Joseph, this pain has become a part of me." She shuddered in agony.

Tears filled Joseph's eyes.

Anna rose and began to rub Ester's shoulders, motioning with her head for Joseph to leave. She reminded him, "The water. Can you boil the water, now?"

"Yes, of course." Joseph gave Ester a kiss before leaving the room. Passing through the narrow sitting room, he took time to cover Michel with a second blanket before going into the kitchen.

Using the last of the precious kerosene, Joseph heated a small amount of water over a small burner. Not only were the citizens of war-torn Jerusalem short on food, but water supplies were at a critical low point.

Joseph visibly flinched when he heard the sounds of Ester's muffled screams. He began to pray aloud for the safety of his wife. "Hear my prayer, Oh God. Keep her from harm." He closed his eyes and rubbed his forehead with his fingers. "Ester's life is all I am asking for." Hesitating with emotion, he whispered, "You decide upon the child."

Michel Gale awoke from his nap and began crying and calling for his mother.

Joseph held his precious child in his arms and offered to play a game, but nothing he could say or do comforted the boy. Just as Joseph was thinking the situation could not possibly worsen, Ari Jawor knocked determinedly at the front door, bringing Joseph unwelcome news.

Ari Jawor was Joseph's closest friend, and a member of the Haganah, the Jewish Defense Force. Ari was a squat, broad-shouldered man with a hard-exterior, soft-interior kind of character. And he tended to be overly dramatic. Today he was speaking even louder than usual. Without taking time to greet his friend, Ari filled the house with his unmistakable passion, "Joseph, they did it again!" He slapped his open palm against the wall. "The old man is furious!"

Joseph quickly locked the door before turning his attention to Ari. He wasn't sure who "they" were, but he knew that the "old man," as he was affectionately called, was David Ben-Gurion, the leader of the Jews in Palestine, and the man who would surely become the first Premier of their new country.

Joseph stared at Ari and almost laughed aloud, thinking that with his nervous eyes, grimy face, ill-fitting clothes, and thick red hair standing straight and stiff from dirt, Ari resembled a demon. And, his unexpected visit clearly meant bad news. Joseph tried to keep the alarm out of his voice, "Ari, what has happened?"

Ari curled his hands into fists and looked as if he wanted to strike out. His face, already red from the cold, grew redder still. "There's been a massive bombing at the bus station at Jaffa Gate. Just a short while ago. Only God knows how many are dead and injured." After a moment's hesitation Ari added, "I was told the street looked like a slaughterhouse."

The Jaffa Gate area was the main commercial artery of Jerusalem and was usually crowded with shoppers.

Joseph answered softly, "God...how easy it is to be alive one moment and dead the next." Since leaving Europe and coming to Palestine, Joseph had often thought the old hatreds that had percolated on the land promised the Jews by God now threatened every living soul, Arab and Jew.

Ari leaned his M-1 rifle against the wall. "Our sources tell us the Irgun gang was responsible. They managed to steal a police van. Then, those bastards rolled two barrels of TNT onto a crowded Arab street. Women…children…all turned into shredded meat."

Joseph spoke in a low voice and did not look into Ari's eyes. "Dear God." He then asked, "Did they capture the men?"

Ari nodded, "After throwing a second bomb at the intersection of Mamillah Road and Princess Mary Avenue, members of the gang crashed the van and tried to escape on foot through the cemetery. The British police and an American Consulate Guard followed the men, killing three of the gang."

The Irgun gang was an illegal military group, led by Menachem Begin, a man whose unassuming appearance gave no indication of his murderous anger. His followers consisted of hardened Holocaust survivors willing to kill anyone trying to block the creation of a Jewish homeland. These men believed their miraculous return to the Promised Land was a sign of God's devotion to their cause, and they justified every terrorist action with a biblical verse. The Irgun gang violently disagreed with the idea of compromise with the British, Americans or the Arabs, and their reckless acts had caused David Ben-Gurion many sleepless nights.

Joseph suddenly remembered. "The water!" He rushed into the kitchen.

Ari gave him an uncomprehending look but followed.

Taking little notice of the two men, Michel Gale sat silently on the floor, playing with a small metal soldier.

"Michel, Ari is here."

Michel pursued his lips but he didn't look up. He only wanted his mother. No one else would do.

Joseph stuck his finger into the water. "Almost."

Ari helped himself to a small amount of the precious water, savoring the drink with a loud swallow.

The two men were silent for a minute but they were thinking the same thing: Arab retaliation was sure to come, and the Musrara area where the Gale family lived was particularly vulnerable to Arab snipers. The neighborhood was adjacent to the old city of Jerusalem and sat squarely between the Eastern-Arab-side and the Western-Jewish-side of the city. And while their street was solely occupied by Jews, only one block away the street was occupied by Arabs. The few Arab snipers presently in the area had done little more than to irritate and isolate their Jewish neighbors, but the sniping had escalated into full-blown fighting in the Sheikh Jarrah quarter, which was only a short distance from Musrara.

The thought of an even greater threat caused Ari to make a motion with his hand toward Michel and announce, "You have to think about the child, Joseph. Pack a few things. I'll try to get a truck and get you out of here."

Joseph slowly shook his head, "No. It's impossible."

Ari's eyes were inquisitive, and when he opened his mouth to protest, Joseph explained, "Ester's been in labor for the past six hours."

"Well, then, that paints a different picture." Ari pulled on his thin mustache, thinking of their options. "If you can't leave," he said finally, "then we'll have to bring a few men into the area to protect you."

Fully understanding the grave shortage of Jewish fighters, Joseph protested, "I can take care of myself."

Ari gave a wide grin, "I don't doubt that." In battle, no soldier was fiercer than Joseph Gale. He slapped his friend on the arm, "There are other Jews in the area to worry about besides the Gales."

Joseph looked thoughtful for a moment, then brightened, changing the subject, "How is Leah?

Leah Rosner was Ari's new bride, and like Ari, she was serving full time in the Haganah. While the Arabs Leah fought called her a fair-haired devil, her Jewish comrades considered her to be an extraordinary soldier.

In her presence, Leah's restless green eyes never revealed the tragedies that had marred her life. She was the sole survivor of a large Czechoslovakian-Jewish family. As the end of World War II drew near,

German soldiers marched six-thousand prisoners out of the Auschwitz Death Camp and away from Russian liberators. The retreating Gestapo had shot the prisoners unable to keep pace. After Ari's father was executed, and Leah's last remaining sister died from starvation, Ari and Leah drew strength from each other. Surviving against all odds, they had become inseparable, and had recently married.

Ari smiled with pleasure and his voice rang with pride, "Leah is wonderful, Joseph. I'm the luckiest man alive!"

Michel began to whine, and as quickly as he arrived, Ari left, leaving Joseph with something new to fret about—Arab revenge for the Irgun's vicious attack.

The hall door creaked opened and Rachel's shoes made a clicking noise as she walked across the tiled floor into the kitchen. She had failed to close the door and Ester's stifled cries escaped from the hallway.

Terribly frightened, Michel began to cry once again. Something awful was happening to his mother. He didn't bother to wipe the mucus running from his nose onto his lip, but instead used the tip of his tongue to lick his upper lip, swallowing the salty liquid.

When Rachel entered the kitchen, Michel grabbed the bottom of her skirt and refused to let go.

"Come now, turn loose!" Rachel tugged on her dress, but when she looked down and saw the boy's twisted face, she raised her voice, "Michel! Where are your toys?" She shot an accusing look at her brother, "Joseph, why isn't he playing?"

"I've tried everything, Rachel. The boy won't be satisfied until he sees his mother." Joseph began to pour boiling water over the knife, scissors, and other metal objects entrusted to him by Anna.

In a thin high voice, Michel insisted, "Mommy! I want my Mommy! Now!" His fear made him determined.

An impatient edge crept into Rachel's voice, "Oh! Michel! Later. Later, you can see mommy." She wiped his face with the edge of her skirt and told him, "Run along. You can see mommy soon. I promise."

Seeing the open door, Michel dashed into the forbidden room. No one was going to keep him away from his mother. "Mommy!" Michel yelled as he ran toward her bed.

Rachel stuck her head in the doorway, "Sorry Ester, he got away from us."

At the sight of her young son, Ester Gale moved her lips into a smile, though the painful grimace which shadowed her face neutralized the smile. "Michel! Darling, come here." She weakly held out one hand.

Michel held tightly to her hand, viewing her huge belly with a trace of suspicion, vaguely recalling that somehow, a baby had gotten in there. Confused about a world that no longer revolved around him, Michel wanted to climb onto the mat with his mother, to snuggle close, the way they used to do. Just as he started to make a playful leap, his mother arched her back and gave out a high-pitched shriek.

Michel screeched in terror!

Anna Taylor jumped to her feet, shoving Michel toward the door and Auntie Rachel. "Rachel! It's time!"

Michel heard his father roar in a tone that he had never heard in all his two years of living, "Ester! Darling! I am coming!"

After Miss Anna told him in an impatient, sharp voice, "Michel! Find something to do," he lay down behind his father's sitting chair and fell into a troubled sleep.

Haifa, Palestine

Palestinian teacher and scholar George Antoun enjoyed a passion for ancient history, and in particular the writings of the Greeks. George often said that the Greek culture had spread throughout the world as a swelling stream of culture and learning and that every modern man benefited. He was enjoying a moment of solitude with a treasured copy of the *Iliad* when he heard a purposeful pounding on the front door.

Mary will see who it is, he thought to himself. Suddenly struck with a painful memory, he closed the pages of his book. Mary had suffered yet another miscarriage the day before and was confined to bed. George was beginning to realize that Mary would never carry a pregnancy to full term. Only married for six years, the couple had suffered through ten heartbreaking miscarriages. They had no living children.

"One moment," he called out. A reluctant George stood to his feet and walked out of his office and up the hallway.

The knocking grew even more determined. "George! Answer the door!"

George recognized the voice. His visitor was Ahmed Ajami, a member of George's reading group who was also a long-time family friend.

"Yes? Ahmed? What is the rush?" George asked with a smile as he flung open the door.

The mournful expression on Ahmed's face alarmed George. Something was dreadfully wrong.

"George, my friend, where is Mitri?"

George's stomach plunged. Was Ahmed bringing the most terrible of all news? Had his beloved father been in an accident? He clutched Ahmed's arm and pulled him into his home. "Papa walked down to the coffee shop over an hour ago. Has something happened to him?"

Ahmed took a deep breath and closed his eyes. "George. There has been a terrible attack in Jerusalem." Ahmed leaned his head against the wall.

"What?"

Ahmed took a second deep breath before looking closely into George's eyes. "My friend. We just received word from my cousin in Jerusalem that many people were killed."

George began to tremble. His two brothers and one sister lived in Jerusalem. Combined, those three siblings were the parents of ten children. From Ahmed's reaction he knew that members of his own family must have been seriously injured in Jerusalem. The city was the scene of increasingly violent acts between the Jews and the Arabs. George clutched at his own throat. "Who? Just tell me who."

Ahmed slowly shook his head and pointed toward the sitting room. Tears came into his eyes. He was afraid that his friend might faint. "Sit down, George. You need to sit down."

George Antoun was a gentle man and no one had ever heard him raise his voice. George startled Ahmed when he shouted, "Just tell me! Who?" George took a step closer to Ahmed. "Ahmed! You must tell me, now!"

Ahmed began to weep and wave his arms around. "George, my friend. There was a deadly bombing at the Jaffa Gate. You lost them all there. Peter and James and Emily. They are all dead."

George stood without speaking. His limbs began to go numb. As he sank in a heap to the floor, he heard the familiar sound of his father's footsteps on the stone walkway.

George began weeping. He covered his eyes with his hands, muttering, "How can I tell him this news? How?"

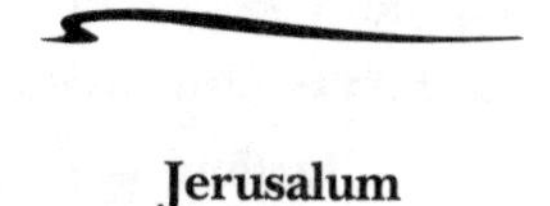

Jerusalum

Several hours later the sound of his father's triumphant voice woke Michel.

"Blessed are You, Lord our God, Ruler of the universe Who is good and does good."

Rubbing his eyes, Michel wandered out from behind the chair.

Joseph beamed affectionately at his son. "Michel, did you hear the good news? You have a baby brother!"

The thought of a new brother did not strike Michel as terrific news. Everything was too unsettling. Michel's dark eyes brimmed with tears, but his father didn't seem to notice.

The knowledge that his beloved wife was safe, and that she had given birth to a healthy baby boy, caused the tension to seep away and brought tears to the eyes of Joseph Gale. He was not going to lose Ester! God was fair, sometimes. Joseph picked Michel up in his arms and recited once again, "Blessed are You, Lord our God, Ruler of the universe Who is good and does good."

The sound of a crying infant sent Michel into a grip of fear. He began to whimper at the cataclysmic changes going on around him, knowing that nothing would ever again be quite the same.

By Friday evening Michel felt slightly more friendly toward his new brother. The baby lay sleeping in Michel's old cradle, which had been set in a corner of the center room. Their new Bedouin maid, Jihan, a woman who used to work for Miss Anna, but was now going to attend to the Gale family, sat crouched on the floor by the side of the crib, her hand lightly touching the infant's back as she gently rocked the cradle. Jihan was singing a plaintive melody.

Standing with his back against the wall, watching Michel play and his new son sleeping, Joseph was happier than he had been in a long time. In spite of the Jaffa Gate attack, the Arabs had not avenged the deaths of their loved ones. He was surprised, but encouraged, hoping that the Gale family would not be the ones to pay the price in the never-ending cycle of revenge. He cheered himself with the idea that before too long, perhaps Jews could move beyond a time when survival was unexpected and death was commonplace. And, since this morning, when three men of the Haganah arrived to guard the area, the sniper fire in the neighborhood had ceased.

Rachel interrupted her older brother's thoughts. She looked at Jihan with glaring disapproval. "Really, Joseph. A *blind* maid?"

Joseph's face was free of expression when he glanced down at his sister. "She's very capable."

"Capable? How can a blind maid be capable? Are you joking? What help can she be to Ester?" Rachel's voice grew louder. She was furious that she had not been asked about the arrangement. "Anna is mad to suggest such a thing!"

Joseph's voice remained patient. "Rachel. Jihan has lived with Anna since she was a young girl. She is wonderful with children."

"No! I can't believe it." Rachel lowered her voice. "Obviously, Anna is weary of feeding a useless mouth!"

Joseph spoke in a vaguely disappointed tone, "Rachel. Don't be unkind. This is Ester's wish. And, mine."

Rachel Gale was a stubborn individual who liked having her way.

Added to that misfortune, she was a plain, dumpy woman born into a family of tall, handsome men. Without a suitor in sight, she understood she would never have a family of her own to nurture. Rachel had looked forward to playing a pivotal role in the upbringing of her brother's children. Her tone was bitter. "Joseph, you are making a terrible mistake! A blind woman! Mind what I tell you, she'll do harm to the children!"

Looking at his sister's face, Joseph had a quick thought that Rachel was becoming impossible. He gave his sister a hard look and his back stiffened. With angry words he told her, "Rachel, the decision has been made! Now, close your mouth and leave me alone!" Joseph walked away.

Rachel stared at her brother in astonishment. Joseph was a gentle, soft-spoken man, and she had rarely heard her brother raise his voice in anger. Indeed, his kindly manner had encouraged Rachel's sharp tongue. Grumbling under her breath, "Blind maid, indeed!" she hurried into the kitchen to prepare the food.

The dark memory of a time when Rachel was truly alone tempered the argument with her brother. A survivor of Auschwitz, Rachel had hidden in the women's barracks on the day the Nazis emptied the camp. After the Russian Army liberated the camp, she had hitchhiked from Poland to France, sleeping in fields and surviving on the kindness of people she did not know. Months later, and with indescribable joy, she arrived in liberated Paris and waited with excited expectation for returning members of the Gale family. While in Paris, Rachel had joined hundreds of other Jews at the Hotel Lutetia, all searching for news of loved ones separated by the deportations. Notes were posted and bits of information exchanged between concentration camp survivors were eagerly pursued. Week after interminable week, Rachel waited, unwilling to believe that she was the only survivor of her family. Clinging to what others called futile hope, she sat in the lobby of the hotel, carefully examining each Jew with interest, bombarding every newcomer with descriptions of her parents and brothers. After a month, she learned from eyewitnesses that her mother and father had been sent to the crematoriums at Auschwitz. Michel, her oldest brother, was last seen in a work camp located on the perimeter of Auschwitz. Abbi, Michel's Christian wife, made her feelings clear when she refused Rachel's request for a place to stay. During the long occupation of France, Abbi had come to regret her marriage to a Jew. And Jacques? At the time Rachel was deported from Drancy with her parents, Jacques had been a resistance prisoner of the Gestapo in France. The last known news of Joseph, Ester and their child, was that they were still living in the Warsaw Ghetto during the spring of 1942.

Rachel was almost at the point of abandoning all hope and accompany her insistent Jewish acquaintances to Palestine when she recognized a familiar figure reading the posted notes at the hotel. Joseph had returned! After a tearful reunion, Rachel joined her brother and his wife on the journey to Palestine. Europe was no longer safe for Jews.

Only after arriving safely in Palestine, had they learned of Jacques' fate.

With a sad grimace, Rachel began to arrange food on the serving trays.

The Friedrich Kleist home in East Berlin

The same haunting dream came to him every night.

Although Friedrich Kleist tried to look stern as he shouted orders to his men to hurry the family, he was completely distressed. His S.S. superior, Karl Drexler, had put Friedrich in charge of clearing the Moses Stein apartment and putting the entire family on the next transport to Treblinka. Friedrich felt the eyes of his hated superior on his back, although when he left S.S. Headquarters he saw that Colonel Drexler remained in his office.

Friedrich gave a start when he realized that the men of the family were gone. He wondered about the big French Jew—the one who had almost broken Friedrich's jaw during the furor at the apartment earlier in the week. Friedrich had promised the Jewish men time—time for them to save some members of their family—but time had run out. Friedrich decided not to advise Colonel Drexler that the two men had escaped the noose. Let what would be, be, he told himself.

Friedrich stood as in a trance and watched as the weeping women and children continued to file past him. He couldn't help thinking that they were a comely crowd—pretty women and adorable children. But his Colonel said they were not fit to live, and die they would. Friedrich knew that too soon those pretty faces would turn to ashes and go up with smoke in the crematoriums.

Friedrich allowed his eyes to linger on one of the youngest of the children. The girl was only two or three years old and quite beautiful with dark bouncing curls and a sweet smile. She ran toward him.

A hand reached out and grabbed her. "Dafna, come with Mommy, please."

Dafna laughed with excitement. "Are we going to ride a train?"

The mother's voice choked. "Yes, my precious. We will see the trees and the flowers."

As Friedrich stared at the child's face he realized something was terribly wrong. The child's face was beginning to smolder! Her flesh began to shrink. Smoke began to rise above her head. The little girl began to howl and twist in agony!

Friedrich was shrieking as he bolted upright in bed.

Eva was talking in a low voice and trying to soothe him. "Friedrich, it was only the dream. You are in Berlin."

Friedrich was shaking so violently that the bed mattress was moving. He forced himself to get up. He kissed Eva on her forehead and told her, "Sorry. I will get some water."

Eva sighed unevenly and turned over. These dreams were getting worse. Where would this end?

Friedrich Kleist sat up for the remainder of the night, oblivious to his moans as he lived that fateful day over and over—a day in 1942 when he had sent the Stein family of Warsaw to burn in the ovens of Treblinka.

Although it had been six years ago, and he had not actually witnessed the crime, Friedrich could smell smoke created by human flesh. The stench of the smoke was growing worse, night by night, dream by dream.

Friedrich began to weep, wishing that he had not survived the war.

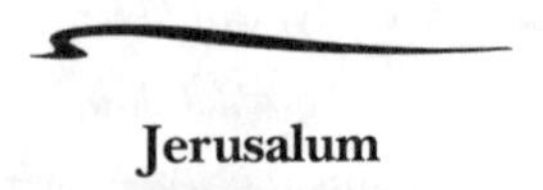

Jerusalum

The house was soon filled with sounds of the celebration of the night of the *Shalom Zachar* (welcome to the male child). Regardless of the deterioration of Jerusalem life, neighbors and friends of the Gale family filled the house.

Ari and Leah Jawor made a last-minute appearance. They were delighted when Joseph asked them to be his new son's god-parents. They began to excitedly discuss the *Brit Milah*, the traditional ceremony held eight days following the birth of a male child, where the child is named and circumcised. Neither Ari nor Leah knew the name chosen for the boy. Such information would be held privately within the Gale family until the *Brit Milah*, but they knew the infant would be named for a departed member of Joseph and Ester's family. Ashkenacic Jewish tradition taught that the memory of the departed would guide the life of the newborn, and due to the Holocaust, Joseph and Ester Gale had numerous possibilities from which to select.

Suddenly, there was loud applause. Rachel brought out three bottles of red wine she had hidden away for the birth of her brother's child. For the first time in months, the kitchen table was loaded with food. Each guest had generously contributed some bit of food they had stowed away for a special occasion. There were cooked beans and peas, some boiled potatoes and even a box of fresh fruit. The fruit had been smuggled into the beleaguered city by Ari Jawor. The precious fruit and wine created more excitement than the birth of the child. There was even a cake, dangerously tilted to one side from the lack of certain ingredients.

While swaying to the sound of the sonorous Hebrew singing, Joseph gathered Michel in his arms, whispering, "You are the light of my life! You are perfection!" Joseph allowed Michel a sip of wine, telling him, "My son! To life!"

A big smile crossed Joseph's lips. New life meant Jewish strength!

Ester smiled the sweetest of smiles, watching her husband delight in their eldest son. She leaned her head against Joseph's shoulder and closed her eyes, reminding herself of the wonderful reality that she was the mother of two healthy sons.

The cantor continued to lead the guests in song, and everyone was smiling and happy, unwavering in their resolve to enjoy the moment and forget about the violence which was overtaking the small country they now claimed as their own. When the sound of gunfire erupted in the neighborhood, two of the men armed themselves and went outside to guard the house. The remaining guests raised their voices and sang even louder, drowning out the chaos of Jerusalem, portraying a perfect picture of people living in a time of peace and harmony.

The moment became bittersweet for Joseph. The scene around him required all the restraint he possessed to maintain his composure. Only a short while ago their future had been intricately intertwined with large and caring families. World War II brought deadly consequences for those whom they loved, and more of Joseph and Ester Gale's past had been lost than saved. Now, too soon, they again found themselves fighting for their lives and the lives of their two young children.

Joseph was fighting the urge to burst into laughter and to cry out in anguish, both in the same instant. His eyes teared with happiness at the safe birth of a son and with sorrow at the thought of the loved ones who had not lived to experience this cherished moment. Yet, Joseph felt some small comfort from the knowledge that the memory of Ester's most beloved brother, Daniel Stern, a good man, a brave man, would now live through their own son. Earlier in the day, Joseph and Ester had made the decision to name their new son Daniel. Daniel Gale.

His mood reached his wife, Ester, and she nodded. She understood: although their sons carried the names of those lost, they would never forget Joseph's brother Michel, or her own brother, Daniel. Looking into Joseph's face, she knew that her husband was seeing another place and another time, and despite the tremendous joy he felt from the birth of two healthy sons, he remained desperately sad.

The traditions of Jewish life called out for the large families they had both lost at Treblinka and Auschwitz. As scarred survivors of the Holocaust, Joseph and Ester had never dreamed the day would come when there would ever again be cause for celebration in their lives, just as in the years before the Holocaust, they never could have imagined the empty void which would come to a culmination at their most significant family events.

Joseph and Ester stood beside each other, hiding their true thoughts, while singing and exchanging pleasant conversation with their friends.

Their guests would have been surprised if they had known Joseph and Ester Gale saw no one standing before them, no one at all.

Part I

Paris-Warsaw:

1938-1942

Character Listing

Part I: Paris–Warsaw (1938-1942)

Stein Family:
Moses Stein *(father)*
Sara Stein *(mother)*
Ester Stein *(daughter)*
Abraham Stein *(son)*
Eilam Stein *(son)*
Daniel Stein *(son)*
Israel Stein *(son)*
Gershom Stein *(son)*

Gale Family:
Benjamin Gale *(father)*
Natalie Gale *(mother)*
Michel Gale *(son)*
Jacques Gale *(son)*
Joseph Gale *(son)*
Rachel Gale *(daughter)*

Miryam Gale *(infant daughter of Joseph & Ester Gale)*
David Stein *(blind grandson of Moses & Sara Stein)*
Karl Drexler *(Nazi S.S. Commander of Warsaw Ghetto)*
Friedrich Kleist *(German S.S. guard at Warsaw Ghetto)*

Minor characters:
Noah Stein *(father of Moses Stein)*
Dr. Shoham *(Jewish doctor in Warsaw)*
Noy *(escaped Jewish prisoner)*
Tolek Grinspan *(Jewish policeman in Warsaw Ghetto)*
Edmúnd *(French resistance fighter)*
André *(French resistance fighter)*
Rudolf Drexler *(father of Karl Drexler)*
Eva Kleist *(wife of Friedrich Kleist)*

Chapter I

The Summer of 1938: Paris, France

Like a virtuous old crone, Sara Stein's Polish mother had guarded her daughters in the same manner that she had been guarded by her mother. As a result, Sara had been married at a young age to a stern man whom she did not know or love. Her first few years of married life had been miserably unhappy. Later, the soft side of her husband had appeared, and Sara's fear had been replaced by affection. Still, those early years had caused a young mother to make a silent pledge: Sara had promised herself that any daughters born of her womb would not be forced to marry against their will. After giving birth to five sons, Sara forgot her youthful vow. That was before she delivered her last child, a delicate girl.

Now that infant daughter was a beautiful young woman, eighteen-years-old last month, and Sara had sided with her daughter against her husband in the choice of a husband for their child.

Second thoughts were now hounding Sara. She appealed, "Moses, I am worried. Will our child find happiness in this union?"

Moses Stein was in no mood for his wife's last minute jitters. "*Woman!* What do I know of the future?" He stared into his wife's face, reminding her. "I suggest that you wait and see what God has in store for a foolish girl that weds one that is not of her kind."

His words struck his wife like a physical blow. Clearly, Moses blamed her for the upcoming wedding.

Sara was right. Moses' devoutly religious father had warned him: "Never break with tradition, to do so is always a mistake." Their five sons had wed women who were chosen by a *shadchan*, or matchmaker, but Moses had always been pliable when it came to his youngest child and only daughter. Ester was the apple of his eye, and he was weakened by his love for this child. Rubbing his eyes with his fingers, Moses tried to console himself. More than likely, it was the accident that made him so vulnerable to the girl. As a child, Ester had been struck by a runaway horse, barely surviving critical injuries. Since that time, the entire Stein family overindulged the girl. His daughter had always gotten her way, and now Ester Stein was a headstrong young woman unwilling to take no for an answer.

Last year, during the family vacation to Paris, Ester had met the youngest of the Gale boys, a good-looking fellow who evidently had a lot of experience with women. The girl had no knowledge of men, but she had fancied herself in love and set her mind on having him. Moses had strongly objected, saying that a girl from Poland had no business marrying a Frenchman, but Ester and her mother had joined forces against him, and now his child was set to wed Joseph Gale and would live in a country far from her parents. They would be fortunate to visit with Ester once a year.

That was not the worse of it. Moses knew that hard times were ahead for the Jews. It didn't take a Prophet to predict that once again, war was coming to Europe. Hitler had already swallowed The Rhineland and Austria. Now he had his sights set on the small Republic of Czechoslovakia. Would Poland follow Czechoslovakia?

If the Germans invaded Poland, Moses knew that the Jews would be the first to pay the price. Seven of his employees were Polish Jews who had once made their home in Germany, men who had lost everything but their lives when Hitler came to power. This very year, the Germans had rounded up all Jews not native-born, forcibly separating families, and expelling those foreign-born Jews back to the country from where they had come. Those people had been separated from their husbands, or wives and children (who were German Jews) put on a train, and sent to the Polish border near Zbaszyn. The Polish Government didn't want them either, and the unfortunate Jews were stuck in a no-man's land! Hearing of the outrage, Moses had used his influence to hire some of the men, freeing them from their predicament. The men felt grateful to their benefactor, and tried to warn him of the coming plague. Moses had heard firsthand from those men how the Nazis dealt with Jews.

Moses was already preparing himself for the inevitable pogroms. European history was stained by the persecution of Jews, and the Polish people themselves were no lovers of their Jewish population. But then, what country made the Jews feel welcome? His own Grandfather had fled into Poland from The Pale, a part of Russia set aside for imprisonment of the Jews. Moses' father, Noah, had only been a child at the time but the horrifying memory had never left him. On his deathbed at an old age Noah Stein had hallucinated, thrashing and screaming about the nightmare of his childhood flight from the Czar's soldiers. Moses had grieved that his father could not find peace, even at the moment of death, but he had reasoned that was the case with all Jews in Diaspora.

Was there no sanctuary for God's own chosen people? Moses was beginning to think not. Already, he was converting part of his wealth into gold and diamonds.

With a troubled sigh, he reminded himself, Ester must be kept close, or how else could he protect her? He had tried to warn the Gales of the coming danger, and now his face reddened at the memory of *that* conversation.

While Sara Stein and Natalie Gale had discussed wedding plans, their husbands fell into a political discussion which naturally centered around Hitler.

Moses brought up the latest news from Berlin. It seemed nothing would keep the Huns from swallowing Czechoslovakia, not even the threat of war. "Will France intervene?" Moses asked.

Benjamin Gale looked startled at the question. "You mean, fight?"

"Yes."

Benjamin was emphatic. "No, no. French citizens will never support another ruinous war."

Moses snorted. "Better to stop the Germans in Prague than at the Arc de Triomphe."

"Be serious."

"I am very serious," Moses retorted. "Are you making preparations?"

Natalie Gale overheard their dialogue and interrupted the two men, laughing at Moses Stein's words, telling him, "Moses, you sound like the voice of doom!"

Moses smarted at Natalie's sarcasm, but out of politeness, he smiled thinly and didn't reply.

Feeling smug in his Frenchness, Benjamin answered Moses' question, "French citizens have no need to make preparations, our own government has taken the necessary precautions. If the Germans are so ignorant as to make their second attempt to conquer Europe, the Maginot Line will keep them at a safe distance from French citizens."

Moses furrowed his brow, "I wouldn't be so sure, Benjamin. I recently read that most military experts deem the Maginot Line nothing more than French folly."

Benjamin flicked his hand in dismissal of that theory.

"No, really. It has been predicted that the Germans will bypass the fortifications by invading Belgium and attacking France from that country."

"No!" Benjamin declared, in spite of the fact that he himself had recently read a magazine article saying that the German military had laughingly nicknamed the Maginot Line the "picket fence."

Moses wouldn't let go. "Hitler hasn't exactly made a secret of the fact that he hates the French only slightly less than he hates the Jews." Moses was getting excited. "Listen to me! Don't be blind in the face of such hatred!"

Both men knew that hatred stemmed from the harsh terms of the Versailles Treaty, dictated upon a defeated Germany at the end of World War I.

Natalie Gale shifted in her seat.

Benjamin glanced at his wife and then changed the subject, saying, "We are disturbing the ladies, Moses."

Moses had tried to warn them, but nothing could penetrate the Gales' gay unconcern, which they wore like armor. Moses could hardly bear the possibility that his most beloved child was now going to live with a family that was too foolish to understand that Jewish cunning and strength was their only protection against the coming plague.

It was too much to endure!

Now, Moses glared at his wife and when she started to speak, his face darkened with fury.

Sara closed her mouth and looked away. In all their years of married life, never had she seen her husband so angry.

Moses recalled his wife's words, calculating how he could use them against her. Employing female tricks, she had brushed up against him, circumventing his disapproval with her pretty smile. "Moses, times have changed. Nowadays many girls marry for love. Besides, he is a nice young man from an affluent family. We would be hard pressed to find a better match for Ester in all of Poland." Sara had wrinkled her nose, making herself resemble the young woman he had wed, not quite sure how to break the news that the Gale family had forgotten they were Jews. "Naomi hears they are well liked and highly respected, even if they don't keep a kosher house."

Moses knew now that his wife and daughter had conspired against him. The law of God ensured that every deception must be paid for, and he feared that his daughter was going to pay dearly.

As far as the Gale family, Moses had done some discreet checking on his own, and he didn't like what he had discovered. Having lived in France for six generations, the Gale family considered themselves purely French, a family that had forgotten their Jewish background. He mumbled to no-one in particular, "They are obviously making up their morals as they go along in life." How else could a non-believing Jew define the guidelines in his life?

The Gale's modern lifestyle did not please Moses Stein, a man reared in a wealthy but religious Jewish family.

Now, here they were, a year later, back in Paris for a wedding Moses did not want to take place. He was maddened by the idea that the girl had insisted upon getting married in Paris, calling it the "City of Love!"

Moses grunted. It was too late now, the engagement had been formalized by *t'naim,* the signing of the legal document that states both parties were obligated to keep their commitment of marriage. If he were to call off the marriage at this late date, it would be a disgrace to his family name.

Moses was mostly haunted by the fact that he could have said no, ending the romance before it ever began. He began to breathe heavily just thinking of his stupidity. Moses clapped his hands together in front of his face and muttered, "Oh God! What could I have been thinking?"

Still, unwavering in his determination not to accept any of the blame, he had barely spoken to his wife since they returned from that day's luncheon with the boy's parents. It had been their third meeting, but the first occasion they had spent extended time alone with the Gales, and the luncheon had quickly turned into a disaster!

The gathering had started off well enough, though Moses was discomfited by the posh restaurant chosen by their hosts for their meeting. Moses shifted uncomfortably in his seat as he astutely observed the mirrored walls and plush velvet draperies. The restaurant made him think of a bordello. Not that he had ever visited such a place, but he had heard tales from those who had. Moses looked all around but failed to spot another Jew in the crowd. Of course, he told himself, in France Jews have a miraculous way of turning into Frenchmen, unidentifiable as Jews.

Moses was proud to be a Jew, one of God's chosen people, and had often heard his father say that due to their unique status, Jews were born to suffer. And suffer they did, with quiet dignity and without appeal to their enemies.

Moses simply did not understand the desperate need some Frenchmen had to conceal their Jewish identity. Such attitudes puzzled and angered him.

The Gales were fashionably late, but hard to miss when they did arrive. Moses carefully scrutinized their hosts as they walked toward him. He had to admit, Benjamin and Natalie Gale were an impressive couple. Benjamin Gale was a tall, well-built man. He was quite obviously intelligent, as Moses had heard that he was a well-respected attorney, proudly claiming some of the biggest *goyim,* or gentile, names and businesses in the city as his clients. Natalie Gale was still trim and attractive, even after giving birth to four children. By what they knew of the woman, it was apparent that she was a leader in her social circle.

Once again, Benjamin and Natalie greeted the Steins with enthusiasm, and Moses felt some degree of self-satisfaction. If the Gales were displeased that their son was marrying a girl from Poland, they managed to hide their emotions perfectly. While it was known that French Jews felt superior to their Eastern European brothers, Moses had gathered at their first meeting that the boy's family must have had some knowledge of the Stein family of Warsaw. Otherwise, why would they be smiling and acting as if Ester were the daughter-in-law of their dreams?

The Stein family had once been poor, but that was no longer the case. Moses' Russian grandfather began with very little. In Russia he had been the village ritual slaughterer, though he hated the sight of blood. But in those days, a son had to follow his father's line of work, regardless of the son's ambitions. After escaping to Poland, he made the happy discovery that the Warsaw *Kehillah,* an elected Jewish body, licensed ritual slaughterers. Unable to obtain a license for his known trade, he decided to set himself up in business, opening one small flour mill. Business was lucrative and from that humble beginning he had built an enormous chain of flour mills, feed stores, and dry goods stores. His business was inherited by his son, Noah, who had a flare for business. Noah soon expanded into money-lending ventures that exceeded his wildest expectations. Moses was the only surviving son of Noah Stein, and he was now a rich and powerful man, highly regarded in the large Jewish community of Warsaw.

Before the luncheon ended, Moses understood that his wealth had nothing to do with the parental approval of the Gales. Benjamin and Natalie Gale were thoroughly modern parents, neither having nor insisting upon a say in their children's choice of a partner.

That was completely clear when Natalie confessed, "You know, I told Benjamin yesterday, I am so excited! We haven't had a wedding in the family in four years! Not since Michel, our oldest, married that nice Christian girl, Abbi." She said archly, "They had a huge Catholic wedding. The priest who performed the service has family in Warsaw!" She looked at Moses with a smile, misinterpreting his fixed look as one of interest. "Perhaps you have heard of the family? The Chaillet family? Of Warsaw?"

Moses was struck dumb, unable to recover from the shocking revelation that his precious daughter was joining a family that allowed their children to marry someone out of the Jewish faith! A Catholic wedding, indeed! He had heard of such goings on in Paris or London, but until now, Moses had never met Jewish people who had turned their backs on the most basic of Jewish belief: mixed marriages are contrary to Jewish tradition.

He looked at Sara with alarm. This was a scandal!

Benjamin Gale threw his wife a look of irritation, wondering why she was purposely trying to annoy the Stein couple.

There was a long silence.

Sara gathered her wits with a visible effort. She tried her best to continue the dialogue but looked incredulous when Natalie Gale quickly suggested that as far as she was concerned, the two children could skip the week-long pre-wedding separation!

The silly woman's words still rang in Moses' ears, "Joseph and Ester have been separated for a year. It is cruel to keep them apart. Joseph was absolutely miserable when we returned yesterday, wanting to hear every single morsel about his love." She turned her face to Sara, "Sara, send Ester out for shopping and Joseph will meet her in a café. Leave the arrangements to me." She giggled and winked, patting Sara on the hand as though the two women were joint conspirators against all that was respectful in Jewish life.

After that, Moses and Sara barely spoke, letting Natalie Gale talk until she could think of nothing else to say.

The luncheon continued to deteriorate, with the social gathering ending in embarrassment.

Benjamin Gale seemed to understand the cause of the discomfort. He was a more sensitive character than his wife, and he tried to ease the situation by assuring the family that the Gales were flexible, and that the parents of the bride were in charge of the entire affair as far as he was concerned. He laughed heartily, slapping Moses on the back. "Just tell me when and where to show up, and I'll be there."

"Benjamin, does it mean so little to you? Your son's wedding?"

Benjamin's face turned bright pink, but he made no response to Moses, filling the strained silence with a great pretense of figuring the bill and snapping his fingers for the waiter.

Natalie looked askance, hoping the Steins would not take their conservative ways too far. All of Natalie's close Jewish friends were secular. More and more she pursued Christian friendships, encouraging her husband to move from the Western part of the city, where most native French Jews lived. It had been a moment of great pride when Michel married Abbi, a girl from one of the most prominent Catholic families in Paris. Natalie thought that the old ways were a terrible burden and did nothing more than to harm the Jews in French society, and she often told her children that Jews were wrong to live in religious and communal isolation. Since Benjamin had no religious beliefs, having left his Jewish faith long ago, he did not complain about his wife's instruction to their children.

She often pointed out to her husband, "Jews bring on most of their problems by their manner of dress and the way they act."

The truth of the matter was that Natalie was ashamed of her Jewish heritage, and the hateful taunts endured as a child still tormented the adult she had become. She had been brought up in a strict Jewish home. Once married to a secular Jew who rescued her from her stern father, she rebelled against everything Jewish. She had fought against naming her children traditional Jewish names, but only Jacques had escaped the taint. Benjamin had insisted with Michel, Joseph and Rachel. She supposed that Benjamin had persisted in order to appease his despairing mother. Natalie received some solace from the fact that Michel's two small children were being named and raised as Christians.

Now, anytime Natalie Gale walked past Orthodox Jews with their hanging earcurls and dirty black caftans, she made a point to glare at them. The way they looked was enough to make people hate them. She wanted no association with *those* people. In Natalie's mind, the Benjamin Gale family of Paris was French, rather than Jewish. She had hoped that the Gale link with their Jewish heritage could be severed, but now, Joseph had fallen in love with a Jewish girl!

Thinking of the upcoming wedding, Natalie consoled herself, grateful that Moses Stein was completely bald and that only two of his five sons wore the offending earlocks—and those two were tending to business back in Warsaw, unable to attend the wedding. Frankly, she didn't want her son to marry into the family, but Joseph had a mind of his own, though he seemed to have lost it over the girl. She comforted herself by the fact that once the parents returned to Poland, the girl would be under her control. In Natalie's reasoning, anyone who had the opportunity to escape the contamination of being Jewish would jump at the chance.

In parting, she did ask Moses and Sara over for dinner, and looked surprised when they declined. Slightly ruffled, she stiffly told the Steins, "I will inform Joseph that a meeting with Ester is not possible."

Benjamin and Natalie Gale had then breezed off, two very carefree and happy French people, as contented and secure in their French citizenship as Moses and Sara Stein were in their Jewishness.

Moses had not spoken civilly to Sara since the luncheon.

Just as Sara thought to confess her misgivings, and to ask her husband to accept her apology for encouraging the union, she heard the sound of her daughter's footsteps.

Ester Stein came into the room.

The worried expressions on their faces instantly softened. Moses and Sara Stein loved their daughter fiercely.

Ester Stein was an unusual girl for the times. Growing up in an indulgent family, with five protective brothers, she carried herself with a serene sense of security. Behind her father's testiness lay a brilliant mind, and Ester had inherited Moses Stein's intelligence. Her proud parents insisted that she receive a good education, and she had made them prouder still by being the brightest female student ever to attend the Hebrew secular Gymnasium, which was a school for the aristocratic Jews of Warsaw. Ester was proficient in languages and fluently spoke and read Yiddish, Polish, German and French. She could speak and understand English and Italian, though she had some difficulty reading those languages. Due to the increasing discrimination against Jews at Polish Universities, Moses had hired a tutor so that Ester could continue her education at home.

Ester was a beautiful girl, with her mother's sweet nature, always thinking of those less fortunate than herself. Still, Ester did have a couple of unflattering traits: she was stubborn like her father and tended to be naïve, the same as her mother. And at times, it seemed that Ester Stein was at odds with a world that made no allowances for the innocent.

Thinking of this, Sara considered that she should have protected her child from youthful emotions, reminding herself that Ester was nothing more than a guileless girl from a puritanical Jewish background. Joseph Gale was a worldly Frenchman who had no difficulty charming women. Sara herself had been enchanted by the man, and could easily understand her daughter's attraction. With a heavy heart, Sara knew that she was to blame if misfortune visited the marriage.

Gazing at his daughter's lovely face, Moses cursed himself for going along with his wife. A marriage brought about by love was a recipe for disaster. He was the father, the ruler of his home. How could he blame a woman, when he had the power to veto any and all requests of his wife and children? Certainly, he would carry a massive burden of regret if his child did not find contentment with this man.

Ester was so caught up in the excitement of wedding plans that she failed to notice the glum expressions suddenly mirrored on her parents' faces. She was breathless with enthusiasm, her face luminous, as her lips parted into a happy smile. "Mummy, the dressmaker has arrived. The gown is beautiful! Come! Quickly!"

Remembering her father, Ester threw her arms around him, "Papa, isn't it wonderful!"

Moses grimaced, forcing himself to respond to his daughter. "Of course, darling. If you are happy, then it is wonderful." He leaned and planted a quick kiss on the top of her head, his lips brushing her dark curls.

Without a backward glance, Sara rushed off with her daughter, leaving her husband in a miserable mood.

Moses stared at the empty doorway for a moment. His poor daughter. She was too young and foolish to separate the French from France. Moses had been told by his brother-in-law, Jacob, that anti-Semitism was on the rise in the country and that while France was hospitable, the French were not. In Jacob's opinion, if the Nazis did conquer France, the French would do little to protect their Jewish citizens.

Moses then began to pace and worry. The Nazi threat occupied his mind, bringing him thoughts of Hitler's rise. He suddenly remembered the book and began to search through his suitcase. One of his employees, recently turned Zionist, was determined to brief the world about Hitler's deadly plans. The man had come to Moses with a mad scheme about smuggling the Stein family into Palestine! With the recent anti-Jewish mood sweeping Germany, and other Eastern European countries, many European Jews were beginning to listen to those who saw no future for Jews except in Palestine. Moses Stein thought the Zionists were fools. Jews had to make themselves acceptable in Europe, and forget the ridiculous notion of traveling half-way around the world to fight the Turks and the Arabs and the British, and God only knew who else, for a small strip of dusty land that couldn't hold half of Europe's Jews in the first place!

In a Zionist zeal, the man had partially translated a copy of the Nazi dictator's book, *Mein Kampf*, begging Moses to read the book, going so far as to force the translation upon Moses when Moses told him about his upcoming trip to Paris. Moses had intended to glance through the book, for the sake of a promise given. Now was as good a time as any, he told himself. He supposed it wouldn't hurt to read Hitler's own book, considering the fact the dictator was casting his evil eye toward Poland.

With the book in hand, Moses settled himself in the chair nearest the window. He let out a tired breath and then wrapped his reading glasses around his face.

Remembering the man's plea, "Alert the Jews of France! Hitler must be stopped!" Moses thumbed through a few pages.

Trying to decipher the man's handwriting was going to be difficult, he decided. Moses Stein slowly drew his fingers along the pages as he read aloud.

As he read, his fears grew and the peace of mind he had sought eluded him.

"The cleanliness of this people, (the Jews) moral and otherwise, I must say, is a point in itself. By their very exterior you could tell that these were no lovers of water, and, to your distress, you often knew it with your eyes closed. Later I often grew sick to my stomach from the smell of these caftan-wearers. Added to this, there was their unclean dress and their generally unheroic appearance.

All this could scarcely be called very attractive; but it became positively repulsive when, in addition to their physical uncleanliness, you discovered the moral stains on this 'chosen people.'

In a short time I was made more thoughtful than ever by my slowly rising insight into the type of activity carried on by the Jews in certain fields.

Was there any form of filth or profligacy, particularly in cultural life, without at least one Jew involved in it?

If you cut even cautiously into such an abscess, you found, like a maggot in a rotting body, often dazzled by the sudden light—a kike!...

When thus for the first time I recognized the Jew as the coldhearted, shameless, and calculating director of this revolting vice traffic (prostitution) in the scum of the big city, a cold shudder ran down my back....

...I had at last come to the conclusion that the Jew was no German.

Only now did I become thoroughly acquainted with the seducer of our people.

A Jew could never be parted from his opinions.

The more I argued with them, the better I came to know their dialectic. First they counted on the stupidity of their adversary, and then, when there was no other way out, they themselves simply played stupid. If all this didn't help, they pretended not to understand, or, if challenged, they changed the subject in a hurry, quoted platitudes which, if you accepted them, they immediately related to entirely different matters, and then if again attacked, gave ground and pretended not to know exactly what you were talking about. Whenever you tried to attack one of these apostles, your hand closed on a jelly-like slime which divided up and poured through your fingers, but in the next moment collected again. But if you really struck one of these fellows so telling a blow that, observed by the audience, he couldn't help but agree, and if you believed that this had taken you at least one step forward, your amazement was great the next day. The Jew had not the slightest recollection of the day before, he rattled off his same old nonsense as though nothing at all had happened, and if indignantly challenged, affected amazement; he couldn't remember a thing, except that he had proved the correctness of his assertions the previous day.

Sometimes I stood there thunderstruck.

I didn't know what to be more amazed at: the agility of their tongues or their virtuosity at lying.

Gradually, I began to hate them.

Hence today I believe that I am acting in accordance with the will of the Almighty Creator: by defending myself against the Jew, I am fighting for the work of the Lord."

Moses' hand trembled as he folded the pages and laid the book on his lap. Then panic started within him and wrapped around his body like a vise. As surely as he knew his name was Moses Stein, he understood that something awesome was going to strike the Jews of Europe.

Chapter II

Joseph Gale

Joseph Gale's bachelor years had never been tranquil. Most people acquainted with the Gale family agreed that while all three of the Gale boys were handsome, the youngest of Benjamin and Natalie Gale's three sons had been blessed with movie star looks that gave him as much trouble as pleasure. Through no fault of his own, he'd earned something of a reputation as a lady's man.

"Are you sure you want to do this?" Jacques Gale chided his brother, who was systematically destroying love letters he had recently received from eight brokenhearted women, each of them pleading with Joseph not to marry Ester Stein.

Joseph raised his eyebrows and smiled, but he didn't bother to answer, knowing that his brother already knew the answer to his question.

Joseph and Jacques Gale had always had an unspoken communication with the other, and their silences indicated a closeness that no one else could penetrate. Only a year apart in age, they had been inseparable since their childhood. Jacques understood perfectly: his brother had met the woman of his dreams and wanted nothing more than to marry Ester Stein.

A melancholy smile flickered across Jacques' face as he watched his brother. He took a small sip of whiskey and soda before speaking, and his voice was tinged with a touch of envy when he declared, "You know Joseph, you are one lucky bastard! Just as you are tiring of too many accommodating women, the most beautiful woman in the world appears!" He exhaled noisily as the memory of Ester came to mind. "I should be so fortunate!"

Joseph's eyes twinkled with amusement. He took the last of the letters and carefully ripped it into small pieces. "You'll meet your own Ester one day, Jacques. Be patient."

A vague and wrenching sadness broke over Jacques, causing him to mouth the words without meaning, "Yeah. I know."

Joseph and Jacques had both spotted Ester Stein at the same moment, though Jacques had always insisted that he had seen her first.

It was only a year ago, this week, when they had met her. They were sitting with three Christian girls, enjoying a sunny afternoon at one of Paris' many sidewalk cafés, when Ester arrived at the café to purchase candies. Though her figure was petite and beautifully shaped, all eyes at the café had seen no further than the girl's face. With enormous black eyes showcased on a perfect face, her beauty was breathtaking. Both boys had instantly forgotten the three French girls, even though the girls made a few catty remarks about the old-fashioned and less than stylish dress of their competitor.

When the girls heard Ester's thick accent, they were cruel in their jealousy, mimicking the foreigner, "Ah! Choc o late candeee, with sweeeet cheeries inside, pleeese sir." The three French girls burst out laughing. "She's straight in from the old country, just your type Jacques!"

None of the three French girls wanted Joseph to have a flirt with the beautiful girl, as each of them had secret aspirations to be his special lady friend. They didn't even care that Joseph was a Jew, which would normally be a strike against him, even in France's tolerant atmosphere. The Gale boys were different, and it was easy to forget their Jewish background.

Jacques had been the first to find his voice. He nudged his brother's arm and whispered, "Hands off brother, I saw her first! She's mine!"

Joseph didn't say a word, but he gave a lopsided half-grin to the girl, who had followed the sound of their laughter and was now staring at Joseph.

Once Ester saw Joseph, Jacques didn't have a chance with her.

The boys quickly excused themselves from their companions, who were maddened by the defection. "Well, see you later, Joseph," the prettiest of the three called out hopefully.

Jacques got to her first, "May I offer my assistance, Madam?" He bowed from the waist.

Joseph towered over his brother's shoulder. He winked at Ester.

Flustered, the girl blushed, not knowing how to handle the unexpected attention from the two sophisticated and determined brothers. "Well…yes. I suppose." Part of Ester's charm was her inability to realize her own heart-stopping beauty, and she was always surprised at the fuss people made over her.

Joseph took charge, reaching for the bulky packet of candies in Ester's hands and with an amused smile, passed the candy to Jacques. "The lady accepts your kind offer of assistance." Then, with calculated leisure, he took Ester's arm and guided her from the café.

Furious at being bested, Jacques hurriedly situated himself on Ester's free side.

Ester glanced from under the edges of her bonnet at Joseph, feeling something close to awe at the most gorgeous man she had ever seen. Her stomach knotted as she desperately tried to think of something clever to say. Her mind was completely blank of a single interesting topic, so she said nothing, letting the young men carry on the conversation as they walked her to the apartment that her father had rented for their summer holiday in Paris.

"Where do you live?" Jacques asked, trying to get her attention and at the same time wanting to know how far they would have to walk. The girl had purchased a considerable amount of candy.

"Warsaw."

Jacques rolled his eyes.

"Poland?" Joseph couldn't conceal his surprise.

"You mean, you don't live in Paris?" Jacques asked, disappointed that the girl was a tourist, and that more than likely her time in France would be short. As he spoke, Ester looked him full in the face and he got the full impact of her flawless features. At that moment he had a feeling that the beautiful girl from Warsaw was going to change their lives in a significant way.

Ester overcame her shyness, confirming that she was Polish and that, "Mummy has a sister who lives in Paris. Auntie Naomi is her only sister. We come and visit every other year. For six weeks." She tilted her head and smiled openly at Joseph.

Joseph couldn't help but notice that Ester's lips were lush and full and her teeth were shining white and perfectly aligned.

They soon learned that she had five older brothers, and a strict religious father who didn't allow her to date.

Too quickly, they arrived at her aunt's neighborhood, the rue des Rosiers, which was in the most Jewish sector of Paris.

Understanding by the boys' manner and dress that they were well-to-do, Ester blushed in embarrassment at their surroundings. Ester had overheard the vicious remarks made by the fashionable French girls, and she wanted to confide to the Gale brothers that their home in Warsaw had thirty rooms. But she didn't. Neither did she explain that her father was very rich and the Stein family could afford much nicer accommodations in the center of the city, even on the Champs-Elysees, if they chose, but that her mother wanted to be as close as possible to her sister.

The rue des Rosiers was unlike any place the Gale boys usually visited. The streets were narrow, crowded and dark, in a neighborhood where many orthodox Jewish newcomers to the city settled. Joseph and Jacques examined everyone and everything around them with great interest.

Ester hesitated on the steps leading to the apartment, biting her lower lip and looking uncomfortably toward the door. Today was the first occasion her parents had allowed her to shop alone. They would never trust her again if they discovered she had permitted two young men to accompany her home. She extended her hands for the packet of candy, "Well, good-bye." Her hesitant demeanor made it clear she could not invite them in.

Jacques handed her the candy but not before taking one of her outstretched hands and brushing it lightly with his lips. "Good-bye, Miss Stein. It was a pleasure escorting you." He flashed a warning look at Joseph. "May I call on you, again?" He cleared his throat. "Tomorrow?"

Ester nervously moved from one foot to the other, waiting to see what Joseph would say. "Well…"

Perplexed, Joseph was staring at her, disarmed by her innocence. Did she really not know how to handle his brash brother?

Ester looked expectantly at Joseph, not wanting to cut the moment short, but she was terrified that her father would appear at the door. Impatient, she glanced at Jacques and then she turned her face to Joseph, her gaze resting on his face. Not knowing what else to do, she nodded and then ran up the steps, pausing at the door to turn back for a final look.

Joseph's eyes were veiled, but he had a shadow of a smile on his face. He would definitely be back.

Jacques carefully noted the apartment number the girl entered. "Number 12. Let's ask around," he suggested. "Find out more about the girl."

"If you say so." Joseph was strangely quiet, thinking about Ester's striking looks and shy manner. She was a refreshing change from the girls he usually met, who were bold and forceful.

Jacques' blunt questions about the beautiful Polish girl to some people gathered nearby were met with hostile looks. Jacques and Joseph looked a bit too dandy for the neighborhood. Nothing about the two brothers seemed Jewish and soon a small crowd gathered.

Joseph kept his attention focused on a couple of neighborhood toughs who appeared rather menacing. "This is looking dangerous," Joseph told his brother, wondering if he was going to have to fight. Generally, his intimidating size was a deterrent to all but the most foolish men.

"Right. Let's get out of here. We'll come back tomorrow." Jacques laughed and both of them took off running, exhilarated by the girl from Poland.

The following afternoon they rode battered bikes that they had borrowed from the Gale family gardeners. Dressed in rough hunting clothes they attracted no attention. Parking their bikes, they slouched on the apartment steps, silently observing the impoverished appearance of the Jewish residents of their fair city while waiting for the girl to come out.

Jacques cupped his hand over his mouth and muttered to Joseph, "I feel sorry for these poor bastards."

Joseph's thoughts never became words, for at that moment apartment door #12 opened and they saw that Ester was coming out hand-in-hand with another young lady and both were dressed for an afternoon walk. Ester was wearing an emerald green dress that clinched her tiny waist and accentuated her swelling bosom. The color suited her dark beauty. Her hair was loose and free, and her curls bounced as she bounded down the steps.

Jacques gasped. "Great God! Joseph, if she is a sample of Polish girls, we must add Poland to our tour." The Gale boys were set to take a world tour the following year.

Joseph was mesmerized, but he kept his thoughts to himself. Ester Stein was even lovelier than he had remembered.

Ester's eyes opened wide, registering pleasure and surprise all in the same instant. "Joseph. Jacques. What are you two doing here?" She was genuinely happy, yet startled and a bit frightened that her cousin might get the wrong idea. She stared at Joseph's attire in astonishment. Judging by the clothes the boys were wearing today, they could easily be from the neighborhood.

Her cousin, Ruth, gave a disapproving look and pulled on her arm.

"Ester, come on."

Jacques quickly stepped in front of the girls and humorously explained why they were attired in rumpled garments. Ruth looked less than impressed, but after getting a good look at Joseph, she allowed the brothers to remain.

The boys fell into step, learning all they could about the beautiful visitor from Poland. Jacques did most of the talking, trying to charm the girl, wanting her to ignore his glamorous brother.

Like everything else they did, the brothers pursued Ester together. Jacques became infatuated with Ester, right along with Joseph, but it soon became clear that despite Jacques' efforts, that Joseph would be the victor.

Jacques Gale was a good looking guy, but Joseph was better looking. Jacques was tall, but his brother was taller. Jacques was charming, but Joseph was more charming. Generally, Jacques had his hands full with the women Joseph didn't have time for, and in the past, that had suited him fine.

When Jacques saw that Ester Stein looked at Joseph, even when responding to Jacques' queries, he gave a short dispirited sigh and turned his attention to the cousin. Taking his loss in good-natured stride, he started chatting with Ruth, who was cute enough to mildly entertain him, while Joseph and Ester dazzled each other.

Ester walked in silence but her thoughts were brilliantly clear: she had met the man she wanted to marry. She knew that her ideas were outpacing the relationship, and that she had no experience with love, but there was no doubt that she had found love with Joseph Gale. How else could she explain the strange feeling of helplessness that overcame her each time she looked into Joseph's face, or the shocks like electricity that ran the length of her body when Joseph held her arm and guided her through the streets of Paris?

She looked up at Joseph and smiled, sexual tension escalating between them.

Captivated by her dark, almost biblical beauty, Joseph proudly escorted Ester to Rue Drouot, a famous café once known as the

Boulevard de Gand, acutely aware that for the first time in his life, his striking appearance went unnoticed. All eyes, male and female, focused on Ester. Once everyone had thoroughly examined Ester, Joseph saw that the men looked at him enviously.

Joseph gently guided Ester to one of the marble top tables, situated in the furthermost corner of the Rue Drouot. The two couples ordered ice cream, but Joseph and Ester couldn't stop talking and their ice cream melted. They talked almost as a reason to keep looking at one another.

Joseph was aching to touch Ester's silky skin, to run his hands through her glossy dark hair, to feel her body up close. But he couldn't touch her.

Ester wanted to know everything about Joseph, to enter his world and know all his thoughts and share his life. But she couldn't tell him.

The moment was so powerful that neither of them noticed when Jacques gave Ruth a sly wink and led her from the table. They walked across the street to a small park, leaving Joseph and Ester at the café, still talking.

Almost as an unspoken agreement, every day for the following nine days, the Gale boys waited on the street for Ester and Ruth, accompanying the girls to various city parks and buying them refreshments at a variety of cafés on the Boulevard.

By the tenth day, Joseph wanted his relationship with Ester to move into a different stage. His passion for the Polish beauty made him careless. Accustomed to women who were more experienced, and conveniently effortless for a man to conquer, Joseph made the fatal mistake of assuming that any woman could be had. He sat quietly, shaping his thoughts as he slowly stirred his tea. As Ester sipped her tea, Joseph admired her bright pink, bow shaped lips. Then he leaned close and whispered, his breath caressing her ear, "Ester, can you escape Ruth? Tomorrow?"

Ester's eyes were alert and inquisitive. She smiled and asked, "Escape?"

"I must see you. Alone."

The smile froze on Ester's face. Alone? She busied herself with her bonnet, studiously avoiding his eyes, pondering his question. Surely Joseph knew that she could not see him alone. Already, she was behaving in a daring fashion. For the first time in her life, she was hiding an important secret from her mother. And Ester knew that her father would angrily forbid her to leave the apartment, or would possibly even take her back to Warsaw, if he had any inkling of how she was spending her afternoons.

Joseph murmured, "My brothers and I keep a small apartment on the Left Bank, away from our parents' home." He put his finger under her chin, lifting her face to his, thinking that this Polish girl stirred him in a way that was almost frightening. Anticipation drove him to recklessness. "Ester, I must have you. Feel you in my arms. No one will ever know."

The smile left Ester's face. Still puzzled, she hesitated. Then she felt Joseph's free hand caress her leg under the table. It was the first time that he had touched her inappropriately. Once she grasped his meaning, Ester's face turned bright red and her eyes blazed with fury. Jumping to her feet, she upset the table, overturning their drinks. Ester was enraged, and her anger silenced the noisy room. "You have made a mistake, Mr. Gale! I am *not* a trollop!" Ester Stein was a small woman, but her slap was impressive. "Ruth! Come!" Ester spun around, running from the room, watery-eyed and furious.

Joseph sat, wordless. He lightly touched the reddened spot on his cheek.

Jacques grinned at Joseph's stunned expression and began to laugh. He laughed so long and so loud that the other patrons began to complain.

"Shut up!" one of the men ordered.

"Can we have some peace, please?" a young man shouted, wishing to himself that he had followed the girls, one of which was a stunning creature. He stretched his neck and stared. The girls were already out of sight. Giving a short sigh, he went back to reading that day's edition of the *Paris Soir.*

"Silly creatures," an aging Parisian beauty whispered to her companion, even as she cast a longing look at Joseph Gale.

Finally, the short, fat owner rushed at them, flicking a small cloth, furiously shouting, "Out! Out!" They could hear him grumbling about the tea-stained linens even as they fled.

Joseph and Jacques Gale had lived carefree lives as long as they could remember. Their father was wealthy and consumed by his work, while their mother was so busy with high society functions that she encouraged her children from an early age to go out and find their own way, laughing while advising them to have fun.

Natalie Gale's easy-going attitude had been just fine with the Gale boys.

Joseph had recently received his law degree from the University of Paris, and his parents had insisted that he take a world tour before he settled down into a predictable career in his father's law practice. Joseph agreed with his parents that a world tour was a good plan but wanted his brother Jacques to accompany him. Jacques was scheduled to graduate from medical school within a year. Until that time, Joseph occupied himself by bouncing from one love affair to the next, idling away his days in a most pleasurable manner.

That is, until he met Ester Stein.

Rebuffed by the Polish girl, Joseph's pride kept him silent. Pretending nonchalance, Joseph attempted to shrug off the unexpected rejection by bedding one girl after another. For some reason, each one bored him more than the one before.

Jacques tried to bring the topic up once or twice but Joseph curtly told him, "If you don't mind, I'd rather not discuss Ester Stein."

After a couple of weeks, Joseph gave in to the restlessness that he knew was caused by Ester Stein. He carefully counted the days on the calendar, knowing the date the Stein family would return to Warsaw. He thought that any day now, he would hear from the girl.

He waited and waited, aching to see her again.

Finding his charade of indifference unbearable, he begin to drink, alone.

It was after midnight one evening when Jacques discovered him in their father's library, thumbing through a book on the history of Polish Jews. Jacques arched one eyebrow when he noticed the half-empty bottle of whiskey. While reading aloud the title of the book, "Jews in Poland," he failed to keep the amusement out of his voice. "Since when have you had an interest in the history of Polish Jews?"

Joseph grunted an unfriendly greeting without speaking, and hastily closed the book he had checked out from the University of Paris Library.

Jacques pulled up a chair. "Looks like you need company."

Joseph shrugged, thinking that his brother knew him too well. Not wanting Jacques to sense his ache for Ester, he began to tell him about his new mistress, a tigress from Nice. "She's half-French, half-Italian and completely wild! Brother, she's even taught me a few tricks!"

They both laughed.

Joseph poured himself a glass of whiskey and downed the drink in two loud swallows.

Jacques looked at his brother for a long time. "You won't hear from her, you know," he said at last. He cleared his throat. "Girls are raised differently in Poland."

Joseph's mouth went dry. He stared at Jacques for a few moments. Saying nothing, he poured himself another drink. He thought about what his brother had said but still could not admit his true feelings. "Let her go back to Poland!" he retorted sharply. Joseph then growled and lit a cigarette, annoyed that Jacques sensed his acute longing for Ester Stein. "She struck me as a bit simple minded, anyhow."

Jacques sat back comfortably. "Really? I didn't get that impression myself." Not for the first time, the idea flashed through Jacques' mind that Joseph was too arrogant about the opposite sex. Since his teenage years, Joseph Gale had exuded sexual magnetism, attracting women of every age. Joseph adored women and they responded in kind. There were simply too many women available, standing in line, all waiting to seduce his handsome brother.

Now this girl from Poland was distracting Joseph to the point of despair. Not that Jacques didn't understand. He thought that the combination of Ester's unbelievable beauty and childlike innocence would haunt any man. Jacques had a quick thought that if his competitor was any man but his brother, Jacques himself would make a serious attempt to capture the heart of Ester Stein.

In an odd way, and for the first time in his life, Jacques felt sorry for his younger brother. Still, Jacques refused to lie to him, even to help Joseph keep his illusions alive. "Joseph, my brother, I must tell you, the words you say and the message in your eyes do not match."

"And you, my brother, are full of shit!" Joseph fired back. He looked away, staring up at the ceiling, debating on whether to be honest or to continue the game. One quick glance at Jacques' face, and he knew that his brother was waiting and judging. Was he ready to poke fun? Joseph took a resigned sigh. To hell with Jacques, he thought, and suddenly any desire he had to fool his brother melted.

Joseph nervously toyed with his empty glass. "How could I be so stupid?" He bit his lip. "I admit it, Jacques. In the beginning, my only motive with Ester Stein was to get her into bed." He slumped over the table. "Now, I cannot eat," he confessed. "I cannot sleep. Jacques, I *must* have her!"

Jacques was startled but pleased. "So! This time you are really in love?" He was good naturedly pulling for the girl. Everything had come too easily for his brother, and perhaps the time had come for Joseph to learn what Jacques already knew—not everything in life comes without effort. "Maybe you should marry her," Jacques suggested with a hearty grin, knowing that Joseph had never considered marriage with any woman, no matter how infatuated he had been. Often Joseph had said, "Why should a man have the same dish daily, when he can enjoy a smorgasbord."

"Really, Joseph," Jacques continued more seriously. "She is going to go back to Warsaw, and you'll never see her again." Their eyes met. "Is that what you want?"

Joseph's face turned bright red. He said nothing for a long time, then he muttered miserably. "No. That is not what I want." He paused and then asked, "Have you seen her?"

Jacques shook his head, and told him in a teasing manner, "No, but I know a lot more about the Stein family than you do."

Joseph gave him a questioning look.

"I still see Ruth," Jacques told him. Jacques was quiet for a mere moment and then made a strange comment. "With Ruth, I have been going around Jewish neighborhoods. Just yesterday I visited the Dos pletzl." The Dos pletzl, known to Parisians as the "little place" was located in the 4th district of Paris and was populated by poor, immigrant Jews. An odd glow came into Jacques' eyes. "Joseph, you wouldn't believe how those immigrant Jews cling to the faith, drawing strength..." He grinned at Joseph's startled expression. "To tell you the truth, I'm a tad curious about those Jews, the real Jews...not shirkers like us..." Jacques laughed and then turned serious. "Let me tell you, it's not easy being a *real* Jew!"

Joseph looked away, showing his impatience. He had little interest in the Jewish life. "Jacques, some other time. Please. Has Ruth told you anything about Ester?"

Jacques humored his brother. "All right. Yes. About Ester Stein." He cleared his throat. "Get this: Ester Stein is an heiress."

Joseph's loud laugh sounded like a strangled bark.

Jacques' words gathered in intensity, "Listen to me, Joseph. Don't let that neighborhood fool you. Ruth swears that Ester is from a prominent Jewish family. The old man is one of the richest Jews in Warsaw, maybe even Poland." He emphasized his words, speaking slowly, "Many men in Warsaw would like to have a chance at this girl. And, my dear brother Joseph, you are the first man Ester has really known, other than her relatives. You've got a head start on every Jewish son-of-a-bitch in Poland!"

Joseph listened with a concentrated sort of desperation, understanding that he was facing a new dilemma. By the way Ester dressed, he had thought that the Steins must be affluent, but he never imagined that the Steins might be wealthier than his own family. "What else did Ruth say?" he croaked.

Jacques squeezed his lips with his fingers, as he thought, then told his brother many facts that Joseph had already learned about Ester Stein during the ten days they had courted. "Well, Ester is an accomplished pianist. She speaks five or six languages. She is well-educated, unlike most Polish girls. Her father hired a private tutor, some woman from England." He recalled a couple of astounding comments volunteered by Ruth. "Uh, seems the Poles give the Jews a hard time in the schools—they have quotas for the Jews. Not only that, they segregate Jews in the classrooms, and make them sit on "ghetto benches" at the back of the class. Can you imagine?" Jacques shook his head glumly before going on. "Anyway, Ester reads a lot. Ruth says she is terribly bright." He glanced at Joseph, who was transfixed, staring into his face. "What else? Oh yes, in her spare time, she volunteers in the Jewish soup kitchens of Warsaw. That's all I can remember." He grinned. "One more thing. Ruth says her cousin is a virgin."

Joseph had no way of knowing whether Ester Stein was a virgin, but after her reaction in the café, he wasn't surprised. His voice lowered and trembled slightly, "Has she mentioned me to Ruth?"

Jacques shook his head. "Sorry, brother. The girl is insulted and angry. She warned Ruth not to speak your name in her presence if she wanted to remain her friend."

Joseph's face turned chalky. The more Joseph learned about Ester, the more he wanted her. She was innocent, sweet, intelligent, and more beautiful than any woman had the right to be. She would make some man a perfect wife. His gut wrenched as he thought of another man having Ester Stein. He wanted her for himself alone.

Joseph sat quietly for a long time.

Jacques got up and opened a bottle of sherry, pouring himself a drink. He sat back down and watched his brother, fascinated by the battle that he saw reflected on Joseph's face.

Joseph looked at his brother skeptically. "Jacques, if I go crawling to her on my hands and knees, how will that look? If I beg Ester Stein, she will think I am weak." Joseph Gale was simply too proud to make an apology. His emotions clearly in turmoil, Joseph changed his mind once again, firmly stating what he wanted to believe. "She'll contact me."

Jacques responded with an impatient shake of his head. "No, this one won't."

With a touch of pride, Joseph reminded Jacques, "They always do, you know."

Jacques sat perfectly still, fighting disappointment as he considered his brother's situation. He knew that Ester Stein would never contact Joseph. Jacques genuinely loved his brother, and he felt with certainty that Joseph was going to be a fool and let the one woman who could make him very, very happy, escape.

The two men continued to sit, neither speaking.

Finally, Jacques squinted at the clock, "Good God! Look at the time! I'm off to bed," he said. Yet, he did not move. Unquestionable affection for his brother caused him to make one final effort. "Joseph, you'll forever regret letting Ester go. Really. Go to her. Tomorrow." He pushed back his chair. "Now, think about what I have said."

Joseph stared at his brother, his lip curling cynically. "Jacques, take your advice to bed with you."

With a sad expression, Jacques shrugged, then walked toward the door. "All right. I will."

After his brother left, Joseph poured himself another drink, and another, and another, and slowly drank himself into a stupor, drowning his raging emotions.

Ten days before the Stein family planned to return to Warsaw, a worried Joseph Gale asked Jacques to deliver Ester Stein a letter.

Ester ripped the communication into two pieces and threw the pieces at Jacques, shouting at him to leave or she would call her father.

Five days before the Stein family planned to return to Warsaw, Jacques and Ruth invited Ester to accompany them to an ice cream parlor.

Ester refused the invitation.

Four days before the Stein family planned to return to Warsaw, Joseph knocked on the Stein door, carrying fresh flowers and chocolate candy.

Ester was not at home. Her parents were icy.

Three days before the Stein family planned to return to Warsaw, Joseph told his stunned parents that he had met the girl he wanted to marry. Would they intervene?

Two days before the Stein family planned to depart Paris, Benjamin and Natalie Gale contacted a matchmaker. After hearing the details, the matchmaker was reluctant, since he thought that the glaring differences in family backgrounds would bode ill for the couple. But, after meeting with Joseph and hearing for himself the depth of feeling the young man expressed for the Polish girl, the matchmaker finally agreed to approach Moses Stein.

Much to everyone's surprise, Moses and Sara Stein refused the offer of marriage, saying that the Gale boy was not suitable for their daughter.

One day before the Stein family planned to depart Paris, a desperate Joseph Gale walked the streets of Paris. He walked and he thought. Slowly, the ideas upon which Joseph had built his life began to fall away. He began rethinking and justifying the rite of marriage, a passage he had always criticized as too stupid for an enlightened modern thinking man. Without knowing how he got there, he found himself in Ester's neighborhood. He stood for a moment, staring up at the windows of the Stein apartment. Suddenly, he understood that if he let her go, he would regret Ester's loss the rest of his life. He walked in a circle, talking to himself, discarding one idea after another, wondering how he could win her back.

People on the street began to laugh, and to make faces at each other and point to their heads. Clearly, this was a lunatic loose in the neighborhood.

Joseph never noticed.

Making a quick decision, Joseph dashed up the stairs and pounded on the door of the Stein apartment. Through the locked door he shouted, "Ester! You must speak with me!"

Moses Stein jerked open the door, thinking a madman was loose.

Sara Stein tried to shield her daughter, believing the young man was inebriated.

Joseph's and Ester's eyes met.

Joseph held out his arms.

Ester pushed her mother aside and walked toward Joseph very slowly. Her face was pale. She had lost weight.

Joseph could tell that Ester was as miserable as he. "Ester," he pleaded, "can you ever forgive me?"

Ester began to weep.

Moses Stein angrily called out for Joseph to leave, threatening to toss him down the stairs.

"Ester, shall we haunt each other forever?" Joseph paused, his love clearly visible on his face. "Darling, you must marry me."

She came closer.

With indescribable gentleness, Joseph tenderly rubbed her cheek with his hand. "Will you marry me, Ester?"

Scandalized, Moses Stein tried to pull his daughter away from Joseph Gale.

Sensing she was witness to a great love, Sara tugged on her husband, trying to disengage his arm from their daughter.

Moses held tight. In his desperation, he had the strength of a superman, and giving a final fierce yank, he pulled his daughter toward him. Joseph came with her.

Moses and Sara were within inches of their daughter's face when she burst into tears, crying out, "Yes, Joseph Gale! I will marry you! I will give you children! I will grow old with you! Yes! Yes!"

Held tight in the iron grip of a horrified Moses Stein, the two lovers wept and kissed, with Joseph whispering, "I love you, Ester, I love you."

A shaken Moses Stein postponed his return to Warsaw. After three days, unable to withstand the determined and tearful assault of the two women he loved, he begrudgingly gave his approval for his daughter to marry Joseph Gale, although he insisted the young lovers endure the traditional one-year engagement period. And he requested a second promise—that if the wedding were going to be held in Paris and his daughter was going to reside in that city, then the couple would return to Poland for the birth of their first child.

"Ester will need her mother at such a time," Moses argued. Moses was a jealous father and not above making use of the situation to get something he wanted.

Joseph's thoughts had not progressed beyond the wedding or the honeymoon. The idea of a family was strangely appealing. He proudly gave his word. Joseph reached out and shook Moses Stein's hand. "It is a promise. At the birth of our first child, I will bring Ester to her mother."

Chapter III

Warsaw, Poland: August 25, 1939

The Warsaw weather was unseasonably warm in August, 1939, but the citizens caught the mood of deep winter. The presence of the gathering Nazi army to the West radiated a chill which drifted across the countryside and into each home and heart.

In a valiant effort to create a festive atmosphere, the Stein family spent a considerable amount of time during the month in their open-air, walled courtyard. Their darling Ester was home for the first time since her wedding, waiting for the birth of her first child.

Despite the feverish insanity that gripped Berlin during that hot summer, Joseph Gale had kept his word to Moses Stein.

Now, Joseph found it hard to believe, promise or no promise, that he had been so rash as to bring his very pregnant wife out of the security of Paris to the uncertainty of Warsaw. Their Polish journey had been against the wishes of his family.

During the past year, Benjamin Gale's optimism for European peace had been smashed. After carefully following the inept attempts of the French and British politicians to appease the insatiable German dictator, he had understood the futility of diplomatic solutions. "Hitler and his goons understand nothing but brute force," he told his youngest son.

"I'm afraid we're in for a bit of a fight. Don't go to Poland, son, that is where the conflagration will begin."

Benjamin Gale's words were now haunting his son: during the past twenty-four hours, the massive German Army had begun to stir.

Joseph was sitting in the courtyard with his father-in-law. The discarded pages of the *Nasz Przeglad*, a Polish-language daily newspaper, lay strewn on the cobblestone floor. Both men were brooding, listening to the wireless radio, waiting for additional news regarding the German military buildup on the Polish border. More than an hour had passed since the excited broadcaster had announced to the Polish people that, "Our sources in Germany inform us that Adolf Hitler has threatened to wipe Poland off the map! German soldiers are poised to boil over the Polish border. Long live Poland!"

Since that announcement, the radio station had been playing the Polish national anthem over and over, *Jeszeze Polska nie zginela* (Poland Is Not Yet Lost). Suddenly, the newscaster broke in, his excitement now verging on hysteria, as he screeched, "Polish intelligence sources have just this moment verified that, during the morning hours, the German Foreign Office wired the German embassy and consulates in Poland requesting that German citizens in Poland leave the country by the quickest route!"

Joseph and Moses stared at each other, wordless.

Curtly, Moses at last spoke. "There is only one explanation for such an order."

The sarcastic look in Joseph's eyes was clear and sharp, "Yes. What a pity that would be! Germans killing Germans."

Once again, the Polish national anthem played across the airwaves.

Moses stood and leaned over the set, fiddling with the dials until he picked up the British Broadcasting Corporation. The British newscaster's announcement sounded the death knell of Poland, his voice concerned yet calm, reflecting perfectly the emotions of his own country which was absorbed by the gripping events, yet did not want to participate. "Our London correspondent reports that Berlin Radio proclaims that there have been Polish "attacks" on German territory, and that the Polish Government has turned down the Fuehrer's offers of peace. Earlier information that the German army is moving closer to the Polish border has been confirmed." The announcer went on to explain how British Prime Minister Neville Chamberlain had exhausted himself in his efforts to discourage a Polish/German clash.

With a growl, Moses set the dial back to Warsaw Radio. The station was temporarily off the air and the wireless gave off a noisy buzz. He then tuned the set to pick up Berlin. The radio announcer in that city was even more excited than his Polish counterpart. "Germany's beloved Fuehrer," he thundered, "a man of great decisions, had made his last generous offer to the pigheaded Poles. Peace was put in the hands of our Polish neighbors! The stupidity of the Poles knows no bounds: they have opted for total war!"

Not knowing what else to do, Moses sat back down, deeply concentrating. The moment that Moses had dreaded for the past two years was now upon him.

Joseph's face was as black as thunder as he looked into his father-in-law's face. "I suppose we are in for it now," he said.

Moses agreed, a touch of pride in his voice. "Poland is no Austria or Czechoslovakia. The Huns won't strut into Poland without a bruising fight."

Joseph raised his eyebrows.

Moses' face flashed in anger. "I tell you right now, Joseph, we won't let them take a button!"

"Yeah, I know." Joseph replied warily. Not for one moment did he think the Poles wouldn't fight. He had learned quite a lot about Poland in the past year and knew that after centuries of tragic wars and brutal occupations the Polish people were steadfast in their resolve not to undergo yet another occupation. For the past few days he had heard the stubborn Poles bragging on the streets about what they were going to do to the Germans if they dared set one foot on Polish soil. Even children boasted of hanging German soldiers from the city gates.

Joseph thought that the plucky Poles were admirable, yet their bravado was foolish.

Moses stared into space, thinking. He was consoled by one fact: after years of timid and half-hearted negotiations with the German despot, Great Britain and France had finally recognized the hard truth—Hitler's appetite could not be satisfied. The Rhineland, Austria and Czechoslovakia had been nothing more than mere appetizers. The leaders of Western Europe were finally discovering what Moses Stein had thought all along: the German dictator would not stop until he had all of Europe in his iron grasp. Now, finally, Poland's powerful allies had reluctantly understood they had no alternative but to fight.

Moses grunted, smiling grimly when Warsaw Radio returned to their news programming and the announcer repeated, for the hundredth time that day, that, "The Ambassadors from Great Britain and France have notified Hitler that their respective countries will honor their commitments to Poland." Moses knew that with the British and French ultimatums, a chain of events had been set in motion that meant real war. His words were blunt. "Hitler's bloodless conquests will end if he attacks Poland."

Joseph's limbs felt numb at that thought. He hoped Moses was wrong. "Rather a bloodless conquest than a bloody one."

Moses' face showed surprise but he attributed his son-in-law's tepid words to Joseph's love for Ester. He decided to ignore the comment. "Now, it is time to pull up the moats," Moses trumpeted. Moses grabbed a pen and paper from the table top and wrote out a message. He stood up and talking to Joseph over his shoulder, walked quickly toward the house. "The issue is settled. For sure, we'll be attacked by morning."

In spite of the tense moment, Joseph almost smiled, thinking that the old man continually surprised him. There was no telling what Moses Stein had in mind. His father-in-law's confidence further reinforced Joseph's determination to bring his wife and unborn child safely through the impending invasion.

Moses stood in the doorway and impatiently called out for Jan, one of the three Polish boys who made deliveries and carried messages for the Stein household. Jan was the smartest and quickest of the boys.

The skinny boy came running, his face flushed from the excitement. "Yes, I am here!"

"Jan," Moses ordered, "Take this message to Abraham." He slapped the boy on the back. "Quickly!" Moses watched to see that the boy was following his orders and then spoke to Joseph. "My boys will be here for dinner."

Moses had sent Jan with the written orders for his five sons to pay the employees their salaries and then send them home. Trusted supervisors were to be sent to the mills, stores, and money-changing operations spread around Warsaw, with the same instructions to be carried out. The employees were to be reassured that they would be notified when the Stein family businesses reopened. After shutting down and locking up, the Stein men were to come immediately to their father's home.

A spine-tingling shriek came from the upstairs.

Joseph felt his pulse quicken as he stumbled from his chair, a horrified look of fear flooding his handsome features. He stared up at the second floor bedroom window and whispered, "Ester."

Ester Gale had gone into labor the night before.

Moses' color paled but he pointed to the chair with one finger and ordered his son-in-law, "Sit down. I'll check with the doctor." He quickly disappeared inside the house.

Joseph followed, intending to protest, but then he simply began to pace, his hands clasped so tightly together that his knuckles whitened. There was no use arguing with his father-in-law. Not after what happened earlier in the day.

While he was waiting for Moses to return, a telegram arrived for Joseph from his father in Paris.

Joseph's lips moved as he read the message.

URGENT
To: Moses Stein - Warsaw, Poland
For the attention of Joseph Gale
Joseph, leave Poland immediately

```
by any route possible.
War is imminent!
Benjamin Gale - Paris, France
```

Joseph held the telegram in his hand and closed his eyes for a moment. He made a small noise in his throat, and then spoke aloud. "Shit! If only that were possible!" He held the telegram tightly to his chest, longing to be with Ester in Paris. After a short moment, he once again began to pace anxiously.

When Moses returned to the courtyard he raised his eyebrows in a questioning gaze when he saw the telegram.

Joseph's heart began to race. First he must know about his wife. "Ester?"

Moses stonily replied to Joseph's question. "Doctor Shoham said the same thing an hour ago, son. Ester's long labor is normal for a first birth."

Joseph followed Moses and stood impatiently over him as he slumped into a chair. "What *exactly* did the doctor say, Moses?"

Moses blew out a deep breath and looked hard at his son-in-law. He had never seen a man so worked up about birthing. A few hours before, Joseph had actually *pushed* Dr. Shoham, demanding in a threatening manner that the poor man stop Ester's pain! Immediately! Thank God Abe Shoham was a friend of the family or there was no telling what might have happened.

Moses gave a tight smile and patted Joseph on the arm. "Abe did request, considering your size and strength, that I keep you away from him."

Joseph apologized. "Sorry, Moses. I don't know what got into me."

Moses knew. The sound of his daughter's pitiful shrieks and moans was hard to take. He reassured Joseph once again, partially in an effort to bolster his own confidence. "My daughter is going to be fine! Just fine!"

Joseph's eyes remained locked on Moses' face, wondering if he was hearing the truth about Ester.

Moses expression was impassive, giving nothing away.

Joseph leaned his head to the side, quietly listening. He heard nothing more.

Throughout the day, Ester's cries had slowly weakened, and now her sobs could barely be heard. Every hour or so her moans would turn into screams. Joseph was deathly afraid for his young wife and now he had additional trouble, for it looked like the German army was going to come down on their heads.

Joseph handed the telegram to his father-in-law, and then groped around in his shirt pocket for a cigarette. His hands were remarkably steady, considering the anxiety he felt for his wife. Joseph drew the smoke deep into his lungs and then glanced at his father-in-law, who was staring at the telegram.

Moses raised his voice in frustration. "It is too dangerous. Ester cannot be moved."

"I know." Joseph replied, taking the telegram from Moses' outstretched hand and putting the paper into his shirt pocket.

Joseph sat back down and continued to smoke. He looked once again at Moses who seemed to have forgotten Joseph's presence. Moses' face was drawn and Joseph thought his eyes now showed fear. Every Jew in Poland probably had the same look, Joseph reckoned. If Hitler got loose in Poland with its three-and-a-half-million Jews, he would be like a fox in a hen house.

Too immersed in his own sudden crisis to linger on Poland's problems, Joseph's eyes narrowed to a slit, and his thoughts began to race. Just yesterday he was a young man with no worries at all, and today he was distraught over Ester and worried sick about her safety in the event of war. He inhaled loudly, blowing smoke from the side of his mouth. He sat back down, asking himself a very important question: just what would he do if Poland were invaded? Alone, it might be a bit of an adventure. He would join the Poles in fighting or he could make a run for it, returning to France and joining the French military. He could then fight the Germans from the West. But with a wife and newborn baby, fighting or running was not a possibility.

Joseph cursed himself for the hundredth time for leaving France and traveling to Poland in the middle of a European crisis. He had been following the German dictator's fiery speeches and it didn't take a genius to predict that Hitler would eventually attack Poland. Joseph tried to recall his rationale for making the trip, ticking off in his mind the reasons he had come to Warsaw: war had seemed so far away from Paris...Joseph Gale was a man who kept his promises...fearful of her first childbirth, Ester had desperately wanted to be with her mother.

There was little that Joseph could refuse Ester.

Their marriage was blessed, and they loved each other more with each passing day.

With Ester's gentle guidance, Joseph had begun to explore something of his Jewish heritage, much to his mother's chagrin. Natalie Gale had done her best to loosen the girl from her Jewish traditions but had failed miserably. Joseph chuckled, remembering his mother's surprise that her daughter-in-law possessed a will stronger than that of her own. While Ester's quiet personality and sweet ways gave the impression that she was a woman who could be easily swayed, Natalie had quickly discovered that was not the case. Ester was respectful to her mother-in-law, and always made a point of listening carefully to her advice. Afterward, Ester followed her own conscience, paying no heed to Natalie's strong-arming tactics. For once in her life, Natalie Gale was stumped, but her daughter-in-law was so diplomatic in her dismissals of Natalie's demands that there was little Natalie could complain about without appearing a bigger shrew than she already was.

Joseph was pleased that Ester had a mind of her own. He would be bored with a woman who said "yes" to everything and everybody.

Last November, when Ester shyly confided that she was pregnant, he had literally whooped with joy, sweeping her into his arms, and kissing her lips...her neck...her belly.

Joseph almost smiled, recalling those happy times. Remembering his dilemma now, his expression quickly returned to a scowl. By dismissing the warning signs that clearly pointed to war, he had foolishly placed Ester and their unborn child into genuine danger.

Just at that moment, one of the Polish maids came out of the kitchen with a pot of coffee and a plate of cookies. She had been sent by her mistress, Sara Stein, who was by Ester's side. Strangely, the girl seemed surly, different from her usual pleasant disposition, reporting to Moses in a spiteful tone that there was a new problem: "Miss Ester's baby is turned wrong. Dr. Shoham is trying to twist the baby around in the right position. He said if the baby is placed correctly, your daughter will give birth within a few hours."

Thinking of the pain that Ester must be enduring, Joseph leaped to his feet. "I must go to her!"

"Leave women's business to women," Moses ordered in a tired voice, bracing himself to restrain his son-in-law physically, if necessary. He stood up and positioned himself between Joseph and the entrance to the house. In his opinion, the place of birthing was off-limits to men, in particular men such as Joseph who couldn't control their emotions. "We have done all we can do by hiring the best doctor in the city," Moses added. "Now, the rest is up to the doctor, Ester, and," he hesitated for a brief moment, "God."

Moses stood next to his towering son-in-law and patted him on his back. He came as close as he could come to giving Joseph an affectionate look. Moses had a quick thought that he had absolutely nothing in common with Joseph Gale except they were both Jews and they both loved Ester. Moses supposed that was enough for him. During the last month, his estimate of Joseph had changed. Regardless of what the boy had been or had done in France, once married to his daughter, he had turned into an indulgent husband, completely devoted to Ester.

In an effort to prove to Moses that she had been right about the marriage, Sara had proudly told him some of what the girl had confided to her mother. Moses had been astounded, thinking that he had never known a man so infatuated with a woman. He would have called any other man a fool, but since this man was his daughter's husband, he was pleased. Joseph's behavior only confirmed what Moses already knew. His only daughter was recognized as an exceptional woman even outside her immediate family.

Moses and Sara had breathed freely for the first time since the wedding, putting the ugly disagreement behind them, knowing that their daughter was greatly loved and genuinely happy.

Without knowing it, Joseph had unanimously won over his wife's family.

"Go, get some paper," Moses said to the servant girl. Thinking to get his son-in-law's mind on other matters, he guided Joseph back to his chair and handed him a pen. "Joseph, you must send a reply to your father. He will be concerned for your safety."

Joseph nodded in agreement, knowing that his family in Paris must be frightened out of their wits. "You are right, Moses."

Moses fidgeted slightly, thinking of what lay ahead. "Who knows when communications will be cut?"

Gauging from the latest press releases from the French Government, Joseph had little doubt that if Hitler attacked Poland, France would definitely declare war against Germany. Knowing Jacques as he did, Joseph knew that his brother would be one of the first men to don a French uniform. With one son in the military and another trapped in Poland, his parents would be in a hard spot. Thinking of that, Joseph wrote the words he knew his panicked family needed to hear.

URGENT
To: Benjamin Gale - Paris, France
Ester about to give birth. Impossible to leave Warsaw. Will return as quickly as events allow. Do not worry. We are safe.
Joseph Gale - Warsaw, Poland

Once the telegram was off, Moses once again began to tinker with the wireless but there was nothing more than a continuous repeat of what they had already heard.

Joseph continued to smoke and pace, keeping an ear tuned to his wife's bedroom. He decided that if Ester lived through this difficult day, he would insist they have no more children. One child would be enough. Once back in Paris, he would seek the best medical advice, making sure that Ester was never again put in such danger. Childbirth was simply too risky.

Both men remained silent, each grappling with his own problems.

When he heard the sound of voices, Joseph raced over the stone path to the back door of the villa. He recognized the voices of Moses' sons and called out, "We are in the courtyard." Joseph waited by the door and solemnly greeted his brothers-in-law. "Gershom, some news huh? Daniel, good to see you." He nodded, "Abraham. Israel. Eilam." Watching the men embrace their father, Joseph couldn't help but stare in fascination at the Stein brothers.

Like their father, all five men were of average looks and height, with small bone structures, in contrast to the tall, brawny, and handsome Joseph. He had met Abraham, Eilam, and Daniel at his wedding the year before and at that time had noted their striking similarity to each other. When he and Ester arrived in Warsaw, he was introduced to Israel and Gershom. In spite of their earlocks, Joseph had been stunned to see that Israel and Gershom looked exactly like their three younger brothers. And all five brothers were nearly identical in appearance to their father, if one allowed for his age and absence of hair. Even more disorienting to Joseph were their similar voices, soft, restrained, yet confident—they were men obviously accustomed to the respect of their peers. When in a room with all six men, Joseph often felt that he was in a house of mirrors—the experience was surreal.

At first glance, the brothers appeared average in looks, with light skin, brown hair and dark eyes, but a closer look revealed the sensitive faces of scholars. While they had followed their father in the lucrative Stein businesses, Joseph had discovered that each of the brothers had been educated in the best Jewish schools in Warsaw and that they were well above average in intelligence.

So much for his opinion of Polish Jews. Like most Frenchmen, Joseph had always had the idea that Poland was a back-water populated with ignorant peasants. In comparison to France, the country was backward, yet Joseph had been pleasantly surprised and slightly awed at the Jewish intellectual community that thrived in Warsaw. He soon discovered that his wife's family was highly regarded within that community.

Joseph had had little contact with the Polish Catholic population, which was predominant in the country and held the political power. Jews were still second-class citizens, and the country had a long way to go before Polish Jews could assimilate into the general population, as they had done in France. The Stein family rarely spoke of the injustices Polish Jews had stolidly endured for generations, but Joseph could easily see that there was a tragic split in Poland's population. The Jewish and Christian communities of Poland were like two separate nations of peoples, neither venturing very far into the other's territory. From what he had seen and heard, Joseph had a sense that the Polish Catholics hated their Jewish population, treating them as if they were intruders in the land in which they had lived for seven-hundred years. Joseph had a sinking feeling that if the Germans did invade, the Jews of Poland would have no help from their own countrymen.

He thought about the dismaying change in the Polish Catholic maid who had reported on Ester's condition. In the short time he had visited the Steins, Joseph had witnessed a complete reversal in the attitudes of the housemaids. Now he knew why. The Stein employees, believing that the Germans would over run Poland and strike out at the Jews, were becoming increasingly hostile to their employers.

Not for the first time since coming to Poland, Joseph recognized how fortunate he was to have been born in France, where anti-Semitism had been on the wane since the days of Napoleon, who had given Jews full rights in French society.

He returned his attention to Moses and the five Stein boys. Moses' sons made a circle around their father, ready for his instructions. Moses was *the* law in the Stein household. Any time Moses entered a room, every family member would stand in respect. No one would resume sitting so long as Moses did not sit. Daniel, the boldest and youngest of the sons, was so apprehensive of his father discovering his smoking habit that he went to great efforts to conceal his tobacco.

It was evident that Moses Stein was greatly loved and respected by his children.

"Papa, what now?" Gershom asked.

Moses spoke in a soft, but commanding voice, "We have much to do," he told his sons.

Joseph watched in amazement as Moses Stein changed before his eyes. Moses' pale complexion darkened, and his eyes turned icy black.

Moses repeated his words. "We have much to do, too much." He pointed at the wireless, motioning with his hand for Israel to cut the set off. "Now, come inside," he ordered.

Moses walked briskly ahead and once they had entered the library, Moses turned back into the hallway and looked up and down to make sure no servants were around. He re-entered the room and stood behind his large wooden desk. He told Daniel to close and bolt the door.

Everyone was curious, waiting to see what Moses had to say. Out of consideration for Joseph, Moses spoke in French, a language all the Steins understood. "Sit down, all of you."

They sat.

His voice was hushed but clear. "I don't need to tell you what you already know. Poland will be attacked by Germany. If not tomorrow, then next week, if not next week, then the week after. And, in spite of our brave military, Poland will lose. This will not be like the first war…the Germans are more determined and better equipped now than then." He shook his head very slowly and rubbed his chin with his hand. "And, meaner. Under the last occupation, I knew some Germans. They were not so bad and had nothing against the Jews. In many ways, they were our friends, dismantling many of the harsh regulations set in place by the Russian occupiers. But now Germans feel differently toward Jews. It seems that under their mad leader, the German soldier is proving to be compliant, easily shaped by those men who follow Hitler's wishes to the letter." He shook his head in sorrow. "I fear we will be a witness to a German slide into evil. And, if what has happened in Austria and Czechoslovakia is any example, the Nazis will arrive with a sinister plan for the Jews.

"The Polish Government says we can hold them off until the British and the French come. I disagree. Our allies seem unprepared. We'll have to wait for a while before we see any British or French soldiers. We may fight a day, maybe a week, but whatever happens, we cannot win." His voice lowered. "Horses cannot defeat tanks. Following the German army will be the Gestapo. We won't have much time to prepare ourselves."

The thought ran through Joseph's mind that there was at least one Jew in Warsaw who understood Hitler.

Moses paused, looking directly at each son in turn and then glanced at Joseph. He drummed his fingers on the desk top. "I have a buyer for the businesses."

The five Stein boys blinked their eyes in surprise and several shifted in their seats, but no one said a word.

A terrible thought overtook Joseph. Suddenly he understood that he was witness to a way of life that was disintegrating. If his father-in-law's predictions came true, there would not be so much as an echo left of Jewish culture in Poland.

Moses explained. "Once the Germans have put a government in place, Jewish bank accounts will be frozen, and most importantly, all Jews will lose their businesses, just as they have in Germany, Austria, Czechoslovakia, and The Rhineland. It is better to sell and make a profit than to have them taken from us for nothing. The buyer was to come by tonight, but with all this war talk, I will have to see him later." Moses put his fingers to his face and made a dent in his lips before adding, "For now, we will take the money from our businesses and buy gold and diamonds. And, tomorrow, I will close our bank accounts." Seeing the stricken look on the faces of his sons, he assured them, "After the war, we'll rebuild, start anew."

After the war! Joseph was struck by the certainty in Moses Stein's voice. Not only that, but they were Jews trapped in a country where people hated Jews, surrounded by a foreign military poised to destroy them. At that moment, Joseph wanted to be anywhere in the world but in Poland. He felt himself break out in a sweat.

Moses turned his back and to everyone's surprise, swung open one of the wooden book cases. Behind the case was a secret panel, built into the wall.

Joseph exchanged glances with Daniel. Daniel shrugged his shoulders. He knew nothing.

Moses busied himself with the lock and then pulled out two bags at a time until he had eight bags piled on the desk. A momentary flash of pride washed over his face. "This," he said, "will save our lives."

There was a buzz of excitement as Moses opened the bags, revealing gold coins and numerous diamonds.

"I'll tell you a small story. My father's life was saved by a gold coin. The Czar's soldiers were greedy and would spare a life for gain. My grandfather had planned ahead and saved for years for the next pogrom. When the Jewish persecution started, he had ten gold coins. Two for the children, and one each for him and his wife, with six coins set aside to begin a new life. With those gold coins he paid off the soldiers, making his way clear to come to Poland."

"Pa, do we need so much?" Daniel asked, his voice awed by the wealth spread before them.

Clearly, Moses had been dwelling on the German threat for some time now. "Who knows? Perhaps the German occupation will last longer. Perhaps our lives have increased in value." His eyes flashed in determination, and his voice hardened as he promised his sons. "But whatever the price, the Stein family will survive!"

Several hours later, three Polish maids served the Stein household cold cuts for dinner. Joseph tried to eat a small slice of beef, but the food lodged in his throat. He had slipped out of the room earlier to check on Ester and was told that the doctor had successfully turned the baby. Soon, his child would be born. Soon, he would see his beloved Ester.

After their earlier meeting, Moses had instructed Abraham to bring the wireless radio into the library. During the meal, the stations continuously played the Polish national anthem. After thirty minutes an announcer broke in with the promise that more news would soon follow. Once their meal was completed, the seven men hovered around the set, waiting for the latest news about the movements of the German troops.

At eight o'clock, news reports were bleak: "Bands of German criminals have crossed the Polish border and are attacking customs posts!"

At nine o'clock, cheerless voices announced, "Motorized columns are advancing on the Polish border."

At ten o'clock, animated newscasters reported the unexpected: "The German advance has halted! Poland will live forever!"

The radio station once again began to play the Polish national anthem.

Moses switched the set off.

The seven men excitedly speculated, wondering if the firm statements from Ambassador Henderson of Great Britain and Ambassador Coulondre of France had stopped the Nazi aggressor in his tracks.

Joseph asked himself, was it possible? Would they be saved at the last hour? He allowed himself to think of Paris and had a flash of desire: he and Ester pushing their child in a pram down the sidewalks of Paris.

Daniel interrupted the wonderful image, personally thanking his brother-in-law for French intervention. "Benjamin Gale must be an important man in France, to persuade the French government to threaten war just to save his son!"

Joseph gave a relieved laugh and punched out at his brother-in-law. Daniel raised his arms and challenged Joseph, and the two men squared off, feigning a boxing match.

"He'll kill you, Daniel," Israel teased.

The tense atmosphere left the house as suddenly as it had entered.

Moses smiled, for the first time in two days. Even though he sensed that the attack was merely postponed, he now had a much needed reprieve. He would have more time to prepare for the evil that he knew was coming.

"The Germans have stopped," Moses reminded them, "for now. But, they have not gone away. Now that we have heard their warning, we will get ready. We need to gather food and plenty of water. We can store part of the supplies here and a portion at Abraham's apartment."

The Stein men began making plans for the following day.

"We won't be the only Jews looking for supplies," Daniel said. "We need to split into groups and cover more than one market."

Moses agreed, giving instructions. "Abraham and Eilam will go to Gesia and Twarda Streets. Israel and Gershom, you two take the open markets on Grzybowski Square and Zelazna Brama Square. Daniel, go to our friend on Towarowa. See if Farbstein can guarantee additional deliveries if we come under siege." He paused before adding, "Offer whatever is necessary."

Moses remembered his son-in-law. "Joseph, since you cannot speak Yiddish and understand little Polish, you can remain in the house with the women."

Joseph blushed. He knew that he had no idea how to get around town or to bargain with Polish Jews, but he was a man's man, not accustomed to being treated softly, like a woman. "No," he insisted, "I will go with Daniel. I can load and haul."

"All right." Moses smiled at his son-in-law, pleased at his reaction. Besides, none of his sons were as strong as Joseph. He would be a big help.

After a while the brothers broke up, declaring that they must go to their families. They would return in the morning to collect Joseph and go about the business of preparing for war.

At the last minute Gershom recalled that his sister was in labor. Any other time, the brothers would have shared Joseph's anxiety over Ester's well-being. With the Germans ready to strike, they had forgotten their younger sister. "And, Ester?" he asked.

"Anytime now," Joseph told them, "Dr. Shoham says the baby will arrive soon."

Abraham grinned at Joseph, remembering how he had felt at the birth of his first child. "Joseph, just remember, the worry you feel now is nothing compared to your worry in the years to come!" He slapped Joseph on the back and teased. "Your troubles are just beginning, brother!"

"Thanks for that, Abraham," Joseph said with a strange sound that little resembled the laugh he intended. "I had no idea you were so sentimental!"

The house seemed large and silent when the men left.

Moses and Joseph remained in the library, saying little while waiting for news of Ester.

At eleven o'clock, they heard the front door slam, and a haggard Sara Stein stumbled into the study. "The doctor has returned home to his family," she told them. "He said he would do his best to come by in the morning."

Joseph tensed. Would Ester never have this baby? He gripped his hands together, promising himself to be strong.

Sara smiled at her son-in-law. "Ester is resting." She looked at Joseph with wistful affection before announcing, "Joseph, you have a beautiful daughter."

Moses and Joseph jumped from their chairs. Joseph had a wide grin on his face. Moses reached to shake his son-in-law's hand, who was standing as though suddenly paralyzed. "Blessed are You, Lord our God, Ruler of the universe Who is good and does good," Moses recited. He slapped Joseph on the back two or three times in quick succession and then dashed toward the book cabinets, yanking at one of the bottom drawers and quickly bringing out a bottle of good red wine. He waved the bottle in the air, giving orders to his son-in-law. "Go! Go to your wife! I will prepare the wine for celebration."

Joseph took the stairs two at a time.

The room was dark and oppressive and he could smell the odors of childbirth. He groped his way to the bed, his eyes slowly adjusting to the candlelit room. Ester was sleeping, her breathing shallow. She looked pale but lovely. Joseph thought that nothing could taint her beauty, not even twenty-four-hours of grinding pain. "My darling, you have worked so hard." He leaned down and lightly kissed her forehead, his large hands tenderly stroking her cheek.

Ester opened her eyes and grimaced, attempting to smile. Her voice was so low that Joseph had to bend his head, touching her lips with his ear. "Have you seen her?"

"Not yet, my love," he answered. Joseph turned his attention to the tiny bundle at Ester's side. He was desperate to lift his daughter in his arms, but feared the trembling in his hands would cause him to drop the infant. He pushed the white cotton cloth away from the baby's face.

Joseph heard himself gasp in the silence. The infant was no larger than his hand, and utterly lovely. At that moment the girl yawned, and her tiny mouth rounded in a perfect O. Afterward, her eyes seemed to focus on his face, and Joseph could have sworn that she stared serenely at him, as if she knew he was her father, her protector. Though he told himself that his daughter was much too young to understand what she was seeing, Joseph felt his eyes tear.

Joseph's lips trembled as he smiled at his wife, searching for the words to match his emotions, thinking that there were no words in his vocabulary to accomplish that task. Finally, in a husky voice, he spoke. "Ester. She is perfect, just like her mother." Once again, Joseph brushed his hand across her face. "Now, my darling, I have two beautiful women to love!"

Ester smiled and fell asleep, her head resting on his arm.

Awed by the tremendous love he felt for his wife and for the child that she had given him, Joseph could not leave Ester's side. Hour after hour, he watched Ester and the baby as they slept, promising himself that no harm would touch those whom he loved more than his own life. He bargained with God, making an agreement with the Master of the Universe, vowing to return to the Jewish faith in exchange for the safety of Ester and his baby. Thinking that perhaps God would find him unworthy, undesirable in the transaction, he whispered to himself, "If God has no interest in reclaiming Joseph Gale into the Jewish faith, then I will die to save my family."

During that long night Joseph finally left behind his carefree, youthful ways and assumed the daunting responsibilities of a man confronted with the greatest crisis of his life. It was there that Joseph Gale's years of maturing came to a completion.

His father-in-law waited patiently in the study, knowing that he had been forgotten. He longed to see his daughter and new granddaughter, but he held himself back, not wanting to interfere in a most private moment.

Sara retired. "Call me if I am needed," she told her husband. Sara Stein went to bed without worry, despite the momentous events, fully confident in her husband's ability to protect their family.

Little by little, Moses finished off the full bottle of wine, getting drunk for the first time in his life. In his inebriated state he swayed from happiness to fear, from relief to reality. Moses clearly sensed danger ahead for his family. He prayed to God, asking Him for the strength to fight the battles ahead to keep his loved ones safe from the coming peril. Sitting straight up at his desk, his head fell against his chest as he drifted off to sleep. His chin quivering, he reminded God of his faithful life. "I have been a good Jew, God," he murmured. "Now, let us live. I ask nothing more. Just let us live."

Chapter IV
War

August 26, 1939 at 1:30 AM: Having called off the invasion of Poland, a despondent Adolf Hitler sat at his desk in the Reich Chancellery. He was shocked that the British and French had issued an ultimatum of war over Poland. Long ago, Hitler had concluded that the British and French politicians were men of paper, and could be bullied into accepting his world vision. Had he miscalculated? Hitler prided himself on his uncanny ability to judge character and predict actions.

Yet another surprising blow had been delivered by courier: Mussolini, his Italian Axis partner, had lost his resolve and was now questioning Hitler on the necessity of attacking Poland at all!

On the eve of war, Adolf Hitler was truly alone.

Growing even more agitated, he decided that world Jewry was to blame! The Jews had too much influence with the British! Hitler stared at the clock. The late hour further enraged him. If not for the Jews, his Army would be inside Polish territory by now!

In one of his characteristic rages, Adolf Hitler shrieked to an empty room, "Nothing will stop me from attacking Poland!"

Nothing at all.

Before pulling on his trousers, Joseph Gale glanced at his watch. The hour was four o'clock on Friday morning, September first. He had tried to sleep, but with rescue so close at hand, sleep had been impossible. Rather than disturb Ester with his restless tossing and turning, he had decided to get up and wait for the sun to rise. Joseph wanted the hours to pass like seconds, but time seemed to be standing still.

Would the day never arrive?

While buttoning his shirt and combing his hair, Joseph found himself thinking about the Germans, wondering what the men of the famed Wehrmacht might be doing. Joseph had a sudden, unwelcome vision of Hitler's blond warriors, with their steel helmets gleaming and their pounding boots marching over the green, quiet land that was Poland.

For the past six days, their war-like activity had all but stopped, and the menacing Nazis had simply sat on Poland's border.

Their sinister quiet had driven the Poles crazy.

But embassies and war departments throughout Europe had been anything but quiet. Frantic politicians had hurried to conferences, made treaties, broken treaties, cursed, plotted, and finally gave up in a shattering collapse, leaving Poland in the path of the greatest war machine ever known to man. Last evening Warsaw radio had broadcast the latest disastrous news: the German dictator refused to compromise, and the British and French had all but given up on peace, though they repeatedly warned the dictator that war was inevitable if he attacked Poland.

Common sense told Joseph that nothing short of full surrender to Hitler's outrageous demands would satisfy the German ruler. Although Joseph was certain Hitler would give out misinformation to the German people for starting another war, it was plain that he needed no excuse for attacking his neighbors: the good people of Austria and Czechoslovakia could attest to that fact. As an excuse to send troops into Austria, Joseph Goebbels, Hitler's Propaganda Minister, informed the German people that German Austria had been saved from chaos by Germany, that there was fighting in the streets of Vienna! Later, when Hitler made the decision to invade Czechoslovakia, German citizens were fed additional lies. Goebbels released information that Czechoslovakia would fall into dissolution without the assistance of the greatness of the German people. For that reason, Czechoslovakia would have to be occupied!

In the insanity of Hitler's world-view, the victim would be blamed by the perpetrator.

Time was running out for Poland. And, while Poland was surely doomed, Joseph needed only a few more hours of peace in which to whisk his family to safety. Their bags were packed, and all arrangements had been made. They would flee this threatened land in a horse drawn cart. The men Moses had hired to transport them out of Poland were coming at noon. The German Third Army had Poland's Western borders sealed, so they had to go East. For the past few days, Joseph had studied the map until he knew the route by heart: he would take Ester and Miryam through the Soviet Union, into Turkey, and from there by boat to Western Europe.

The trip would be dangerous, but there were no other options.

Joseph looked at his watch the second time, and then pulled back the lace curtains, pressing his forehead against the cold pane, staring futilely at the empty street. The night was black and frightening. He strained to see a telltale gleam of dawn before heaving a worried sigh.

Joseph tried to shake off the feeling of doom that continued to haunt him, regardless of the carefully planned escape, as he walked softly out of the room, down the stairs and into the kitchen where he found his father-in-law sitting alone at the table. Moses was intently counting out the amount of money he believed it would take Joseph to bribe Russian and Turkish officials.

Joseph greeted his father-in-law. "Moses. Good morning."

The old man acknowledged him with a slight nod while continuing with his accounting. There was a tall stack of Polish *zlotys* on the table.

After preparing a cup of coffee, Joseph slipped into a chair and began to study his father-in-law. The previous week had taken a toll on Moses. His eyes were bloodshot and his face pale. He looked exhausted. Still, Joseph knew that as physically drained as he might be, nothing had crushed Moses' fierce will to protect his family. Poland's close call on August 25th had given Moses wings! The old man had accomplished miracles during the week's reprieve. He had sold the Stein mills to a rich Pole who thought the Germans would leave him to his business since he was of the Catholic faith. The man had taken the deeds to the Stein mills, leaving Moses with an enormous bundle of *zlotys.* Moses had refused a bank check, insisting upon the cash. That cash now joined the currency Moses had taken from his bank accounts, along with gold and diamonds in the hidden panel in the library. The Stein sons had followed their father's instructions and had stockpiled food and water. Moses' household employees had spent the week sandbagging the first floor of the house.

The Stein family was ready for a lengthy siege.

Moses Stein was a tenacious old man, and if anyone could survive the Nazi occupation, Joseph figured it would be his father-in-law. In spite of his confidence in Moses' ability to come through, Joseph thought that the Stein family should leave Poland. Joseph had a strong feeling that soon Poland was going to be a very unpleasant place.

His hand automatically groped in his shirt pocket and brought out a packet of cigarettes. He took his time lighting a cigarette, thinking about what he wanted to say. Joseph watched the smoke rise about his head, and then after clearing his throat, he made one last attempt. "Moses. Come with us. For the sake of the women and children, if nothing else."

Moses studiously avoided his eyes, slowly shaking his head. "Joseph," he retorted, "you know that I cannot leave."

Joseph pulled the smoke deep into his lungs before approaching the topic again. This time he became impassioned. "But the Nazis, Moses. The Nazis…"

"Jews have survived worse," Moses answered tonelessly, thinking of the Russian pogroms.

"But Ester will be frantic for your safety," Joseph stubbornly argued.

Moses was quiet for a long time before saying, "You will take care of Ester. She is your wife, your responsibility. Ester belongs with her husband and child in France. The Stein family belongs in Poland."

After the summer's visit, Moses Stein had come to realize that what he had once deemed impossible was now true: Joseph loved Ester as much as Moses loved her. His daughter was safe as long as his son-in-law was alive. That knowledge gave Moses great peace of mind about Ester's well-being.

Joseph stared at Moses for a full five minutes. He flicked his ashes on the edge of the saucer before taking another sip of coffee. It was futile. He knew that he could never convince Moses to leave his beloved Warsaw. But he worried that if the Steins did not leave Poland before the Germans made their strutting entrance, the family might not ever leave Poland again. Still, understanding that Moses had his own plan, Joseph rubbed his forehead with his hand and mumbled in a low voice, "Then, I will pray for your safety."

Knowing that his son-in-law had been raised a non-believer, Moses was touched. He finished counting the money and snapped rubber bands around three separate piles, stacking them together before turning to face Joseph. He smiled faintly, then laid a hand on his shoulder, his crusty manner gone. "Thank you, son. I am glad."

Both men stopped speaking and began listening.

There was a strange humming noise in the atmosphere.

They froze.

The humming grew louder and louder.

"Planes?" Joseph asked in a hushed voice.

Moses sat utterly silent, listening and thinking. After a short pause, he whispered to himself, "Germans." Suddenly, he pulled his hand away from Joseph, stood up and raced to the courtyard, his son-in-law on his heels. Together, the two men stood side by side, staring into the sky, watching the darkness of war come to Poland.

The planes of the German Luftwaffe resembled black crosses, and the bombs they dropped made thumping noises when they hit their targets. Breathtaking explosions and instant, enormous fires began to brighten the Warsaw skyline.

The flash of lights outlined the two men's faces, exposing their expressions of grim horror.

The war had begun!

Hitler had defied the world!

Joseph's hopes of rescuing Ester and their daughter vanished.

Moses Stein moved his mouth in an effort to tell his son-in-law to take cover, but Moses found that for once in his life, his tongue failed to respond.

Insane with fury at the German machines raining death and destruction on civilian Warsaw, threatening his own wife and child, destroying their opportunity to escape, Joseph stood defiantly in the open, shaking his fist at the intruders, screaming obscenities at men he did not know. "Assholes! Fucking German assholes! Goddamn you!"

Moses rushed inside to warn his family, leaving the younger man alone.

Bitter tears rolled down his cheeks and his voice cracked as Joseph Gale cried out, *"Nooooo! Nooooo!"*

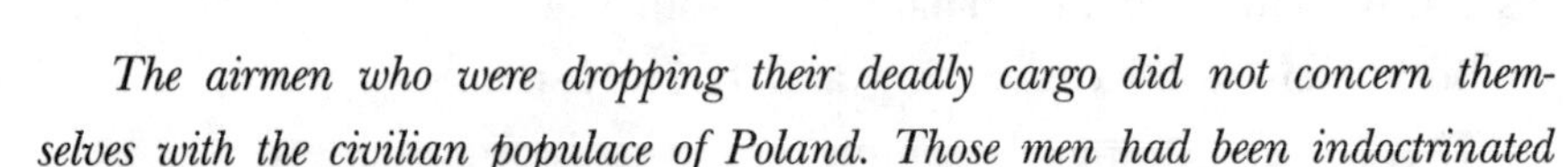

The airmen who were dropping their deadly cargo did not concern themselves with the civilian populace of Poland. Those men had been indoctrinated to believe totally in their mission.

Days in advance of the Luftwaffe attack, and before the German armies penetrated the Polish border, Adolf Hitler delivered a speech to his Generals in a supreme effort to invigorate their waning appetite for war.

Hitler's words were empathic, his orders specific. "Close your hearts to pity! Act brutally! Eighty million people must obtain what is their right, and the stronger man is right. You must be harsh and remorseless, steeling yourself against signs of compassion! Whoever has pondered over this world knows that its meaning lies in the success of the best by means of force."

Hitler's sense of destiny was catching, like an infectious disease, and quickly contaminated the entire Germany military.

And, like the exceptional fighting men they were, the German soldiers followed their orders.

In Paris, the Gale family had gathered in the salon. During this emotional conference, they tried to conceive a plan to rescue Joseph, his wife, and baby from the Germans.

All sorts of wild schemes were put forward.

"Jacques and I will follow the path of the German Army," Michel offered, "taking in enough money to bribe whatever officials necessary to bring them out." After looking at Rachel's worried face, he added, "The entire Stein family if possible."

Benjamin Gale vetoed that idea. "Shall I have all my sons in danger? Besides, if money will save their lives, there is no lack of money in Moses Stein's safe."

Jacques asked, "Can't our government render aid?"

Benjamin glumly shook his head. "I think not. We'll be at war with Germany before morning. I suspect all diplomatic channels are already seriously strained."

A bitchy Natalie Gale blamed the Steins for Joseph's dilemma. Natalie had become increasingly uncomfortable with her religious daughter-in-law and her family. In France there were signs that the wave of anti-Semitism working its way from Germany was beginning to have an effect. Only yesterday Natalie had witnessed a small demonstration against immigrant Jews when Christian French citizens cried out, "France should be returned to the French! Jews go home!" Such scenes only reinforced her idea that no good could come from being branded a Jew. "If the Steins had stayed in Warsaw where they belong," she muttered, "my son would be safe in Paris!"

"Mother!" Jacques sputtered. "Don't say such things." Gently he reminded her, "Have you forgotten that we, too, are Jews?"

Natalie's laugh was artificial as she denied her heritage. "Jews? We are not Jews my darling son, we are French!"

Jacques' mouth hung open as he gaped in amazement, first at his mother and then at his father. "Whatever is mother talking about?" he asked, mystified.

Benjamin patted his wife's hand. "Don't be so hard on your mother, Jacques. Can't you see she is distraught?"

Natalie rewarded her husband with a smile, but tears glistened in her eyes. Just that evening she had decided that of her three sons, Joseph was her favorite. And now her most beloved son was in grave danger.

While pouring drinks for her father and two brothers, Rachel fought back tears. "Joseph may be wounded, perhaps dead…even as we speak!" She wailed, "And the baby!"

Just the day before, Benjamin had received a second telegram, advising him of the safe birth of a grand-daughter.

Michel looked in horror at his sister. "Rachel! Don't even suggest such a possibility!"

"It's true! It's true! Didn't the news say that Warsaw was being bombed?" Rachel collapsed into tears, overturning and spilling a bottle of brandy in the process.

Jacques tried to reassure his sister. "Rachel, you know your brother. Joseph can take care of himself."

A million thoughts were going through Natalie's mind. She looked accusingly at her husband. "Benjamin, I told you we shouldn't circumcise the boys. Remember?"

Benjamin threw his hands in the air. "For God's sake, Natalie!"

"It's true! Joseph will never be able to convince the Nazis he is not Jewish." Natalie, like most Europeans, had heard rumors that the Germans were so obsessed with locating Jews they actually forced grown men to remove their pants and be inspected. Her son looked gentile, but if physically examined would be counted a Jew. Natalie's angry breathing could be heard throughout the room. "A handful of dust means more to the Nazis than the life of a Jew," she declared. "And if you had only listened to me, Joseph wouldn't be in danger!"

Benjamin jumped to his feet, reaching out with his hand for his wife. "Natalie, you are over-stressed." His voice was firm. "Come, we will retire."

Natalie didn't leave the room without protest. "No!" she exclaimed. "We must think of a way to rescue Joseph." As Benjamin guided her away, she turned. "Save Joseph," she told Michel and Jacques. "Leave his wife and child if you have to, but save Joseph."

Jacques watched his parents leave the room. His mother's eyes were making him more and more uneasy. "Wouldn't you say Mother is acting strangely?" he asked. When no one responded, he added, "There are times when mother blames every problem upon her Jewish past."

Michel avoided family quarrels, at all costs. "We don't know what her life was like, before," he said, then paused. "But, it does seem that the Jewish culture which shaped mother also drove her away."

"Every life has its tears." Rachel said bitterly.

Jacques looked at his sister, surprised. He admitted to himself for the first time that his sister's life had been difficult. Rachel was completely overshadowed by her attractive mother and handsome brothers. Jacques had often heard older aunts cruelly remark, in Rachel's presence, that it was a pity the Gale boys got all the looks and charm.

Michel looked at his pocket watch and stood up. "I have to get home. Abbi was expecting me some time ago."

Jacques asked. "Are you joining the military?

Michel was hesitant. "I don't think so. I'll wait for them to call me." He gave his brother a penetrating look. "And you?"

"Tomorrow."

"I thought as much. Medical Corps?"

Jacques gave a small laugh before whispering confidentially, "Not a chance. I want to see those bastard's eyeballs."

Michel looked admiringly at his younger brother. He was not surprised, yet he felt a bit envious of Jacques' detachment from fear. Joseph had that same trait. Older than Jacques by four years and Joseph by five years, Michel had grown up quiet and lonely, seeking comfort from reading and quieter pursuits. "Well, take care of yourself," he said, before embracing his brother and walking away.

"Tell Abbi hello," Jacques replied. He then smiled. "And, inform my two nephews I'll be around to see them tomorrow evening."

"Right."

Rachel was silent as she watched Michel leave the salon. She then gave Jacques a searching look before putting her head on the game table, weeping uncontrollably.

Jacques rubbed his sister's neck and back. "You're worried about

Joseph? He's a bull! Don't you know Joseph can take on ten Germans and not even lose his breath?" Jacques chuckled, remembering a few times when Joseph had scared the hell out of him.

In spite of Jacques' comforting touch and soothing words, Rachel couldn't stop crying. Deep inside she was gripped with a terrifying knowledge she could not explain.

Rachel Gale knew that the Nazis were about to shatter their wonderful world.

Chapter V

The Warsaw Ghetto

Within a week of attacking Poland, the German Army sped across the countryside and arrived at the outskirts of Warsaw. The nearly defeated Polish Military reorganized and 160,000 troops fiercely defended their capital city. The German Blitzkrieg faltered, then stopped.

Hitler's surprise at the brave tenacity of the Poles turned into fury. The dictator ordered that in addition to continuing air raids, the hapless city was to be targeted with heavy artillery bombardment.

On September 17th, the Russian Army attacked Poland from the East. Warsaw was under siege.

By September 25th, lacking military supplies and food, Warsaw prepared to surrender. On that day the Germans made their final assault on the city, attacking with such ferocity that the terrified citizens of Poland thought the Germans meant to kill every living creature.

On September 27, 1939, Warsaw fell.

While singing Heili Heilo, their song of victory, the men of the victorious German Army marched into the destroyed city.

A reign of terror began for the 350,000 Jewish residents of Warsaw, bringing to a tragic end the accumulation of a treasure house of centuries of Jewish art, education, and culture that had enriched Warsaw.

German violence was numbing in its intensity.

Starving Jews were pulled from food lines.

Jews were kidnapped for forced labor.

Jewish bank accounts were frozen.

Jewish businesses were closed.

Jews over age ten were forced to wear a white armband with a blue Star of David.

Jews were banned from using sidewalks, entering public places, or using public transport.

Jews were put under a curfew.

A daily food ration was enforced: 2,613 calories per day for Germans; 669 calories per day for Poles; and 184 calories per day for Jews.

On November 16, 1940, the Warsaw Ghetto was sealed, effectively locking 30% of Warsaw's population into 2.5% of the city's living space. Inside this city "within a city" the Jews worked, shopped, and struggled to keep from starving.

World War II lasted 2,076 days. No city in Europe suffered more than Warsaw, and no people more than the Jews.

February, 1942

When Joseph Gale came out of the ghetto bakery, he saw the most extraordinary sight. About four feet in front of the bakery, there was an emaciated figure, naked except for a small blanket pulled around it, jumping up and down in the snow. The skin of the figure was ghostly white and stretched tightly over bones. Joseph had a quick, hideous thought that he was looking at a little skeleton covered with white dough.

Joseph knew that something was happening, but he didn't know what, and that worried him. He stopped to take a good look. The moment he paused, a small boy jumped out of hiding and grabbed the bread from Joseph's arms. Joseph was so startled that he yelled, "Stop! Thief!"

The child ran away. Joseph followed, quickly grasping the pitiful child in his arms. The boy fought like a wild animal, kicking and clawing, and at the same time stuffing as much of the bread into his mouth as possible. The figure in the white sheet suddenly appeared and grabbed a portion of the bread, pushing the bread down its throat, swallowing large pieces of it. The strange figure in the blanket proved to be another young boy. Joseph had no intention of taking the bread away from the boys and he tried to quiet them. "Stop fighting! Stop fighting!" he said. "I am going to take you to my wife. She will prepare you a hot soup."

The boys thought the offer was a trick and continued to struggle with Joseph.

A crowd began to gather. Joseph quickly realized the danger to everyone. Joseph wrapped the two boys close to his body with one arm and dug into his pocket with his free hand, bringing out a 50 *zloty* bill. He held the money above his head, tempting the children with the money. "If you will stop fighting, I'll buy you plenty of food, and warm clothes."

Finally realizing Joseph had no intention of harming them, the boys' wildness began to evaporate.

At that moment, a German soldier rounded the corner and spotted the threesome.

The ghetto swarmed with orphans. The children first sold their clothes to buy food and later traveled in packs, banding together to beg or steal food. The German command had made such acts a serious crime, and the German soldier quickly realized the children were thieves. He decided to take the boys into custody.

Walking toward Joseph, the soldier swung his truncheon in a menacing manner. Without saying a word, he tried to strike the boys.

Instinctively, Joseph pulled away from the man, folding the bill in one of the boy's shrunken palms, before releasing the two. *"Run!"* he warned them.

Joseph's good deed brought him the full attention of the German. The soldier was enraged. "You!" he shouted. "Germans command! Jews obey! You cannot give orders!"

Joseph intentionally kept his face impassive. He shrugged.

The German was a S.S. guard battalion officer, a soldier, naturally suspicious, who, after years of diligent brainwashing by the Nazi party, truly believed that all Jews were foul inferior beings. Looking at Joseph, he had a quick thought that the tall, well-built man before him could not possibly be a part of the disgusting Jewish race. He squinted at Joseph. "Are you a Jew?" he asked in a demanding tone.

"Do you think I'd be wearing *this*, otherwise?" Joseph pointed at his armband, the identifying emblem of Warsaw Jews: a blue-colored star of David sewn on a white armband.

The Nazi circled Joseph, thinking. Joseph's good looks and decent clothes were a complete mystery.

Joseph wondered if he could disarm the soldier, who was perhaps fifty pounds lighter than Joseph, and make a quick getaway.

Before Joseph could act on his thoughts, the soldier pulled his hand-gun and called out for reinforcements. The German wondered if he had captured a Polish smuggler. Any number of Poles were willing to assist the Jews, for the right price.

Joseph soon found himself sitting on the hard ground, surrounded by Polish police. The German fitted some type of metal instrument around Joseph's head, taking a measurement. The size and shape of Joseph's head did not match the German guidelines for Jewish heads, so the soldier decided his prisoner was definitely a smuggler.

Smuggling in the Warsaw Ghetto was a crime punishable by death.

The soldier gave a smug look to one of the Polish policemen. "I was right! This man is not a Jew."

Joseph shouted an outraged objection at the Nazi. "I most certainly am a Jew!"

The Nazi shook his head vehemently. "You are no Jew!"

The irony of the situation made Joseph break into ironic laughter. "I tell you, I am a full-blooded Jew!"

Jews passing on the street couldn't believe what they were hearing. With their pale complexions and sunken faces, they looked at Joseph with amazement. They had not heard anyone in occupied Poland proclaim himself a Jew, or seen anyone with the courage to speak harshly to a German in a very long time.

Joseph knocked the metal object off his head. His voice was dripping with venom. "Surely you don't believe your own ridiculous propaganda." The German government had utilized the bizarre gadget for years to prove that Jews were of a lesser intellect than other races.

The Polish police exchanged uneasy glances as they slowly moved away from the prisoner. They were surprised at Joseph's bold behavior and fully expected him to be shot by the Nazi soldier.

The Nazi's eyes glinted with curiosity, thinking perhaps there could be profit here. This man might lead him to other, more important Polish smugglers, or wealthy Jews. Such a catch might mean a promotion.

Joseph felt his entire body flash hot when the Nazi soldier said, "Take him to Pawiak." Whether he was tortured and killed, or sent to a labor camp, Joseph feared that his wife and child might never know what happened to him. He knew such a situation would cause Ester unimaginable grief. He cursed himself for being so reckless.

Surrounded by the police and marched into Pawiak Prison, Joseph was unceremoniously dumped into a small dirty cell already holding four other Jews.

Expecting the worst, Joseph waited but nothing happened. Evidently he had been forgotten! While his cellmates were taken out on a daily basis and interrogated and tortured, Joseph was ignored. Still, he overheard the vicious beatings, the horrible screams, and the heartbreaking pleas for mercy.

The three days Joseph was held prisoner were unlike any other, yet he knew the days were no different from days lived by so many other Jews. Like prisoners who came before him, and prisoners who followed him, Joseph sat in his cell, wondering how he would die and when he would die, and praying to his newfound God to let him die with courage.

While waiting, Joseph decided that one way or another, before he died, he was going to kill as many of the bastards as he could. Somehow, the death of a few Germans would help sweeten the horror of his own premature death.

And then Moses Stein came with a bag of diamonds, postponing Joseph's confrontation with the Nazis.

After much negotiation, five of Moses' largest diamonds were required to save Joseph's life.

Joseph was greatly distressed at the price paid for his life, thinking about the large quantity of food those diamonds would have bought on the black market. The times were unimaginably bleak, and nothing was as valuable as food in the Warsaw Ghetto. The Germans were trying to starve the Jews to death and without hard cash to purchase extra provisions from the food smugglers, the Stein family would be forced to subside on ghetto rations of 184 calories per Jew per day. A cat would starve on the German enforced ration of 184 calories.

Joseph couldn't stop thinking about food, even as Ester laughed and cried all at the same time, touching his face, his hair, his hands, babbling to her mother that Joseph was not an apparition, that he was alive and had been returned to her.

Rarely did a Jew make it out of Pawiak Prison alive.

Ester jumped from Joseph to Moses and embraced her father. "You saved him! Oh, Papa, thank you! You saved him!"

"Miryam! I must tell Miryam!" With a shining face, Ester ran to get Miryam, to wake the child from a troubled sleep. The girl had been comfortless since the day her father had disappeared.

Looking at his granddaughter's rush of happiness at the sight of her father, Moses knew that he would have given the Germans all the diamonds, if that is what it would have taken to bring Joseph Gale out of Pawiak unharmed.

Sara Stein studied her son-in-law's face. "You look so tired, Joseph. Moses, can't you see how tired he is?"

"The boy's more hungry than he is tired." Not wanting to upset Ester, Moses whispered in Sara's ear. "He's been fed nothing but hard bread and watery soup, since the day they took him."

Sara patted Joseph's cheek. "I'll prepare a hot dish," she promised.

"That would be wonderful," Joseph said, unconsciously licking his lips. He was ravenous.

Soon Sara could be heard in the kitchen, preparing a bean stew.

The delicious aroma drifted through the apartment, arousing Joseph's hunger to a point of actual pain.

While stirring the pot of stew, Sara glanced over her shoulder through the open door now and then, looking at the happy reunion. Sara moved her lips in prayer, vastly relieved that they had not lost yet another member of their family. At that thought, Sara's stomach knotted. Joseph's safe return had cast the memory of her lost sons in motion once again.

Since the 25th day of the German attack, the blows had fallen, one after the other, until the Stein family had been devastated.

The Pole's unexpected and brave defense had infuriated the Nazi dictator, and Hitler had given a command to level Warsaw. Even as Warsaw had been on the verge of surrender, the Germans had continued to rain death upon the city, with the bombings reaching a new height of terror on September 25, 1939.

They had later heard that seventy tons of incendiary bombs were dropped on Warsaw during that one day. And that was the day their luck ran out: Abraham, Eilam, their wives, and seven of their eight children had been burned alive in Abraham's apartment home.

At the time, Moses and Sara were still living in their three-storey neo-classical villa located in the Zochodnia district, situated between the Polish southern and Jewish north-western district. Abraham lived only two blocks away. Even as they hovered in the cellar, they had heard the blast. Rushing to the first floor, they had seen the fire and smoke coming from the direction of Abraham's apartment.

In a blind panic, Sara, along with the rest of the family, had rushed to try and save them. Both floors of the apartment house had partially collapsed and were ablaze. Eilam, with his eight-month-old son clasped tight in his arms, was discovered by Joseph and pulled alive from the burning building. Eilam, horribly injured, died in Moses' arms, pleading with his father to save his wife and children.

That had been over two years ago, but Sara could still smell the awful stench of burning flesh…the flesh of her flesh.

And, the boy…David… His small body had been sheltered by his father and was free from injury. But David had suffered ghastly facial burns and injuries. They quickly discovered the horrifying truth: David had been blinded!

Warsaw was in chaos after 25 days of bombardment, the hospitals were destroyed, and no doctors were to be found. By that time, the Red Cross was useless. Sara had seen with her own eyes Red Cross personnel abandoning the wounded to take cover from German shells.

Sara had done what she could to ease David's suffering, and she had succeeded in saving her grandson's life. Sara often wondered if she had made a mistake, for still, after all this time, the boy was easily frightened. Still, he cried for his mama. For hours on end, the boy would swing his little head from side to side, whimpering like a frightened and uncomprehending animal, acting as if by changing his direction his vision might return.

David was a most heartbreaking sight. Only Miryam could get the boy to smile. With her sweet ways she teased and coaxed her little cousin to forget—if only for a moment—the drastic turn his young life had taken.

Sara went into the sitting room to tell Joseph his meal would be ready shortly. Her eyes fell on the rickety furniture, reminding her of the beautiful home and furnishings they had lost. About a year after the invasion, the dreaded rumors of a Jewish ghetto came true. On November 16, 1940, the Jews of Warsaw were sealed behind a walled ghetto. Every Jew in the city was forced to move within the old Jewish section of Warsaw, which the Germans were careful to call the "Jewish quarter," forbidding the use of the term ghetto. But as Moses had said, "A ghetto is a ghetto, no matter what the Germans might call it." At last count, there were nearly 400,000 Jews living in the confinement of the Warsaw Ghetto. The population continued to swell as the Nazis transported Jews from the countryside into the ghetto.

Moses had managed to get them a good apartment on Chtodna Street where the apartments were quite large, big enough for the entire family to live together, even though they were terribly cramped. But no one complained, for some poor souls were living 20 persons to a room!

The Germans had forbidden Moses to move their expensive furniture, and they had heard later that their home was occupied by a top-ranking S.S. officer. Unexpectedly, they had been allowed to keep their clothes and even Moses' extensive library, which was a shocking but pleasant surprise.

Sara leaned against the doorframe, watching but no longer listening, while taking a silent accounting of her shrinking family. Israel had disappeared last August. In the wrong place at the wrong time, Israel had been abducted off the streets. After frantic investigation, Moses had been informed by a member of the Judenrat, the Jewish Council appointed by the Nazis to keep order in the ghetto, that Israel had been taken to work in a labor camp far away from Warsaw.

Israel Stein was a slave laborer.

When told, Sara had screamed, "No! Moses, no!" She had heard about the beastly conditions endured by Jews in such circumstances: Germans forcing Jews to carry frozen lead pipes with their bare hands...Jews made to push carts loaded with rocks up hills...Jews beaten for no reason other than that they were Jewish. Everyone knew that the German or Polish supervisors devised particularly harsh assignments for Jews who appeared intelligent or wealthy.

Men just like Israel Stein.

Once the invasion ended and the occupation was completed, Sara had assumed that her three remaining sons were safe, for Moses had paid a steep price to keep his sons and Joseph off the registry for slave labor.

The labor battalion registry had been started to appease the Germans, to keep them from snatching men off the streets. Wealthy Jews paid to keep their names off the list. And while it was not an uncommon practice for certain families to receive preferential treatment, there were occasions when their wealth and influence could not save them. Random selection for labor camps was still a danger for Jewish men between the ages of sixteen and sixty.

Moses had done everything in his power to locate the camp, but no one seemed to know, or to care, just where Israel had been taken. Then, only last week they had learned from an escaped laborer what had happened to their son.

Moses' contact at the Judenrat had been wrong, the labor camp was located only 15 miles south of Warsaw.

The escapee's name was Noy, meaning ornament, probably named because of unusual beauty at birth. Now he looked anything but beautiful with his thin, wasted body, and his head balding from malnutrition. Sara thought he looked like a young child suddenly overtaken by old age.

Savoring some hearty soup that Sara had prepared for him, Noy told Israel's story slowly, a hacking cough interrupting his words. His eyes remained fixed on the soup, but in the telling, a terrible sadness darkened his face. "The camp was so near to the city that many men tried to break out. The large number of escapees angered the Polish supervisor—I think because the Germans beat him each time someone escaped. He warned us that the next man who ran would be severely punished. But it was so harsh in the camp that nothing could stop us.

Last December, your son, Israel, and two other men tried to break out. Two of the three were successful. Your son was caught."

Noy became absorbed, remembering Israel. He gave Sara a warm look. "Your son, he was a good person. He was always looking after somebody, sharing his blanket, encouraging us to survive...yes...Israel Stein was a decent sort."

Sara's heart plunged as she remembered the story they had heard.

"I tell you, that that Pole was angry! He had lost two more men, and knew what was coming. All of that anger fell on your son. He decided to make an example of Israel Stein."

Sara made a soft guttural sound, deep in her throat. At that point, Moses had made her go into the kitchen, insisting that Noy needed a real meal. But Sara knew that Moses was merely trying to protect her, and she had stood behind the door and listened to every word.

"The Pole hadn't been too bad, up until then. But the Germans threatened him, telling him they were going to send his family to a concentration camp if he didn't stop being soft on the Jews. So he turned sadistic...beating your boy with a pipe, until we didn't know how he could still be alive. Later on, when we passed by him, Israel called out and asked that someone tell his family...said he knew you'd be worried sick...not knowing...he tried hard to live...but the cold took him."

In terrible pain from his wounds, the most gentle of Sara's sons had been tied to a stake and left to die a hard, slow death in the bitter cold of a Polish winter. Completely alone.

Three sons, two daughters-in-law, and seven grandchildren: all dead.

Ester laughed loudly at something Miryam said, jerking Sara back to the present. She watched as her daughter took the child back into the bedroom, all the while assuring her, "Miryam, papa will still be here tomorrow morning. I promise!" Ester gave her daughter a loud kiss. "Now, darling, I want you to be a good girl and go back to sleep."

Sara returned to the kitchen.

Joseph poignantly watched his wife and child until they were out of view. He was silent for a few moments, digesting the implications of his close call. What would they have done if he had not returned? Unconsciously, he squared his broad shoulders and turned to his father-in-law. "Moses, thank you. For life."

Moses, his face alive with the victory, gave Joseph an enormous smile. "Your face is like a medicine to us!" Moses tilted his head from one side to the other and looked at his two surviving sons, Daniel and Gershom, giving them each a wink.

Daniel and Gershom had been awakened by the loud noise and laughter and were now hanging about Joseph.

Gershom patted his brother-in-law on the back. "Joseph, thank God you are safe."

Daniel kissed Joseph on both cheeks, then stood back and stared into Joseph's face. "You don't look too bad." He paused, then added sorrowfully, "Israel was right, you know."

Moses shot his son a questioning glance. "Israel?"

Daniel ran a hand through his hair before he replied. "About a week before he was taken, Israel told me he had come to the conclusion that few Jews would live through this dark time. I'll never forget what he told me. He said, 'Daniel, under the Nazis, you don't know how your life will end, or why it will end, or when it will end, but you do know it will end.'" Daniel controlled himself with an effort, for he had been closest to Israel. "He was right. We'll all die before this occupation is over."

There was a moment of silence.

Joseph whitened. The past two years made it clear to him that the Nazis were capable of committing shocking inhumanities. Now, after what he had witnessed in Pawiak Prison, he was afraid that Israel had been right. If the war didn't end soon, it would be a miracle if a Jew in Poland survived.

Moses' face hardened in determination. "No! Your brother was wrong, Daniel! We *can* survive. If I had known your brother's whereabouts, I could have saved his life." He held up a hand in protest. "Remember, the Russians took gold in lieu of your grandfather's life." He pointed at Joseph. "The Germans returned this life, for diamonds. I tell you, they can be bought! Our enemies are men of greed." Moses smiled faintly. "And…their greed will be our salvation."

Daniel, his arms behind his back, clenched and unclenched his fists, trying to keep the anger from flooding his face. His father was dead wrong, and Daniel knew it. He tried to keep his voice respectful. "Pa, the only way we can survive is to fight! We should take part of the money and send our wives and children out of this ghetto…through the sewers…in the garbage wagon…anyway that we can!" Daniel looked at Joseph and Gershom, trying to gain their support. "I have heard that there are Polish farmers who are willing to take Jewish women and children into their homes, for a certain price. We can get them out, a few at the time! They will be safer in the countryside, anyhow. The men will remain in the ghetto and fight." He looked imploringly at Moses. "Pa, we can buy hundreds of guns with the money you have. Just give me the word!"

Moses was unmoved, and he answered cautiously, "Daniel, we will wait this war out, without joining in the fight." He gave his son a probing look. He had recently heard worrisome reports that Daniel had joined a group of young toughs who thought violence should be met with violence. Now, looking at his son, Moses had a strong feeling that what he had heard was true, and it worried him. Attacking Germans was the surest route to attracting the attention of the Nazis. He couldn't save a single member of his family from the S.S. if Daniel behaved like a fool.

The two men were locked in a staring match.

Daniel knew that his father was living in a fantasy world if he thought the Germans could be reasoned with, for any amount of money. Perhaps a few of the Germans could be tempted, but the vast majority possessed a deadly appetite for killing Jews. As a direct result of German hatred, Poland was becoming one vast Jewish graveyard.

Daniel broke the silence. "Pa. We won't be defeated without a struggle!"

Moses tried to be calm. "Son. First we must survive the German occupation. To fight them now means certain death. Soon, the war will go to Germany. Hitler was insane to attack Russia." He shook his head from side to side. "Fighting the East...fighting the West... Germany has made too many enemies. In the end, they will lose this war, and their enemies will devour Hitler and free the planet from the marauding Germans." With an edge of triumph in his voice, Moses declared, "When the Huns begin their inevitable decline, *then* we will fight."

Daniel was tired of the old and timid Jews in the Ghetto. Jews were dying like flies while men such as his father thought the Germans could simply be outlasted. He became excited. "When? When? When the war is over. At the moment of peace we will fight?"

"And why not?" Moses said. "Tell me, son, when in history has the last day of war been the first day of peace?"

Gershom had heard his father and Daniel go over the same territory too many times. Gershom didn't know what to think, so he followed his instinct and put his life and the lives of his wife and children in God's hand. He quietly announced, "If God means for us to live, then we will. If not, then we will die." He expelled a long breath. "Our fate is that simple."

Joseph was beginning to think like Daniel, but he didn't believe the evening was the appropriate place to have such an important discussion. Emotions were too strong. Deciding to stop the exchange between Moses and his son before their disagreement flared into a shouting match, Joseph changed the subject. "Moses, I am sorry. About the diamonds."

Moses shrugged his shoulders. "Joseph, you might as well stop worrying about those diamonds. That's what they are for…to keep the Stein family alive." Anxiously he glanced at Daniel and his voice took on a hard edge. "Not for killing Germans."

Daniel's large brown eyes took on a shattered look. He did not want to spoil his family's happiness over Joseph's return, so he gave up the argument. Waving his arms in disgust, Daniel left the room without saying good-night.

Moses stared off into space. Daniel's deliberate rudeness would have been unimaginable before the war.

Joseph was dismayed at the rift between the father and son, but he masked his feelings, returning to the business of the evening. "I will never forgive myself. I was stupid to get arrested." Joseph voiced what they both secretly feared. "This war may go on for years. You will need all that you have saved, and more."

Joseph's regret went much deeper than the loss of diamonds. His arrest had put the family into grave danger.

Since the first moment the ghetto was closed, and the Nazis had concentrated their most hated victims in one area, the Stein family had done their utmost to live inconspicuously, making a desperate attempt to remain anonymous to their S.S. guards. That was no longer possible. After today, the S.S. was now aware that Moses Stein was a very wealthy Jew.

That was most unfortunate.

Moses gave a dry, humorless laugh. "That S.S. officer, Captain Kleist, told me it was the fault of a child. That you would never have been arrested had it not been for a boy. Is that so?"

Sara suddenly reappeared. She frowned and asked, "Child? What child?"

Moses prodded him. "Exactly what happened? Captain Kleist didn't give me the details. And," he gave a dry laugh, "I didn't wait around to find out."

Ester came into the room and sat next to Joseph, her hand holding his. "Miryam and I gave thanks to God," she told him. Quickly she motioned for Joseph to go on with his conversation.

Joseph began to relax a little. The entire episode had been so ridiculous that he now could hardly believe a trip to the bakery had almost cost him his life. He smiled wryly and then began to speak. "That Captain was right. I was arrested because of a child. A hungry child." He gave a rueful chuckle, reminded of another detail. "There were two boys, actually. They set me up." Pausing for a moment, he thought back and then with deliberate slowness, he told the family the tale.

Scarcely breathing, Moses, Gershom, Sara, and Ester peered at him intently, listening. Each was aware of the homeless children of the ghetto, the pitiful youngsters whose parents had either been killed by the Germans or had died from disease or starvation. Those little ones had no way to live except to steal or beg, or if they were lucky, they were taken into one of the orphanages set up in the ghetto. Only last week they had heard about a small boy who had stolen bread and had allowed himself to be beaten to death rather than give up the bread.

Ester quietly wiped the tears from her face. She had fed many street urchins over the past couple of years. As a mother, she thought nothing was so terrible as the hungry band of orphans roaming the ghetto streets.

"The soldier saw what happened," Joseph continued, "and he tried to take the two children into custody. I argued with him, telling him that they were nothing more than two hungry children." Joseph raised his eyebrows and groaned, "That's when I got into serious trouble."

"Ah, yes," Moses murmured, he understood perfectly, knowing that the Germans would never let such a thing pass. "All Germans are sticklers for the law. In that S.S. guard's mind, a child stealing bread was just cause for punishment."

An angry Ester spoke up. "Those babies were starving!"

Sara finished her daughter's thoughts. "Yes, and due to the German policy of withholding food!"

Moses interrupted, "Don't ever forget, in the Nazi mind, a private citizen should never assist in the escape of a hooligan but should hand a criminal over, without a struggle. Remember that, all of you!" he warned them sternly.

"Never would I hand over a child!"

Ester looked accusingly at her father. Moses made a gesture of resignation with his hands. "To the Germans, the world is either black or white."

Joseph scratched his head, then quickly pulled his hand away and looked at it with horror. "Shit!" he yelled out, "I have the lice!"

Joseph dashed into the kitchen, heartily cursing the filth of Pawiak Prison.

Ester rushed behind him. "I'll boil some water," she volunteered.

The Stein household was one of the few that could claim victory over the parasitic and insidious insect which plagued the citizens of the Warsaw Ghetto. The Steins hard-won success was attributed to nothing less than Sara's insistence that each time a member of their family ventured into the streets, a full bath and complete boiling of their clothes would be awaiting them upon their return.

Once Joseph washed, he polished off his pot of stew.

Then the family retired.

The past three days had been hideous and Joseph was exhausted, but he could not rest. Long after Ester had gone to sleep, he lay awake and stared blankly at the ceiling.

With acute longing, Joseph began to think about his family in France, still struggling, even after all this time, to understand that Paris was under German occupation. Joseph had wept in humiliation when he read how the German Army marched down the Champs Elysees. His only comfort came from the knowledge that Michel and Jacques had both safely returned from the Western Front.

The last communication from the Gales had arrived over six-months earlier stuffed in the center of a block of cheese. Joseph had read the one-page letter so many times that the message was now a part of him.

His father had written:

Our Darling Son,

We pray each day for your safety, and for that of Ester and Miryam, and for all the Steins. What we hear of Warsaw is frightening. We fear for your very life. We are living for your return.

Even in France, the noose is tightening. Many French citizens have joined the Germans against our people. Blue-shirted French Fascists now picket Jewish shops. Your mother has refused to leave the house since her identity card was stamped Juif. We are personally safe for the time being, but due to French collaboration, many immigrant Jews are languishing in Internment Camps. Such news has come as a shock to your mother and me, to say the very least, for we had not expected a single Frenchmen to join hands with the Germans against the Jews.

Your brother Jacques no longer lives in Paris. We have not seen him in nearly three months. But we hear he is well. Michel, his family, and Rachel are safe. The moment the war ends, please hurry home. We will be waiting at the door.

Papa and family.

Joseph gave a deep sigh. He had no doubt that Jacques had joined the resistance. That would explain why he no longer lived at home—he did not want his family to be endangered. Jacques was a bold, inventive man and would undoubtedly volunteer for the most dangerous assignments. Joseph turned restlessly from side to side. How he longed to be fighting by his brother's side! Together, they would be formidable foes against the Germans. Locked in a ghetto and helpless, he could only hope Jacques would survive the war. Would he ever see his brother again?

To distract his mind from that disturbing possibility, he allowed his thoughts to drift back to his own confrontation with the Germans. Joseph had managed to avoid such an encounter for the past two years. He had purposely eluded the Germans soldiers by staying in the

Stein home day after day. Joseph found wearing the armband insulting. And the preposterous regulations requiring Jews to show their German masters homage by stepping off the sidewalk and doffing hats enraged him to the point of violence. On the rare occasions when he did walk outside, he had watched in disbelief as Polish Jews did the Germans' bidding, seemingly without a struggle. He decided that after years of Christian Polish intimidation, the Polish Jews had learned to disguise their contempt. But Joseph Gale was no Pole. His French upbringing blocked any possibility of showing such deference to any man, and in particular to the hated S.S. guards. Joseph knew the Germans might kill him for the slightest offense. His love for Ester and Miryam made him want to survive. Avoiding the Germans seemed to be a wise strategy. Moses Stein's large sums of money made it possible for Joseph to lock himself away in Moses' library, reading one book after another, waiting for the second world war to end.

Joseph now realized he had been naïve.

Daniel Stein was right. The time had come for Jews to resist...to fight their oppressors.

Joseph turned on his side and stared at Ester as she slept. In his eyes, Ester was one of God's sweetest works. Joseph lightly touched his wife's face and hair with his hand. At that moment, he decided to join Daniel's militant group. Tomorrow morning, Joseph Gale would begin to kill Germans. After all, he told himself, each dead German was one less threat to his beloved wife.

After kissing his wife's cheek and covering his young daughter with an extra blanket, Joseph slept a peaceful sleep.

Chapter VI
Resistance

In early 1942, Adolf Hitler decided the time had come to find a final solution to the Jewish problem. Even though the Wehrmacht had suffered setbacks in Russia, Hitler believed the war would soon be won. He saw himself as the undisputed ruler of all Europe. Along with military victory, he insisted upon the elimination of the Jewish problem. Nothing less than total extermination of the Jewish race would satisfy the Nazi dictator.

Reich Marshal Hermann Goering was listening closely when Hitler said, "The Polish Jews are the easiest to get to, and besides, the Jews in Poland are the greatest danger to Reich society. Those Jews are bearers of disease, black-market smugglers and are generally unfit for slave labor."

Goering eagerly agreed. The Reich Marshall set about to ensure that the Fuehrer's orders were followed to the letter.

The Warsaw Ghetto: On the Sabbath - April 19, 1942

"We are becoming the filthy creatures the Germans proclaim we are," Joseph muttered to no one in particular, as he walked around and over the miserable Jews who lay sleeping on the sidewalk of the ghetto. His breathing was purposely shallow. The streets of the ghetto stank with the sharp odors of urine and unwashed bodies wracked with bloody diarrhea. Joseph took in the pathetic scene, searing the images on his brain, vowing that one day soon ghetto fighters would seek justice for every man, woman, and child who died in the Warsaw Ghetto.

Just the night before, Joseph had attended his first meeting of the Jewish underground. The group had no more than four weapons, and so the most gentile looking man of the group would soon be leaving the ghetto to meet with Polish resistance. Everyone had high hopes that the man would return with additional weapons.

The thought of taking action, any kind of action, made Joseph's insides surge with adrenaline. He flexed his muscles, thankful that he was still young and strong. Joseph had awakened slowly, but now his fury was formidable, as if the simmering of his emotions had come to a full boil.

Out of the corner of his eye he saw the form of a skeletal woman in a doorway, huddled over two small babies, their cries as weak as newborn kittens. His anger rose to new heights. He began to walk faster, whispering, "Sorry, so sorry," each time his foot accidentally made contact with a bundle of rags covering the body of a wretched Jew.

Joseph turned his mind back to the problem of the moment. His father-in-law's life was in danger, and Joseph felt the blame was his own.

Since Joseph's arrest two months before, the Germans had tightened their strangle-hold on the Stein family. Within a week of Joseph's release, Moses had received orders for the family to vacate the apartment on Chtodna and move into a much smaller unit on Nisko Street.

After that, the Gestapo targeted Moses' two remaining sons.

First they had come for Gershom, saying that he was needed at a work camp. At the last moment, the S.S. guard had accepted three pieces of gold for Gershom's release.

Daniel had been arrested last week, but the Germans were unaware that they had apprehended a major participant in the Jewish underground. The S.S. had charged Daniel with hoarding money. Daniel's incarceration was nothing more than a crude method of blackmail, and Moses had paid the Germans in *zlotys*, even as he insisted that the money he gave them was the last of his riches.

Since Daniel's release, the Stein family had waited for the S.S. to make their next move. "Pa," Daniel warned his father, "until they are certain we are impoverished, the Germans will be like a dog with a bone." He paused before adding, "Then, they will kill us all."

"Bone?" Moses fired back, "What good is a bone! Enough already, the Germans have already gnawed my flesh to the bone."

Nothing was going according to Moses' well-thought-out plan. Until now, he had never considered the possibility of defeat. Yet, as his hoard of coins grew smaller, his fears grew larger.

Daniel pressed on. "Pa, haven't you figured the Nazis out? The Germans are like a wall you can't climb, you can't break through, and you can't by-pass." Daniel's thoughts festered into hatred. "Pa, we have to meet them face to face and fight to the finish."

Moses knew with sinking certainty that his riches provided the only ray of light that had illuminated their darkening world. He shook his head but said nothing, stubbornly holding on to the hope that his money would last until the war ended.

Now, only one week later, the Stein family was caught in yet another crisis not of their making.

The previous week, a German soldier had been murdered in the no-man's land between the ghetto wall and the Aryan side of the city. When that happened, whispered rumors had made the rounds that the S.S. was going to avenge the soldier. No one knew what form the revenge might take, but the Jews had already had enough experience with the Germans to know that sooner or later a blow would fall. The ghetto population was stricken with fear, and when the Germans finally struck, the Jews paid dearly.

The night before, on the eve of the Sabbath, the S.S. had entered the ghetto, and a terrible massacre had taken place. The S.S. came with a list, a register of names that struck every segment of the ghetto community. Prominent Jews, former Judenrat officials, along with poor Jews from the lowest level of society, were pulled from their beds and executed.

Moses Stein's name was on that list.

One of Moses' numerous contacts saved his life. A Jewish policemen, Tolek Grinspan, formerly an attorney for Moses' pre-war business interests and a man who had been in Moses' pay since the day he was appointed a policemen, had warned Moses in time for him to seek shelter in the home of a friend.

In a rush to kill all the Jews on the list, the S.S. guards had quickly searched the apartment and said nothing to Daniel's weak lie that Moses Stein had recently died after a lethal bout of pneumonia.

Even as they watched the S.S. men leave the apartment, Daniel pulled Joseph into the hallway and said, "We haven't seen the last of them." Daniel's voice was alive with hostility.

The next morning, Tolek Grinspan sent one of the street orphans with the message that Moses must meet him that evening, at the corner of the Moriah Synagogue, on Karmalicka Street. Afraid the meeting might be a set-up, that Tolek's fear of the Germans over-powered his greed, Joseph insisted on making the contact.

Joseph slowed his pace as he neared his destination. He saw Tolek before Tolek saw him. Even in the darkness it was easy, since Tolek wore the distinguishing starred cap and high boots of the Jewish force. Tolek was leaning against the synagogue and he had a rubber club in his right hand, which he was beating rhythmically against his left palm.

Joseph stood in the shadow, watching. He is nervous, Joseph thought. That is a good sign, making Joseph think that Tolek was anxious about his rendezvous with Moses Stein. If the assignation were a ruse arranged by the Germans, Tolek would not be in danger and therefore would be more relaxed. It made sense.

Joseph looked all around and then sauntered toward Tolek. He stood a head taller than Tolek, who was a short, plump man in his mid-fifties. He nodded and looked down at the man, "Tolek."

Unable to mask his surprise, Tolek asked, "Where is Moses?"

"With friends."

Tolek studied Joseph's face for a moment, scratching the end of his nose with a dirty fingernail. He made a quick decision, deciding to deal with the son-in-law. "I have some good information for him." He stared up at Joseph, his silence long, the implications clear. Tolek wanted compensation prior to providing the information.

With a great effort, Joseph kept his bitterness from showing.

During the early days of the ghetto, the Germans had forced the Jews to form their own police force, which dually reported to the Polish Police and the German authorities. And, in the very beginning, the Jews who made up the force had been responsible and well-behaved. As time passed, they exploited their position and used their authority to enjoy special privileges, slowly becoming hated symbols of power. Moses was tolerant of their weakness for bribery, for he used the situation to his advantage, but Joseph was less forgiving of Jews who bled other Jews, even though the Steins themselves benefited from corruption.

Joseph's eyes narrowed. Tolek was fat and sleek. The sight of the man's oily flesh disgusted him. Joseph would bet a thousand *zlotys* that Tolek Grinspan ate meat every day. Sara Stein no longer served meat at her table, and the Stein babies had milk only once a week. Miryam had begun to lose weight. Joseph clenched his teeth. Finally, he asked, "How much?"

Tolek gave him a funny look. "Moses didn't tell you?"

Joseph shook his head, "No."

"The fee is set." Tolek nervously looked over his shoulder. "Are you sure he didn't advise you?"

"Moses is in hiding, my friend."

Tolek carefully appraised Joseph Gale, thinking how he could benefit. Despite his intimidating size, Moses Stein's French son-in-law was not known as a man of violence, and Tolek felt Joseph could be pushed. Besides, doing business with the Steins was becoming too dangerous. Tolek knew for a fact that the Germans were going to kill Moses Stein. Once the Germans got fixed on a Jew, the Jew died, sooner rather than later. Believing this was his last chance at the

Stein cache, he inflated the amount. "Five pieces of gold."

Joseph smiled slightly. Tolek was lying. The fee was one piece of gold. He decided at that moment that he was going to kill Tolek Grinspan and eliminate one of the rats plaguing the ghetto's occupants. "Five?" Joseph dug in his pocket and brought out the gold, counting the pieces one by one.

Tolek grabbed the gold with his pudgy hands and put the five pieces in a small bag attached to a string that wrapped around his chest.

Joseph heard the tinkle of coins as Tolek tucked the bag under his armpit, and realized that he was right: Tolek's pockets were bulging with money from many other Jews.

Joseph spoke softly, "Tell me."

Now that he had the gold, Tolek quickly announced what he had heard. "Advise your father-in-law to leave the ghetto, any way that he can. I overheard my Captain say that Colonel Drexler is furious that Moses Stein eluded capture." He spoke urgently. "Tonight. Tell Moses they'll be back tonight."

His brow furrowed, Joseph asked, "And the rest of the family?"

Tolek paused, wondering just how much he should reveal. He had heard a rumor that the Germans were going to execute Moses, his two sons, and his son-in-law, and then evict the women and children onto the streets. If the whole family suddenly disappeared, the Germans would start looking for an informer, and that might lead them to him. Quickly deciding that he had fulfilled his obligation to Moses Stein, Tolek retorted, "No. Just Moses."

Intuitively, Joseph knew that Tolek was lying. He was so angry he felt like he might explode, but his face was smooth and free of any emotion.

Tolek quickly looked all around and started to move away.

Joseph shook his head, then squeezed Tolek's shoulder with one hand. "Just a moment."

Tolek licked his lips and his face reddened. "What's this?" He shifted nervously from one foot to the other, suddenly unnerved by the big man's manner.

Joseph gave Tolek a small smile. Without raising his voice he said, "Tolek, I don't believe you have received *everything* you have coming." He then forced the man backward toward the synagogue.

Tolek's brown eyes betrayed surprise and then fear. He had misjudged Joseph Gale. Suddenly, the man looked positively fierce, his gray eyes alive with vengeance. Tolek gave a small kick, but he knew he didn't stand a chance against the obvious prowess of the much younger, larger man. "Let me go," he whined. "You got what you wanted."

"Shut up!" Joseph hissed.

Just as Tolek felt Joseph's huge hands around his throat, he made a feeble effort to strike his opponent with the rubber club.

The brief struggle ended as quickly as it began. Joseph felt Tolek shake violently and then go limp. Joseph slowly eased Tolek's body to a sitting position and propped him against the wall. After making sure that Tolek was dead, he ripped the man's shirt and snapped loose the cord that held the bag of gold coins.

Joseph paused and looked behind him. Despite the ghetto curfew, he had the eerie sensation that he was being watched.

Joseph had no way of knowing that Daniel Stein had followed him and was in the shadows waiting to make sure Joseph was in no danger.

Daniel Stein was surprised but pleased that Joseph had killed Tolek, and a smile slowly crossed his face. Understanding that Joseph's mission had been a success, Daniel quickly made his way back to the Stein apartment where his father was waiting.

Unable to shake the feeling that unknown eyes were staring at him, Joseph took the time to look up and down the empty streets. He saw no one. Slowly he stood up and walked away, strangely unmoved by what he had done. As he disappeared into the darkness, his fingers caressed the gold pieces. There were 29 coins.

As Joseph made his way along Zomenhota back to Nisko Street, a lovely thought suddenly occurred to him. After slipping twenty-four gold coins into his pockets, he kept the remaining five in his hand. Moving quickly, he sought out the woman he had earlier seen in a doorway off Mila Street, and slipped those gold coins into her palm,

"Here," he whispered, "buy your babies some food."

Joseph heard the woman give a small cry and felt her startled look as he briskly walked away.

For the first time in years, Joseph was free of tension.

Soon he was on Nisko, and as he climbed the steps to the Stein apartment, Joseph saw that Daniel and his father-in-law were waiting. He took the steps three at a time. The two men faced him in the shadowy hallway outside the apartment.

"And?" Moses' black eyes searched his questioningly.

The expression on Joseph's face was answer enough.

A low moan escaped Moses' lips.

Joseph shook his head sorrowfully. He had an odd feeling, knowing that after this night, their lives would be changed forever. He told them. "The situation is not good. The Germans will be back, tonight." He stared at his father-in-law. "Moses, you must bribe your way out of the ghetto."

Moses slumped and stared glumly at Daniel.

"Are you absolutely certain?" Daniel asked. "Exactly what did Tolek say?"

"The S.S. Colonel is sending his men back tonight to claim the fish that escaped the first net." Joseph paused for a moment, thinking how he would cover Tolek's death. "Tolek believes the Germans are onto him. That his days are numbered."

A small spark came to Daniel's eyes, but he said nothing. Joseph Gale was going to make a hell of a ghetto fighter.

Moses dropped his chin onto his chest, whispering in a low voice of disbelief. "Then, this is really it." He turned his back and then stumbled into the front room, making a quick decision while thinking that sometimes a man is forced to decide the most important things in the flash of a moment.

Joseph and Daniel followed him into the apartment without another word.

Sara and Gershom were waiting in the sitting room, fearful of the worst but hoping for the best.

Moses looked at his wife. "Sara, my dear, the time has come to pack my things."

Sara shook her head vehemently while giving a small cry. Seeing the look of despair on her husband's face, she stifled that cry by stuffing the end of her apron into her mouth. Sara nodded and arose from her chair.

Moses followed his wife from the room.

Ester, still awake, joined the family in the sitting room. Dazed, she didn't speak but rushed into Joseph's arms.

Joseph, Daniel, and Gershom were silent, knowing that Ester was within a moment of hysterics.

Moses abruptly re-entered the room, carrying a small case. His face flushed when he saw his daughter. "Ester. You should be sleeping."

Ester ran to her father. "Father, please don't go."

With her pleading eyes, Moses thought that Ester looked like a little girl. Moses' own eyes spoke volumes, but he said little. "Ester, if I stay here, I will endanger you all." He guided his daughter back into her husband's arms. Moses stared intently into Joseph's face. "Joseph will take care of you. And the child." As an afterthought he added, "Until I return."

Gershom held his mother, who was now weeping openly.

Daniel stood to the side, not knowing what to say.

Moses faced his family and smiled bravely, thinking that until Hitler got the insane idea to conquer the world he had been the luckiest of men. He had lived a full life. Until the Nazis came to Warsaw, he had envisioned his end quite differently, believing that he would die a peaceful death as an old man, in his bed, surrounded by his children and grandchildren. But nothing was guaranteed, and it seemed a peaceful end was not to be his destiny.

He stuck his hand out, gripping Daniel's hand. He stared for a long time at his warrior son, wishing for one more chance to convince Daniel to refrain from violence. But time had run out, and now he could only hope for the best. Moses nodded and drew his son close, kissing him on first one cheek and then the other.

He turned to Joseph and patted him on the shoulder. Joseph Gale had proved to be a blessing from God. In a wistful voice Moses murmured, "Joseph, you were right. I should have taken my family out of Poland, long ago."

Joseph wondered how the family would ever manage without Moses Stein. The man was like a tank, standing between his family and the hated Germans.

Moses looked at Gershom. Gershom would be all right. He had his faith.

Ester's grief burst into heaving sobs. "Father, father."

Moses' wrinkled face grew pale. "I must go." Then he hugged his family again, one by one, saving Sara until the last.

Tears rolled down Sara's cheeks. "Moses, I..."

Moses placed his finger on her lips, silencing her. Suddenly, without thought, he knew. "Sara, we shall meet again. In a better place."

For the first time in her life, Sara Stein threw herself into her husband's arms.

Sara's anguish was the crushing blow. It took all the strength that Moses possessed to pull himself away.

Before closing the door, Moses looked at Gershom and Daniel in turn and then commanded, "You know what to do." He was referring to the last of the valuables carefully hidden in three different locations.

With a gentle smile on his face and a quick wave of his hand, Moses Stein carefully closed the door, not telling his family where he was going, not wishing to endanger them with the knowledge of his whereabouts.

An inconsolable Sara Stein groped her way from the room.

Daniel and Gershom went to tell their wives what had happened, agreeing to meet Joseph back in the sitting room within thirty-minutes-time.

Joseph gently picked Ester up in his arms and carried her to bed. He sat beside her until she cried herself to sleep.

In a half an hour, after deciding on a plan with the two brothers, Joseph returned to his bedroom, but he didn't sleep. Instead, he sat on the large trunk next to the bedroom window that faced Nisko street, quietly waiting, knowing that soon the Germans would come looking for Moses Stein.

Joseph Gale didn't have long to wait.

Paris

Jacques Gale was now living out of a suitcase. He never stayed more than one night at any location. His bed might be a luxurious suite in a grand hotel or a thin mattress in a closet. Once he had even slept curled in a wash tub with only his jacket for a pillow.

Jacques was jubilant when he received the news that his old resistance cell in Paris had finally captured *"The Cat,"* a French collaborator who had caused the deaths of many of Jacques' resistance comrades. Jacques had been told that while under torture, *"The Cat"* had revealed a ghastly bit of information that spelled doom for Europe's Jews.

Jacques quickly made his way to a safe flat in the heart of Paris. After greeting Edmúnd and André, two of his comrades, and laughing at jokes about the "cat's claws being clipped," he devoured a meal of bread, soup, and cheese.

Edmúnd handed Jacques a two-page document. "Now, chew on this," he told him.

A disbelieving Jacques Gale read and reread the papers thrust into his hand.

"The Cat" has the complete confidence of his contact, a Nazi Captain. This Nazi enjoys bragging about his personal knowledge of high-level meetings where policy decisions are made concerning Hitler's one-thousand-year plan for European rule. The Captain confided to "The Cat" that a special meeting, the Wannsee Conference, held at the Berlin suburb of Wannsee on January 20, 1942, was attended by fifteen leading Nazi officials. Decisions reached during

that conference are now believed to be generally known throughout the Nazi bureaucracy.

Although not in attendance at the Conference, Reich Marshal Goering issued orders through S.S. General Heydrich to those present that the Jews of Europe were not dying at a rate fast enough to ensure the demise of the Jewish race.

After much discussion of the Jewish question, a decision was reached to build gas chamber camps in Poland to speed the death process. All Jews, including women and children, who have not yet died of starvation or disease, are to be gassed to death.

The Jews of Poland are the first on the elimination list. Once Polish Jews are eliminated, the Jews of Western Europe, including French Jews, are to be transported in cattle cars to those death camps.

Jacques gazed into the distance and whispered, "Joseph."

Edmúnd and André were both aware that Jacques Gale was a Jew and that the information clearly meant danger for his family in Paris. Edmúnd's fingers plucked at the paper and his voice shook with anger. "I told André, the Germans are mad dogs!"

André tried to hide his own fears. He had a Jewish fiancée. "Try not to worry, Jacques. The Germans will die facedown in puddles soon."

"And," Edmúnd added. "Don't forget, there's a host of Polish Jews between the Nazis and your family."

Jacques surprised the men with his cold, stony look. "I have a brother in Warsaw," he whispered, "married to the loveliest woman I've ever known. My brother, and his beautiful wife have a baby daughter."

His words were greeted with silence.

Jacques' voice was almost inaudible when he spoke. "My brother, his wife and their child are the sacrificial Jews of whom you speak."

Ashen-faced, Edmúnd and André exchanged glances. Trapped in a realm beyond words, the two men turned their faces away.

Chapter VII
The S.S.

In 1933, when Adolf Hitler became Chancellor of the German Republic, a republic he had sworn to destroy, the ever-faithful Heinrich Himmler had already demonstrated his ability as an organizer by building the S.S., Hitler's personal bodyguard unit, from 300 men to 50,000 men. The former poultry farmer had accomplished this daunting task in only four years. Under Himmler's skillful management, the S.S., short for Schutztaffel, meaning "defense echelon" and known as the black order, steadily gained power and prestige.

When Germany attacked Poland in September, 1939, there were nearly 100,000 men in the S.S. Adolf Hitler bragged to his staff: "I have ordered my Death's Head Units in the East to kill without pity or mercy all men, women and children of the Jewish race or language."

When asked whether those men had the stomach to murder innocent women with babes-in-arms, Hitler slapped his knee and guffawed at the question, secure in his knowledge that the "brave troops of the Waffen-S.S. are like no other men." Indeed, he had often repeated his conviction that through grueling Spartan training, Himmler's S.S. had produced a race of men whose obedience to Hitler was unquestioning, and if told by their Fuehrer to attack a tank with their bare hands, they would do so.

Karl Drexler, like all human beings, entered the world programmed by his own unique genetic codes acted upon by people destined to shape his life.

Karl Drexler was molded into a monster by his father, Rudolf Drexler.

Rudolf Drexler was born in Munich on March 8, 1892, to a middle class family. His father was a university professor and his mother a home-maker. He was one of four brothers, and his childhood was idyllic. He attended university and during his second year in school Rudolf married the pretty daughter of a neighbor. Their first child, Karl, was born in 1913.

Life was uneventful until the Drexlers, like other Europeans, were overtaken by a tragedy of history: the first world war. Rudolf and his three brothers left Germany to fight on the Western front. Before the war was lost, one brother was killed, a second lost both legs, while a third was blinded. Only Rudolf survived without any physical injuries. After Germany's bitter defeat, Rudolf returned to a devastated country and to a family broken by personal and financial disasters. Rudolf withdrew into himself, trying to find an explanation for the horrible agonies inflicted upon the country he loved and the family he adored.

In this dark period of his life, Rudolf Drexler discovered Houston Steward Chamberlain, a British citizen who had denounced his own country, married the daughter of Richard Wagner and became even more dogmatically Pro-German than the most fanatical native-born German. During World War I, Chamberlain published anti-British propaganda, infuriating the British, who branded him a turn-coat.

Chamberlain was the author of *The Foundations of the Nineteenth Century,* which took the extreme stance that Germans were a master race and their mission was to rule the world. A vicious anti-Semite, Chamberlain's twisted views held that the Germans were the creators and bearers of civilization while the Jews were the destroyers.

As Germany and Germans became more mired in the chaos of a lost war and ruined economy, Rudolf Drexler, under the influence of the writings of Steward Chamberlain, found a scapegoat for his troubled life: the Jews. He seethed with anger each time he saw a Jew walking the streets of his homeland or working in a job that in his mind had been taken from an Aryan.

With the help of his wife's father, Rudolf returned to the university and obtained an advanced degree in philosophy. In 1922, he became a salaried lecturer at the University of Berlin. Five years later, after a bitter quarrel with a colleague, he was fired from his post. The colleague was Jewish, and the head of his department who recommended Rudolf's termination, was also a Jew.

In order to support his growing family, Rudolf was forced to work in a dry goods store for a small salary. The owner of the shop was a Jew.

With a great anger consuming him, Rudolf lectured his young children on the evils of the Jewish race. "My children," he warned them, "if we do not act, our beloved Germany will be lost to an inferior race!" Rudolf was tireless in his quest to teach his children to despise Jews, declaring that "Jews should be interned, kept from the general population, and if that does not solve the problem, then Jews should be deported from Germany! Germany's very future is at stake!"

Of Rudolf's six children, Karl was the most malleable. He soon came to think of Jews as abnormal and terrifying. As a youngster, Karl pleased his father by cursing and spitting at Jews they passed on the street, startling them by calling them "murderers of Christ."

When he became a teenager, Karl joined a roving gang of neighborhood boys who attacked helpless Jewish children on the street. At his university, Karl was the leader of a group of young men who protested the large number of Jewish students and physically attacked Jews who scored high marks on exams.

When the National Socialists came to power, Karl Drexler and his father wept with joy, knowing that their savior was at the helm. *Mein Kampf,* the book written by Hitler outlining his political program, along with naming Jews as parasites in the bodies of Germans, became their bible.

With his father's blessing, Karl Drexler applied for membership in the S.S. Karl's Aryan pedigree demonstrated that the Drexler family's blood-line had been pure since the year 1750, a necessity if Karl were to be accepted as an officer candidate. Tall and blonde, with blue eyes and striking Nordic features, Karl Drexler easily met the S.S.'s important criteria of correct racial appearance.

When Karl left home to undergo his training, he was a hero to his family. He was going to protect The Fatherland from the Jewish swine draining the wealth from his country.

Once his rigorous training was completed, Karl watched with great interest as the underside of his upper arm was tattooed with the lightning S.S. insignia. The following day he was presented with his uniform-black breeches, black belt, brown shirt, black tie, black jacket and black jackboots. His black cap and chinstrap were set off by the silver Death's Head insignia.

On April 30, 1937, on the Fuehrer's birthday, Karl gave his oath as an S.S. man:

"I swear to Thee, Adolf Hitler
As Fuehrer and Chancellor of
The German Reich
Loyalty and bravery.
I vow to Thee and to the
Superiors whom thou shalt appoint
Obedience unto death,
So help me God."

After swearing a second oath which committed Karl Drexler and his descendants to marriage only if "the necessary conditions" of race and health stock were fulfilled, and after giving his solemn word that he would not marry without permission by Himmler himself, Karl received his pride and joy: his S.S. dagger.

Following Himmler's advice, Karl chose to become a member of the Gestapo. The Gestapo was a branch of the S.S. which quickly became a dreaded symbol of the Nazi reign of terror.

The day he was to return to his home in Berlin, Karl Drexler took great care arranging his dagger and cap. He turned and posed in front of the mirror, knowing that he presented a handsome, imposing picture.

Karl's family was waiting at the train station for his arrival. The most rewarding moment in Karl Drexler's young life came when he saw the proud look in his father's eyes.

Rudolf Drexler hugged his son and wept. "My son. My son, the soldier!" Up until that instant, Rudolf had always felt himself a failure, but at the sight of Karl, he knew he had succeeded in raising a splendid son who would bravely fight to restore all that had been stolen from him and from his beloved Germany.

Once the war began, members of the Gestapo followed the German armed forces into occupied countries, using their own brutal methods to destroy anyone hostile to German rule. In working for the annihilation of Reich enemies, the Gestapo's natural prey was the large numbers of helpless Jews who became trapped in ghettos.

After suffering a leg wound when his military vehicle ran over a Russian mine, Karl Drexler was sent to Berlin to recover. Once fit, he was reassigned to the Eastern Front in order to assist with the growing Jewish problem at the Warsaw Ghetto.

As Karl Drexler stared at the list in his hands, a slight twitch played across his lips.

His subordinate, Friedrich Kleist, stood facing Karl, his hands behind his back, his expression devoid of the apprehension he felt. He told himself that his superior had become increasingly irrational since the tragic winter campaign in Russia. Nowadays, Karl Drexler lashed out at everyone around him. Colonel Drexler had a younger brother fighting west of Smolensk, on the Eastern Front. The week before they had learned Soviet partisans had established a line east of the German line, setting the stage for a massacre of German soldiers. Friedrich wondered if that accounted for Drexler's attitude.

Stuffing the paper into his pocket, Karl asked, "German soldiers outwitted by moronic Jews?"

Friedrich purposely kept his voice impassive. "That appears to be the case, Sir."

Karl grunted. He walked around his desk and picked up a few documents, playing for time as he thought about the Jews in the Warsaw Ghetto. The Jews were a crafty lot, doing everything they could to hang on to their miserable lives.

Karl begrudged them every breath.

The night before, fifteen of the beastly Jews on the execution list had escaped. Since that time, his men had tracked down only three of the escapees. Karl himself had overseen their torture before execution, and while that had given him momentary pleasure, nothing seemed to completely satisfy his desire to see Jews humiliated and broken.

With the Russian campaign faltering, Karl felt the urgency of his task. He and his men must have time to exterminate all Jewish swine. Karl knew that in the mind of his superiors in Berlin, the resolution of the Jewish question was as important as winning the war. If only one Jew survived, then Karl's mission was a failure.

He turned his anger on Friedrich. "Do I have to do everything?" He snapped his fingers, "Go! Gather your men and come with me." He personally would go into the Ghetto and search out those wily Jews! Then, right before their families, he would pump a bullet into their brains.

A smile colder than the icy cold of his eyes played on his lips, as he reconsidered that possibility. He decided not to kill the Jews outright. Seeing them beg for mercy while under torture was much more gratifying. Karl felt a rush of excitement at the thought of spilling Jewish blood.

The night was an orgy of killing. Karl's method was simple. He held Jewish children as hostages. He curtly informed the Jewish dogs that they had five minutes to tell the whereabouts of the wanted man. After that, the killing began. It didn't take long for the cowards to reveal the hiding places of their men.

Within hours, Karl had arrested ten of the twelve men he sought. Unfortunately, it had been necessary to kill one of the men. When the Jew saw his bloodied, dead child, he had howled like a hyena, and with bare hands outstretched had lunged at Karl.

As they walked toward the final apartment on Nisko Street, Karl reached over and patted Friedrich on the back. Karl felt immense pride in his success, for he had an image of himself as a brilliant strategist in the deadly game with the Jews. Still, Karl had a touch of concern about Friedrich Kleist. Friedrich was new to the Warsaw Ghetto, and Karl often felt that the man's heart was not in his job. Karl understood. Often it took some time for his men, particularly the less experienced, to see the Jews as they really were, and to understand the absolute necessity of eliminating them from European life. Part of the Jewish danger came from their ability to win people over to their cause by their sly and insidious conduct.

Karl spoke loudly, making his points with his truncheon jerking up and down in the air, bringing to Friedrich's mind an enthusiastic instructor in front of his pupils, except the lesson was like none a student should ever learn.

"You see Friedrich, the Jews are quite simple-minded. Through various intelligence tests performed by reputable Reich scientists, it has been discovered that the Jews have a brain that is equivalent to that of a horse."

Seeing Friedrich's look of disbelief, Karl laughingly added, "Not as big as a horse, but as dumb as a horse. Really! It is true!" Then he gave a little chuckle. "Friedrich, tell me, does a man discuss his ideas with a horse?"

Friedrich gave the expected response. "No, Sir."

"No, of course not. A man must beat the beast to show it the way he wants to go. That's the way it is with Jews. It is necessary to show them what they must do in a very basic manner." Karl Drexler then grinned at Friedrich, waiting for his reply.

Not knowing what to say, Friedrich mumbled, "I suppose you are right." Friedrich blushed with shame, feeling that a thousand eyes of his ancestors were watching him, judging him during a time and place destined to show a man's true merit. Friedrich heaved a terrible sigh, sensing that he was helpless, caught in an unbelievable situation with a bunch of lunatics.

Friedrich wanted no part of the night's grim work.

Friedrich had been led to join the S.S. by a cousin, who had convinced Friedrich's parents that their only son would be much safer in the S.S. than fighting in an army that was suddenly taking terrible losses. Friedrich was a medium sized, fairly attractive man, but he was a child in many ways, being overly protected by his indulgent parents. His mother had urged him to consider the S.S., since she, like many uninformed Germans, considered the S.S. responsible for nothing more than the morals of Germans and of the prisoners whom they guarded. As the war entered its third year, the S.S. had relaxed some of its most stringent requirements in recruiting. For that reason only, Friedrich had been accepted as one of the elite.

Admiring the uniforms and the confidence of S.S. soldiers, Friedrich had been pleased...at first. He had told himself that every able-bodied man in Germany was in uniform, so he had no choice, and one branch of service was the same as another.

Friedrich was dead wrong.

Once in training, he had realized that he was not emotionally equipped for the type of assignments given the S.S. units. Friedrich quickly grasped he was being trained to be a murderer, not a soldier! Trained to murder Jews! At every opportunity, Jews were targeted as the root of Germany's problems. Jews started the war and now deserved the catastrophe awaiting them. Jews were the reason for every German defeat.

Even today, while walking beside Colonel Drexler, Friedrich's former S.S. instructor's words rang in his ears: "The danger to our country has not yet been removed. Our enemies want to press ever further onto German soil! The biggest menace to German life is filthy Jews!"

While the instructor had clearly meant what he had said, his icy eyes emotionless, Friedrich mouthed the response he knew was expected, but his heart was not in his answer.

Though no Jews were personal friends of the Kleist family, Friedrich had nothing against the Jews and often felt sorry for the way they were being treated. He was not so naïve as to express his doubts and had ended up assigned as a concentration camp guard in Poland. His parents had been delighted, thinking no further than that their son would be safe from the guns of Germany's growing list of enemies. Yet Friedrich knew that if they really understood what was happening to the Jews, and the role their son was forced to play, they might rather he were in a snow-covered trench in Russia, fighting for his life.

As far as his superior, Karl Drexler, was concerned, Friedrich thought the man was completely mad, committing ghastly acts against innocent women and children. The Colonel's obsession with the Jews caused Friedrich dismay and horror, but he knew the futility of speaking his mind. He knew that prior to Warsaw, Colonel Drexler had served on the Eastern front. In Kiev, he had flown into a rage at two of his own men for refusing to carry out orders to set fire to a barn that held one-hundred Russian Jewish women and children captives. Friedrich had been told that those two men had been severely punished.

The Colonel was a dangerous man, and Friedrich knew better than to go against one so powerful. Friedrich believed that the consequences of disobedience would be his own punishment.

Anyway, he thought the Jews were as good as dead and there was nothing Friedrich could do to help them. Recently, Drexler had privately informed him that their superiors had held a meeting in January at Wannsee, on the outskirts of Berlin, and at that meeting they had made a decision to adopt the *Final Solution,* which was the code name for the extermination of European Jews.

Mad! The whole world had gone mad, Friedrich often told himself.

But for now he braced himself for further violence, for he saw that they were almost at the apartment on Nisko Street, the home of one of the ghetto's wealthiest Jews, Moses Stein.

Friedrich had more than one reason to dread an encounter with Moses Stein. He had met the old Jew a couple of months before and had accepted a bribe to free one of his relatives, a man who had been arrested on charges of smuggling. Friedrich had never accepted a bribe before, but he had, just that day, received a disturbing letter from his wife, Eva. The British had increased their bombing raids on Berlin and Eva told him of the hardships she and her family were undergoing. Food prices were now exorbitant in Germany. Thinking of Eva and of his parents, Friedrich had been seduced by Moses Stein's large diamonds, rationalizing that the Jews of the Warsaw Ghetto would soon be dead anyway. And, after discovering that the guard who had arrested Moses' relative had been called back to Germany for the funeral of a brother, and that the arresting officer had not filled out the necessary forms, Friedrich had taken five diamonds and released the Jew. Without the signed forms, Friedrich hoped that no one would ever know the Jew had been arrested in the first place.

Keeping only one diamond for himself for possible future use, Friedrich had arranged with a trusted S.S. comrade to deliver two diamonds each to Eva and his mother.

But, others must have known of the old Jew's wealth, for somehow, Moses Stein's name had been placed on the extermination list when Colonel Drexler decided to avenge the death of a murdered German soldier. Since Colonel Drexler treated Friedrich as he always had, Friedrich hoped that meant his superior had not discovered the illegal transaction. Otherwise, Friedrich would be in serious trouble. Karl Drexler was deeply committed to the oath he had taken. No one had ever known the Colonel to take a bribe.

When the Jew managed to escape the first round-up, Karl had told Friedrich that "Moses Stein will be the last man we will arrest." Karl always saved the best for the last.

Friedrich had discovered that Karl especially enjoyed degrading rich Jews. "The rich bastards mistakenly consider their wealth as protection from German justice," he'd say. Karl had laughed as he remembered what was to him, cherished memories. "The wealthy Jews always look so stunned, just at the moment of death!"

Friedrich felt his stomach heave as they climbed the stairs to the Stein apartment. At four o'clock in the morning he suspected that the Stein family was sleeping, unaware of the menacing Karl Drexler on his way to destroy their lives. Sensing that the Colonel was watching his reaction, Friedrich tried to look enthusiastic.

Karl Drexler straightened his back and felt a deadly calm wash over him as he stood at the apartment door of Moses Stein. He was fulfilling the wishes of his beloved Fuehrer. "Break the door," Karl ordered.

Chapter VIII

Death on Nisko Street

Joseph Gale had been waiting for the past four hours. He had heard the echo of Karl Drexler's voice and the thump of heavy boots, as the S.S. men walked through the ghetto, making their way to Nisko Street.

Joseph quickly locked Ester and Miryam in the bedroom. "Ester, do *not* come out, no matter what you might hear!" he told his frightened wife.

His heart thumping loudly, Joseph then rushed to join Gershom and Daniel in the front room. The three men were offering themselves as a sacrifice to save their families.

Joseph and Daniel exchanged determined looks and suddenly, Joseph felt calm and cold.

With a crash, the door burst open and S.S. men swarmed into the apartment.

Karl Drexler seemed perplexed to find the three Jews waiting for him. He raised his eyebrows, then carefully looked them over, his eyes resting on Joseph Gale. He studied the large man for a few moments before sauntering through the broken door, as casually as if he were an invited guest.

He gave a small cold smile and asked in a nonchalant manner. "Moses Stein? Is Moses about?"

Daniel answered, giving the response agreed upon by the men of the family. "My father recently died. He was buried only last week."

For the past year, Jews in the Warsaw Ghetto were dying at a rate of 200 persons per day. It was entirely possible for Moses Stein to be one of the numerous unfortunate.

Karl Drexler flicked an imaginary speck off his black jacket. "Really?" He turned to Friedrich Kleist and winked, before walking past the three men to Moses' bookcase. The room was utterly silent as Karl studied the large selection of classics displayed in more than one language. "What's this?" he muttered, as he flipped through the essays of Montaigne. Knowing that the Jews were thieves, he decided the Stein family must have robbed some Polish aristocrat of his book collection. Later, he would have Captain Kleist return for the entire library.

Returning the book to its proper place, Karl turned his attention back to the three Jews. He nudged Daniel's back with his truncheon. "Your name?"

Daniel stiffened. "Daniel Stein."

"Ah, yes! *Daniel.*" Karl chuckled before quoting a verse from the bible, "Daniel, servant of the living God, has your God, whom you serve continually, been able to deliver you from the lions?"

Daniel didn't answer.

Several of the S.S. guards laughed.

Karl smiled at the guards then cleared his throat. "Daniel. What ailment took, uh, your father, I presume?"

Daniel nodded his head. "My father was Moses Stein." He swallowed, calming himself, so that he did not curse the German instead of answering his question. "My father died of pneumonia."

"Pneumonia, yes, of course." Karl Drexler walked between Daniel and Joseph. He stopped and stared up into Joseph's eyes, peering closely at his face, and studying the shape of his head. He squeezed one of Joseph's upper arms with his hand, all the while thinking that the man possessed none of the normal physical characteristics of a Jew. Uncomfortable with Joseph's large size and extraordinarily handsome demeanor, his eyes narrowed. "And, your name?"

Joseph answered very distinctly. "Joseph Gale."

Karl Drexler continued to stare. Joseph stood over Karl Drexler and steadily stared back. Karl Drexler was a tall man, but Joseph Gale was slightly taller.

At one time in his life, Joseph Gale had been an admirer of the German race, in spite of the first world war and the misguided German military that kept making war on their European neighbors. The Germans were filled with contradictions: on one hand they produced musical geniuses, extraordinary writers, intellectuals, and scientists, and on the other created monsters that sought to destroy all that was good in civilization.

However, since the start of World War II, the attack and occupation of Poland, and the formation of the Warsaw Ghetto, Joseph hated every German bastard alive or dead.

Scrutinizing the German, Joseph decided there was nothing behind the icy blue eyes of the S.S. man. He was an empty shell, programmed for nothing more than killing. Joseph wondered if Nazi doctrine had managed to suck the good out of all Germans, the way it had done with the man standing before him.

If so, they all deserved to die.

Joseph almost smiled, thinking of the large number of German soldiers doing exactly that in Russia. The Eastern Front was bleeding the German war machine, and for some time now Joseph had known that the Germans would lose their frantic race to rule the world and massacre all their enemies. He just hoped that a German defeat happened in time to save the Jews of Warsaw.

Suddenly, a strange sense swept through Joseph—that one day, the man before him would be at *his* mercy.

The two men remained locked in a staring match.

Karl's face began to turn red, angered at the audacity of the Jew to challenge him, even with a look.

Joseph was itching with the desire to kill Karl Drexler. He had a terrible thought that his hands had a will all their own and would reach out and strangle the man, with the ease with which they had squeezed the life out of Tolek Grinspan. Knowing that reaction would mean the death of everyone in the apartment, Joseph stuffed his fists in his pockets and clamped his teeth together, forcing himself to lower his eyes from Drexler's face.

Karl was pleased. Admittedly, it was only a small victory, but he refused to be bested by any Jew. There was much he would have liked to ask Joseph Gale, but he didn't. He decided that there would be ample time for a lengthy interrogation later.

Turning to Gershom for the first time, he asked, "May I see the death certificate, please. For Moses Stein."

Gershom shifted his feet before answering. "We don't have the document. Not yet." The uneasiness that suddenly crept into Gershom's voice was clear to everyone present.

Daniel quickly interrupted. "The doctor says the report will be ready tomorrow."

Karl shook his head and made a tskking noise with his tongue. He looked at his adjutant. "See what I mean, Friedrich. The truth and a Jew are strangers. *A Jew simply cannot tell the truth.*"

Karl's face reddened and he suddenly shrieked, "Liars, every stinking Jew is a liar!"

The small game was over, and Karl was no longer amused. "Find the women and children," he ordered briskly, snapping his fingers at the S.S. guards standing at attention behind Friedrich Kleist.

Five of the guards went in different directions throughout the apartment.

Karl ordered the three Jews to remain where they were, but Joseph disobeyed, following quickly on the heels of the guard going toward his bedroom. Joseph outpaced the guard to the door of the room where his wife and child were hidden, and he held back the guard while he unlocked the door. "Ester. Darling, bring Miryam and come with me."

Karl Drexler decided at that very moment that he was going to take a long time before killing the big Jew.

Crashing doors and the crying of small children filled the apartment.

The wives of Daniel and Gershom, along with the widow of Israel herded their children before them, cringing in terror at the S.S. men in the room.

Sara Stein held her blind grandson David in her arms and stood calmly between her two grown sons.

Joseph held a whimpering Miryam close to his chest while Ester clung to his side. Joseph could feel Ester's entire body trembling. He turned to her and gave a small smile, whispering, "Don't worry, darling. This will soon be over."

Karl looked from one Jew to the other, hatred twitching his face. He was particularly incensed at the sight of the big Jew with his wife and child. While the Jewess was no doubt lovely, with her dark eyes and olive skin, she was obviously a full-blooded Jew. The child was blonde, with pale skin and light eyes. She could pass for a German. The man mystified him. Karl thought that he might be Aryan. If so, Joseph Gale had committed the worse kind of crime against the state: entering into sexual relations with a Jewish whore. Karl studied the picture of the happy Jewish family a moment longer. He couldn't quite put his finger on why he hated the big Jew more than the others. Then he realized that the reason was that Joseph Gale looked so damned sanctimonious, giving Karl the feeling that he, the Jew, felt superior to him, a German!

On the spot Karl changed his mind, deciding that he wanted to punish Joseph Gale more than he wanted to kill him. He just hadn't decided what to do or how to do it. Yet.

Friedrich edged uncomfortably toward the door. He had been relieved to find that the old Jew was dead or gone, but he felt sick to his stomach, knowing someone was about to die.

Watching Joseph tenderly cradle his child, Karl had an idea. He suppressed a smile, feeling a little more cheerful.

He swaggered over to Daniel, speaking directly into his face. "Get a message to Moses Stein. He is to turn himself in at Pawiak Prison within eight hours." He paused, and the room was still for one long heartbeat. Then he spoke very softly, his voice filled with evil promise. "Otherwise, I will kill you all."

Filled with a rage that shortened his breath, Daniel nodded his head, knowing that the German meant what he said. It was futile to continue to deny his father's existence.

As Karl looked directly at Joseph, a spiteful smirk crossed his lips.

Joseph watched and listened without moving a muscle. He sensed that he had become the focus of the man's hatred.

The room turned to instant bedlam when Karl pointed at Miryam. "Bring the blonde child," he ordered briskly. He hesitated, glancing quickly at the other children. "And the small boy there." He motioned toward David, Sara's blind grandson.

"No!" Ester screeched.

Joseph clutched his child with one hand while using the other to wrestle with the S.S. man who attempted to seize Miryam.

Friedrich clenched his teeth so hard that the veins bulged in his head.

Over the din of increasing pandemonium, Karl called out, "Do not kill the big Jew!"

Giving a loud groan, Sara turned and ran with David to her bedroom. Blind, not knowing the cause of his grandmother's alarming behavior, the child began shrieking.

Daniel and Gershom went after their mother with two S.S. men in pursuit.

Sara's three surviving daughters-in-law pulled their children to a corner of the room, shielding the hysterical youngsters with their bodies.

Joseph succeeded in shoving the S.S. man to the floor and he took that moment to pass Miryam to Ester, pushing her and the child to the wall. Standing in front of his wife and baby, he fought like a man possessed, his bloodcurdling shouts piercing the air. Two additional S.S. men joined in the struggle, but Joseph's fear for his child had given him the strength of ten men.

With the greatest interest, Karl observed the Jew's determined resistance. In Karl's experience, most Jews meekly obeyed any order given by their German masters. No doubt, the Jew was a powerful fighter. Three of Karl's men were out of the fight, and Joseph was beating the fourth man badly. Joseph's fierce manner of fighting reinforced his earlier thought that the man was not a Jew. Karl pulled his revolver and took two steps backward toward the exit. Regretfully, he thought he was going to have to give the order to kill Joseph Gale. What a pity!

With a quick movement of his hand, Karl motioned for two more of his men, one of the men being Friedrich, to assist in subduing the Jew. Friedrich was not prepared for the force of a physical encounter and was astonished when Joseph's huge fist shot out toward his face. Blood spurted from Friedrich's nose and the pain was like nothing he had ever known. He staggered backwards, landing hard on his buttocks.

Karl gave a frantic order for his remaining men to join the battle. Finally, Joseph was beaten to the floor. Then the men began to kick and stomp him.

With Joseph unconscious, Karl walked across the room as one of his men reached for Miryam. Miryam was shielded behind her mother's back and was crying pitifully. A hysterical Ester kicked and clawed the man, fighting like a tigress. Karl stared at Ester stonily, and then knocked her out with one swift blow to her jaw. He received a jolt of malicious pleasure watching the Jewess crumple.

Miryam kicked and screamed, calling out for her mama.

Karl grabbed the baby by her blonde curls, pulling her along the floor. He slapped her twice in the face to silence her and then ordered Friedrich to pick her up.

Friedrich was dazed, sitting with a bloody handkerchief to his nose. His reply was a distracted, "Yes, I will. Give me but a moment."

A shot was fired at the back of the apartment, and two S.S. men returned with David, who was deathly white and still. The boy had fainted in terror.

Holding the sobbing girl, Friedrich fought the urge to vomit. He awkwardly tried to comfort the child, but Miryam had known nothing but love and kindness from the moment of her birth and could not fathom the night's events. "Mommy! Mommy!" she screamed to an unconscious Ester Gale.

Karl glowed with pride as he surveyed the unspeakable scene that he had brought to life. Joseph Gale was sprawled on the floor, his face and head bloodied. Karl decided that his injuries were not serious. He would survive. Karl knew that with the loss of his child, the Jew would live out the few months of life Karl had decided to allot him in a special kind of torment.

Ester Gale was unconscious. Her jaw hung loosely and was more than likely broken.

Karl almost laughed aloud when his gaze rested on the daughters-in-law of Moses Stein. The three Jewish whores hovered around their bastard children, all of them frozen in fear.

Loud sobs could be heard from the back of the apartment.

For the moment, Karl was satisfied. He gave another one of his cold smiles.

He wasn't finished with the Stein family. Not quite yet.

Paris

With one quick glance, Benjamin Gale decided his wife had lost her mind. She was going through the pages of the Gale family album, removing photographs of Jacques, Joseph and Ester. One by one, she threw the pictures into a garbage can.

A protesting Rachel was retrieving the pictures, crying out to her mother. "Mother! What are you doing? Mother! *Stop!*"

Benjamin heard Natalie mumble a reply and thought he heard her repeating the words, "lonesome album, lonesome Jewish album," but he couldn't be certain. Walking across the room, he grabbed Natalie by the shoulders before forcefully removing the album from his wife's hands.

A sobbing Rachel began to retrieve the photographs and replace them in their rightful place.

Benjamin tried his utmost to offer comfort to his grieving wife. He knew the reason for Natalie's anguish. The previous evening they had received word that Jacques was a prisoner of the German Gestapo. At the same time, they had learned their son was a highly regarded member of the Resistance and had been stationed in Lyon, the city which had become the capital of French Resistance during the past year. From what they had been told, their son had killed a large number of German soldiers and French collaborators before being captured.

Benjamin had been warned to take his family and escape Paris by crossing the border into Switzerland. A favorite Gestapo tactic was to torture innocent family members before the eyes of resistance prisoners.

Natalie lifted her head and looked into her husband's face. With an urgent and overwhelming sadness she said, "I want my sons! Benjamin, I *must* see my sons! I have something important I must tell them!"

Benjamin held his wife tighter. A lump came into his throat and his eyes teared. He struggled not to break, knowing that if one of them did not remain strong, the family might never recover from the shock of losing both Jacques and Joseph.

Natalie broke loose from his grasp and collapsed into a chair. "I have been wrong all these years!" she confessed as she stared up and into her husband's face.

Contemplating his wife, Benjamin thought Natalie seemed unhinged.

"Benjamin, I refused to let my sons live as Jews." She paused, and with empty eyes looked over his shoulder at nothing. "But now it seems, they will die as Jews."

Desperate to turn his wife's mental state around, Benjamin gave a small cry before kneeling at Natalie's feet. He kissed her hands and placed his head in her lap. "Natalie. You must not torture yourself."

Natalie gently rubbed her husband's head with her hands. "Benjamin. I strayed from the faith. I kept my children from their heritage. I have committed an unforgivable sin." Her voice was bitter. "Now, I am being punished by the loss of my beautiful sons."

Unable to bear her mother's agony another moment, Rachel rushed from the room, the picture album clasped tightly against her chest, wishing to herself that she was missing from the family, rather than Jacques or Joseph. Rachel knew her mother had always favored her handsome sons over her plain daughter.

Benjamin heard the door slam as Rachel left the room. He remembered that Jacques' arrest meant they were all in danger. Bracing for a difficult time, he said, "Natalie, we must prepare to leave. We have to think of Rachel, and Michel, now."

Natalie's wild look had been replaced by one of utter misery. "Let the Germans come." She flapped her hands before her face. "My soul is dead, what good is my body?"

The circumstances stripped Benjamin of any indecision. "Natalie. We have two other children. To ensure their survival, we *must* leave Paris."

Natalie gave a slight nod. Her husband was right. She thought of her two remaining children. Rachel was a young girl. She shuddered at the thought of crude German hands on her daughter. And although Michel was married to a gentile, she knew that would matter little to their occupiers.

Even though she felt a tired vagueness in her mind, she took a deep breath and said, "I will pack a few things."

Benjamin quickly rose to his feet. He felt a stirring urgency—they could not lose any time.

Before they could arrange their departure, the telephone rang and a hysterical Abbi informed them that Michel had been taken away by three German men in a black car.

Within moments, there was a persistent ringing of the door chimes. Benjamin gathered his wife and daughter in his arms and waited in the hall entrance. When the dour-faced men of the Gestapo entered their home, Natalie struggled to release herself from her husband's embrace. She stepped forward and with the mad look of a woman unleashing demons in her soul, she announced, "I am the one you want. I am the Jewish masquerader."

The following morning, when Moses Stein overheard his protectors anxiously whispering that something horrible had happened to his family, he immediately came out of hiding and ran through the streets of the ghetto. Ignoring the danger to himself, he returned to the apartment on Nisko Street, not bothering to check the area for a sign of S.S. surveillance.

"What have I done?" Moses cried in anguish, when he saw the appalling condition of his remaining family, and heard about the abduction of two of his grandchildren.

The damage was considerable.

Gershom was dead. One of the S.S. men had shot him in the face during their struggle over David. His heartbroken wife and children were cloistered in their bedroom, devastated at the loss of their gentle husband and father.

Daniel was not in the apartment, having gone to a meeting of the ghetto fighters to try and convince the men to stage an attack on Gestapo offices.

Joseph was alive, but terribly battered. With deep gashes and enormous bruises covering his face and head, he was conscious but confused. Hearing the sound of his wife's weeping, he forced his eyelids open, not remembering for one short blessed moment the scene of the earlier nightmare and the fact that his beloved child had been kidnapped by brutal murderers. He shook his head in bewilderment as he looked around the room, praying to God that he was wrong.

Ester's jaw was shattered. Sara tied a wide strip of cloth around her chin and over her head. Ester's eyes overflowed with tears but her feeble moans had nothing to do with her painful injury.

Sara's face was drawn as she told her husband what had happened.

Tight-lipped, Moses said little as he listened to his wife. Once he learned the demands of the S.S. Colonel, Moses comforted his daughter. "Darling, your child will be returned shortly," he promised. Moses was going to do the only thing he could: turn himself in to the Gestapo. "I am old," he said, "I have lived my life. It is the young who must be saved." Moses would do whatever he had to do to ensure the release of those precious, innocent children.

Knowing for certain that he would soon die a horrible death, Moses bade farewell to each member of his rapidly diminishing family.

"Moses!" An impassioned Sara cried as her husband stood stoically at the door of the apartment, saying goodbye for the second time in twenty-four hours.

Moses stared for a long moment at his wife. Moses had a quick thought that he had become immune to his own death. The deaths of four sons, the deaths and abductions of his beloved grandchildren, and the uncertainty of the lives of his family members, had finally defeated him. Moses was ready to go to God. God would have to sort out the fate of his family left on earth.

When the door closed and Moses Stein left, the sound of his fading footsteps was quickly lost in the distance.

Then the apartment was very quiet.

To those whom he loved, it was as if Moses Stein was already dead.

Part II

The Levantine:

1952-1982

Character Listing

Part II: The Levantine (1952-1982)

Antoun Family:
George Antoun *(father)*
Mary Antoun *(mother)*
Demetrius Antoun *(son)*
Mitri Antoun *(father of George)*
Sammy *(Demetrius' toy donkey)*

Bader Family:
Mustafa Bader *(father)*
Abeen Bader *(mother)*
Walid Bader *(son)*

The Gale Family:
Joseph Gale *(father)*
Ester Gale *(mother)*
Michel Gale *(son)*
Jordan Gale *(daughter)*

The Kleist Family:
Friedrich Kleist *(former S.S. guard at Shatita Camp)*
Eva Kleist *(wife of Friedrich)*
Christine Kleist *(daughter of Friedrich & Eva—working as nurse at Shatila Camp)*

Amin Darwish *(Palestinian baker living at Shatila)*
Ratiba Darwish *(long deceased wife of Amin)*
Ahmed Fayez *(Fatah freedom fighter)*
Hala Kenaan *(fiancée of Demetrius)*
Maha Fakharry *(Headmistress of Shatila school)*

Minor Characters:
Yassin & Hawad *(Fatah fighters)*
Mahmoud Bader *(Uncle of Walid)*
Rozette Kenaan *(mother of Hala)*
Nadine *(younger sister of Hala)*
Omar *(younger brother of Hala)*
Majida, Nizar & Anwar *(nurses at Shatila Clinic)*
Stephan Grossman *(deceased fiancé of Jordan Gale)*

Public Figures:
Yasser Arafat, also known as Abu Ammar *(Head of Fatah)*
Menachem Begin *(Israeli Prime Minister)*
Bashir Gemayel *(assassinated President of Lebanon)*

Prologue: Part II

April 21, 1948: Haifa, Palestine

George and Mary Antoun were awakened by a loud voice speaking heavily accented, imperfect Arabic. The words came from a loudspeaker mounted to a rapidly moving truck. Arabs were being advised to leave Haifa. "Escape while there is still time! Jewish forces have surrounded Haifa. Accept the last offer of safe conduct. Terrible consequences will overrun your family if you do not leave immediately. Escape! Escape! Remember Deir Yassin!"

The Jewish man's blaring voice grew smaller and smaller, until it faded away completely. Worried, George lay in bed, trying to decide what would be best for his family. Thoughts of Deir Yassin and the possibility that his wife and son could be murdered in their beds caused him to break into a sweat.

Every Arab in Palestine knew the story of Deir Yassin. The Arab village had declared its neutrality and refused to join the fight against the Jews. Nevertheless, on April 9, 1948, the Jewish renegade Irgun gang had attacked the village and massacred over 200 Arab men, women, and children. Since then, frightened Arab civilians of Northern Galilee had fled Palestine, seeking safety in Lebanon and Jordan.

Sighing, George reached for his wife and pulled her to him.

Mary said nothing, but the rapid beating of her heart expressed her fear more accurately than words.

The moment George dreaded most had arrived. Soon, the battle for Haifa would begin and George did not know what to do. Should he stay and fight? Should he take his family and flee to Lebanon? As he considered their dilemma, his eyes became fixed and his thoughts drifted. If only the Zionists had not come to Palestine...

The Jews were defeated by the Roman Army in 70 AD and Jerusalem was destroyed. Captive Jews were taken to Rome as slaves. Those Jews who escaped Rome's wrath scattered throughout Palestine. For nearly 2,000 years, through wars, invasions, and occupations, the Jews and Arabs of Palestine lived together in peaceful coexistence.

But toward the end of the nineteenth century, tensions between Jews and Arabs in Palestine began to appear. European Jews, fleeing persecution and discrimination in Europe, began arriving in Palestine seeking sanctuary. Jews purchased large tracts of land from feudal absentee Arab landlords living in neighboring countries. Palestinian tenants and sharecroppers were forced off the newly purchased land by owners who wanted to cultivate their own soil. Random acts of violence began to occur between the two peoples.

Jews began founding Zionist colonies and forming political parties. The Arabs responded by establishing anti-Zionist societies. Using the Old Testament as evidence, Jews began to assert that Palestine was their rightful homeland. The Arabs, both Muslim and Christian, categorically rejected the idea that Jewish settlement during biblical times gave present day European-born Jews a legitimate claim to Palestine which overrode Arab birthrights. Influential Arabs petitioned the Ottoman rulers, demanding that Jewish immigration into Palestine be halted. The Jewish immigration was slowed but not stopped.

When World War I began in 1914, there were 690,000 citizens of Palestine living under the rule of the Turkish Ottoman Empire. Of these 690,000 people, 535,000 were Sunni Muslim Arabs, 70,000 were Christian Arabs, and 85,000 were Jews. When the war ended in 1918, war and famine had taken a toll, and while the population figures had not increased, the political structure of Palestine had changed dramatically. Great Britain had driven the Turks from Palestine. The Ottoman Empire's 400-year rule ended, and the 30-year British occupation began.

During the early days of British rule, colonial officers attempted to please both Arab and Jew. They promised Jews they would have a homeland. They assured nervous Arabs that Jewish immigration quotas would never exceed the economic capacity of Palestine. Neither Jews nor Arabs were satisfied and both began venting their anger against the British Government by attacking British soldiers.

During the 1920's, the Jews of Europe faced increasing anti-Semitism. By 1933, Jewish immigrants from Europe were flooding Palestine. Three years after Adolf Hitler came to power in Germany, the Jewish population of Palestine had exploded to 400,000.

Palestinian Arabs, reeling in anger and fear, demanded that the British rulers turn back the Jewish tide.

Although the British government claimed Palestine could economically support a much larger population, they placed quotas on Jewish immigration.

European Jews denied entry into Palestine by the British quota evaded authorities and entered the country illegally. Violence between Jews and Arabs increased.

A Royal Commission for the British Government investigated the situation in Palestine and concluded that Arabs and Jews could not peacefully reside in the same country. The commission recommended that the area be partitioned into two separate states. The Jews accepted the recommendation. The Arab's response was to begin an open rebellion against the British occupiers.

In 1939, the outbreak of World War II forced the British government to assign the Palestinian problem a low priority, and the Arabs and the Jews settled into a temporary and uneasy truce.

When World War II ended in 1945, the Jews renewed their demand for a homeland in Palestine. Throughout the world community, there was widespread support for the Jews. The unspeakable crimes committed against the Jews of Europe by the German Third Reich had given the Holocaust survivors a moral license to be heard. The Jewish population of Palestine now stood at 550,000 and they owned 20% of the land. The remaining 80% was owned by the 1.1 million Muslim Arabs and 140,000 Christian Arabs also living in Palestine.

U.S. President Harry Truman began to push for the creation of a Jewish State in Palestine. He believed his own future political interests would be well served by supporting Jewish demands for a homeland. Largely as a result of the Truman administration's efforts, the United Nations voted to partition Palestine, giving the Jews 55% of the land area. There were vehement protests from the Arabs. The UN also voted for Jerusalem to remain an international city, which infuriated the Jews who claimed that the formation of a Jewish state without Jerusalem was impossible.

Once again, neither Arab or Jew was appeased.

From the date of the UN vote, November 29, 1947, Jews and Arabs set out to exterminate each other. Attacks followed by reprisal attacks became commonplace. Hardened Jewish survivors of World War II and the Holocaust were tenacious fighters. In battle after battle, Palestinians were losing Palestine.

Without warning, a blast of noise louder than anything George had ever heard burst into the room, numbing his hearing, rattling every object, and shaking the entire house. He leaped to his feet, screaming, "The Jews! The Jews are blowing up Haifa!"

Without speaking, Mary reached into the wooden cradle lying close to her body and lifted their infant son, Demetrius. The child began to cry.

The echo of the huge blast faded only to be replaced by the sounds of rapid gun-fire coming from all directions. George was breathing rapidly. The time had come to make the decision he had sworn never to make…to leave Palestine. One quick look at the innocent face of his child and his decision was made.

George hurriedly told his wife to pack. "Just a few things," he said. We must leave at once!" He paused at the door and turned to his wife and child. "I'll get Pa. Be quick!"

Mary nodded to her husband. Tears filled her eyes. She clasped Demetrius to her breast as she began to pile their clothes into a brown suitcase laying open on the floor.

George and his father gathered the family's important documents, family photographs, a few treasured books, several carpets, some copper trays, Mary's favorite cooking pots and kitchen utensils, some food supplies and placed everything on the stone walkway in front of their house. Then they walked through the house, closing shutters and locking doors.

After putting everything into the car, the Antoun family paused for a long parting glance at their home from the front garden. Then they climbed into the automobile and drove away. They planned to return.

The sounds of war startled the baby and he began to cry once again. Mary soothed her son, all the while turning her head to look over her shoulder toward the wonderful home she was leaving. She had planned to raise Demetrius in that house. Now she wondered what would happen to their dreams? What would happen to them?

Seeing his wife's distraught face, George tried to assure her, "Don't worry. We'll be back." He paused before repeating what Palestinians had been told. "We'll be back in one week." Neighboring Arab governments had promised to come to the Palestinian's defense…promised to defeat the "Zionist gangs"…promised to toss them into the sea. George repeated the words, this time as much for himself as for Mary, "We'll be back…in one week."

Mary sat silent. Sorrow came flowing over her. She could not control her tears, which rolled down her cheeks.

George's father, Mitri, sat ashen-faced, refusing to speak or even to look back at the house where he had lived most of his life. He had hoped the British could keep the peace…at least until the British forces left the country later in the year. But the British, claiming they could not implement a policy which was not acceptable to both sides, had opposed the UN vote and were planning to leave Palestine the following month.

Votes, and mandates, and partitions, and legal talk all swirled through George Antoun's thoughts—they were all useless, he concluded. Nothing could change the fact that he had been forced to leave his home in order to protect his family from the fighting.

Frightened and angry, George drove his family out of their beloved city of Haifa, up the Coast North, through the cities of Acre and Nahariya, and across the border into Lebanon.

Two days later, on April 23, 1948, the Jews captured Haifa.

On May 14, 1948, the State of Israel was proclaimed. Later that same day, the British high commissioner, Sir Alan Cunningham, lowered the Union Jack and departed Palestine.

Total war arrived.

During the fighting, the Jews lost the prize they most coveted, the old city of Jerusalem. But the entry of Arab armies into the conflict failed to defeat the Jews. By June 1, 1948, the Jews had doubled the size of their small state by securing the upper Galilee, the Coastal Plain, and the Negev.

The Jews celebrated.

The Arabs mourned.

On December 13, 1948, the Trans-Jordanian Parliament voted to annex the portion of Palestinian land not captured by the Jews, doubling the size of their own small country.

The ancient name of Palestine ceased to exist. In the eyes of the world, there was no longer a Palestine, and no longer a Palestinian people.

During the fighting, over 700,000 Arabs fled into neighboring Arab countries. Following the war, various delegations representing the Arabs and the Jews negotiated to find a solution to the Palestinian refugee problem. All attempts to repatriate the Palestinians failed. Arabs who had unwittingly left their homes during the war, believing their flight to be temporary, were stunned to discover that the new Jewish government had passed a law on "abandoned property" which legalized a policy of "no return of Palestinians."

Among those stranded and homeless Arab refugees were the George Antoun family, formerly of Haifa, Palestine.

Chapter IX

Four years later, February, 1952
Nahr al Barid Refugee Camp
(16 km North of Tripoli, Lebanon)

In a land of ten million prayers and ten thousand martyrs a young boy sat motionless on a large rock. With his face to the South and his eyes closed, Demetrius Antoun strained to see with his mind what could not be seen with his eyes...Palestine. "The most beautiful of all God's lands," his father would say. And then, hallucinating on hope, his father would tell of a wonderful land which Demetrius could not imagine. But, now, he was trying to do as his father asked: to see his home in his mind.

Demetrius' lips began to pucker as he squeezed his eyelids ever tighter, remembering all that his father had told him of his lost inheritance. The images were vivid: the street in front of their home was patterned with dark-colored, smooth cobblestones. The front gate was painted pale pink and covered with a vine-draped trellis. The Antoun's small home was built of shimmering white stone. Demetrius saw the gate...the steps...the front door...each room...the rugs...the furniture...the pictures...the books...smelled the cooking odors...heard the sounds of their neighbors...saw the school where his father taught...his father's office...and the small park in front of their home where the children of the neighborhood played.

The vision was so realistic his breathing became irregular from a rush of excitement. Thinking he had succeeded in wishing himself back to Palestine, Demetrius quickly opened his eyes, but he saw he had gone nowhere. Struck with heartsickness, he recalled that, for reasons he could not fathom, none of his family could return to that wonderful place. Old beyond his years, Demetrius truly believed he had lived in Palestine for all of his life and was nothing more than a temporary visitor to the squalor of Nahr al Barid Camp.

Overcome with a wrenching sadness, Demetrius took a deep breath.

Beating a tin pan with a small stone, George Antoun called out in a singsong voice, "Demetrius! Demetrius! Where are you?"

Demetrius' solemn mood vanished when he heard the familiar sound of his father's voice. He pulled himself to a standing position atop the rock, searching for his father in the mass of humanity crowding the curved pathways winding throughout the camp. George Antoun was a small man, but he looked huge to his four-year-old son, and the boy easily picked his father's fast-moving figure out of the multitude.

A smile washed across the boy's face at the sight of his doting father. He cried out, "Papa!"

Demetrius leaped down from the rock, losing his balance and tumbling on the hard soil of mountainous Lebanon. His high spirits burst when he saw he had broken the strap on one of his new sandals and he began to weep. Holding the highly prized sandals in his tiny hands, he ran to his father, crying "Papa, papa!"

When George saw his son weeping, he began running, and tossing the tin pan aside, he swept his son into his arms. "Demetrius! Precious one! Why are you crying?"

Sniffling, Demetrius held out a sandal. "Broke! Papa, I fell and broke my sandal!" Demetrius remembered receiving the new sandals for his birthday just three weeks earlier. His father had traveled to Tripoli and traded a silver coin for food to supplement the family's monotonous rice and bean diet provided by the United Nations agency operating the camp. As a birthday surprise, his father had also purchased the sandals.

Papa had beamed with pleasure watching Demetrius slide his tiny feet into the new sandals.

Mama had baked a small cake and prepared a special chicken dinner.

Grandpa had given him a box of chocolates.

The day had been happiest of Demetrius' young life.

George's expression sobered at the sight of the broken sandal. Demetrius began to shake his small head, his pitiful cries rending the air. "I broke my sandal!"

George Antoun hugged his son and forced himself to smile. "Stop crying, Demetrius." He caressed the boy's head. "It's only a sandal. Besides, Grandpa can repair it." George settled himself on the rocky ground, using his hands to remove soil and dried grass from his son's clothing. "Remember when grandpa put Sammy's broken leg back together? You remember that, don't you, Demetrius?"

Demetrius shook his head, his child-like voice whispering, "Yes, papa."

Sammy was Demetrius' wooden donkey. The year before, the refugees had received a large shipment of clothes and toys from people in France who had heard about their life in the camps. Each child had received one toy and one set of clothes. There had been a wonderful moment when Demetrius embraced the donkey, screaming out the name, "Sammy," as if the donkey were a long-lost friend. Demetrius had insisted that he should carry the donkey himself. His father had shaken his head in wonder, patiently walking behind his small son as the boy dragged, pushed, and pulled the bulky toy from the camp director's office to their home. Demetrius was devastated later when he discovered that one of the donkey's legs had suffered a crack during the journey to Lebanon. The leg fell off within a matter of days. When his grandfather repaired the donkey and made the toy as good as new, the boy had whooped with joy.

The child cried, "Sammy is not broke," and then shook his sandal in the air, "my shoe is broke!" Nothing could comfort him. Rubbing the damaged sandal with his finger, he sucked in his breath and began to cry even louder.

George gave a ragged sigh and took the sandals from his son, tucking them into his pants pocket. He pulled Demetrius toward him. "Come little one, dry your tears." He rocked the boy in his arms. "Stop crying. For papa?"

Staring at the child, George's eyes began to water. For a long time now, George had understood that the boy was too sensitive for his own good and was often in an emotional turmoil over something. There were other characteristics of the boy which troubled George. Although Arab culture did not encourage a love of beasts, Demetrius was fascinated by animals and nature, often spending hours alone exploring the rocky knolls surrounding the camp. Lizards and bugs scurrying through the sand, butterflies and bees feeding on the flowers, and birds chirping in the trees occupied Demetrius for hours on end. The boy's great love of such creatures was an oddity often mentioned by adults in the camp.

George made a noise in his throat which sounded like a croaking frog. He knew his son was different from other children and had been so from the very beginning.

Roused from his thoughts by whimpering noises, George sighed despondently and stared admiringly at the boy. Demetrius had been born a beautiful baby and was now an exceedingly handsome boy, but he looked nothing like his father. George had no doubt that one day Demetrius would grow into a strikingly handsome man.

Demetrius buried his head in his papa's arms, quaking with emotion.

Unable to endure Demetrius' unhappiness one minute longer, George began making a funny noise like a snorting donkey, kissing his son's cheeks, nose, and tummy until the child began to giggle. Finally Demetrius laughed aloud and the tension broke.

George smiled. "Come, let's go and find grandpa."

George leaned forward and pushed himself to his feet. His eyes fell on Nahr al Barid and he blinked at the sharpening outlines of the camp. He thought the setting sun cast an ugly light on the place he now called home. Home! He laughed bitterly as an image of his real home flashed through his mind. Heaving a long sigh, he bit his lower lip, muttering to himself, "All ended…all that was good has ended." George glanced at Demetrius. Except for the child…the boy was the only good thing left in his life. George turned his full attention back to Demetrius and with amazing tenderness gathered his son in his arms. Erect as a statue, he made his way back to the camp.

The Antoun house, consisting of one small room made into two smaller rooms when divided by a hanging blanket, had only recently been built. And without the assistance of the United Nations Relief and Works Agency, the family would still be living in a small tent. Sadly, due to the lack of funds, few homes had been constructed and the majority of the refugees were still miserably housed in tents. The Antoun family was fortunate to have a house made of cinder-block and covered with a tin roof. Still, their humble dwelling offered little relief from the icy winds which blew from the Northern snow-covered mountains of Lebanon.

The front "room" was decorated with scant personal belongings the family had managed to salvage the day of their hurried departure from their home in Haifa, Palestine. A few cushions precisely arranged made up the sitting area, and a half dozen copper pots were carefully spaced between the cushions. A worn carpet, brightly colored with a black and burgundy design, covered the floor. An ornately patterned copper serving tray which held tiny porcelain coffee cups sat conspicuously in the center of the carpet. A group of treasured books were carefully organized on crudely built wooden shelves, while a pile of dog-eared family photographs lay stacked against the row of books. A large house key, tied with a black velvet ribbon, hung from a large nail on the wall.

The second "room," even smaller than the first, was cluttered with family bedding and served as the sleeping area. A faded fabric curtain strung on a wire cordoned off an additional, smaller space, making a private dressing area for George's wife, Mary. A battered, brown suitcase functioned as a clothing bureau, and a large barrel held the food supplies. Bent cooking utensils and chipped plates were stacked high on the barrel.

George paused under the door-frame of the first room. "Mary?" he called.

Squirming in his father's arms, Demetrius freed himself and slid to the floor. His small feet made no noise as he padded over the carpet and through the house. He parroted his father, "Mary? Mary?"

Frowning, George turned and glanced into the sky. The setting sun told him that the hour for the night meal was near. He motioned with his head to his son. "Come, Demetrius, mama is cooking."

Holding hands, father and son walked around the outside of the house to a small tin-covered space in the back, Demetrius' short plump legs almost running to keep up with his father's pace.

They saw Grandpa Mitri first, smoking his pipe and reading a recently issued news bulletin describing the continuing crisis in Palestine. From the first day of exile, Grandpa Mitri had closely followed the news from his homeland. He truly believed the world would come to see that Palestine had been stolen from its legitimate owners and that soon this terrible wrong would be righted. Four years later, Grandpa was still waiting.

Mary Antoun was sitting with her back to the house, squatting in front of the fire, stirring a meal of rice with tomatoes, pine nuts and onions.

Mary was in a rare bad mood. On most days she pretended to her burdened husband that she did not mind the squalor of their home, but her forced, noncomplaining attitude was a mockery of the truth of her feelings. No matter how she had tried, adjusting to the difficulty of life in the camp proved impossible for her.

The daily problems were insurmountable. As soon as she arrived at a solution for one problem, another took its place. Today, the difficulty of obtaining water was the cause of her distress.

When their house was first constructed, George had rigged a large tin pan to catch the rain water, which was convenient when the winter rains came. But the rain water was used for baths and for washing clothes and did little to relieve the numbing chore of hauling and carrying drinking and cooking water, which was a woman's duty.

Earlier in the afternoon, Mary had made two long trips to the communal well to fill the family drinking and cooking pots. She had stumbled on the first trip, spilling half the water in her jug. Discouraged to the point of tears, she had turned her eyes toward heaven and startled the other women by angrily shaking her fists and crying out, "God! Why have you deserted us?"

As soon as she had completed that chore, Mary had hurried to light a fire under the black cooking pot. She was in a rush to prepare the last and largest meal of the day, for with the setting of the early winter sun, the Mediterranean coastal sea breeze quickly became frigid.

Mary hated working in the cold outdoors. She shivered as she stirred the contents of the pot, telling herself that if not for her son, she would turn her face to the wall and wait for death to claim her weary body.

"Mama!" Laughing aloud, Demetrius ran to his mother, wrapping his small arms around her back. "Mama! Guess what? This afternoon, I saw a bird with blue feathers and guess what? That bird talked to me!"

Laying her wooden stirring spoon on a small piece of broken cinder block, Mary turned and stood, lifting her son in her arms. Her face was unusually stern as she told him, "Demetrius! How many times do I have to tell you? Birds don't talk! Cats don't talk! Donkeys don't talk!"

A capricious Demetrius argued, "They do too talk! They do! They talk to me!" With a scowl, he leaned his upper torso away from his mama's face and declared, "I did just what grandpa told me to do. I said: speak bird, speak! And, it did!" Leaping from his mama's arms, he ran to his grandfather. "Grandpa, tell mama! Birds talk to you, and they talk to me! Remember, grandpa?"

Grandpa Mitri shot a guilty look at Mary. He had promised his daughter-in-law he would help her discourage the boy's over-active imagination. Now, with the boy's words, he was caught between his promise and his deed!

"Tell her, grandpa!" Demetrius continued to insist.

Grandpa Mitri rubbed his beard, looking away, trying to think of a way out of the situation. He could think of nothing to say and finally wiggled his eyebrows at the boy, trying in vain to give the child a message.

Demetrius' response was to make a buzzing sound in his throat, flying motions with his arms and a downward jerking movement with his head, his lips pushed out to resemble a sharp beak. He laughed before staring up at his mother and declaring, "Grandpa says when we move back to our house in Palestine that I can have a caged bird!" Excited, Demetrius tugged on his mama's dress. "Will you bake a birthday cake for my bird, mama?"

Mary raised an eyebrow, looking at George with an "I told you so" expression. "Well?" she asked her husband.

George gazed at his father, whose face had suddenly drooped in dread of his son's forthcoming words. George's voice was low and apologetic, for George Antoun was not a man who could easily criticize his own father. Gently he reminded him, "Try not to fill the boy with nonsense, papa. Please."

Grandpa Mitri brushed nervously at the wispy hair on his head. He then pulled on the boy's arm. "Demetrius, that was our special secret. Remember?"

Confused, the child looked at each of the adults in turn. His mother's face was rigid and she looked angry. She returned to her squatting position and sat hunched over the cooking pot. His grandpa began to beat his pipe against the side of the house, ignoring him. His father stood perfectly still, staring at the sky, eyes blazing, feet apart, with arms folded tightly across his chest.

Demetrius' chin quivered. Instinctively, he knew that he had said something wrong. Fretful, he began to cry, knowing somehow that the place where they lived now, and the home they had lost had everything to do with the incredible sadness of the moment. With a shaky voice he asked, "Why can't we go home, papa?" Getting no response, he shouted and stamped his foot. *"I want to go home!"*

Putting aside their earlier discord, all three adults gathered around the sobbing child. "We'll go home one day, I promise," George assured his son, giving the child a weak smile.

Mary patted her son on his back, making soothing sounds with her tongue, reminding herself that she must keep her unhappiness from spilling over and hurting those whom she loved.

Knowing that he had caused the unpleasant episode over the bird, Grandpa Mitri knelt before his grandson, knees apart, arms outstretched, and motioned for the child to come to him.

At a loss, the child hurried to the spot between his grandpa's legs where he had stood so many times before. He wrapped his arms around the old man's neck, sobbing so hard that he began to hiccup.

Grandpa Mitri negotiated with the boy. "Don't cry, lad. If you won't cry, after dinner grandpa will tell how he saved his pet lamb from a hungry wolf. And I was not much bigger than you are now." Toothless, he grinned at the child while digging in his pocket for a small sweet he had been hoarding for a special occasion.

While the men of the family continued to comfort Demetrius, Mary stared over her husband's shoulder at the stark ugliness of the small patch of brown dirt that now served as her garden, calling to mind the fragrant bushes which lined her terraced patio in Haifa. Soon those carefully tended bushes would begin to bloom, and she wondered what woman would claim them as her own.

These days, Mary often felt that her life in Palestine had been lived by another and was nothing more than an interesting story told to her by someone else; but now, homesickness overwhelmed her and she was swept back to Palestine. Mary Antoun's prize rose garden had been the envy of her friends. Her home and yard had been immaculate, and her husband proud of the tempting creations which came from her kitchen. She didn't hear the soft moan escape her own lips as she recalled the pleasant moments spent in her lovely home with George, their families, and their friends. Then Mary's lips tightened as the precious memories evaporated and she remembered the horrible war and the unexpected exile. Grunting, she shook her head, trying to clear away those images, cautioning herself that it was dangerous to think such thoughts or even admit to having them. In their four years of banishment she had come to recognize the harsh reality of their situation. At the very beginning of exile, Mary had believed that one day they would be allowed to return to their home, to recapture their way of life, but over the years an increasingly desperate sense had grown inside her that the Antoun family would never again be allowed even to visit Palestine, let alone live there.

She glanced at her son. Her husband and father-in-law continued to fill the child's head with visions of Palestine. That was a foolish mistake. She was certain the boy would never live in Palestine. Knowing she was helpless to change the future, she closed her eyes to the bleakness of her surroundings, and bitterly muttered, "This is our life, now."

Sighing regretfully, she used her hands to push herself to her feet. Her face was white and tense as she looked at the three men in her family. "All dreamers," she complained under her breath. "The three of them are dreamers."

Bending straight from her waist, she lifted the handle of the heavy black pot and slowly walked into her home. With unaccustomed abruptness, she called out, "Now, the three of you, come inside before dinner gets cold."

Later that evening George was subdued, and he sat silent, his face drawn and tired, watching but not seeing, as Mary fed the boy and then put him to bed. He heard the sounds but not the words, as Grandpa Mitri fulfilled his earlier promise, giving an exciting rendition of wolf howls and sheep noises to a well-known bedtime story that soon had Demetrius squealing with laughter.

Mary watched her husband's face for the briefest of moments, knowing him so well that she understood his thoughts as easily as if they were her own. She knew that her husband was once again reliving the events of 1948. Many times George had said he had made a mistake: that they should not have run from their enemy, that Palestinians should have stayed in their homes and fought, even if staying had cost them their lives. But like cowards they had fled, and in the process, had lost their possessions, their means of livelihood, and their country. Now, George could blame no one but himself, and at least once a day he made the wistful remark that Palestine did not leave him, but rather, he had left Palestine.

The smallest of reminders of that fateful year drove George into the deepest despair. Mary said nothing, for she knew that no words could relieve his suffering. For a frightening moment Mary wondered if a man could die of grief. Certainly, that seemed to be the case in Nahr al Barid, for there were a number of men who had dropped dead for no apparent medical reason.

Unlike the Antoun family of Haifa, most of the camp inhabitants were farmers from the Lake Houleh region in Northern Palestine. These were men who had once been active members of thriving farming communities who suddenly found they had nothing to do but walk aimlessly about the camp, waiting first for sunrise, then for sunset. They were men who struggled to meet a day they knew would be exactly like the previous day. The situation was different for the women. Women of the camp were as industrious in exile as they had been in their homes in Palestine. There was no end to cooking, cleaning, and care of children. Women had no time to sit still and shrivel up inside.

Mary felt real fear for George's well-being. With a sad quickening inside her, she paused and took a moment to touch his shoulder before stepping behind the private curtain to prepare herself for bed. Hidden from her family, Mary allowed herself the luxury of mourning. She pressed her forehead against the wall and wept softly for all that was lost.

Some hours later, a cold wind born of the pre-dawn blackness whipped through the cracked walls and creaking door, whirling around the shivering inhabitants with indifference.

George watched his family and saw that his father slept fitfully. The continuous and troubled movements of Grandpa Mitri's thin body suggested he was bothered by the cold air on either side of his tattered blanket. George's stomach plunged. His father's comfort was his responsibility. An aged man should be sleeping in his own bed.

Wrapping his arms around his shoulders and leaning his back against the wall, George shook his head in sorrow. He had refused to go to bed, even at Mary's repeated urging, and now he sat upright on a small cushion instead of laying his body across one of the thin mattresses he found so uncomfortable. There was a nervousness about George Antoun, a sense of uncertainty. He was in the process of making a decision he knew would affect his family for the rest of their lives.

George was fully dressed, his creased face deeply troubled, as he turned to stare at his wife curled instinctively around their son. George thought that at least the child is warm. His small body was protected from the cold, tightly bound in his coverlet and wrapped snugly in the blanket meant for his father. Demetrius had been given a cup of warm goat's milk before saying his prayers, and was now sleeping comfortably and soundly with a hint of a smile on his young face.

Without rising from his seat, George bent his upper torso toward his wife. He saw that Mary's eyes were open, wide with worry, he supposed. George raised his thick eyebrows just a bit, thinking how he would break the news to his wife. He prodded her back with one finger and spoke softly. "Mary? Are you awake?"

Mary slowly twisted her body, careful not to wake the sleeping child. She looked at George, her eyes searching his face. She adored her gentle husband and had a fleeting thought that George Antoun was one of those steady and decent men history fails to record, yet life could not endure without such men. She had faced the bad times with him and knew he had tried his hardest to adapt their lives to the difficult circumstances. Before "The Catastrophe of 1948," her husband had been a teacher of men, an educated, quiet man who longed for peace in his land. The storm of violence had caught him off-guard, and then they had lost everything.

Mary lifted her chin and made a silent gesture with her lips and tongue, meaning, "no," she was not sleeping. She patted the mat on which she lay, issuing an invitation.

On his hands and knees, George slowly eased his body next to his wife, his chest touching her shoulder. "I have made a decision," he whispered. George then paused, thinking, slowly, slowly, I'll break the plan to her. "Mary, we must leave this place."

"George, where can we go?"

George's brow was furrowed as he studied his wife's face. "We must go far away." He pinched his bottom lip with his fingers. "I thought of Tripoli, but the city is too close. We would be discovered and returned to the camp." Suddenly he was a man who had made up his mind. "Beirut. There is more opportunity for us there."

Afraid of her own voice, afraid it would only betray doubt, Mary said nothing, but she thought of Beirut. The city was an impossible dream for refugees of the Nahr al Barid Camp. Finally she whispered longingly, "Beirut." The city inspired enormous hope in her heart. The Lebanese were schooled people; they insisted upon good educations for their children. Schools required teachers. They had heard George could find work in a private school there. With work, her husband could renew his dignity. His salary would earn them the right to live as free citizens. Her thoughts raced ahead: they could rent a small apartment in the city, far away from the camps. In two years, her son would be six-years-old, and they would enroll him in a good school. She rubbed the worn shirt on her husband's back. She would buy a sewing machine and make the men in her family some decent clothes.

She smiled at George and nodded her head. "Beirut." Their lives would be transformed if they went to Beirut.

In the very beginning of their exile, George and Mary had made many attempts to move out of the camp, but as the Palestinian population swelled in the small country of Lebanon, restrictions had quickly been enacted, making travel difficult for the Palestinians wanting to move from one refugee camp or city to another. Economic independence was required for freedom of movement, and the Antoun family had escaped with little other than their lives.

They had been destitute since 1948.

In her darkest moments, Mary did remind herself of the good fortune that they were alive. In January of 1948, George had lost two brothers and his only sister in a terrorist attack at the Jaffa Gate in Jerusalem. Now, he was the sole surviving child of his father. As the only child of her parents to survive infancy, Mary had no siblings to lose in the fighting. She often thanked God her parents had died of natural causes, each within a year of the other, several years before the war broke out. They, at least, had not lived to experience the pain of exile.

Remembering their past difficulties in leaving the camp, Mary wondered what her husband might be thinking. "How, George?" she asked. Her question turned into a plea. "Tell me, how?"

The blood rushed to George's face. Now came the hard part. Embarrassed by what he had to say, he pulled away from his wife. His trembling turned into a rattle, and he was unable to speak.

"George?" Impatient, she coaxed him. "What? Tell me."

George lowered his eyes and gestured toward her chest. Making several unsuccessful attempts to speak, his words finally came out in a rush. "Mary, I... Your jewels. I need the jewels from your dowry. I have heard talk in the camp. There are men who will prepare the proper papers and slip us into Beirut. For your jewels." With tear-blurred eyes, George stared down at the simple woman who had brought so much happiness to his life. Asking her for the only possessions she would ever own, the jewels which would protect her from starvation if he were to die before her, made him deeply ashamed.

Smiling sweetly at her husband, Mary felt surges of the strange and wonderful love she shared with this man. She did not hesitate for a moment. She struggled to sit upright, unbuttoning the three top buttons of her shabby blouse. Reaching inside, Mary retrieved a small, nut-colored pouch which was tied with a leather drawstring. She held out the pouch to her husband.

"Here. Take them." Seeing the acute anguish on his face, she assured him, "What good are jewels, George?" She teased. "Come now, am I going to a ball?"

His hands shaking, George leaned toward his wife, and with an urgency withdrew from her hand the gifts of gold and precious stones he had offered her ten years before as a token of his everlasting love. Unable to look at Mary, he turned away and muttered, "Tomorrow. Tomorrow, I will contact the men."

Hearing soft sobs, Mary rubbed her hands up and down his back, praying silently that God would allow George Antoun another chance at life.

One week later, Mary prepared a special meal of lamb and rice. Rarely did the family enjoy meat with their meals and the child grinned with happiness, wiping his plate clean with his pita bread and stuffing himself with the last delicious bite.

After supper, Mary knelt before her son and motioned for the boy to come and sit in her lap. "Demetrius," she said in a serious voice, "tonight we are going to play a special game."

While standing over Mary, George instructed the child, "Demetrius, you must be very quiet." George himself appeared uncharacteristically stern. "You are going to hide. No one must hear you. No one must see you. Can you hide? For papa?"

"A game!" Demetrius laughed aloud, and then jumped from his mother's lap to his grandfather, bouncing up and down in his arms. "Hide, grandpa! Hide!" he happily chanted, grabbing his grandfather's beard and then closing the old man's eyes with his fingers.

Mary stood and began to gather the child's warmest and best clothing into a pile.

With a determined edge to his voice, George told Mary, "Hand me the basket." He carefully prepared the large straw container, placing the child's clothing and sandals Grandpa Mitri had managed to repair inside. When the packing was complete, Demetrius eagerly crawled inside, but when George covered him with a blanket, shutting out the dim light of the single lantern, the child began to whimper, "Sammy, I want Sammy!"

The three adults exchanged pained looks. The wooden donkey was the only real toy the child had ever owned. The donkey was heavy and awkwardly shaped; they had hoped to leave the toy in the house, along with other bulky possessions they would not be able to carry during the long walk to Beirut.

"Demetrius. You must be a big boy," Mary admonished him. She told a small lie, asking God for forgiveness even as she spoke the words, "Sammy will follow us later."

"Sammy! I want my Sammy!" The child began to chant. "Sammy! I want Sammy!" Then he screamed and began kicking his legs.

George shuddered. Rushing away from the child's piercing howls, he hurried to bring the donkey from the bedroom and spent precious moments fitting the toy into the basket under the blanket with his son.

The child's sobs quickly sputtered and stopped. He whispered, "Sammy! Now you must be very quiet!" He tossed the blanket off his face and grinned happily at his papa.

With a pale face, Mary looked at her husband. "George, you are impossible when it comes to this boy."

"That I am, mother, that I am," George responded, a warm smile softening his worried features.

Once the child was settled, the Antoun family prepared to creep quietly from the house. Who knew what neighbor might report them? Each of the adults had packs wrapped around their backs, stuffed with clothing. George hoisted the basket with their most precious cargo, while Mary carried the brown suitcase, crammed with important documents, family photos, a few books, and some cooking utensils. Grandpa Mitri was responsible for the blankets and three of the cushions. Earlier in the day, Mary had sewn the porcelain coffee cups inside the cushions.

As they took one last look around the room and started to close the door, Grandpa Mitri gave a small cry. Rushing into the sitting room, he retrieved the key to their home in Palestine. With a sheepish smile at his daughter-in-law's disapproving look, he carefully draped the black ribbon around his neck, tucking the key inside his shirt. "We will need it one day," he explained.

George led the way. He walked quickly through the camp and then slowed down on the narrow path. The basket swayed slightly in George's arms.

Feeling secure, Demetrius wrapped his arms around the wooden donkey and fell into a deep sleep.

No one spoke, but Mary was dazed with anxiety, and her heart pounded wildly. The possibilities were endless: what if the guides did not meet them? The men could have easily lied to trick George out of the last of their possessions. The stray dogs hanging around the camp might bark, alerting the authorities to their flight. They would be forced to return, without any hope of bettering their bleak future. Mary knew that at any moment, danger could erupt. She told herself to think of something else, and she thought of her beautiful son. Demetrius was nothing less than a miracle. After six years of desperate longing, miscarriage after miscarriage, after hope had died, the boy had been sent, straight from God's hand. George often told her their son was nothing less than a heavenly dispensation.

Her lips parted with a hint of a small smile.

Mary caught a quick breath as Grandpa Mitri stumbled, almost tumbling on the hard earth. The stony foot-path was difficult to maneuver. Only George walked with a sure foot. He was so certain they were doing the right thing that for the past few days his dour mood had lifted and he had become something similar to the man he had been prior to their flight from Palestine.

The night air was cold. Soon Mary's fingers felt frozen. She moved the heavy suitcase from one hand to the other, warming her free hand in the folds of her skirt.

The meeting place was two-kilometers south of the camp. Mary breathed more easily when she saw two men appear from behind a large rock. Both men were wearing black baggy pants, with broad sashes. Black turbans covered their heads. Looking at the men, she remembered what George had told her. Their two guides were brothers, members of the highly secretive Druze religion.

During the twelfth century, the Druze sect had broken away from traditional Islam, and since that time, the rites of their religion were a well-guarded secret, known to no one but adult males of the sect. Druze men were known throughout the area for their ability to track and for dependability. The Druze were incredibly loyal to their friends, but the most vindictive of men to their enemies.

Mary saw that both men were armed with rifles and large knives. They looked sinister and dangerous, and though she knew that the Druze were men who would not attack unless attacked, Mary felt a keen sense of relief that the men were paid to protect them.

Their manner was one of brisk efficiency. Both men greeted George and Grandpa Mitri with a raised hand signal. When they looked at Mary, the oldest brother placed his hand over his heart, while the youngest one simply nodded. Without speaking, one of the men took the suitcase from Mary's hand while the other quickly hoisted Grandpa Mitri's load upon his own back. The older man motioned for them to fall into place. With the older taking the lead and the younger walking in the rear, the group began their long trek to Beirut.

Keeping a steady pace, the five adults walked all night, through the ancient hills and valleys of Lebanon. Finally, just as Mary was on the verge of telling George she could not go on and Grandpa Mitri was gasping and pale, the child awakened, popped his head out of the basket and looked all around. The oldest of the guides laughed at Demetrius, whom he said "looks like a baby bird waiting for a worm." Then he commanded, "We will rest until night falls."

Coffee was boiled on a small fire, and while the adults drank the steaming brew and ate bread and cheese, Demetrius was given milk from a tin container and ate two of the six boiled eggs Mary had prepared for the trip.

The two guides teased Demetrius but otherwise said little while eating. Afterward, they disappeared, climbing to the highest point around where they would take turns resting and keeping watch.

Grandpa Mitri curled into a fetal position and began to snore almost immediately.

George looked at his wife and smiled. "Mary. Get some sleep. I will take our son for a short walk."

Looking at his eyes, red from lack of sleep, Mary protested, "No...no...you rest first. I will tend to Demetrius."

Seeing that his wife was pale from fatigue, George was adamant, taking Demetrius by the hand and walking away. They wandered to a small hill and spent more than an hour watching a small hare nibble on the wild Mediterranean vegetation. After the hare went into a hole, George and Demetrius leaned against a fir tree, dreamily watching the sky. Suddenly a flock of Kingfisher birds begin to circle above their heads, and after a few moments of watching and with a lost, soulful look on his face, George told Demetrius, "My son, you and I are like those birds, circling aimlessly, looking for a home."

With a terrible awe, Demetrius watched the birds circle and dive, circle and dive, waiting for the feared intruders to leave their tree so they could go home again.

Pink dawn was breaking as the group reached the outskirts of Beirut. Mary stopped in mid-stride and gasped, staring at the beautiful city with its white gleaming buildings nestled among the green of terraced hillsides and gracious mountains reaching to the deep blue of the Mediterranean Sea. Beirut was as lovely as she had been told. Looking about, she quickly decided Beirut was even more dramatic in appearance than their home city of Haifa, the most beautiful city in all of Palestine.

With a soft, almost imperceptible touch on her shoulder, George leaned toward his wife. They looked at each other and smiled, knowing they had made the right decision.

Somehow, in that moment, many of the hardships of the past few years slipped away.

Chapter X

The 400-year-old Turkish Ottoman Empire collapsed in defeat in 1918, along with Germany and its other allies, with the signing of surrender papers ending World War I. Victorious Western nations divided the empires of the defeated countries among themselves. The Ottoman Empire in the Middle East was divided between England and France. The British became the new rulers of Palestine. The French assumed control of the newly created country of Lebanon.

Between the World Wars, many citizens of the new Lebanon prospered under French rule. Without the divisive issue of the "Jewish question" which tormented Palestine, Lebanon enjoyed political stability and social calm.

In 1946, Lebanon was granted independence. Lebanese leaders, both Christian and Muslim, responded to their new freedom by forming a national pact, vowing to maintain unity between the numerous religious factions within the country. Although Muslims complained that the new President, a Christian Maronite, favored his Christian friends, the pact held during the early years of independence.

Jewish victory in the 1948 War for Palestine had serious repercussions for Lebanon. Palestinian refugees from Northern Galilee fled into Lebanon seeking safety. The mountainous terrain of Lebanon had always served as a refuge for various ethnic and religious groups and the tolerant Lebanese sympathetically welcomed their Palestinian brothers.

An exact count of the number of fleeing Palestinians arriving in Lebanon could not be made, but estimates placed the number near 250,000. There were already over two-million citizens of Lebanon living in a country only 135 miles long and 55 miles at its widest point. The arrival of Palestinian refugees overwhelmed the economic and social resources of the small country.

The Palestinian refugees also presented a political challenge to the delicate balance of power between religious groups in Lebanon. The Christian population held a slight political advantage based on religious groupings. But the majority of the Palestinian refugees were of the Sunni Muslim faith. Lebanese Christians feared the increased number of Muslims would tilt the political balance of the country away from the Christians and toward the Muslims. Partly because of this Christian fear, Palestinian refugees were given only minimal legal and political rights in Lebanon.

When Palestinian refugees moved into caves, mosques, old military barracks, and whatever else offered shelter, the Lebanese government began to establish refugee camps throughout the country.

In the city of Beirut, the government created refugee camps by simply confiscating privately owned undeveloped land sites and giving them to the Palestinians. One of the main camps, a camp named Shatila, was located in the Southern outskirts of Beirut.

Shatila residents lived in tents for several years. Gradually the tents were replaced by crudely constructed cement-block buildings. The camp slowly began to lose the look of a refugee camp and to acquire the look of a poor suburb of Beirut.

George and Mary Antoun raised their beloved son, Demetrius, in Shatila Camp.

The Antouns tried unsuccessfully to merge into Lebanese society. But without full citizenship and permission to participate in the country's economic system, they, like other Palestinians, were forced to live quiet lives in poverty. Their comfort came from their Greek Orthodox Christian faith and their happiness came from one another.

Greatly loved and spoiled by his parents and grandfather, Demetrius Antoun grew into a soft-spoken and dutiful young man who dreamed of one day lifting his parents into the luxury of a middle-class life.

Demetrius developed, as his own father had predicted, into an exceedingly handsome young man with an imposing persona. He was tall and broad chested, with a slender body. A wide brow, gray eyes so dark they appeared black, a straight nose and full lips topped by a well-trimmed mustache combined to elicit favorable attention for Demetrius wherever he went.

In 1968, Demetrius graduated with honors from high school. As a special present, George and Mary Antoun made their son's first graduation wish come true. They presented Demetrius with a small sum of money, each coin having been diligently saved for this moment, to pay for his long-desired sightseeing trip into Jordan and Syria with his best friend, Walid Bader.

16 Years Later
The Road to Karameh
March 20, 1968

Demetrius Antoun and Walid Bader had been walking since early morning and now the sun glared noontime hot and heatwaves danced in the air. After coming upon a lone fig tree, they decided to wait in the shade beside the road west of Kerek, hoping for a free ride down the mountain to the Dead Sea Highway. In spite of the heat, the waiting was not a burden, for they were young, carefree and close friends since childhood. The early afternoon passed rather quickly.

The week before, the two young men had left their parents' homes in Beirut and traveled to Jordan on a greatly anticipated sightseeing trip. After touring Petra, the ruined capital of the Nabataeans, they were making their way across the Hashemite Kingdom, intending to visit the refugee camp of Karameh, where Walid had relatives, before returning to Amman, the capital city.

Demetrius and Walid exchanged glances of relief when an approaching truck stopped. Seeing that the driver was not going to come to a full stop, they scrambled to leap into the cab of the truck.

Walid shouted, "To Karameh?"

The driver nodded, then ignored the two while occupying himself with getting his truck back on the road again. He was middle-aged and the physical opposite of his worn and rusting truck. Small, thin, and quick in his movements, he seemed the complete master of the brutish and sluggish 10-ton vehicle. He spoke only after satisfying himself that everything was in good order with his truck, which was his sole means of livelihood.

The driver then gave a brief look at Walid before bending forward and studying Demetrius. After turning his attention back to the road, the driver asked him, "Are you a wrestler?"

Walid gave a gleeful laugh. Demetrius was over six-feet tall and had a powerful body. Strangers were always struck by Demetrius' size.

Demetrius attempted to keep his irritation from showing, but he was unable to keep a scowl off his face. "I am a student," he retorted sharply. Demetrius intensely disliked such automatic assumptions that he made his living by means of his physical prowess, when in fact he desired nothing more than to make his way in the world by using his considerable intellectual gifts. Deciding to change the subject, he softened his tone and added, "My friend and I are temporarily residing in Beirut."

"Until Palestine is freed," Walid interjected.

Now the driver laughed. Every Palestinian in exile truly believed they would return to Palestine one day. He had Palestinian neighbors in Amman who talked of little else. With the fingers of his right hand, the driver gave a flick of dismissal. "Forget Palestine! You'll rock your grandchildren in Beirut!"

Walid changed the subject. "After we see Jordan and Syria, we will return to Beirut." He smiled. "This fall, my friend and I will begin university schooling."

The driver looked into the rear-view mirror before commenting. "Ah! Scholars!"

"Some day, God willing," Walid responded.

Demetrius remained silent, gazing out the open window beyond the driver. The sun was still above the horizon and gray clouds had begun to gather. Shafts of sunlight created great pools of light and shadow, some stretching three or four miles across the entire width of the valley. The beauty and serenity completely absorbed Demetrius' attention.

The conversation lapsed between Walid and the driver as the truck continued down the mountain road then north along the Red Sea Highway.

Even in silence, time and distance seemed to pass quickly. The driver paused as he lifted his foot onto the brake pedal and pressed down with determined strength. "We are at the village of Shunet Nimrin. If you want to go to Karameh, you must get out at this intersection."

Demetrius nodded. "Good, then. We will get out here."

As the truck rolled to a stop, Walid thanked the driver. "From this point, can we arrive in Karameh before nightfall?" he asked.

The driver grinned. "Maybe yes, maybe no. Anyway, sometimes it is better to travel than to arrive!" As the driver pulled away, he looked back and shouted, "May God go with you!"

Smoke and dust from the truck billowed around Demetrius and Walid, causing them to dash from the highway toward the small buildings of Shunet Nimrin. After gagging, coughing and clearing their lungs, the two men stood silently for a moment, looking about. Two elderly men sat sipping coffee and playing a board game in front of a small open market. A mechanic, his head and most of his upper body underneath the open hood of a truck, called out instructions to his assistant sitting behind the steering wheel. Several rusting automobiles, parked pointing in all directions, obscured the view of any other activity.

"Shunet Nimrin is a small, quiet place," Walid observed. He gave a fixed stare to the occupants, hoping for a friendly greeting. Neither the old men, the mechanic, or his assistant welcomed them. Walid sighed and told Demetrius, "It is good we did not plan to spend the night here."

"Yes," Demetrius replied. "You are right about that." Demetrius then looked up and down the highway, before starting to walk toward Karameh.

Walid's shoulders slumped in disappointment. His legs were much shorter than Demetrius' long limbs, and the morning walk had tired Walid considerably. Walid remembered Karameh was seven miles from Shunet Nimrin. He rushed to match Demetrius' stride. "We should offer money to that mechanic," he suggested hopefully. "He could drive us to Karameh."

Demetrius' eyes sparkled as he looked down at his friend and his mouth widened in a smile. He flung his arms out and began to shake his head slowly from side to side, taunting his friend. "Walid, tell me, how could we smell the sweet aroma of the valley from a car…or feel the stones beneath our feet…or hear the partridge's song…or…"

Walid blinked, then laughed. He had a quick thought that it was just like Demetrius to sing the praises of nature. Still, Demetrius' sunny mood was infectious, and not to be outdone, Walid joined in the small game, "Yes! Of course! How right you are! How could we smell the perfumed dung of the camel…or look upon the bony sheep…or gag upon the odor of unwashed sheep herders."

"Walid, your heart in not in the right place."

"No, it is my *feet* that are not in the right place!" Walid bent over double and laughed at his own small joke.

Before long, Walid dug a small scrap of blue cloth out of his pocket and wiped his forehead. "I am tired!"

Demetrius chuckled and then responded with a gentle insult. "You are too small, my friend. Your tiny legs tire easily."

Walid glared at Demetrius. "That's not funny." He rolled the blue fabric into a ball before stuffing it back into his pocket. Looking pale and frustrated, he marched ahead, refusing to speak. Walid hated being short and slight. Since childhood, he had wanted to be large and strong like Demetrius.

Unconcerned, Demetrius once again chuckled, staring at the back of his friend with undisguised affection.

Demetrius Antoun and Walid Bader had been best friends since the first moment they had met, sixteen-years before when the Antoun family fled Nahr al Barid Camp and traveled to Beirut. Extending a hand of friendship, Mustafa Bader and his family had offered the exhausted Antoun family food and bedding. Both families had four-year-old sons and those sons took an immediate liking to each other. They were always together at school and at play, bringing the two refugee families even closer.

Over the years, George Antoun and Mustafa Bader accepted the resigned, regretful lives of exiles, while their sons met life with a defiance, almost an aggressiveness in their insistence they would overcome the poverty and hopelessness that had consumed their fathers.

There was now an unbreakable bond between the two young men.

Recently graduated from high school and on a trip which they had long anticipated, with tentative arrangements to attend college in the fall, Demetrius and Walid both felt the early stirrings of victory over their hated exile.

Demetrius and Walid were happy young men.

Thirsty, Demetrius paused and uncorked his water bottle.

Walid kept walking.

Demetrius took a long swallow of the tepid liquid. He called out in a teasing manner, "Walid! Water?"

As Demetrius knew, Walid couldn't stay irritated with him for very long.

Walid looked back and then retraced his steps, reaching for the water bottle and taking a drink. Satisfied, he wiped his mouth with the back of his hand and asked Demetrius, "Where are the cars? Where are the trucks?"

Demetrius examined the sun, "Soon it will be dark."

Walid sighed in disappointment but kept walking. After an hour passed there was still no ride in sight. "I must stop soon," Walid told Demetrius.

"While there is the smallest amount of light we should press on." Demetrius looked at his friend and smiled before continuing, "A bed of sand and stone has no appeal to me when a village is near."

Between breaths, Walid replied, "At this moment, a bed of sand and stone would feel like the softest cotton. I am finished. Karameh can wait until morning."

Demetrius looked at Walid's fatigued face and changed his mind. They had slept in the outdoors before. "You are right. We can find a spot off the road...perhaps on the hillside. We will rest until the first light of the new day." In an attempt to make Walid feel better, he added, "Anyway, walking beside the road in the dark is not such a good idea."

Walid pointed toward two large limestone rocks protruding from the hillside several yards above the highway. "Look there…on the right."

"I see."

The two men climbed the distance without speaking.

Once they reached their destination, Walid placed his jacket on the soil between the two large rocks and slowly lowered himself to the ground.

Demetrius unfastened his back-pack and retrieved a half-eaten sandwich. He leaned his back against the side of a rock and offered the sandwich to Walid who shook his head, no. "I am so tired that I am not hungry."

Demetrius began to munch. "We can rest here." He glanced at Walid. "You sleep first, I am not so tired."

"I won't argue with you," Walid responded. "I will sleep, beginning now." Walid curled into a ball-like position and was quickly asleep.

The night passed slowly for Demetrius Antoun. As he sat, time became somewhat distorted, and to keep himself awake, he thought of Palestine. The knowledge that he was no more than a short distance from his lost homeland made his heart beat faster and his breathing grow shallow. Palestine had always been a constant shadowy presence in his life, a reminder of the prosperity that had been lost to his entire family. Demetrius wondered what that land was really like and wished he could see it for himself. For the first time in years, the dreams and stories he had been told as a child came back in a rush and he had a thought that tomorrow they would travel to the border and at least peer into the homeland that Palestinian refugees were not allowed to enter. Then he would relate with great detail all he had seen to his family and friends. With that happy thought, his eyes closed and he rested his head against the cold side of the stone, allowing himself the relief of what seemed only a few minutes of sleep.

The very loud and distinctive sounds of a low-flying helicopter burst upon them with a suddenness which jolted both Demetrius and Walid into instant alertness.

"What?" Walid shouted, trying to be heard above the beating of the rotor-blades and the whine of the engine.

"Helicopter," Demetrius replied as he lifted himself to his feet and turned his eyes toward the sky.

"Where?" Walid called out anxiously as he rose to stand beside Demetrius.

The sounds began to fade. Demetrius waited a few seconds before responding, "The helicopter is flying low. Over the road toward Karameh."

Walid looked once again in the sky and then turned to Demetrius. "What is the time?"

"Almost daybreak, I think."

"Daybreak!" Walid's voice contained a hint of irritation. "You were supposed to wake me!"

Demetrius shrugged his shoulders. "I drifted."

Their conversation lagged as Walid scanned the sky and Demetrius repeatedly turned his body, slowly from left to right, retracing the flight path of the helicopter.

"The light is coming quickly..."

Demetrius interrupted, speaking in a whisper, "Quiet." He paused. "Listen closely. What do you hear?"

Walid closed his eyes and held his breath. After several seconds had passed, he answered. "Trucks...more than one truck."

"Yes, maybe trucks, also...but the heavy engines...the rattling and squeaking...those are the sounds of tanks."

"Tanks!" Walid spoke at full volume.

"Quiet! Listen once more."

The two men stood listening, straining to hear, trying to distinguish the sounds in the distance.

Demetrius began turning his head, to the left for a few seconds and then to the right for a few seconds, and then repeating the motion.

Walid's breathing was labored as he gaped at his friend. "What are you doing?"

"I am looking with my ears."

Perplexed, Walid did exactly as Demetrius did. Finally, he muttered,

"I am looking with my ears, also, but I see nothing." He stared into Demetrius' face. "What can you hope to see with your ears?"

Demetrius repeated the head motion a final time before responding. "I have seen enough. It is the Israelis."

"The Israelis!" Walid reacted with disbelief and urgency in his voice. "You can see Israelis?"

Demetrius was patient, as he would be with a child. "Walid. It is not necessary to see their flag to know their identity. The sounds come from the South and from the West. The Jordanians are to the East. The Palestinians have no tanks." He took a deep breath. "That leaves only the Israelis."

Walid protested, "But...but, we are in Jordan!"

"So are the Israelis. They must have crossed the King Hussein Bridge and entered Shunet Nimrin. It is good we did not stay in that place."

Walid did not want Demetrius to be right, so he continued to argue, "There is nothing in Shunet Nimrin to interest the Israelis, Demetrius."

"Correct. Their target is Karameh."

"Karameh!" Walid repeated in an anxious whisper, "Why Karameh?"

Demetrius stooped and picked up Walid's coat and small bag, tossing both to him. "Because, my friend, Karameh is the home of Palestinian Fatah fighters."

Walid stood silently for a moment, pondering the implications of the remark and watching as Demetrius calmly buttoned his jacket and connected his satchel around his back. "Should we move away from the road?" he asked.

"Yes."

Demetrius led the way. The two men turned toward the steeply slopped hillside and began climbing.

"Move to the left as you climb," Walid advised. "Then the slope will not be so steep."

"The climb might be easier, but each step to the left will take us closer to Karameh."

"Exactly," Walid replied. He wanted to know what was happening to his father's brother who lived in Karameh. "Perhaps we will be able to view the village from a high vantage point."

As Demetrius opened his mouth to respond, the unmistakable whine and thunder of jet engines in full throttle at low altitude burst out of the sky and rolled across the valley. Both men instinctively dropped to the ground and lay prone, their chests pressing against the ground. They waited for the peak of the sound to pass before looking upward.

"Nothing! I see nothing!" Walid yelled into Demetrius' ear. His words were hurried. "There is too little light…and too much fog."

"And too much speed," Demetrius replied calmly as he rolled to his side and stood, pulling Walid to his feet in the process. He looked skyward. "They passed before we even heard them."

Walid slipped several inches downhill as he tried to gain his footing. He tried again, this time firmly grasping the branches of a small bush and was able to pull himself back to his feet before speaking, "So much noise! How many, do you think?"

Demetrius tersely replied, "Two…maybe more. There is no way to be certain unless we see them."

"If we cannot see them, then perhaps they cannot see us." Walid sounded enormously relieved. "We are invisible!"

Demetrius had a frown on his face as he carefully observed the spot from which they had come. "Perhaps from the sky, but not from the road."

"The tanks! For a moment I forgot the tanks…" Walid followed Demetrius' gaze. After listening, he muttered, "The sounds are louder."

For the first time Demetrius seemed worried. He began climbing even as he told Walid, "We must keep moving away from the road. Hurry!" On hands and knees, Demetrius crawled up the hillside, through the thick undergrowth of brush. "Come on!"

For several minutes the men climbed the hillside without speaking, occasionally giving a backward glance downward, toward the road. Grabbing onto anything stationary for leverage, the men pulled themselves upward.

"The tanks are close," Walid warned Demetrius.

"When they pass below us, we will hide behind the rocks. Keep your eyes on the road..."

Demetrius was interrupted by the high-pitched whine and whistle of jet engines. Startled by the unexpected loud volume from the planes, both men suspended their movements. Demetrius began climbing once again as the passing sound waves pounded against the hillside.

"Are these the same planes?" Walid cried out as he too began to climb.

Demetrius shouted, "Perhaps. But the clouds protect us. They can see nothing." His voice was intense. "Now, *climb!*"

Walid had taken several more steps forward when he gave a hurried look over his shoulder toward the road and Shunet Nimrin. "Demetrius!" Walid sounded frightened. "I see a tank!"

Demetrius abruptly stopped and turned his eyes to the road. "I see it. Quickly! Here!" Demetrius threw himself to the ground behind a large rock.

Walid, his feet slipping in the loose soil and small stones, pulled himself toward the rock by digging his fingers into the ground beside Demetrius. Breathing heavily, he fell down beside Demetrius.

"Their eyes are elsewhere," Demetrius said. "We should be safe behind this rock. Keep close to the ground."

Walid tried to shift his body for a clear view of the road as the roar of the tank engines grew louder. "Now, two tanks," Walid said softly.

Demetrius peered at the tanks. "Now, three."

A new whining, whistling sound overhead drew the men's attention away from the road and toward Karameh. Both were staring at the sky when the sound stopped and was replaced by the dull thump of an explosion. The earth beneath them trembled. Small pebbles were still rolling down the hillside when the sounds were repeated—again, and again.

"God, Walid. The Israelis are shelling Karameh!"

Walid began to bite his lower lip, hoping that his uncle and cousins had proper shelter.

Demetrius was still conceiving a plan, trying to think of a way out of their dilemma. "The shells are coming from the West...across the Jordan River." Between explosions, Demetrius spoke, "When they find the proper range, there will be many more shells."

Walid was almost weeping, as he placed his head in his hands. "But, there are many women and children in Karameh, Demetrius. How can they do this?"

Demetrius was silent, his eyes focused on the Western horizon. Several seconds passed before he understood what he was seeing. "Walid."

"Yes."

"Walid, look. Do you see helicopters coming toward us from the West?"

Walid lifted his head out of his hands and stared toward the Jordan River. "Yes! Oh, God! There are six...seven...many, too many helicopters! And, they are low in the sky!"

Without blinking once, Demetrius stared, suddenly realizing the scope of the attack and their own personal danger. He spoke louder than he intended. "Soldiers." Demetrius lowered his voice. "Walid, those helicopters are bringing in soldiers to attack the Palestinians in Karameh."

Walid felt his stomach churn in fear. "We have to get out of here!"

Demetrius appeared lost in his own thoughts and his eyes remained on the approaching helicopters. Everywhere I look, there is danger, he thought.

The still distant sounds of the beating rotary blades were replaced by the hissing of large numbers of incoming artillery shells. The explosions which followed shook the ground beneath the men, as if jarred by giant footsteps.

"Demetrius!" Walid cried out. "I am not liking my visit to Jordan so very much!"

"Keep down!" Demetrius shouted as loudly as he could. Seeing Walid's expression of sheer terror, Demetrius pulled Walid close to him. He could feel Walid's entire body shaking from fear.

They waited.

The shelling suddenly stopped. Demetrius and Walid exchanged a quick glance and then both looked toward Karameh.

Black smoke marked the center of the village. Three tanks, moving slowly, were now only a few hundred yards from the first houses. Helicopters began landing on the Eastern edge of the village. The gunfire began. Soldiers leaped from the doors of each helicopter as it touched down, some firing their weapons as they moved away from the huge machine. The helicopters lifted off and were away within a few seconds.

Demetrius knew what was happening. He told himself that their personal danger increased with each passing second. "Walid, the Israeli soldiers from the helicopters will try to stop anyone from escaping into the hills."

"Demetrius! Look!" Walid shook Demetrius by the arm. "The Palestinians are resisting! They have weapons! They are firing from holes in the ground! See! They have hit a tank!"

"They will all be killed," Demetrius muttered.

Bursts of gunfire alternated with exploding shells fired from the tanks. There was hardly a moment quiet enough for Demetrius and Walid to speak. For several more minutes the two men lay watching the fierce battle for Karameh as the smoke mixed with the slowly lifting fog.

The sounds of rifle fire and exploding shells suddenly became intermittent. Palestinian fighters began to retreat, running toward the hills above the village. During a moment of relative quiet, Walid turned his eyes away from the battle and toward Demetrius. His voice was low and sad. "The battle is lost. See, the Palestinians are running from Karameh."

Demetrius shook his head in regret as he stared at Karameh. A mixture of slowly rising black, white, and gray smoke obscured the view of most of the buildings. East of the village, several tanks, followed by Israeli soldiers, had dispersed and were now climbing the steep slopes of the mountain base.

"The Israeli soldiers are chasing the Palestinians," Demetrius said flatly. "They will kill them all."

A series of muffled explosions coming from within the village caught Demetrius' ear. He gave a long sigh. "Walid, they are blowing up the buildings. Karameh will soon be destroyed. And, that's not all. If the tanks turn South, you and I will be in great danger. No one will ask why we are here."

"Perhaps we should move."

"Where? No place is safe."

Walid's color went from light brown to pale white. "Then we must remain unseen where we are."

"Yes. That will be best. But we must watch the tanks. If they turn toward us..."

An unusually loud explosion caused Demetrius to pause and stare toward the tanks climbing the mountain.

"Walid! Look!" he hissed. "The Palestinians have destroyed a tank!"

"I see it!"

Shells began exploding near the other tanks as they continued to move slowly up the mountains.

"Jordanians!" Demetrius whooped with joy. "Jordanians are coming to help. They are firing on Israeli tanks!"

"Praise God!" Walid called out. "Praise God! We are saved!"

Demetrius knew what had happened. The Jordanians had obviously been watching the battle, but to them, Karameh had no value. Only when the Israeli tanks turned in the direction of Amman did the Jordanians begin to attack.

"We are seeing a real war!" Walid was now more excited than frightened. With the Jordanians in the battle, the possibility of Palestinian victory had increased.

The Israeli tanks began to turn back. "The Jordanians have won!" Walid screeched.

"No. I think not. They are turning back only because they did not come here to fight the Jordanians. They were surprised when attacked by a tank instead of a rifle."

"Then, the Jordanians will allow them to continue their attack on Karameh?"

"The fighting inside Karameh is finished. Ask yourself, why should the Jordanians risk a larger confrontation over a destroyed village when they did nothing to protect an intact village?" He exhaled. "Now the

Israelis will want the ones who have escaped."

"Demetrius! There are more Israeli tanks on the road below us!"

"I see them. They are coming from Shunet Nimrin."

"Israeli reinforcements?"

"Yes. Soon the Jews will be everywhere." Demetrius' tone became more urgent. "Walid, now, we must leave this place."

Walid moved abruptly and began pushing him. "Go! Go! Go!"

Demetrius refused to be hurried. He raised himself cautiously, looked up toward the mountain slope, then stood transfixed, his eyes fixed on a single spot some hundred yards away.

Walid was impatient to run away. "What is it, Demetrius?"

Demetrius did not answer immediately, but when he did, his voice was low and his words sounded as though they were being pushed through clenched teeth. "We are not alone."

"Have you been seen?"

Demetrius continued his motionless stare without answering.

Slowly, cautiously, a man wearing a khaki uniform stepped away from a large rock and began walking down the slope of the mountain. He held a Kalashnikov AK-47 rifle in his right hand. A string of hand grenades hung from a belt at his waist. His movements were strong, confident, and very precise.

"I believe our guest is a Palestinian freedom fighter."

His friend's tone, as well as his words, caused Walid to spring to his feet and stand fully upright.

Standing side-by-side, they watched the man approach.

"Keep down!" the soldier called, his words commanding, but neither Demetrius nor Walid reacted.

"Keep down!" The man repeated his instruction and added a motion with his left arm to signal his meaning.

Walid lowered himself into a squatting position.

Demetrius' eyes never left the stranger. As he watched the soldier, Demetrius had a rush of thoughts, recalling his father's warning to forgo the visit to Karameh, a stronghold for the most fanatical of Abu Ammar's (Yasser Arafat's) fedayeen.

Except for brief intervals, Jews and Arabs had not stopped fighting since the 1948 War. Encircled by Arabs, Israel had been forced to defend every border. Full-fledged wars had broken out in 1956 and 1967. During the 1967 War, the Jews quadrupled the size of the territory they held, capturing East Jerusalem, the West Bank, the Golan Heights, and the Sinai. The Jewish victory not only succeeded in demoralizing the Arabs but also created 500,000 new Palestinian refugees. During the past year, border incidents had escalated, and tensions had increased. Even knowing all of this, Demetrius had nevertheless ignored his father's sound advice because Walid was anxious to visit his uncle and cousins.

Walid's quiet, hopeful voice interrupted Demetrius' thoughts. "It is good for us that he is a freedom fighter, don't you agree?"

"Yes, much better an Arab than a Jew."

The man was much closer now, moving slowly down the mountainside, crouching over his weapon. He slid to a stop every few yards and glanced about. When he was fully shielded from the road by the large rock, he spoke. "I am Ahmed Fayez."

Demetrius nodded. "And I am Demetrius Antoun." He looked down at Walid. "This is my friend, Walid Bader."

Ahmed seemed to take no notice of the introduction. He leaned his back against the rock, took a deep breath, and then turned to look at the road. A few seconds passed before he turned again toward Demetrius and Walid. "Where are your weapons?" he asked.

"We have no weapons," Walid told him in a high-pitched voice.

Ahmed paused. His eyes moved from Demetrius to Walid and then back to Demetrius.

"What are you doing here?"

"Our business is our own," Demetrius replied.

The barrel of Ahmed's weapon moved slowly until it pointed directly at Demetrius' chest.

"Today, my friends, *everything* is my business. I have heard that there are Israeli spies about." He gave them both a hard, determined look. "Now, you will answer my questions. You are Palestinians, yes?"

"Yes," Demetrius told him. "But, we are not guerrilla fighters."

"Once more. What are you doing here."

Walid spoke in a rush, not wanting Demetrius to get into an altercation with an armed man. "My father's brother, Mahmoud Bader, lives in Karameh. We are here to visit him."

"Why is he not with you?" the soldier asked suspiciously.

"We had not yet arrived," Walid said.

"Yesterday we began walking from Shunet Nimrin late in the afternoon," Demetrius explained to a perplexed Ahmed, "but we could not reach Karameh while there was still light." He waved his arms toward the battle scene. "Now, this."

"We spent the night near the road," Walid added.

No one spoke for a time as Ahmed further scrutinized the men, weighing whether or not to believe them. Although Ahmed appeared to be near their own age, there was an unfamiliar edge of hardness in his manner that most men would find intimidating.

Still, neither Demetrius nor Walid offered anything further as they waited for the fighter's next question.

Ahmed Fayez seemed to taunt them as he moved his rifle from Demetrius' chest to Walid's chest.

Walid loudly inhaled.

Ahmed smiled, then said, "I believe you." He smiled even wider. "But the Jews will not. They believe that every Palestinian is a commando fighter."

Walid jumped to his feet and glanced toward Demetrius before speaking. "We saw the battle from the beginning."

"Did you?" Ahmed's voice was low and carried the sadness of loss. "Many brave fighters are dead. Forty…fifty…maybe more…"

"How could this happen?" Demetrius interrupted. "Was there no warning?"

Ahmed chuckled quietly before answering. "Warning? I suppose…before the attack, an enemy helicopter passed over the village…very low…dropping pieces of paper." He reached into his shirt pocket and withdrew a crumpled piece of yellow paper with printing on both sides. "See. This is the warning. This paper says that civilians should leave the village." He nodded his head vigorously and laughed. "We have known for several days that Karameh would be attacked, but we wanted to stand and fight. Even when the Jordanians told us to flee into the hills." He laughed again, louder this time and his satisfaction was evident. "We have killed many Jews."

Demetrius was curious. "But the Israelis have tanks and planes. How could you hope to win such a battle?"

"Those who wished to leave were permitted to do so." Ahmed's lips spread into a happy smile as he leaned back against the rock. For the first time ever, Ahmed Fayez had seen the blood of his enemy. "Those who stayed and fought have won a great victory."

"A Victory?" Walid said. "But Karameh is destroyed...and many people are dead."

Ahmed wanted them to share his vision. "You are wrong. It is a great victory. Soon all the world will know that the Palestinians...the fedayeen...will fight forever for their homeland." He paused as his great passion overwhelmed him. "This is the victory!" he declared fervently.

Demetrius lowered his eyes. "I do not understand such a victory."

The sound of a shell fired from a tank on the road below made Demetrius and Walid suddenly freeze.

Ahmed reacted by throwing himself onto the ground and calling out, "Get down!"

Demetrius and Walid fell to the ground beside Ahmed. The shell exploded on the mountainside several yards above them. Shock waves lifted their bodies several inches before gravity slammed them back against the hard earth. Small rocks began falling through the lingering black smoke and struck the men with the sting of sharply thrown stones.

Ahmed lifted his head and carefully peered past the edge of the rock hiding them. A tank, its smoking gun barrel still pointing toward the mountain, sat in the middle of the road. Israeli soldiers surrounded the tank, some standing, others crouching, all with their weapons held at the ready and pointed toward the mountain.

Ahmed turned toward Demetrius and Walid. His voice was calm. "They know our position. We must move away quickly. I will go first. You will follow, but not together. Keep a distance of at least ten yards between each man. Move from rock to rock."

Demetrius and Walid both nodded, letting him know that they understood his instructions.

Without further conversation, Ahmed moved to the south side of the rock, glanced toward the road, then ran to a small mound of earth and stones several yards away.

Demetrius nudged his friend. "We must do as he said, Walid. You go now. I will follow."

Walid crawled to the edge of the rock and looked toward the tank. Several of the Israeli soldiers had left the road and were climbing the mountain. Walid gasped and looked toward Demetrius. "The soldiers are coming!"

"Follow Ahmed. Now!" Demetrius gave the reluctant Walid a hard push. He knew if he went first, Walid might not have the courage to follow.

Walid ran toward the spot Ahmed had chosen.

Before making his move, Demetrius located the soldiers. He saw that they had separated into groups of four and five and had climbed several yards above the road. Demetrius told himself that they needed to escape, and quickly!

Walid ran toward Ahmed.

Demetrius darted toward the spot where Walid had been. As he leaped toward the protected ground, he heard the tank fire. The ground, lifted by the explosion from the shell, seem to rise to meet him. He landed hard on his chest and knees. Dirt filled his mouth. Demetrius spat and coughed before raising his head to see where the shell had landed. Curling black smoke was slowly lifting from freshly turned soil and stones near a small depression a few yards in front of him.

There was utter silence.

Demetrius told himself that Walid had gone ahead. "Walid!" He waited for a reply—waited until he could no longer wait. Demetrius called once more, peering through the thick dust. *"Walid! Answer me!"*

Finally, Demetrius bolted, screaming as he ran toward the smoking depression the shell had created. He leaped into the hole, falling to his knees. Then he climbed out, pulling himself through the loosened soil with his fingers, crawling forward on his hands and knees, still calling Walid.

Demetrius saw the empty shoes first. He gave a guttural cry. One shoe was upside down. The other shoe was lying on its edge a few inches away. Then he saw the small feet, the short legs, the slim body…face down…still.

"Walid?" Demetrius gently lifted Walid's shoulder to turn him. Demetrius was numb, unable to breathe. He sat upright, taking Walid's head in his arms and weeping. "Walid. Oh God, Walid, please get up." Demetrius brushed his friend's face with his hand as he softly asked, "Walid. Oh, Walid, how will I ever tell your mother?"

"Demetrius!" Ahmed Fayez's voice came like an echo from God. A strong hand pulled at Demetrius' arm. "Leave him. We must go."

"Leave him…" Demetrius mouthed the words without actually voicing them. "Leave him?"

"Yes. Leave him." Ahmed reached out his hand. "There is nothing to be done for your friend."

Demetrius took Ahmed's hand in his own then released it. He pulled himself erect. Suddenly, without even thinking, Demetrius grabbed Ahmed's weapon and twisted it from his hand.

Ahmed's eyes constricted, but stunned by Demetrius' strength, he did not react.

Demetrius turned his eyes toward the tank and the soldiers climbing the mountain. His face twitched in fury as an uncontrollable rage overwhelmed him. Demetrius ran down the mountainside, cursing, screaming, and firing the weapon.

For a moment, Demetrius' mad charge froze the soldiers in place. Then they dropped to the ground and began firing.

The tank's gun turret swiveled…the barrel lowered… the gunner waited.

Demetrius automatically fell to the ground before rolling to the side and firing his weapon. A bullet struck a soldier in the face. The soldier's body began slowly sliding down the mountain, feet first. Like a filtered voice in a dream, Demetrius heard the soldier's comrade call out, "Abe!"

Firing and screaming, Demetrius plunged toward a soldier who was lying face down, holding his helmet in place.

Demetrius fired as he ran past. The soldier's hand dropped from his helmet.

As Demetrius passed through their line, the soldiers stopped firing from fear of hitting one of their own men. The soldiers nearest the road retreated to positions behind the tank.

Demetrius stumbled and fell backward down the slope.

An Israeli soldier raised himself onto one knee and lifted his weapon.

A burst of bullets from Demetrius' AK-47 struck him in the chest. Demetrius heard the wounded man call for his mother.

In the stillness of that moment, the rear of the tank was suddenly lifted by a small explosion. A second later the tank exploded in a huge ball of fire and black smoke.

The force of the blast threw Demetrius backward and the weapon fell from his hand. Shouts and bursts of gunfire replaced the receding roar of the explosion.

Demetrius struggled to stand.

A few yards farther down the slope, a soldier tried to lift himself. He was hit by a volley of bullets.

Demetrius made no attempt to retrieve the AK-47. He immediately lunged toward the soldier, who was standing in stunned silence, staring down at his mortal wounds.

The unexpected collision threw the soldier onto his back. Demetrius leaped astride the man's chest and grasped the soldier's throat with both hands, squeezing…five seconds…ten seconds…fifteen seconds… The man's face turned red, then white, then blue. His eyes bulged from their sockets.

"Demetrius!" Ahmed yelled as he rushed down the mountain.

Thirty seconds…

"Demetrius!"

Sixty seconds...

Ahmed placed his hand on Demetrius shoulder. "Enough!" Ahmed's voice was calm, steady, reassuring. "Demetrius. He is dead, already." Ahmed had shot the soldier, who died as Demetrius pushed him to the ground. Ahmed looked around with satisfaction. "They are all dead."

Demetrius' grip loosened. He continued to stare at the soldier's distorted features. He had been choking a dead man! Slowly, his mind began to clear. He could hear shouts and feel Ahmed's firm grip. He could smell the stench of burned flesh mingled with gasoline.

Ahmed asked, his voice nearly hushed, "Are you injured? Can you stand?"

Demetrius moved each limb slowly as he raised himself off the body of the dead soldier.

A cry, "Praise God!" seemed to come from all directions, followed by bursts of gunfire.

Demetrius looked at Ahmed and then toward the Palestinian fighters who were beginning to gather around him.

"This is Demetrius Antoun!" Ahmed spoke for all to hear. "And these men," Ahmed gestured toward the fighters, "they are your brothers."

A grim Demetrius remained silent.

"And this one," Ahmed motioned for one of the men to come closer, "is Yassin, the man who fired the rocket into the tank." Ahmed laughed loudly. His obvious joy was shared by the others. He looked proudly at Demetrius. "Demetrius." Ahmed smiled and patted him on the shoulder. "With ten more fighters like you, we could defeat the entire Jewish army!"

The Palestinians began to jostle each other, laughing and cheering.

When they calmed, Ahmed told them, "Enough! We will continue our celebration later." He gave an order, "Gather their weapons. We must leave at once."

Ahmed turned to face Demetrius and spoke quietly. "My brother, you must come with us. We will hide in the hills until the Jews return to claim their dead. Then we will kill them all!" Ahmed laughed at the thought of dead Israelis.

Demetrius did not respond. An idea flashed through Demetrius' mind that Ahmed Fayez was a man who laughed more easily than he smiled.

Images of the bulging face of the dead Israeli soldier came to Demetrius' mind, only to be replaced by the words of his beloved father. "Demetrius, to take a life is the greatest sin against God and man."

"Demetrius!" Ahmed called out. "You have done enough for this day. Now, you will rest. Hawad! You will take Demetrius to our hiding place."

Ahmed placed his hand on Demetrius' shoulder. "Go with Hawad, Demetrius. The others must know of your bravery...such courage brings inspiration."

Demetrius turned away from Ahmed and watched the man called Hawad as he walked toward him. When Demetrius spoke, his voice was soft and his words trailed away. "Yes...a rest would be good."

Demetrius stepped forward to meet Hawad, but even as he exchanged greetings, his thoughts clung to Ahmed's words: bravery and courage. Demetrius knew the truth, that he had not acted out of bravery, or out of courage, but rather, at that moment, dying had seemed easier than living.

"God go with you, Demetrius Antoun," Ahmed called out.

Demetrius was lost in his own dark thoughts. He was a man who had been taught that violence and killing was wrong. He was not an expert with weaponry. What had happened to him? Despite the shock of Walid's death, how was it that in a matter of moments he had found the courage and knowledge to become a warrior?

Understanding nothing of the day's sorrow, Demetrius silently followed the man called Hawad.

Chapter XI

Shatila Refugee Camp

When the State of Israel was created in 1948 and the State of Palestine disappeared, the powerful national movement for Palestinian independence withdrew from the political scene by transferring responsibility for Palestinian rights to the Arab League. Still in exile ten years later and feeling neglected by Arab regimes which promised to liberate Palestine, a young Palestinian engineer named Yasser Arafat formed an organization called Fatah. Relying on Palestinians to fight for their own independence, Fatah turned away from all Arab Governments. In 1965, members of Fatah's military wing began attacking targets inside Israel's borders, raising the hopes of Palestinians still confined to refugee camps.

During the 1960s, with Arab nationalism on the rise across the Middle East, Palestinian intellectuals began pressing Arab regimes to recognize the Palestinian movement. In 1964, the Arab League created the Palestine Liberation Organization. In the beginning, the PLO was under the direction and control of Egypt's President, Gamal Abdel Nassar. The PLO was a political organization rather than a military organization, and their demands for the return of Palestine was largely ignored by Western governments.

In 1967, following the third searing defeat of Arab armies by the Zionists, desperate Palestinian refugees turned to Fatah in the hope that a more radical approach would win the attention of world Governments. At the same time, the defeated and demoralized Arab masses of Arab nations who had lost three wars to the Jews began blaming Palestinian refugees for their own loss of self-esteem. Arab governments, looking for some way to withdraw as leaders of the movement to free Palestine, encouraged the integration of the PLO and Fatah and named Yasser Arafat as the PLO's new President.

After drawing Jewish blood at Karameh, Palestinian fedayeen of the Fatah suddenly became the champions of the Arabs. An explosion of Arab support swept the entire region.

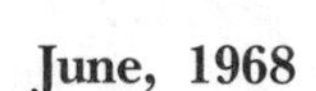

June, 1968

A bereaved Demetrius Antoun made his way from Karameh to Amman, Jordan, and from there to Damascus, Syria. Remembering Walid's almost desperate yearning to visit Damascus, Demetrius moved around in an emotional turmoil, finding little to celebrate in the beauty of the ancient city. After only one day of browsing in the old city and the Souq al-Hamadiyyeh, he began to find the cobblestone streets of Damascus a gloomy place. Walking past a row of coffee houses filled with men having loud conversations, he stopped at the one least crowded. Taking a table at the back of the café, he ordered a cheese sandwich and strong Arabic coffee.

While sitting in the café, Demetrius became a reluctant witness to a heated argument between two Turkish businessmen and a Lebanese student. The topic was the 1917 Ottoman-inflicted-famine of Lebanon which brought about the starvation death of 300,000 Lebanese citizens. The men from Turkey were outspoken and quarrelsome, and Demetrius quickly saw that the shy student from Beirut was overwhelmed by the unexpected confrontation.

Educated at the foot of his modest but learned father, Demetrius became enraged when he overheard the fattest of the two Turks shout at the student, "You son of a donkey! The famine of 1917 was nothing more than a plot by the British and the French Governments to undermine the Ottoman rulers." He waved his hand at the young man, "Bah! Go back to school."

The fat man gave a smug smile to his friend before pointing to his head and muttering, "Arabs have stunted brains." The man liked nothing better than to ridicule former subjects of the Ottoman Empire, sons of the men whom his own father had once commanded.

Demetrius' face reddened in anger. He had observed early in life that the more ignorant a man, the more arrogant. Demetrius took a deep breath, telling himself to stay out of the disagreement, but after glancing at the student and witnessing the humiliation on his face, Demetrius was unable to restrain himself. He swiveled in his seat and caught the fat man by the shoulder. "You'll have to apologize," he said, the softness of his voice belying his seriousness. "The Lebanese famine of 1917 was man-made by your own people. The Turkish army commandeered *all* the food in Lebanon, leaving the civilians to eat grass."

The fat man hesitated for a split second. He tried to pull free, but Demetrius' grasp tightened. Telling himself he would be protected in a country that had chosen state-sponsored tyranny over public anarchy, the man looked around for someone in uniform. Spotting three policemen, he turned back to Demetrius, his voice dripping with sarcasm. "Ah! A *second* Lebanese donkey!"

Demetrius' eyes narrowed and his lips tightened, but he said nothing.

His silence gave his opponent courage. The man jerked his chin in the air and hissed, "Or maybe you are the son of a whore!"

Demetrius Antoun was a man on edge. Without thinking about the consequences, he acted on impulse. In a single swift move he stood and struck a single heavy blow to the top of the man's head.

The fat man's surprised expression slowly shut down as he crumpled, sliding out of his chair onto the tiled floor and falling into a heap at Demetrius' feet.

Panic gripped the crowd. Several old men stumbled over one another as they made their way out of the coffee shop.

The fat man's friend began to shriek. "Police! Help!"

Shouts of "What's happening?" and "A fight!" filled the café.

Demetrius dug in his pocket and threw a 50-Syrian lira note on the table. He winked at the student saying, "Leave. Now."

The student fumbled nervously, gathering his papers. Before running away, he gave Demetrius a quick smile of appreciation.

Demetrius then took a last sip of coffee and calmly waited for the authorities.

The three policemen, along with several onlookers, stood circling the fat man as he lay on the floor. Apparently the officers preferred to use the time allotted for their break to drink coffee. Taking someone to the Police Station would require forms to be completed.

Nudging the unconscious Turk with his boot, the oldest of the policemen wearily asked, "What happened?"

"He insulted me, officer," Demetrius volunteered. "I responded."

"And how were you insulted?"

"The honor of my mother was attacked."

The officer nodded, understanding. He looked at Demetrius with interest. No true man would permit such an insult to go unpunished. Besides, most young men would have run at the first sight of authority. The boy looked like a good sort, just the type who would defend his mother.

One of the onlookers began to laugh, demonstrating with his closed fist. "I saw everything, officer. The big guy there." He pointed at Demetrius. "He hit the man on the head with his fist. One clean hit, and he knocked him cold!"

After looking at Demetrius with a tinge of admiration, the men focused again on the unconscious figure. Mucus had spurted from his nose, running down his lips and chin.

One of the younger policeman scratched his head. "Knocked the snot out of him, too."

Everyone began to laugh.

The friend of the unconscious man began to sputter, "He attacked us! Arrest him!"

The officer in charge made a quick decision. Looking at Demetrius, he commanded, "Go on. Get out of here. And, don't hit anyone else."

He glanced at Demetrius' muscled arms. "You might kill someone."

Demetrius left. Once on the street, he decided the time had come to return to Beirut.

The unpleasant incident took Demetrius back to his youth. Like all boys, he had been involved in his share of disagreements and minor brawls. He had discovered years before that he could not hit a person with even half his full strength. During a friendly rumble, he had accidentally broken a classmate's ribs. Demetrius had done nothing more than hold the boy tightly to prevent him from fighting with Walid. Later during the same year, Demetrius had broken a boy's jaw. The two youngsters were participating in a neighborhood boxing tournament. After that incident, Demetrius had shunned physical violence of any type, dissociating himself from his own strength—that is, until the last few months when his anger and frustration had overcome his common sense.

Demetrius walked rapidly, returning to the small hotel where he was staying. Taking less than an hour to tidy his things and close his small valise case, he paid the bill and hastily made his way to the taxi stand, hoping to save money by sharing a cab back to Beirut with several other passengers. When the taxi finally pulled out of the station, Demetrius told himself he shouldn't have worried. In order to increase his profit, the taxi driver had rounded up four passengers. Five adult males were crammed into the rusted and battered black Mercedes. Two of the passengers, an old man and his grandson, were Lebanese Shite Muslims. They were poor men returning to the slums of Beirut.

Trying to clear his mind of his troubles, Demetrius sat quietly and listened.

The elderly man's daughter was married to a Syrian. He and his grandson had gone to Syria to celebrate the birth of his daughter's newborn child. They had been shocked to discover the male infant had been born with a large head which was growing larger by the day. Without asking, Demetrius knew the infant had severe hydrocephalus, or water on the brain. His heart sank, knowing the baby would die, but only after much suffering.

Demetrius desperately wanted to be a doctor, but he didn't have the courage to tell anyone of his ambition, knowing that the poverty of his family made such a dream impossible. Instead, he consoled himself that he would be content to become a teacher of men, the same as his father.

After the men finished their sad story, the taxi driver mentioned that his throat was dry and his stomach empty. Glancing at the man's gaunt face and ill-fitting clothes, Demetrius felt in his pocket, seeking the last of his lira notes. He offered to buy everyone a meal.

The taxi driver stopped at a road food stand and all the men got out to stretch their legs and relieve their bladders. Demetrius bought a dozen hard-boiled eggs, five tomatoes, five slices of pita bread, and five sodas. The owner of the stand added a handful of green olives at no cost.

After sharing the meager snack, the men continued on their journey.

Demetrius was the only passenger who remained awake as they crossed the Anti-Lebanon mountain range along the Syrian border. As the taxi driver skillfully maneuvered the road's hairpin curves, Demetrius gazed at the red-tile-roofed homes clinging to the craggy mountains. In the Druze villages, he saw men riding donkeys and mountain women bustling to finish their chores. As they descended the mountain on the Lebanese border, he caught a glimpse of the sparkling blue Mediterranean Sea shining through the green trees sloping down from the mountains.

To Demetrius' eyes, Lebanon was a beautiful country, much lovelier than Jordan or Syria. As Demetrius leaned his face against the dirty, cracked window pane and looked at the lush Aleppo pine forests, he thought about his father. Once his father told him that in every way, Lebanon was a country of contrasts; there was a place for every man, from the richest to the poorest. If God smiled, a man might begin his life in the slums of Southern Beirut and end his life living in a hilltop mansion. Anything was possible in Lebanon. Longing for a less complicated life, Demetrius momentarily wished he had been born Lebanese instead of Palestinian.

Demetrius sighed. Thus far, God had laughed at the dreams of Palestinians.

The sadness reflected on Demetrius' face began to fade as the cab approached East Beirut, passed through the Christian enclaves and into the outskirts of West Beirut. While passing walled villas surrounded by palm trees standing beside small shops, Demetrius noticed that the pink and white oleander bushes were in bloom. Summer had arrived.

The streets of Beirut were crowded with people from around the world. Demetrius smiled as he watched beautiful Lebanese women dressed in the latest Parisian fashions bargain with old bearded men at vegetable carts. Druze tribesmen with red tarboosh hats and baggy pants walked stiffly by the sides of Maronite priests in long white robes. The aroma of roasting coffee beans drifted in the open window of the car, causing the sleeping passengers to wake from their naps.

The traffic was jammed and Demetrius began to think he could walk the remaining distance faster then the taxi could maneuver through the blocked streets. He was becoming impatient. Never had he been so long separated from his family.

Finally, they were at Shatila. After paying his share of the fare and telling everyone farewell, Demetrius got out of the cab and walked into the camp.

Shatila Camp was no more than a mile square, but it was home to over 7,000 people. And, in spite of their proximity to bustling Beirut, Shatila refugee camp was the poorest of all the refugee camps in Lebanon. Surrounded by rolling hills, the camp was located in a basin which turned into a muddy river when the rains came, overflowing the open sewers.

Looking nothing like the wealthy sections of Beirut, Shatila was made up of small shabby structures, built of cinderblocks and concrete. Few of the buildings were painted and water pipes and electric wires hung on every frame. Most of the men originally were farmers in Palestine having turned to menial labor as refugees. Even though many now worked as painters, carpenters, or plumbers, maintaining the beauty of the homes of rich Lebanese, nothing of Shatila spoke of their skills.

During Demetrius' three-month absence, nothing about Shatila had changed, but he didn't see the squalor of the place he called home. He could think of little besides his family and the shock they would receive at his unexpected return. He had written to them only one month ago, saying he might remain in Karameh for another year or more.

Thinking of the happiness his arrival would bring, Demetrius' spirits lifted and he began to whistle.

Shatila was always a crowded place, but on this day every street was packed with people. Demetrius searched his memory but could not recall seeing such a large multitude. What was going on? Suddenly, he heard the noise of cheering voices and saw youthful soldiers. A large group of small boys were marching through Shatila Camp. The boys were in single file formation, proudly holding small sticks, calling out "Palestine! Palestine!" Camp inhabitants lined the narrow winding streets, chanting, "Young Lions! You will save us! Young Lions! You will save us!"

Not yet recognized by friends or neighbors, Demetrius leaned against the block of a small tenement building and stared at the spectacle. To the delight of the crowd and at the signal of their leaders, the youthful troop suddenly crouched to the ground and then began to run before tucking their short legs under their bodies and rolling, turning complete somersaults. As they came out of the somersault, the boys jumped atop a readied sand dune and roared, trying their best to sound like beasts of the jungle. The crowd thundered their approval, laughing and crying at the same moment, and their hysteria spun through the air like a whirlwind.

"Fatah! Fatah! Fatah!"

After a few moments of watching, Demetrius began to push his way through the masses, understanding completely what the fuss was about. He muttered under his breath, "Karameh." Before the battle of Karameh, the Palestinians were pariahs in the Arab world. To a man, the Palestinians were despised. But, now, after killing a few Jewish soldiers, they were heroes to every Arab who had ever felt the sting of humiliating defeat at the hands of the Jews!

Demetrius had a strong desire to shout out that Fatah's single victory was less than it seemed. He longed to herald the truth: that a few Israeli dead would never alter the outcome of the ongoing struggle between Jews and Arabs. And yes, those dead Jews had names too, names like Abe. Demetrius involuntarily winced.

Walking through Shatila Camp, the vision of those he had seen killed, including Walid, overwhelmed him. Demetrius heaved a huge sigh, thinking that Arab and Jew disunity bound the two peoples together in a way that neither would ever admit. Arab and Jew—Jew and Arab.

Demetrius threaded his way through the large gathering toward his parent's home, tuning out the boastful street gossip about how, finally, the Arabs were going to throw the Jews into the sea.

Demetrius began to walk faster, stooping down as he passed under overhead dwellings which had been built over the narrow streets. In the damp heat, he began to perspire. At times he found himself in alleyways that were no more than three-feet wide. The people of Shatila had built their homes on every available spot of land.

Finally, he was home.

Mary Antoun was standing outside, her back to the street, her long dark hair knotted into a neat bun, silhouetted against the sun. Demetrius stopped and stood, watching as Mary lovingly tended to a single, exquisite purple flower blooming in a tin can.

His mother had always loved flowers.

Demetrius remained unnoticed as Mary watered the plant before bending her body to gently brush the fragrant blossom with her nose and lips. As she turned, Demetrius saw indescribable pleasure washing across his mother's face.

Then she saw him.

Their eyes met and held, before an outburst of joy erupted from her. A wondrous smile crossed her face. "Demetrius!" She ran into his waiting arms, her heart pounding with excitement at the touch of her son. "My son! My life!" she purred. "You are home… You are home…" She brushed his face with her fingers. "Papa and Grandpa will be home soon. They will be so happy."

The moment grew silent and Mary became aware of her son's fixed gaze, and she instantly knew that the death of Walid Bader hung between them. Without a word, Mary led him inside their simple home.

Once the door was closed, Mary looked up at her son, rubbing his face, encouraging him. "Tell me, Demetrius. Tell me all about Walid."

Demetrius tried to speak, opening and closing his mouth several times. Then, without a word, Demetrius sank to his knees and buried his head in his mother's bosom, sobbing, releasing the anguish he had kept buried for so long.

Mary Antoun was a wise woman. She knew that many men often could not speak of something which meant everything. Walid had meant so much to Demetrius. Rubbing Demetrius' heaving shoulders, a terrible sadness came over Mary—remorse that she could not protect her son from life's sorrows.

Seeing Demetrius' terrible anguish, Mary began to weep with her son, until neither had any more tears.

Chapter XII

Amin Darwish

The following afternoon Demetrius closed the door to his parents' home and stepped outside. From the first instant he was out of his parents' sight, a pale cast of worry settled upon his classically chiseled features. Demetrius was going to visit Walid Bader's parents and with each leaden step, a terrible sense of dread overtook him. Today would be the first occasion he had seen Mustafa and Abeen Bader since their son's death three months earlier. In an effort to raise his sinking spirits, Demetrius whistled a shaky half tune beneath his breath. Still, the memory of Walid rankled in his conscience.

The day after the battle of Karameh, Mahmoud Bader had carefully collected his nephew's mangled remains and buried Walid at the side of Mahmoud's own daughter, a young girl who had lost her life the year before, in November of 1967, when the Israeli Army shelled Karameh and hit a group of girls leaving school.

In a strange twist of fate, the murder of Walid's cousin had ultimately brought about Walid's own demise.

The Palestinian community at Karameh had been enraged by the death of the young girls, and the fedayeen had retaliated by infiltrating Israeli territory and laying mines. On March 18, 1968, an Israeli school bus ran over one of the mines, resulting in the deaths of a schoolboy and a doctor and injuring 29 other children. The incident further escalated the ongoing violence, causing the Israeli Government to commit to a large-scale military intervention, designed to permanently rid their borders of Arab terrorists. The Israeli attack occurred on the day Walid and Demetrius were in the area.

After Walid's funeral, Mahmoud Bader made the sad journey to Shatila to inform his brother of his youngest son's death. Stricken with guilt that Walid had died while he had lived, Demetrius did not go with Mahmoud. Furthermore, the devastating event propelled Demetrius to a place he had never been, confusing him more about his Arab identity and purpose. Undecided about his future plans, he became caught up in the jubilant fellowship of the victorious Palestinians. Doubtless, the influx of Ahmed Fayez's ideas of liberating Palestine had some seductive influence. Demetrius had remained in Jordan with Ahmed Fayez and the fedayeen warriors near the border of Israel. He did send letters to his parents and the Bader family, telling what had happened on that fateful day—that one moment Walid was by his side and the next moment he was with God.

Now, three months later, Demetrius was back in Shatila, disillusioned by the disjointed fedayeen struggle. The mirage of a Palestinian victory had vanished.

Reaching the front door of the Bader home, Demetrius clasped his hands behind him and began to pace anxiously. Two large red patches marked Demetrius' cheeks. He pushed his hand through his thick brown hair before blowing out a noisy breath. With an expression of anguish mingled with determination, Demetrius slowly pushed on the wooden door.

The door was unlocked but the hinges creaked ominously as the door opened.

Mustafa Bader was nearly blind without his glasses, but his hearing was still keen. Mustafa had been resting in a small courtyard at the back of the house when he heard the soft creak of the door. Wondering who might be visiting before supper, Mustafa easily made his way through the familiar rooms of his home while groping in his shirt pocket for his glasses. One of the glass lens had fallen out the year before and was now taped in place. Carefully feeling with his fingers, Mustafa made certain the lens was secure before wrapping the immense dark green frames around his head. Even with the thick glasses perched on the end of his nose, he squinted at Demetrius, gasping when he recognized the young man's unmistakable large figure.

"Demetrius!" Mustafa thrust out his arms in welcome. "Demetrius! You are back!" Mustafa's thick graying hair bounced each time he hugged Demetrius. Becoming increasingly excited, he waved his hands, exclaiming, "We heard a rumor last evening that you had returned!" After kissing him on both cheeks three or four times, Mustafa called out, "Abeen, come quickly! Demetrius is here!"

They heard her cry before she could be seen. "Demetrius! Love!"

Abeen Bader was a thin, short woman, and her stern face gave the mistaken impression that she was a grave, unfeeling person. In mourning since her youngest child's death, she had become even thinner, looking positively gaunt. Dressed in black from head to toe, her coloring appeared ghostly white and her eyes dominated her face.

Demetrius was staggered by Abeen's appearance, thinking to himself that Walid's mother had aged twenty years since her son's death. Still, a sweet smile greeted Demetrius as Abeen examined his face silently, dragging out the moments, as if she were searching for some identifying mark known only to her.

"You are our son, now," Abeen declared with passion, her amber-shaded eyes darkening with emotion as she continued to stare full into Demetrius' face. Abeen spoke with a confident ring, for although frail in body, she was strong in spirit. "Is that not right, Mustafa?" Abeen asked her husband, who was bobbing his head in agreement, his unruly hair dancing over his forehead.

Mustafa looked as though he might break into tears, and Demetrius recalled what Walid had often repeated about his parents: his father was nervous and moody, having the sentiments of a woman, while his mother possessed the logical mind of a man.

Walid once confided that he deeply regretted inheriting his mother's body type and his father's excitable nature. "An unwelcome combination," he had wryly remarked to Demetrius.

Demetrius started to protest to Walid's parents, wanting to shout that he could never take their son's place, but the protest died on his lips when he stole a glance at Mustafa and saw that the man's eyes were glittering with transparent pleasure. Demetrius reminded himself that their affection was genuine, that Mustafa and Abeen had always loved him as one of their own, in spite of the Antouns' Christian faith and the Baders' Sunni Muslim beliefs. More than one of the camp's Muslim families had not looked kindly upon the Antouns' presence in their overwhelmingly Muslim community.

Looking over and beyond Mustafa, Demetrius' silence was accompanied by an audible change of breath the moment he spotted a smiling photograph of his old friend hanging on the center wall in the sitting room. Draped with black cloth, the picture was in a place of honor, and Demetrius could only imagine the long hours of wrenching sadness that had taken place in the Bader dwelling. Looking at the likeness of his friend in better days, Demetrius tried his utmost to shake off the image of a blood-splattered and very dead Walid, but gloomy reality enveloped him. He forced a jocular tone when he turned back to Walid's mother and said, "Abeen, you are looking well. How wonderful it is to see you!"

Abeen took a small bow and her pleasure was evident.

Demetrius sniffed at the air, "What is that delicious smell?" he remarked.

Abeen's face lit up with a dazzling smile. "What do you think? It is your favorite meal, vine leaves stuffed with lamb!"

Mustafa slapped his hands together and leaned his head toward Demetrius. "Abeen has been cooking since dawn on the chance you had not forgotten us."

"Forget you? Never!" Demetrius protested before winking at

Mustafa, teasing, "Mustafa, you will be the fattest man in all of Shatila if you're not careful!"

Mustafa sighed heavily and patted his growing belly. He was a stocky man, but his stomach was beginning to eclipse his broad chest. Mustafa gave a nod. "That is exactly what Walid used to tell me." With an unnatural smile, he asked his wife, "Isn't that right, Abeen?"

There was an awkward moment as Mustafa knew he had said the wrong thing.

Abeen blanched, then shifted her weight from one foot to the other before scolding her husband, "Mustafa, you promised!" She explained to Demetrius, "Tonight we want nothing more than to celebrate your safe return. If God is willing, there will be plenty of tomorrows to remember our Walid."

Demetrius' lips tightened, but he didn't speak.

The large clock on the small sitting room table made a loud, ticking noise.

In spite of her severe appearance and strong personality, Abeen Bader was a women whose nature surged with affection. She slipped beside Demetrius and rested her head on his chest, comforting him. "Tomorrow. You can tell us everything, tomorrow."

Demetrius clamped his teeth together and did not answer. His dark gray eyes grew darker as he looked once again at the photograph on the wall. The shocking loss of his friend was even more acute in Shatila than it had been at Karameh. Demetrius realized with a devastating sadness that never again would the jolly Walid participate in such family gatherings. His eyes teared as he reminded himself once more: Walid Bader was really dead, and Demetrius Antoun had lost the best friend any man had ever known.

Turning to look at Abeen and then Mustafa, Demetrius recalled what was in his heart. "When Walid died, more than one man was taken."

Abeen faintly nodded, knowing exactly what Demetrius meant. Walid Bader had been a beloved son, an adored brother, and a cherished friend.

Mustafa, a visible tremor in his throat, saved the moment. "May God forgive me! I have not offered you coffee!" Mustafa hurried to the kitchen, muttering under his breath about his appalling lack of manners.

Abeen led Demetrius to the only oversized chair in the house. "Amin Darwish dropped by earlier in the day," she said. "He wants to see you."

As quickly as Demetrius sat down, he stood again, looking for any excuse to leave the Bader household. "I will go and get him."

Abeen nodded her head, yes. "Would you?" She added with a smile. "But return quickly. Your coffee will get cold." She looked at the clock, judging the time she would need to prepare the food. "I will serve the meal within the hour."

"Don't worry. I am starving." Demetrius would never confess that he was stuffed from his own mother's kitchen.

After a quick hug and another kiss, Demetrius walked away. At the door, Demetrius turned back. "How is Amin getting on?" he asked.

Abeen brought her hand to her heart and gave a sad shake to her head, "Oh. About the same."

Amin Darwish's three-room shack was no more than a two-minute walk from the Bader dwelling. Demetrius made the distance in half that time, even though he knew he was escaping from one house of mourning only to enter a second one. Still, he told himself it was easier to endure the long-established and seasoned sadness practiced by Amin rather than the Baders' unaccustomed sufferings.

Amin Darwish had been in mourning since Demetrius had known him.

Demetrius smiled when he spotted the brass gong still leaning against the side of Amin's home. Amin had been partially deaf for the past twenty-one years, since November, 1947, the day a bomb blast in Jerusalem killed Amin's childhood sweetheart and young bride, Ratiba, along with the couple's unborn child. Demetrius performed the same routine as all of Amin's visitors: he lifted a short thick cane, striking the gong Demetrius knew was connected to a second gong in the middle room of Amin's tiny home. Demetrius felt the vibration from his fingertips to his shoulder.

Within seconds, the door flew open, and short, fat Amin came running out, wiping his hands on a small kitchen towel. Squealing, he grabbed Demetrius around his waist and danced around the young man, giving Demetrius a view of his receding hair—too long in the back and carelessly tangled.

Demetrius lifted the smaller man to his eye level, affection visible on his face. "Amin!" he shouted, "You are getting shorter and rounder by the day!" Laughing, he set Amin on the ground.

Amin was the image of sheer joy. "I missed you!" Amin reached up and pinched Demetrius' cheeks, looking worried. "It is as I thought, you have lost weight."

Demetrius denied what he knew was true. "No! You are wrong."

"You must think I am as blind as Mustafa Bader!" Amin fired back.

To Demetrius' undisguised pleasure, Amin waddled back into the house, announcing, "I baked almond cookies. Just for you. Come along."

No woman in the camp could match Amin's talent for baking sweets. Demetrius followed Amin inside. As a sign of respect and courtesy to the older man's unusual sentiment toward his long-dead wife, Demetrius stopped in the front room and faced the small shrine dedicated to Ratiba Darwish. While most Arabs kept a special place in their homes in remembrance of lost loved ones, Ratiba's shrine was noticeably elaborate. "Amin. How is Ratiba doing?" Demetrius asked.

Amin shouted from the kitchen, "What?"

Demetrius shook his head, chuckling to himself.

"What did you say?"

"Ratiba. How is she?"

"Oh yes. Ratiba." Amin scurried toward Demetrius, holding a large plate of freshly baked cookies in one hand and motioning with the other for Demetrius to sit on the largest of the cushions strewn around the room before placing the cookies at his feet. "Eat! Eat!" he ordered, his high pitched voice getting louder. After straightening his back, Amin bunched his eyebrows together and stared at the photographs of Ratiba as a happy child, Ratiba as a smiling young girl, and finally at Ratiba as a radiant bride, examining the photos as though he were comparing them with what he remembered. Amin made a small sound in his throat when he saw that one of the vases of bright pink plastic flowers placed beneath the shrine had overturned. "One of the Yassine children, I suppose!" He took the time to rearrange a couple of the plastic flowers, before answering Demetrius' query, but for once the mention of Ratiba didn't seem to strike a melancholy chord.

"Ratiba? Poor darling, this was one of her bad days."

Demetrius munched on the delicious cookies, while gazing at Ratiba's likeness, wondering as he often had how the rather plain woman had won such a love from her husband...a love that lived on even two decades after her death. "A bad day? How so?" Demetrius asked, perfectly serious.

Amin drummed his fingers on the side of the wall. "She misses her home in Jerusalem. Still."

"Ah. Of course."

Amin sat beside him, hovering close, waving a short stubby hand in the direction of the shrine. "Enough of Ratiba. Once we return to Palestine, her good health will return. For now, I must know about you."

Amin's concern brought unwelcome thoughts to the forefront of Demetrius' mind and suddenly a muscle next to his right eye began to twitch, out of control. He placed a hand over his eye to quiet the muscle.

Amin refused to be ignored and decided to get past the subject that he knew was haunting the young man. "Demetrius, all our hearts are broken about Walid. But what can we do?" He patted Demetrius' shoulder. "Rest your hurt for a few days, then you can tell me what happened."

"You are right," Demetrius agreed. "The wound is too fresh."

Amin jumped to his most favorite topic, second to Ratiba. "Never forget what I am to tell you: the return of Palestine will not come about from a gentlemen's agreement. Each of us must be prepared to sacrifice."

Demetrius nodded, yet he did not agree with the logic, knowing that Walid's death had done nothing to further the liberation of Palestine.

Amin drew closer. "Did you go into Palestine?"

Demetrius' silence along with his thin, knowing smile confirmed to Amin that he had. Still, not wishing to speak of the disappointing experience, Demetrius selected the largest of the remaining refreshments and popped the entire cookie in his mouth.

Amin's eyes were burning with emotion, and his voice was gleeful. "Wonderful!" Lonesome for the very smell of Palestine, for its precipices, hills, and deep ravines, Amin leaned so close that Demetrius could see every tiny line on the older man's face, "And, did your blood run hot, seeing all that beauty?"

Demetrius shifted his weight on the cushion, hesitating to tell Amin the truth that he now knew: in their dispersion and exile, Palestinians had spun exaggerated tales of Palestine. From his earliest memory, Demetrius had been told of the beauty of his homeland, but when he was confronted with the harsh truth and barren wastes that greeted his eyes, Demetrius had staggered, slumping to the ground, speechless. "This," he thought, "this was the land mourned nearly to the death by my father? This was the land of promise?"

Amin's fingers lightly touched his arm. "Well?"

Demetrius' lips parted in a thoughtful smile, before he glanced once again at his friend. As he examined Amin's eager face, a strange web of obligation wrapped around Demetrius, giving him a sense that he must protect the older man's dreams. And so in his mind, Demetrius gathered the truth of what he had experienced, suppressed that truth, and put it aside. Then he did the only thing he felt he could do—he lied. "Amin! What a land! From the moment my feet touched the soil of Palestine, all I could see was the color green. Green hills...green trees, their branches literally touching the ground, heavy with ripening fruit... And the streams of sweet water...I tell you, there is enough water in Palestine for a country of many millions."

Demetrius told himself that the power of word and of myth was far greater than the truth, for Amin's round face grew pink with pleasure. He hung on every word, and the laughter burst out of him. "I must know. Tell me. Did you taste the Jaffa oranges?"

His voice rising, Demetrius assured him, "My God! Those Jaffa oranges are delicious!"

Amin's entire body bounced as he nodded in agreement. "The sweetest oranges in the world!" At the thought, Amin's tongue touched his upper lip, savoring the memory. Reminded of forgotten things, Amin's eyes wandered from Demetrius' face to his own hands that were clasped together so tightly his knuckles whitened. Amin was thinking of the golden time in his life when he had a home in Jerusalem and was part of a large family that took memorable vacations to the coast to obtain sweet oranges from the groves of Jaffa and fresh fish from the port cities on the Mediterranean Sea.

While Amin remembered his past, reliving the happiness from which he had never recovered, Demetrius glanced around the room, recalling the numerous times he and Walid had skipped school, hiding out from their parents in Amin's home. Demetrius found it reassuring that nothing had changed since the days he was a child.

Like most refugees, Amin had few personal possessions. His home was sparsely furnished with a few colorful cushions for seating and a couple of maroon-colored braided rugs covering the cement floor. There was a small brass coffee pot sitting on top of a wooden crate. Beside Amin's favorite cushion lay a worn and creased copy of the Koran. Pictures of Ratiba covered the walls. Demetrius knew the bedroom was nothing more than a bare room with a small cot, for he had once tried to hide there from his father, but his feet had protruded from beneath the cot and he had been discovered. The tiny, walk-in kitchen was cluttered with the favorite utensils of a skilled cook.

Before the 1948 war, Amin Darwish had owned a small bakery in what is now known as West Jerusalem, the Jewish section of that sprawling city.

Demetrius couldn't forget that Ratiba was killed at that very bakery. He had heard the story a thousand times, as Amin recounted the fact that it was Ratiba's insatiable appetite for sweets and his determination to provide his beloved with anything she desired, that brought about Ratiba's "serious injuries."

Growing up on the same street in Jerusalem, Amin and Ratiba had known each other since they were children. Amin decided he would marry Ratiba the first time he saw her. He had gone into Ratiba's yard to retrieve a ball, thrown there by his younger brother. Ratiba had met him at the gate, holding tightly to his brother's toy, stubbornly demanding a sweet, saying that the ball had struck her on the head and that she was going to hold the ball as a ransom. Amin was shocked at her audacity but liked her spirit; however, that had not kept him from grabbing the ball out of her hands and running away. He couldn't get the spunky girl out of his mind and he came back later in the day with a small cake he had stolen from his mother's table.

Taking a cue from the girl's own schemes, Amin had insisted upon a kiss for the cake.

One peck on the cheek and Amin was in love.

When Amin was twenty and Ratiba sixteen, they became engaged. During the period of engagement, Amin secured a small loan and purchased a shop in the Jewish section of the city. He had no personal gripes with the Jews, and the Arab quarter was saturated with bakeries. Besides, many Jews loved Arabic sweets. The bakery became prosperous and soon Amin had to employ two assistants.

One year later, Amin and Ratiba were married. The wedding took place in her father's garden, on the very spot the romance had begun so many years before. By this time, tension over the ownership of Palestine was building between the Arabs and the Jews and there was wild talk of war. Random attacks of violence involving Arabs and Jews had already become commonplace. Amin was so complacent in his married bliss he ignored sound advice that he should sell his small shop and discontinue his daily journey to the Jewish side of the city. Besides, Amin Darwish truly believed his Jewish acquaintances would shield him from Jewish assaults.

After three months of marriage, Amin announced the wonderful news that Ratiba was expecting their first child. During her pregnancy, Ratiba craved sweets even more than usual. One evening after dinner, Ratiba mentioned she craved some *Atif,* Arab pancakes dipped in syrup and sprinkled with pistachios. Ratiba declared that no one could produce pancakes as light as Amin, that only her husband could make the favored dish to her satisfaction. Nothing would do but for Amin to take Ratiba to his bakery to select some of the *Atif* he had baked earlier that day.

Just as a proud Amin was about to lead Ratiba into the bakery, a group of three Jews in a speeding truck passed the sidewalk where Amin and Ratiba were standing. The truck tires were squealing and the truck was careening out of control. Amin was transfixed by the racket, unsure of what the commotion was about. He did notice that a tawny-haired Jew was hanging dangerously to the side of the truck door. Just as Amin's eyes met the eyes of this man he did not know, the man smiled demonically before screaming, "Arab Dog! Get out of Jerusalem!" Then the man drew back his arm and tossed an incendiary device filled with gasoline.

When Amin awoke in the quiet of the hospital, his tearful family was gathered around his bedside, telling him a truth that Amin refused to accept: neither Ratiba nor their unborn child had survived.

From that time on, throughout the period of war, flight, and exile, Amin Darwish created his own world, pretending that Ratiba was still alive, though he often said she was in the back room, resting from a headache or some other minor ailment. In every other way, Amin behaved rationally, and in time, the people of Shatila accepted his odd behavior, careful always to inquire about Amin's beloved wife,

Ratiba, a woman dead for over twenty years.

Amin supported himself by baking special dishes which he sold on the streets of Beirut. He was a favorite of the camp children, for Amin Darwish always had a special treat hidden in some pocket or bag and a ready smile for any child.

An apologetic knock on the door interrupted the thoughts of both men.

"Damn! It must be Mustafa," Demetrius said, with a grimace. "I forgot, he was preparing coffee."

Amin squinted his eyes. "Are you sure? I heard nothing."

Demetrius laughed, pulling his small friend to his feet, speaking louder than was necessary. "Amin, let me take you into the city." He put his lips close to Amin's right ear and yelled. "There are devices nowadays that will help your hearing!"

Amin jerked backward as he retorted, "Well, there's no reason to shout!"

Mustafa's head appeared in the doorway as he timidly peered inside. He had always taken care not to surprise Amin Darwish, for Mustafa was of the opinion that Amin would one day slip into total madness. Mustafa often asked anyone who would listen what form Amin's insanity might take. Besides, Mustafa Bader was a cautious man, and he truly believed that a lowered head lasts longer.

"Is coffee ready, Mustafa?" Demetrius asked.

Mustafa's blank expression was more telling than a scowl, and Demetrius, perceptive to every vibration, knew he had behaved badly. Hurtfully, Mustafa told him, "Coffee is not only ready, coffee is waiting."

Demetrius pulled on Amin's arm. "Come, Amin." He smiled at Mustafa. "I apologize for letting the time slip away." At twenty-years of age, Demetrius Antoun was reaching the height of his charms. With his handsome face and dark gray eyes sparkling with sensitivity, no one could stay irritated with Demetrius for very long.

Mustafa smiled back. "Oh, never mind." He motioned with his hand. "Come on. Abeen is waiting."

Mustafa and Amin slipped contentedly by Demetrius' side. With Demetrius in the middle, the three men linked arms and made their way back to the Bader home. The two older men looked first at Demetrius and then at each other, seeing in Demetrius Antoun the combination of strength and intellect needed to recover their homeland. Turning despair into hope, they built their dreams on the younger man.

Chapter XIII

Demetrius' Future

A few weeks after his return to Shatila Camp, Demetrius felt as though he had never been away. Walid's glaring absence was the one difference.

Returning from a visit with Hala Kenaan, Demetrius reached his home in Shatila after nightfall, and he stumbled more than once on the neglected pathway winding through the camp. As he approached the light shining through cracks in the curtains of the Antoun home, the sound of a friendly quarrel reached his ears. The familiar voices of Mustafa Bader, Amin Darwish, and Grandpa Mitri rang out above the noise of children playing in a neighboring yard.

Demetrius gave a relieved sigh. Perhaps company would provide him cover from his family's insatiable prying into his relationship with Hala Kenaan, a young woman whom Demetrius had been courting since he was seventeen. For as long as Demetrius could remember, his doting parents and grandfather made grandiose assumptions, and due to recent events, they had begun to think of Hala as their daughter-in-law.

Demetrius sensed that his close call at Karameh and his three-month-stay in Jordan had shown his family the reality of a fighter's life.

Out of fear their beloved Demetrius would join the fedayeen, his parents had independently concluded that the time for him to marry had arrived. The idea was fixed, regardless of Demetrius' adamant protests that he could not afford to support a wife and children before completing his education. Respectful of his parents, Demetrius pretended an interest in their wearisome plots and plans to provide him with the money needed for schooling and family, yet he never seriously entertained the idea of a marriage made in haste. Demetrius wore a face of patience, understanding that his family had difficulty reconciling the boy he used to be with the man he had become, an adult fully capable of making his own decisions.

As Demetrius entered the house, the shouting voices grew louder, and of the four men in attendance, only his father made a quick sign of greeting, blinking his eyes and waving with his hand for Demetrius to come and sit beside him.

Grandpa Mitri was ruthless in his determination to be heard, finally shouting at Mustafa and Amin, "Have you no respect for your elders?" and causing both men to blush in shame.

"Of course, you are right," Amin said in a sober tone, while waving his short arms in invitation. "Speak, speak, my ears are waiting."

Mustafa Bader's eyes opened wide, registering surprise. "When have I ever insulted the aged?" A hurt Mustafa looked about with an expression of pained offense, wanting someone to insist that such a breach of conduct had never occurred at his instigation. He looked hopefully at George Antoun but received no response, for George's attention was focused on his son.

Trying hard not to laugh, Demetrius grinned at his father before motioning with his finger that he would return in a moment. He walked to the side of the over-crowded sitting room and went into the kitchen, thinking to prepare himself a small snack before joining the group. Demetrius was still hungry, even after the dinner he had shared with Hala's family.

The Kenaan family was large but their income was small, and Demetrius had eaten sparingly, knowing that the three younger children had probably been told to eat rice and vegetables and to forgo chicken until Demetrius had been served. Demetrius had taken one small piece of dark meat, quietly reminding Hala's mother, "Rozette, I am unable to eat as before. My appetite was lost at the moment of Walid's death."

Hearing the remark, Omar, Hala's five-year-old brother, had squealed with delight, asking, "Mama! Does that mean I can have a piece of the chicken?"

His suspicions confirmed, Demetrius had turned his attention to the youngest of the girls, two-year-old Nadine, pretending not to notice as an embarrassed Rozette pinched the unfortunate Omar on his arm, causing the boy to squeal even louder.

While thinking about the evening and pouring himself an orange soda, Demetrius overheard the soft voices of his mother and Abeen Bader flowing down the hallway from the small chamber Mary Antoun had set aside as her sewing and knitting room. He told himself that the two women were most likely knitting socks or patching the worn clothes of their husbands and children, small chores they often accomplished while their men-folk drank coffee or tea and plotted the return of their homeland.

Grandpa Mitri's voice was raised in consideration of Amin Darwish. "As I was saying, the cruel man who conquered and ruled an unwilling country first slaughtered as many of its citizens as he could catch, then he exiled the remainder, before bringing in his own tribe to till the soil." Grandpa Mitri raised his thick, gray eyebrows, and sat watching his listeners for a short time. He maddened the men by slowly stirring his tea before taking a small sip.

"So, go on," Amin prodded, trying to remain polite. His plan to return home in time to bake extra pastries for the morning sales slipped away as Grandpa Mitri lingered.

"You don't know this story?" Grandpa asked.

George Antoun spoke out. "Pa!"

When he smiled, Grandpa Mitri's eyes disappeared into his deeply lined face, and he chuckled with pleasure. "Oh, all right, then."

As Demetrius searched through the kitchen cabinets for a snack, the voices of the four men blended together, and with his mind on other matters, Demetrius did not follow their words. Finally he found some shelled nuts. Leaning his elbows on the small wooden shelf which separated the kitchen area from the sitting room, he chewed on the nuts while looking fondly at the four men before him. Just as Demetrius began to listen, the men grew silent.

Grandpa Mitri looked pleased with himself as he started to go through the mechanics of lighting his pipe.

Uneasy laughter escaped Amin's lips, but he said nothing.

George massaged the back of his neck with his hand. For once in his life, he could think of nothing to say, but he couldn't avoid the thought that his father was becoming more and more eccentric with age.

After a moment or two of agitated reflection, Grandpa Mitri clenched his fist in excitement. "This is what I have been trying to tell you all evening: an unjust ruler can be defeated, even without an army. It only takes *one* determined man!"

Mustafa looked wildly around the room before turning to Grandpa Mitri, "Let me understand," he said, raising his voice, "Are you suggesting that Demetrius should somehow slip into Jerusalem and assassinate Israel's Prime Minister, Levi Eshkol?"

Demetrius gasped, choking on a nut.

George jumped toward his son, beating him on the back until the nut was dislodged.

"What the hell is going on here?" a red-faced Demetrius insisted. Demetrius had a sudden thought they were all insane. "And, what have I got to do with Levi Eshkol?"

Amin and Mustafa began speaking at the same time, while Grandpa Mitri looked rather pleased at the unpleasant scene he had created.

A fidgety Amin sprang to his feet, his pudgy fingers squeezing Demetrius on the shoulder. "We have been discussing your promising future as a leader in the movement."

Demetrius was doing his best to understand what Amin was talking about. "What movement?" Demetrius asked, unable to hold his temper, glaring at each of the men in turn, suddenly realizing that he had been the main topic of conversation.

Mustafa's voice faltered. "Why, the Fatah of course, the movement to liberate the homeland. We..."

Amin interrupted, almost shaking in excitement, his voice pleading, "You have said yourself that Ahmed Fayez said you would go far, if you wanted. He even offered you a leadership role in his fighting unit!"

Mustafa and Amin stared up hopefully at the young man who looked every inch a warrior.

George chastised the men. "You are speaking without thinking. My son does not belong in the Fatah."

Demetrius' anger evaporated. He felt a chill pass through his body as a terrifying revelation was revealed to him: Mustafa Bader, Amin Darwish, and his own grandfather truly believed he was going to play a role in fighting the Jews and recovering the land they could not forget. In a rush of thoughts, Demetrius knew he should have told these men a shameful truth, that he had made one very important discovery during his time with the fedayeen: George Antoun had raised a son of independent thinking, a man whose soul was influenced by abstract ideas of warfare, rather than a warrior who could persuade himself that murder was not murder.

Shuddering, Demetrius remembered the words spoken by Ahmed Fayez when together they had viewed the body of the only Israeli soldier the Jews had not succeeded in recovering after the battle of Karameh: "Ah, Demetrius! The corpse of our enemy smells as sweet as perfume!"

Yes, Ahmed Fayez was just the type of man desired by the men now standing before him, men who were too old to be heroes except in their dreams. Ahmed possessed the mentality of the perfect killer: he could not get enough of killing. When he was only ten years old, Ahmed's entire family had perished when a Jewish shell landed on their home at Karameh. From that moment, his revenge was so savage he celebrated every Jewish death with palpable pleasure.

In frustration, Demetrius stared into Amin's face and muttered, "I am not the man you believe me to be."

No one spoke.

When Demetrius looked at the three men around him, a terrible sadness darkened his face. The time had come to tell them the things he knew, rather than the things they wanted to know. Firmly, he told them, "I have made a separate peace with the Jews."

Amin recoiled and then gasped.

Mustafa stared at Demetrius skeptically.

From the sitting room, Grandpa Mitri made a harsh choking sound in his throat.

George asked cautiously, "Son. What do you mean?"

"Exactly what I said. I have looked inside myself." Demetrius' face became withdrawn and intense. "I will leave the task of fighting for Palestine to the men who feel the call."

Amin's laugh was artificial. "Dear boy, you don't mean the words you speak!"

Demetrius fought a flash of anger at the older mens' romantic attachment to fighting and violence without themselves being in danger of death. Since Karameh, Fatah's ranks had swollen and their attacks on Israel had increased twenty times over the past year. The border war with the Jewish nation was heating up and Fatah's successes had caused men long exiled from their homes to dream once again of the return.

The uncomfortable silence ended when George wrapped his arm around his son's waist and remarked reproachfully, "I told you before, Demetrius is going to be married soon."

George appeared not to notice Demetrius' startled look.

"And after that, arrangements have been made for him to enter the American University of Beirut." George gazed proudly at his brilliant son, before adding a fact each of the men already knew. "My son scored second to none on the entrance exams. He will begin his college education in the fall."

Inspired, Amin declared, "Each of us knows what military scholars say: that physical force is more apt to be victorious when manipulated by mental power. With Demetrius, we have our champion!"

George Antoun shook his head. "No. No."

His excitement building, Amin made a convulsive movement with his entire body. "I say to all of you, Demetrius Antoun must make his march to destiny!"

"Yes! Amin is right!" Mustafa emphatically stated.

George looked defiantly at the two men. "Only the learned man rules himself, and my son will be a scholar."

Mustafa responded confidentially, "George, the Lebanese don't give an olive that Demetrius is an intellectual, only that he is Palestinian. Demetrius will be regarded as a second-class citizen. Is that what you want for your son?"

George shook his head and then spoke, a trace of self-importance evident in his voice. "Demetrius will be treated with great respect." He lowered his voice. "I have assurances from the highest authorities at the University."

Mustafa looked at him suspiciously. George Antoun was a highly educated man, yet he had never acquired a position of any importance since leaving Palestine. His latest job was a step up from the one before, but really, George Antoun was nothing more than a janitor at the University. Before that, he had swept the streets of Beirut. The Antoun family would starve without Mary's sewing skills.

Demetrius' eyes sparked with anger. He knew exactly what Mustafa was thinking. Humiliated for his father, Demetrius sucked in his breath and with twisted lips shouted, "Enough!" There was a short silence. "You speak as though I am not in your presence!" Demetrius stared at the men intently, thinking to himself that they had heard nothing he had said. "Do I appear simple-minded?"

George winced while Mustafa and Amin followed Demetrius' every movement with their eyes. Still, disarmed by his anger, no one dared answer.

Demetrius' voice trembled when he told the men, "Listen to me very carefully. I do not require your advice. I will answer for my own life."

George shifted uncomfortably as his son directed his gaze at him.

"Pa. How many times do I have to tell you: I cannot ask Hala to marry me until I complete my education! Do you expect me to take the second step before I take the first?" Never had Demetrius spoken so harshly to any of the men surrounding him. Seeing tears spring to his father's eyes, Demetrius stomped toward the front door to keep from saying words he would later regret. "I believe I will request a cot at the Asfourieh!" he shouted, his dark features intense.

Growing alarmed, his father implored, "Demetrius! Son! Do not leave!"

Demetrius vehemently cried out, "Well, at least in the Asfourieh, the advice I receive will be from professionals!"

Grandpa Mitri cast a strange glance at his grandson. He thought the boy's ideas were foolish. A separate peace with the Jews, indeed! If every Palestinian thought as his grandson, they would all rot in the refugee camps. "Child, perhaps that is where you belong," he clucked. "I have been told that the idiots in the Asfourieh are quite clever and can invent more theories about this and that than even their psychiatrists can refute. You will fit there nicely!"

There was a moment of silence while Demetrius stood lost in thought, wondering what on earth his grandfather was talking about.

George understood. "Pa, you talk too much!" He warned his father, suddenly realizing that the evening was taking a turn that would be difficult to reverse.

Hesitating no longer, Demetrius threw his hands into the air and then fled, noisily slamming the door as he departed.

Mary and Abeen came rushing into the room.

"What on earth has happened?" Mary demanded of her husband, who had a fixed and bewildered look on his face. Eliciting no answer, Mary looked around the room. "Where is Demetrius?"

Grandpa Mitri began to move and slowly raised himself upright by balancing with his cane. With grave dignity, he slowly walked toward his daughter-in-law, pausing briefly, and drily speaking almost in a whisper. "Mary, your son said he was going to the Asfourieh."

Thinking she has misheard, a startled Mary Antoun repeated her father-in-law's words, "The Asfourieh?"

Mary and Abeen exchanged puzzled glances. The Asfourieh, meaning Birdcage, was a huge stone building located in the center of Beirut…a dark and fearful place which housed the mentally ill.

Abeen wondered if her husband had played a role in upsetting Demetrius. Her voice hinting of anger, she asked, "At this hour?" Abeen recalled two young men Demetrius knew who had suffered nervous collapses. They were patients at the institution, but the hour was too late for Demetrius to pay a social visit.

Afraid of his wife's reaction to the truth, Mustafa opened his mouth but was unable to offer an explanation.

George answered cautiously for his friend. "He has not *really* gone to the Asfourieh, Abeen." He gave a mournful sigh and in a sinking voice confessed, "It was just Demetrius' way of telling us to stop interfering in his life."

Grandpa Mitri impatiently jerked his pipe in the air. "Bah! Young people today are too independent for their own good. We are his family! We have the right to interfere!"

"Try not to get excited, Pa," George urged.

Abeen looked at Mustafa mistrustfully, sensing correctly that there was more to the story. Much more.

Mary gave her husband a knowing look, understanding something of what had happened, telling herself that George would tell her everything once they were in private. She cleared her throat. "Did our son say when he would return?"

"No," George answered gravely.

Amin's face was drawn and he was experiencing a twinge of regret in his heart for all he had said. His memory nudged him, and he recalled that when in distress, Demetrius often used his home as a refuge. Tonight it seems he was denied that comfort. Amin rubbed his eyes and yawned, looking at the front door. "Bedtime," he muttered, before going to the door, his small feet hardly making a sound. "Ratiba will wonder why I am delayed. Good night all."

Mustafa, wishing to postpone his wife's queries, spun on his heels and quickly followed, calling out, "Abeen, stay as long as you like, my dear. I will accompany Amin."

Abeen stared reproachfully at her husband as he hurriedly left the room.

Chapter XIV

Hala Kenaan

A lace curtain was briefly drawn aside as Demetrius Antoun came into view of the camp kindergarten. A small face peeked out the window. "He's here," Omar Kenaan happily announced.

Maha Fakharry, the headmistress of the kindergarten, felt her anxiety lift as she pushed Omar along. "Wonderful, Omar," she told him. "Now, join the other children. Quickly!" Maha smiled to no one in particular. The presence of a fedayeen hero would significantly contribute to the day's success.

Several children shouted simultaneously as Omar ran into another room, crying out, "Demetrius is here! We can begin!"

Maha stood at the door and located Hala Kenaan with her eyes before calling to the young woman. "Hala! Come!"

Hala gave a last instruction to the young boy cast as the lead rabbit in the play. An instant, luminous smile lit Hala's face as she made her way to the front room of the kindergarten building. Demetrius must have come, after all.

Maha watched Hala with the greatest attention. Hala Kenaan was celebrated throughout Shatila for her extraordinary combination of lovely qualities, and Maha fought to overcome the wistful mood of regret which always struck her at the sight of the much younger and stunningly beautiful woman: regret that a person could not be young forever. Everything Hala was, Maha had once been. A hard life had exhausted Maha. Her once smooth face was now weighed down by wrinkles, her thick black hair had long ago thinned and turned gray, while her slim girlish figure had thickened.

Sudden, unbearable memories flashed through Maha's mind: her beloved husband, the father of her six children, had recently died a slow, dreadful death from cancer. In her late forties, with the memory of her charm buried along with her husband, Maha understood she would likely live out the remainder of her life without the love of a man.

Hala's joy was undisguised as she whispered, "Is he here?"

Maha opened her mouth in a friendly smile, trying to hide her envy and share the younger woman's feeling of anticipation. Maha made a quick gesture with her hand. "Omar saw him walking this way."

Hala gave her raven-colored hair a quick pat and yanked on her new blouse in a futile effort to make the wrinkles disappear. She suddenly became very pensive, almost distracted as she asked the older woman, "How do I look?"

Once again, Maha scrutinized Hala from head to foot, thinking that Hala Kenaan's lack of self-esteem was completely incomprehensible. Confidence should come naturally to one so blessed by God. In her youth, Maha had felt the power of her beauty. After shaking her head and giving a muted laugh, Maha told her assistant the truth. "Hala, my dear, you look lovely." A hint of irritation crossed her face as she added, "Surely, Hala, you must realize that every man who sees you wants you?"

Hala blushed, the pink of her face making her even lovelier. "Stop teasing me!" She looked at Maha in total bewilderment at such an idea.

Maha shrugged her shoulders. "So be it." Her voice grew slightly bitter, "Hala, take a bit of advice: enjoy your beauty, my dear. Too soon, it will turn to dust." Maha started to walk away, but felt Hala's questioning eyes on her back. She quickly turned and gave Hala a friendly squeeze around the waist, whispering, "Don't mind me, dear!" She gave the younger woman a gentle push. "Now, go to your beloved!"

Hala lowered her eyes, "Maha, thank you for building my courage."

Suddenly, a frenzied expression appeared on Maha's face as she remembered her young charges. She was all brisk business. "Now, I must get the children in order. As soon as you seat Demetrius, I will give the signal for the play to begin." With that final instruction, Maha walked rapidly away, muttering under her breath about several things at once.

Hala blew out her breath and looked expectantly at the front street entrance to the school. Where was Demetrius?

Hala had recently been appointed as one of the three assistants at the kindergarten and today the children were going to stage a small play. The assistants had been told that in addition to their immediate families, they could each invite one guest. Hala had invited Demetrius Antoun.

Hala and Demetrius had been in love for three years, and Hala was becoming impatient, wanting nothing more than to become Demetrius' wife. Taking Maha's advice—"to conquer, one must dare"—Hala was hoping that by seeing the adorable children at play, the desire for fatherhood would move Demetrius to propose. The thought made her giddy.

Just at that moment Hala heard a persistent knock on the door. No one but Demetrius announced his presence with such authority. Her insides shook as she went to answer the knock, taking a short moment and moistening her lips with the tip of her tongue before opening the door.

Hala looked at her beloved with flashing eyes, slyly simulating surprise. "Demetrius! You came!"

An entranced Demetrius blinked, thinking to himself that Hala looked especially pretty today. With her dark hair and eyes, Hala's pale skin looked like rich cream against the bright green of her blouse. Demetrius took Hala's hands in his, and the couple gazed intently into each other's eyes. Demetrius was silent for so long Hala became uncomfortable, thinking he was not going to answer.

"Demetrius?" she asked doubtfully.

Demetrius glanced around to be certain no one was looking and then leaned his body forward and planted a quick kiss on Hala's lips. "You are beautiful!" he remarked softly.

Hala laughed. "Demetrius! Someone will see us!"

Demetrius felt the affection in her voice. "Let them," he told her in a husky whisper. "I am an honorable man."

Trying to overcome her delighted surprise, Hala took him by the arm and led him to the last and largest room of the three-room building, seating him close to the stage. Hala felt all eyes in the auditorium upon them and she found her pride difficult to conceal. She had often been told by her girlfriends that Demetrius Antoun was the most desirable man in all of Lebanon, possibly in the world! Not only was he tall, handsome, and smart, but Demetrius was sweet-natured and gentle. Hala didn't need anyone to tell her she was lucky.

Out of the corner of her eye, Hala saw that Maha was frantically signaling to her, pointing to the curtain they had hung earlier that day. The row of white sheets had begun to sway dangerously, being pulled upon by small, mischievous hands.

Without saying another word, Hala ran toward the children.

Demetrius Antoun's appearance continued to cause a slight commotion, and there was a buzz of excitement as the unmarried girls and women grew animated at Demetrius' unexpected arrival.

Although Demetrius was a Christian in a largely Sunni Muslim society, nevertheless due to the respect accorded his family, along with his good looks and charm, he had never suffered from a lack of female attention. There were scores of unmarried Muslim girls in Shatila Camp who longed for the opportunity to capture his heart, even if doing so meant a protracted battle with their own parents over the issue of mixed-religion marriages. The fact that Demetrius Antoun had never seriously dated anyone but Hala Kenaan, an eligible girl from a Christian family, made little difference to those unattached women. Until Demetrius was formally wed, he was "fair game."

The older married women in attendance exchanged winks and raised eyebrows. Each of those women had independently concluded that a very important decision must have been made for Demetrius to be present. They speculated that soon, Demetrius and Hala would announce their engagement. They were thrilled—in the Arab world, an unmarried man was a challenge to be met.

Demetrius was aware of the sensation he caused. He tried to be inconspicuous, murmuring a few courteous words to people he knew and attempting to sit comfortably in the small folding chair.

Maha Fakharry made a point of seeking him out, welcoming him to the play. “Demetrius, it was so good of you to come. You must stay for refreshments afterward,” she insisted, her voice unusually shrill and loud. “I must hear all about the battle at Karameh.” Maha gave what she thought was a tantalizing smile, but in reality it appeared grotesque with her large yellowing teeth.

Not knowing what else to do, Demetrius smiled thinly and nodded, but he shifted uneasily in his seat as he watched Maha return backstage.

He remembered his mother had once told him that in her youth Maha Fakharry had been a great beauty, but that was difficult for him to imagine. Mary Antoun had added that, sadly, after the bloom of her youth had faded, Maha could not overcome an insatiable hunger for the notice she had received as a young and desirable woman. The aging beauty was known to flirt outrageously with other women’s husbands. Demetrius’ imagination could not turn back the years, and in his eyes, Maha Fakharry was just an intense, rather combative woman old enough to be his mother. Recalling what she had said about Karameh, he suffered his first doubts about accepting Hala’s invitation, wondering if he had made a mistake by coming. Who knew what Maha expected from him? Once again, Demetrius shifted uneasily in his seat.

To relieve his mind of vexing thoughts, Demetrius looked around the room and peered into a second room through an open doorway. Much had changed since Demetrius was a boy. He was surprised to see desks and chairs, schoolbooks, packets of yellow paper and brightly colored pencils.

As children in this school, he and Walid had sat on reed mats. There had been no schoolbooks, and discarded paper bags had been their paper. Cardboard boxes held a few donated supplies and broken toys. Demetrius recalled that on sunny days, the school had become stiflingly hot. Demetrius and Walid, along with the other students, were taken outside for their classes. Often, they painstakingly wrote their letters in the sand, using their fingers as pencils. Their teacher, Amal Atwi, had made bittersweet jokes about their poverty, saying that simplicity was good and over-abundance in life created adults without goals.

Demetrius frowned. Riddles, they had been fed nothing but riddles, he told himself before continuing his review of the small building. The walls were still painted a dull gray but were brightened with the clever use of colorful posters, some made by the children. Other posters, heralding nutrition and good health for children, had been donated by the United Nations Relief and Works Agency.

Demetrius' eyes rested on the largest of the posters, moving his lips without sounding the words, "Palestine for the Palestinians." To Demetrius, that poster created a rather unpleasant atmosphere, reminding him that Palestinian adults were still building dreams, dreams Demetrius knew would never come to pass.

The buzz of whispers alternated with silence as Maha gave the signal and the first of the children eagerly ran on-stage. After a scattered outbreak of applause, Maha walked to the center of the stage. "Parents, relatives, and friends. Welcome. Your children have practiced long hours, waiting for this moment." Maha paused and looked around the room. "Although we Palestinians have been tortured by a thousand misfortunes, we no longer view ourselves solely as a people stricken with poverty or disgraced by defeat."

Demetrius winced when he saw that Maha sought him with her eyes.

She continued with her speech. "No! Not after our victory at Karameh!" Looking directly at Demetrius, she smiled brightly, and all conversation drifting through the room ceased instantly. Everyone listened with curiosity. "After our spectacular victory at Karameh, the children were inspired." Maha looked proudly toward her students. "Yes. While our heroes fight with guns, we women fight for Palestine in our own way. And, how is that? By bearing children and then educating those children to be revolutionaries! And, today, these young revolutionaries will honor our martyrs by performing a small skit about the continuing struggle to reclaim our homeland!"

Demetrius groaned, becoming more irritated with every word Maha uttered. He gazed at the innocent children, who were hanging on her every word. Mere babies were being taught that it was an honor to die…for what? He had the unpleasant thought that adult Palestinians were willing to sacrifice their children to keep their own energy and idealism alive.

He flinched when he saw that Maha was staring at him once again. Demetrius had a sinking feeling he had been manipulated, by Maha or Hala, or both. Maha's next comment convinced him that was so.

Maha made a dramatic movement with her arms. "I would like to announce that we are honored to have a hero of Karameh at our small school today."

There was a general buzz of excitement throughout the room.

"Demetrius Antoun!" Maha shouted. "A Shatila hero! Demetrius, stand up!"

Loud applause and cheers rang throughout the room. Rumors abounded in Shatila that Demetrius Antoun had fought at Karameh, but since his return, he had neither denied nor confirmed those rumors, making people wonder if what they had heard was correct. Now those rumors were pronounced true, and women stamped their feet and shouted and men made whistling sounds. Many people present had sons, brothers, or husbands in the movement.

All Palestinians, whether Christian or Muslim, were committed to the cause of freeing Palestine from the Jews, and Demetrius was now a hero to everyone in Shatila.

Demetrius looked about him with consternation, but finally he lifted himself from the chair. He gave an awkward wave and a wry smile to the excited gathering.

Maha continued to speak, but her words were drowned out by the general uproar.

A stunned Demetrius returned to his chair without uttering a word, although he was unable to tear himself away from hands reaching out to hug him or to escape the sound of the congratulatory whispers murmured from all directions. Just as his anger was building toward Hala, he saw she was staring at Maha with a surprised look in her eyes, and Demetrius experienced a twinge of relief, knowing she had nothing to do with Maha's actions. He was glad. He knew he could never forgive Hala if that been the case, for she was fully aware of his reluctance to acknowledge or discuss his experience at Karameh.

Elated by her audience's reaction, Maha's dark eyes glittered and she blurted out incautiously, "Demetrius Antoun will be our special guest of honor at the reception following the day's events. For those of you eager to hear first-hand of the Palestinian Army's latest victorious achievement, please join us!"

Demetrius turned pale and sat silent, trembling with rage, though he presented a perfectly composed face to the crowd. If not for embarrassing Hala and jeopardizing her position at the school, he would bolt.

Becoming more excited, Maha paced the stage. "Thank you, thank you. Now, on with the show!" She began to place the playful children, first in one spot and then in another, causing ripples of laughter to break out as the smallest children began to hop about the stage, believing the play had begun.

Maha began to laugh too and threw her hands up in surrender. Finally, just as the crowd was becoming restless, thinking the woman would never leave the stage, she came forward once more and concluded her introduction. "In understanding our current dilemma, and our children's hopes and dreams, the following stage play, titled, *The Honorable Rabbit Family of Palestine,* will be narrated and acted out by your children and mine." She waved her hands toward her students. "Our children! Our hope for the future!"

Everyone except Demetrius applauded.

A lovely girl named Nadia, who was about twelve years old, charming and obviously intelligent, took her place at the left front of the stage. Nadia was the narrator. Without once looking at a text, she began to tell the story, her voice clear and wonderful to hear.

"Once there was a beautiful meadow. In this meadow all the birds and beasts lived happily together."

Several small girls spread their arms and pretended to fly, while two boys acted out the high jumps of gazelles.

"A certain family of rabbits had lived for many, many years in a special spot in this meadow. The mother and father rabbit built a wonderful home for their baby rabbits. A tree shadowed their nest. An abundance of fresh food grew beside their carefully constructed home. A clear running spring flowed nearby."

Five children hopped on stage. A giggle erupted from the audience when one of the girls began to nibble on a bit of lettuce and made a terrible face, sticking out her tongue and moving her head from side to side.

"One sad day a family of hungry foxes came into the meadow."

No one in the audience could control their laughter when a young boy playing the role of a fox began to cry and shout, "I told you *before!* I don't *want* to be an Israeli!"

Later, when the play came to the desired end with the foxes defeated by the rabbits, the crowd rose and applauded. "Long live Palestine!" they yelled. "Long live Palestine!"

The play was a huge success. Nadia proudly took a bow with the complete cast while Maha rushed about on stage, kissing the children one by one.

Demetrius watched as Hala tried to comfort the young boy who was still crying about being cast as an Israeli. And even though his distaste for the play was palpable, a pale case of respect settled over Demetrius' face. His own people were masters of manipulation. At this moment, there was not one adult in the house who would not sacrifice his or her child in the battle for Palestine. Still worse, every child wanted to become a martyr.

Hours later, after enduring lengthy congratulations from most of the people attending the play, a terribly annoyed Demetrius raised his voice in response to Hala's bold hint that several people had asked her when she and Demetrius were going to announce their engagement.

"Hala!" Demetrius became more and more exasperated. He hated the strain that was becoming evident in their relationship over Hala's determination for them to marry within the year. "Hala, there are times when I feel you and I are like two people dancing together, all the while hearing a different tune!" He motioned with his hand. "You and I are not in step."

Hala's smile turned into a frown. She looked at Demetrius with a calculating glance. Her plan had not worked, and indeed, it seemed as though Demetrius' ideas of postponing marriage had hardened over the course of the afternoon. Still, she was not giving up. "Yes!" she fired back, "and as we dance, I am growing old! Soon I will have as many wrinkles as Abeen Bader! Then you will propose to another!" Just thinking about that horrifying prospect, Hala began to cry in earnest, her words barely coherent. "Demetrius, you are not fair! You say one thing but imply something different with your actions!"

Demetrius recoiled from her accusation. He gave a deep and ragged sigh. Understanding that most of Hala's friends were preparing for marriage, he felt a sudden empathy for her dilemma. "Darling." Demetrius lifted Hala's chin with one finger and his voice brimmed with promise. "To my eyes, you will always be beautiful, even as we grow old together." Demetrius was frustrated, wanting desperately to marry Hala, yet hampered by his poverty. "You know my situation." Dramatically, Demetrius pulled his empty pants pockets inside out. "See? I am a poor man!"

Hala gave a choked laugh and with a pensive and sad expression pushed his pockets back into his pants, wishing for a short moment that her beloved was not so brilliant and less ambitious. "Demetrius, who in Shatila is not poor?" She paused before carefully asking, "Have you thought of joining the fighters? Many of the fighters have political positions and are stationed here in the city. Each month they receive a sum of money for their service." Hala would do anything to marry Demetrius, even ask him to join Fatah, something she knew he did not want.

Demetrius' burning eyes stared at Hala. He started to stalk out of the room, but decided she was not herself. He forced himself to keep his anger in check. "Darling, how many times do I have to tell you? As much as I respect their sacrifices, I will *not* join the Fatah." A dogged determination carried him on. "Hala, every man has to follow his own path. I will help the Palestinian cause by educating myself and making enough money to send our children to the best schools. But do not think for one moment that I will bring children into this world to live as we have lived." His feverish eyes bore in on her as he relived his painful past. "To exist on charity! Every shirt I owned, first worn by another! Each toy, cast aside by a child I did not know before it found a way into my home!"

"Don't excite yourself," Hala begged.

Demetrius couldn't stop. "To celebrate a scrawny chicken as if that chicken were priceless caviar!" Demetrius desperately wanted Hala to share his vision, to long for something other than the grinding life endured by their parents. "Hala, listen to me. Palestinians must stop dreaming and make the most of the lives we have been given. I *must* have a way of earning a living!"

Hala's face fell with her hopes.

Demetrius tried to convince her. "Listen, I will take double courses. You know I can do that. I will graduate as quickly as possible. Then, we will have a wonderful wedding…" He made a reckless promise. "And I'll take you to Paris for our honeymoon!"

They had spoken of this before. "Four years?" Hala's voice was flat and her color had gone pale, as she considered what she would tell her friends and family.

"Three years!"

Hala wailed, "I'll be twenty-two!"

"Hala, put your trust in me. Three years will pass quickly and you'll be your most beautiful at twenty-two."

Hala continued to fret. "What will I tell everyone?" Her voice took on an accusing tone. "I mean, Demetrius, you have never asked me to marry you!"

Demetrius peered into her face, as though recognizing something he had never seen before. "Is that what you are worried about, darling?" He gave a small laugh. In Demetrius' mind, he had never given thought to the possibility that he and Hala would not one day wed. Although there were many young women who made it known that his advances would be welcomed, he had never wanted anyone but Hala Kenaan.

Demetrius had an idea. Smiling affably, he gently put his right hand on her shoulder, pushing her to sit onto the sofa. Then, before Hala knew what he was doing, Demetrius dropped to his knees. His eyes were on a level with hers. This close, he was struck by the extraordinary beauty of Hala's face.

Hala's face reddened.

There was immense love in Demetrius' expression, along with something wonderfully good and kind, as he spoke. "Hala Kenaan, I love you. I have never loved another woman. Hala, will you marry me?"

Hala bit her lip, then giggled.

Demetrius smiled. "Well? I ask the woman I love to marry me, and she giggles?"

"You look so silly on the floor like that."

Demetrius held her face tight in his hands. "Answer yes, now! Or I'll kiss you until you say yes. Then there will be a scandal!"

Hala laughed aloud and then answered, "Yes! Yes!"

Demetrius looked at her hard. "You'll wait for me? Three years?" Demetrius wanted her promise so they could put the topic behind them, once and for all.

"Yes! For three years, only! After that, if you don't marry me, I'll elope with a handsome stranger." Hala felt happier and more self-assured than she had in a long time. At least now, she could tell her friends and family that she and Demetrius were formally engaged.

Demetrius returned the joke. "You marry a handsome stranger and I will be forced to commit murder!"

Hala blushed, wondering if Demetrius loved her enough to commit such an act.

Demetrius stared into her eyes for a long time, his longing for her visible. He pulled Hala's face close to his. "Darling," he murmured.

Hala struggled briefly.

"You are my fiancée, now," Demetrius whispered, before passionately kissing the woman he desperately loved.

Chapter XV

Beirut

Between 1968, the year Demetrius Antoun asked Hala Kenaan to be his wife, and 1982, the year Israel invaded Lebanon, a series of political and military events unfolded in the region which threatened the future of all Palestinian refugees in Lebanon.

After the battle of Karameh in 1968, tensions between Israel and the PLO escalated. Heady with victory at Karameh, the PLO, under the leadership of Yasser Arafat, undertook numerous raids across Jordanian and Lebanese borders against Israel, inflicting large numbers of Jewish civilian causalities. When the Israeli Government began to hold PLO host countries responsible for the PLO's violent tactics, relations between Palestinians and the governments of Jordan, Lebanon and Syria became strained.

When the PLO presence in Jordan became too politically disruptive, the Jordanian military was ordered by King Hussein of Jordan to assert its authority over the PLO fighters. A terrible conflict ensued which imperiled the stability of the entire nation. Following a year of fighting, the Palestinian guerillas retreated from Jordan into Lebanon where they joined PLO forces in that country. Raids into Israel continued from Southern Lebanon.

The Israeli Government, incensed over the loss of Jewish life from PLO raids out of Lebanon, demanded that Lebanese leaders prevent armed PLO factions from attacking Israel. When the Lebanese Government was unable to restrain the PLO, the Israeli military began the first of many attacks against PLO positions in Lebanon.

Even without the Palestinian problem, the sectarian balance in Lebanon was fragile. The Christians held greater political power and the Muslims rightfully claimed they were alienated by the existing political structure despite the fact that Muslims now outnumbered Christians. In an effort to unseat the Christians, the Lebanese Muslims, both Sunni and Shite sects, cast their support with the Palestinians.

The Palestinian problem, combined with the ongoing Christian-Muslim tensions, plunged the small country into political chaos.

On April 13, 1975, an armed attack on Christians occurred in the Christian Beirut suburb of Ain al Rummaneh. Six people were killed. Believing the attackers to be Palestinian, Christian militiamen avenged the assault by attacking a busload of Palestinian civilians traveling between two refugee camps. Twenty-nine Palestinians were killed.

A simmering Lebanon erupted into a vicious civil war.

Muslims fought Christians...Palestinians fought Lebanese...Druze fought Maronites... With no single group strong enough to defeat all others, the government of Lebanon collapsed. Syrian intervention brought Israelis into the conflict.

In 1977, Menachem Begin was elected Prime Minister of Israel. Having lost his parents and a brother in Nazi concentration camps, Begin saw the face of Hitler on any enemy of the Jews. Taking an uncompromising position toward the Palestinians, Begin came to see opportunity in the Lebanese War...an opportunity for Israel to defeat its Palestinian enemies. Using the June 3, 1982, PLO attack on Israel's ambassador to Great Britain, Shlomo Argov, as an excuse, Begin ordered the Israeli Military to invade Lebanon on June 6, 1982.

Although unexpected personal events prevented the marriage of Demetrius Antoun and Hala Kenaan, one of Demetrius' dreams came true when he graduated from the American University of Beirut Medical School in the summer of 1978. When the 1982 Israeli invasion of Lebanon began, Demetrius Antoun was operating a medical clinic in the Shatila Camp.

The Israeli Siege of West Beirut
August 12, 1982

In a crescendo of sound, Christine Kleist heard the wave of Israeli F-16 fighter-bombers approaching low over the Mediterranean Sea. She glanced at the small clock she had set for an early wake-up. The time was exactly 6 AM. Hearing the sound of the planes grow louder, she grabbed her binoculars and jumped from the small cot, not taking time to throw a robe over her flimsy night shirt before rushing to the apartment balcony. While squinting at the sleek planes, she cursed under her breath and wondered to herself what had happened to the truce?

Just the day before, ecstatic Lebanese radio announcers had reported to a relieved city that the long negotiations between the Lebanese, the PLO, and the Israelis had come to a satisfactory end. Yasser Arafat and the PLO fighters would soon evacuate. The Israelis would stop the bombing and quit the suffering Levantine city.

Christine pushed aside the limbs of a lilac tree flourishing on the balcony and positioned herself to follow the route of the planes with her eyes. The Israeli pilots raced across the sea-front toward West Beirut and the Palestinian camps of Sabra and Shatila. Since the first day of the war the most violent attacks had been directed toward the refugee camps. Christine winced at the moment the planes dropped their terrible explosives on the Western part of the besieged city. As the concrete buildings of Beirut disintegrated, black, violent clouds of smoke rose over the city and drifted toward the sea.

Christine clutched her throat unconsciously and whispered, "Demetrius. Oh God. Demetrius." Her limbs numb with fatigue and fear, Christine stood and watched, hour after hour, flight after flight, as the relentless Israeli pilots pounded the refugee camps.

Christine had tearfully departed from Demetrius, Shatila Camp, and

Muslim West Beirut only the day before after enduring over two months of air raids. Though she was now safe in Christian East Beirut, she knew all too well the violence of the Israeli attacks: the ear-splitting bombs and shell bursts, the blue skies raining shrapnel, the gutted buildings, the rubble of stones, the blackened corpses. Yet no day had been so brutal as this day. She could only imagine the horror of being caught in the conflagration.

Three hours after the first bombing raids, an increasingly frantic Christine decided to telephone an acquaintance, a Norwegian reporter who had an apartment on Sidini Street, located in the Hamra District of West Beirut. The man's apartment was on a high floor and he had a clear view of the camps. She had to know what was happening!

Just as Christine was about to re-enter her apartment, an Israeli soldier passed by on the sidewalk, directly below her apartment block. Christine dropped her hands to her side and barely noticed the thump made by her falling binoculars. She stared straight at the soldier, focusing on the man's face.

Michel Gale walked jauntily down the narrow sidewalk, his head held high, whistling a peppy tune. While saturation bombings had been ordered for the terrorists in the refugee camps, life in Christian East Beirut was completely normal. Coffee cafés were doing a brisk business and Lebanese women were sunbathing along the Mediterranean seashore.

Michel gave a happy smile as he decided this was definitely the way to wage war. Sauntering along, trying to decide what he would have for breakfast, he had no idea his movements were being carefully observed by a stranger.

The Israelis were everywhere in East Beirut, and Christine was having difficulty reconciling the cheerful persona of the youthful soldiers with the savagery of the attacks upon West Beirut. Who were these young men who were massacring entire families? Surely the attractive man before her could not be a murderer He appeared to be a man who did not to have a care in the world.

While watching the soldier, Christine asked herself whether Demetrius' father had been right when he declared to Christine that "The German persecution of the Jews desensitized those Jews who survived the Holocaust, rather than sensitized them." At this moment, Christine could see George Antoun's face as surely as if he were standing before her. George had nodded his head in sorrow as he continued, "Sadly, history proves this is often the case, that many victims, after suffering terrible tragedies, are inexplicably driven to inflict pain and suffering on their own perceived enemies." Demetrius' father had smiled sweetly at Christine, whispering in a conspiratorial tone. "You and I are a link in this chain, Christine. The Jews brutalized by *your* people are now brutalizing *my* people."

At the time, Christine had hung her head in shame, wondering if the actions taken by the Nazis were now determining the fate of displaced Arabs, even her own beloved Demetrius.

Now, after the brutal Israeli attack on Lebanon, Christine was beginning to realize that George Antoun was on to something. The Israelis appeared untouched by the horrible deaths and massive destruction they were inflicting upon their Arab enemy. As a people, the Jews had suffered horribly, but now they were causing terrible pain and suffering to another people: the Arabs.

During the past year, once Christine confided that her father had been a S.S. Officer in Hitler's army, she had been the center of many lively discussions while working as a nurse in Shatila Camp. Though a relieved Christine had not been held responsible for the crimes of the Nazis, the Arabs' curiosity was insatiable as to why the Germans had felt compelled to exterminate an entire race of people. Christine had discovered that the convoys of trains, wholesale gassings, and burning ovens filled with babies had been more than an Arab mind could imagine. The Arabs were far too emotional for such European organization in the deaths of their enemies, and their murderous rages ended as quickly as they began. During this time with the Arabs, Christine had been surprised to discover that the Palestinian Arabs felt sympathy for victims of the Jewish Holocaust and were able to separate that issue from their ongoing struggle with the Israelis over the piece of land both peoples claimed as their own.

Christine sighed before focusing once again on the Israeli soldier.

At that very instant Michel Gale looked up. His eyes gleamed at the sight of a pretty girl with large breasts. Her brown nipples were visible through her clothing. He stopped and stared. With her dark hair, he mistook Christine for a local girl. Michel gave an enthusiastic wave and shouted in fluent Arabic, "Come down and have a coffee! We'll celebrate." Laughing cheerfully in encouragement, he said, "After today, there won't be a terrorist left in Beirut!"

Christine clung to the balcony railing so tightly her hands began to throb. She simply could not believe the soldier's words! Terrorists? Did he really *not* know Shatila and Sabra were teeming neighborhoods filled with noncombatants? She gave Michel a long, stony look, while picturing her beautiful, gentle, Demetrius, the man she loved, in the thick of battle, darting from one place to another, tending the wounded and comforting those he could not save. Flashes of what he must be enduring caused Christine to take a step backward and to whimper in agony.

Misinterpreting her intense expression as interest, Michel was persistent. "Come on down!" He suffered a momentary and guilty thought about Dinah, his girlfriend of two years, but Jerusalem and Dinah seemed a long way off. Besides, the Lebanese girls were coy and sexy. Once again, he called up, "Did you hear me? I'll buy you breakfast." He cocked his head to one side, pleased with the day's work. "We are ridding Lebanon of the terrorists." He paused before adding, "You Lebanese should be grateful!"

Christine erupted like an angry volcano. There was no fear in her voice, only a bottomless rage. She spat out the words with withering sarcasm, her face contorted, her heavy breasts swaying, while she waved her hands in the direction of West Beirut. *"You simpleton!* Do you really believe your own lies? Terrorists? You are killing women and children and old men! Not terrorists!"

Michel flinched. Torn by the unexpected conflict with a beautiful woman, he waved his arms helplessly and repeated, "We are killing terrorists!"

Christine exploded once again, "No! You are killing tiny babies!" She held her hands out as if to measure the size of the last bloodied and torn infant she had held in her arms. "Babies! Babies!" Remembering that the Israeli Government was deceiving the Americans who truly believed Israeli propaganda, she added, "And while you are at it, tell the stupid Americans that it is their bombs that are dismembering those babies!"

Michel stood dumbfounded, rubbing his jaw, trying to decide what to do. Until this incident, he had found the Lebanese in Eastern Beirut warm and friendly toward their Jewish occupiers.

Christine paused for breath, her lips blue against the whiteness of her skin. Her anger over the senseless attacks and her very real fear for Demetrius consumed her. She became hysterical, jabbing her chest with her finger and screaming, "Why don't you kill me! I'm as much a terrorist as those you are killing! Kill me! Kill me!" Christine began to writhe against the wall before sliding to the floor. Weeping, her voice barely above a whisper, she cried, "Kill us all…just kill us all…"

With great uncertainty in his eyes, Michel stood quietly, trying to get a glimpse of the woman once again before slowly walking away. No longer in a good mood, he felt his shoulders droop. He tried to rationalize the incident, to regain his happy disposition. Evidently the woman was deranged. Everyone knew West Beirut was swarming with terrorists and that noncombatants had been warned to leave. Anyhow, he grumbled to himself, all he wanted was female companionship and a cup of good Turkish coffee. Still believing the woman to be an Arab, he remembered that in Arab training school he had been warned: the Arabs are either at your feet or at your throat. The woman he had just seen had definitely gone for his throat!

Michel had a fleeting thought that perhaps he should return and arrest the woman. But he didn't.

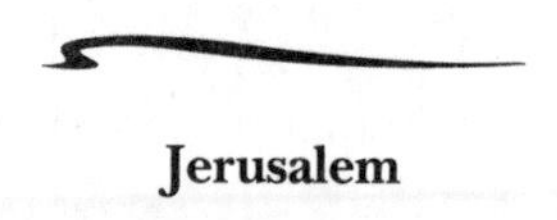

Jerusalem

At her home in Jerusalem, Ester Gale pulled the curtains open before walking outside onto the small balcony attached to their living area. The light had seemed dim from inside the room, but Ester could see that the sun was already bright yellow. She decided the day was going to be hot.

While waiting for her husband and daughter to return from the post office, Ester busied herself in the kitchen, brewing strong coffee. They had not heard from Michel in over two weeks and Ester was worried. The disastrous war in Lebanon was proving deadly. Ester knew that neither she, nor Joseph, could survive the loss of another child.

Ester heard the front door open and hurried to see if a letter had arrived from Michel. Without asking, she knew the answer when she saw the satisfied smiles mirrored on Joseph's and Jordan's faces.

"Joseph! A letter?"

"Yes, darling." Joseph held out the unopened communication for Ester to see. "A nice fat letter."

Even after forty-four years of marriage, Joseph felt his face grow warm at the sight of his wife. In spite of the horrific conditions she had endured during World War II, Ester was still a beautiful woman and looked a full ten years younger than her sixty-two years.

Jordan nudged her father on his back. "Open the letter!" she demanded. She hopped over to her mother, giving her a quick hug, before saying, "Pop refused to open the letter before we got home!"

Ester smiled up at her tall, vivacious daughter, whose face was glowing in anticipation. She stroked Jordan's long red hair. "Come into the kitchen. I have coffee and rolls. We'll read the letter together."

After pouring three cups of coffee, Ester settled into one chair and propped her feet on the wooden prongs of another. With Joseph and Jordan looking on, she opened Michel's letter. Ester frowned in disappointment when she saw there was nothing more than a one-page letter accompanied by a stack of photographs. Before studying the pictures, she read aloud the nearly illegible black scribbles her son had made on the white paper.

August 1, 1982 at 11 PM

Dear Mom, Pop, and Little Sister,

Remember that old saying, it might be easy to get into a war, but it's not so easy to get out of it? That's Lebanon! I feel we have been in Lebanon for two years rather than two months. Trying to clear out the terrorists is a lot more difficult than I had imagined. The slums in West Beirut are filled with Arafat's fighters and until we can go in and clean out the nest of the viper, nothing will be resolved. We know that Shatila and Sabra are teeming with terrorists, so we are concentrating our efforts on the camps. Today, our pilots flew over 120 sorties. Plus, our ground forces are moving in from the West and the South and the good boys of the Navy are bombarding PLO positions.

I've asked myself a million times, why don't the Palestinians just give up and go away? There is no longer a place for them in this part of the world.

I won't bore you with war talk. I'm fat and sassy and no longer in any danger. Actually, to the Lebanese Christians here in East Beirut, we are heroes and even the little girls throw flowers in our path. (Don't tell Dinah, but the big girls make us feel welcome in other ways!)

Seriously, if we can only make the Palestinians vanish, Lebanon would be a terrific neighbor. So, maybe this war will accomplish something when all is said and done.

I'm sending Swiss chocolates and Danish cookies by one of my pals who has a minor leg wound and is being sent home. You would be astonished at the goodies I have purchased: Christian East Beirut is like one big shopping centre. It's hard to believe these people have been embroiled in a civil war for years!

So you see, there is no need to worry about me. I am quite safe. See enclosed pics to prove my point! A big kiss to you all…

Your loving son and big brother,

Michel

Ester carefully appraised the pictures of her handsome son before passing them, one by one, to Joseph. "He does look well," Ester commented, a small smile on her face.

Sitting sideways, Jordan leaned her head on her father's shoulder, peering at her brother standing next to the sea, his weapon in his hand. In the background there were a number of bikini-clad, Lebanese women.

Joseph winked at his daughter and gave a small laugh. "Better not show this one to Dinah."

"Michel looks like a tourist," Ester mused.

Jordan made a small sound with her tongue before lifting her cup for a sip of coffee. Suddenly, unable to restrain herself, she slammed her cup on the table causing the coffee to slosh over the white cloth. Her dark green eyes flashed in anger. "We have no business in Lebanon!" she exclaimed loudly. "Michel should resign from the service. And come home!"

Joseph grunted, wishing his daughter was less emotional. After the death of her beloved Stephen the past year, Jordan had become increasingly disenchanted by the continuous turmoil with the Arabs, dismaying her family by becoming a Jewish pacifist. Jordan's endless talk of senseless Jewish aggression did nothing more than irritate the family, particularly her brother, Michel, who had an opposite point of view. Michel Gale was a military man who intensely disliked Israel's Arab population and was convinced the Israeli nation would never enjoy peace until every Arab was expelled from the country.

With one child a hardened warrior and the other a pacifist, there was no peace in the Gale household.

Much to Joseph and Ester Gale's sorrow, Michel had grown up believing that war and killing were a normal part of life. Only a baby during the 1948 War against the Arabs, with heroic Jewish soldiers filling the Gale home, Michel's earliest ambition was to become a member of the Haganah. When asked why, Michel had shocked his parents and delighted the soldiers by replying in his baby voice, "So that I can kill Arabs."

Deliberately provocative, Jordan repeated the same words she had said many times before, "I only wish the two of you would admit what I *know* you both think…our country is built on injustice!"

Suppressing the retort he longed to utter, Joseph patted Jordan's hand. "Jordan, please." He took a deep breath.

The opposite of her parents and older brother, Jordan reveled in dramatic outbursts. When she spoke again, her tone was spiteful. "War and victory! War and victory! There is no such thing as victory in war. Every victory is full of holes!"

Ester glanced at her daughter. "Oh, stop it, Jordan!"

Hoping to still Jordan's emotions, Joseph returned to the subject of Michel. "Your brother will be home soon, sweetheart. I'm sure when you hear the details of his mission, you'll agree he had no choice but to fight the terrorists." Seeing Jordan's face turn bright red, he continued, "Try not to upset yourself, sweetie."

Jordan's bitter memories overcame her and she snatched her hand away before running from the kitchen and shrilly shouting at her father. "How will Michel come home? In a body bag? Like Stephen?"

Joseph felt the wind go out of his body. He stood up and started to follow his daughter, but Ester said smoothly, "Let her go, Joseph. This is one of her bad days."

Hearing Jordan's sobs through the thin walls, Joseph felt drawn and weary. After a long silence, he finally spoke. "What a pity. Since Stephen's death, our daughter recognizes nothing good about our country."

Ester agreed. "You are right about that, darling. Jordan can see nothing but defects."

Joseph and his wife stared at one another for a moment before Ester returned her attention to Michel's photographs.

While his wife continued to stare at their son's likeness, Joseph walked onto the balcony looking over the rooftops of his neighbors. The thought of his daughter's sorrow and the brutal manner of her fiancé's death blended together and sank into Joseph Gale like a dagger. "Poor Stephen," he muttered.

Like all Israeli men, Stephen Grossman was required to give three years of mandatory military service. During the final six months of his service, Stephen was stationed near Gaza Beach Camp, the most dangerous of assignments.

Unlike Michel Gale, Stephen Grossman was a man too temperate to have been born in a land at war. While at Gaza, Stephen began to question the policies of his own country. He thought the Arabs were treated unfairly, and he often told the Gales that one day, if they wanted to survive, Jews were going to have to accept the Arabs as equal partners.

On his last weekend leave, Stephen had confided to Jordan that he was looking forward to leaving Gaza, that no matter how friendly he was, the Arabs looked at him with faces of pained endurance, like hate biding its time.

Stephen's words had been eerily prophetic. The following week, Stephen Grossman had been kidnapped, tortured, and chopped to bits with a scimitar. Without knowing it, the Arabs had killed one of the few Jews sympathetic to their plight.

Jordan had never recovered from the loss of Stephen. One day she was the happiest woman alive, the next she was consumed by the blackest misery.

Joseph's morose thoughts were interrupted by a loud commotion. His daughter was shouting at his wife. Rushing back into the kitchen he saw that Jordan had packed a small bag. Shocked, he stood and listened when Jordan defiantly told them, her face twisted in anger and grief, "I am leaving this country forever! I am sick of the killing!" She stood and glared for a few seconds before adding, "And, don't look for me! *And, I mean it!*"

The room shook with Jordan's running steps.

Ester stared in grim silence.

Joseph called out, "Jordan! Come back!"

The front door slammed and then a stillness crept into the room. Joseph felt his entire body tremble. He looked at Ester as though he could not understand what had happened. "How can this be?"

Ester was amazingly calm. "Don't fret, darling," she told her husband. "Actually, I have been thinking that Jordan needs a complete change." Aware of Joseph's incredulous look, she added, "You and I came to Palestine because of a terrible tragedy. Here, we found a new life." She paused. "Our daughter must now find her way." She looked at Joseph and tried to console him. "Don't worry. Jordan will be back."

Joseph was not comforted. He could not rid himself of the terrible thought that of four children, only two had survived. Now with Jordan's departure, and Michel's presence in Lebanon, once again, he and Ester were completely alone.

Beruit

Hearing the sound of the soldier's departing footsteps, Christine Kleist dragged herself to her feet working her way toward the interior of the apartment. She crumpled onto the sofa in the center of the sparsely decorated living room, feeling lonely and hollow.

As she lay half-on, half-off the sofa, Christine was overwhelmed by the desire to see Demetrius, to know that the man she loved had survived the day's attack. She buried her face in the musty smelling sofa and cried, "Oh God! Keep him safe!" Christine knew that if Demetrius were to die, she would drift unmoored through the rest of her life.

The force of Demetrius Antoun bore down on her and Christine suddenly knew she could not leave Lebanon. Despite Demetrius urging her to be safe, and in spite of her parents' frantic requests for their only child to return to West Berlin, Christine had just changed her plans. She would not take the ferry from Jounieh, nor was she going to disembark at Cyprus, nor would she board the plane that would take her to the safety of her parents' home in Germany. The moment the bombing and shelling subsided, Christine was going to cross the notorious Green Line separating Christian East Beirut from Muslim West Beirut and return to Shatila Camp.

A small smile smoothed the worry lines from her forehead as Christine had her first pleasant thought of the day: she would soon be returning to the arms of Demetrius Antoun.

Later that afternoon, during a lull between the Israeli attacks and on the way to Demetrius' medical clinic, Christine found herself in a narrow street in Shatila which was clogged with hysterical relatives of the dead and wounded. Disguised as an Arab woman in black garb, the Israelis had believed she was Arab, and Christine had surprisingly little difficulty crossing the Green Line. But now she had a frightening thought that she might be crushed to death by the very people she had come to help, only yards away from Demetrius' clinic.

From her experiences in the camp, Christine knew that between Israeli bombing runs and shelling, the citizens of West Beirut rushed their wounded to medical clinics. The fortunate who were uninjured used the respite to prepare for the next round of fighting. Today was no exception. The threadlike, winding streets of Shatila seemed to be hemorrhaging people.

Looking at the pale excited faces of the Palestinians, which were twisted in misery and splattered with the blood of their loved ones, Christine knew the clinic must be overwhelmed with the wounded and dying. She must get to Demetrius! He needed her!

Christine called loudly in Arabic. "Make room…move!…allow me to pass!…I am a nurse!" But her words made no impact. The sound of her cries was lost amid the general uproar of the Arabic clamor—shrieks, moans and bellows. Losing her temper, Christine began to use her hands and shoulders to push. Raising her voice, she shouted in German, "Clear the way! I am needed at Dr. Antoun's clinic!" Still unheard, Christine began to pinch, shove, and kick, her dogged determination carrying her through the mass of people.

Propelled along by the force of the surging crowd, Christine finally arrived at Demetrius' clinic. With a grateful sigh, she quickly noted that the crude, one-story cement-block clinic had not sustained major damage, though the carnage of battle was evident. Christine ran her hand over the shrapnel-riddled wall of the clinic as she stepped over a stack of empty burlap bags waiting to be filled and used for sandbagging. Without electricity, the interior of the building was shadowy with the dim light of lanterns. Christine stood for a short moment, letting her eyes adjust to the muted light. Her anxiety mingled with relief when she heard the distinctive sound of Demetrius' strong voice. He was shouting for someone to locate blood for a transfusion, quickly!

Christine gave a small cry of joy and ran through the tiny waiting room jammed with families of the wounded. She gasped when she spotted a decapitated child. A woman was holding the body of the child in a woolen blanket while a man cradled the child's head in a bloodied sheet. Christine decided they must be in shock. Both adults wore identical expressions of perfect calm, as if they were waiting in complete confidence for the doctor to put the child back into one piece. Christine shuddered and looked away, wanting only to find Demetrius, to throw herself into his arms and to weep with abandon.

Knowing Demetrius, she knew he would be in the clinic's only operating room, working on the most seriously injured. While making her way through the crowded hallway, several of the clinic volunteers recognized Christine and with questioning looks at her unexpected return, paused for a quick hug on their way to bandage wounds or dispense medicine. Not wanting anyone to call out her name, Christine placed her finger to her lips, motioning that she wanted to surprise Demetrius.

Demetrius' back was to the door. Christine could hear nothing above the tone of his voice, serious and soft, all at the same time. He was always tender with his patients, she thought to herself, smiling proudly. That endearing trait was only one of the reasons she had fallen in love with Demetrius Antoun.

Not wanting to interrupt his work, Christine leaned forward and listened, waiting for the right moment to make her presence known.

Demetrius' patient was a woman. In a single confused moment Christine understood she was intruding on an intimate scene. Demetrius and the unknown woman were having a tormented and complex conversation.

The woman, her voice in a slow measured whisper, was saying some very strange things. "Demetrius. I know. I know life is leaving me. Please, my love, tell me that you forgive me."

Demetrius' powerfully built shoulders slumped. In a pained voice he tried to quiet the woman. "Shhhh. Hala, you will tire yourself. You are not going to die." He gave a short sob and his body went limp. "I won't *let* you die."

Their words made no sense to Christine, no sense at all.

Hala's anguished tone grew louder. "It is written. I am going to die."

The woman named Hala coughed and from the garbled sound, Christine knew she had suffered a chest wound. After only a year assisting Demetrius in treating trauma patients, Christine knew the sound all too well.

Demetrius drew closer to Hala and gently pushed loose strands of hair from her face. "Now, you must stop talking."

Hala's hands clawed the air in her struggle to speak. "Darling, do not look so sad. Death has become my ally."

"Hala, no! Don't say such things."

"All dead. Almost everyone I have loved is dead. Except for you…and mother." She coughed once again, before continuing. "Please, Demetrius, grant me one last wish. Tell me you forgive me."

Demetrius' shoulders heaved with a silent sob, and he suddenly gave in to his emotion, speaking rapidly, as though he was afraid of what time might bring. "Of course I forgive you, darling. Besides, it was my fault that you didn't wait."

Christine sensed the smile she could not see on his face.

Hala became more intense. "No! No! I have been very wicked, to marry one man while loving another."

The woman's voice lowered to a whisper and Christine had to strain to hear her words. "Demetrius, do you believe all of this is a punishment, that God is punishing me? Punishing me for marrying Nicola when I was still in love with you?"

Christine was frozen to the spot, knowing that she should bolt, yet she did not have the strength. She tried in vain to move her legs, but she felt nothing more than a tingling on the flesh of her thighs.

"Hala! *Not another word.* You will weaken yourself. Majida is collecting blood for your surgery. You need your strength to recover. We will talk later."

"One more thing, only."

"Anything."

"Tell me you love me. Please."

In the tight closeness of the room, Christine feared that Demetrius would hear the loud pounding of her heart.

Demetrius drew a deep breath but did not answer.

Hala's voice had a touch of accusation. "Demetrius, after Nicola was killed, I waited for you to come to me."

Demetrius shook his head and gave a noisy sigh.

Hala was persistent. "Tell me, is it because of that German woman? Is that why you did not come back?" Hala tried to raise herself up, to get closer to Demetrius. "Do you love her now, as you once loved me?"

Demetrius pushed her shoulders gently. "Hala. Tomorrow you will regret these words. You are a widowed woman, with two fine children."

Hala's voice was dry, all knowing. "My two fine children are dead. I saw them both before I blacked out. Poor Ramzi lost his head."

Demetrius said nothing. He made a small noise in the back of his throat.

Suddenly, with the force of a woman who has suppressed her true emotions for too long, Hala's words rang out. "Demetrius, listen to me, my husband is dead, my children are dead. Before I join them in the dark grave, I must right this wrong. Demetrius, in my heart, I was always married to you. Never once did Nicola touch me that I did not feel your caress. Never once did I look at him that I did not see your face."

"Hala…"

"Do you still love me?" Her words came out in a desperate rush, almost as if she were bargaining. "If you will tell me that you love me, I…I will do my utmost to live."

At last, succumbing to what had once been, Demetrius drew closer to Hala. His voice was filled with a soft affection which Christine had never heard. "Hala, I will say this once, and once only. I have never stopped loving you, and you know it."

Hala gave the weakest of laughs. "Then, my darling, I die happy."

Christine buried her face in her hands and slipped away from the clinic, running blindly through the maze of the cluttered streets of Shatila, toward the home of Amin Darwish. Amin was her friend. Perhaps he would tell her about this woman called Hala.

Rushing past the brass gong at Amin's door, taking no time to announce her presence, a sobbing Christine pushed the partially opened door and called out, "Amin?"

There was no answer. She cried once more, "Amin! It is Christine!"

Then she saw him.

Christine's face turned white as chalk and her legs folded up beneath her. Then she began to scream. She screeched so loud and for so long she attracted the attention of every neighbor on the street, a street that lately had grown accustomed to the cries of the anguished.

Mustafa and Abeen Bader were the first to arrive. The couple quickly busied themselves with Christine, trying to discover the cause of her distress.

Abeen seized her by the arm, "Dear girl, what is the problem?"

Christine, still unable to speak, pointed a finger toward the center of the room.

Abeen looked first. "God save him!" She quickly pulled the bottom of her apron to her mouth and stood in stunned silence.

Mustafa followed his wife's gaze. "My friend!" He rushed forward.

Amin Darwish's small body lay crumpled beneath the shrine to his wife, Ratiba. His right hand still clasped a photo of Ratiba as a happy bride—held close to his face, as if he took the last precious moment of life for one last look.

By that time, Amin's small home was filled to capacity with the curious.

"Was a woman attacked?"

"I swear before God, the Israeli jets were not so loud!"

"What has happened?"

One old man pointed to his head and explained, "It is the crazy one."

"Shall I fetch the doctor?" someone asked.

Christine spoke for the first time, her voice hoarse and dry. "The doctor is occupied."

A glassy-eyed Mustafa said, "There is no need for a doctor." He failed to control the trembling of his lips. "Amin is dead."

There was a long silence. The little baker would be sorely missed.

"Was it his heart?" the old man asked.

Christine took a deep breath and tried to compose herself. Never had she lost control at a moment of crisis. Embarrassed, she worked her way toward Amin. "Sorry, excuse me. I will see."

There was no blood on Amin's body. After a quick examination, Christine found the small wound. She pointed. "Here. Look. It was his heart, in a way."

Mustafa and several other men bent forward. A single piece of shrapnel had pierced Amin's heart. There were no other wounds, and only a small amount of blood had pooled under his shirt.

George and Mary Antoun burst through the door. They had heard something was amiss at the home of Amin Darwish and came as rapidly as possible.

Abeen wrapped her arms around Mary to soften the blow. "Mary, Amin is with Ratiba."

"Oh, no!"

George Antoun rushed to cradle Amin's head in his lap. George looked first at Mustafa and then at Christine, speaking in a broken voice, "You know, Christine, in a way, Amin has been dead since 1947."

"Yes, I know," Christine answered, softly patting Amin's head.

A saddened George Antoun told them, "Amin Darwish was one of those rare men who knew that time always resolves the problems of every man."

Tears were working their way down the wrinkled crevices of Mustafa Bader's face. He nodded in agreement.

Christine said nothing. She was staring at Amin Darwish. Since coming to Beirut, she had seen many faces of death: fear...agony...and more often than not, surprise, but never had she seen such an expression on a corpse.

A beautiful smile of contentment had transfixed Amin Darwish's face.

Chapter XVI
Death

Amin Darwish's only known living relative was an older brother who lived in Amman, Jordan. Over the years, the brothers had drifted apart due to Amin's insistence that Ratiba was still alive and his brother's lack of patience with such a view. Since no family member was available to attend to Amin, Mustafa and Abeen Bader, along with several other Shatila neighbors, washed and wrapped Amin's body in a white shroud, scenting the shroud with a sweet perfume.

According to Muslim law, the dead should be buried as quickly as possible, therefore, a decision was reached to bury Amin within the next forty-eight hours.

Mustafa Bader reassured George Antoun. "We will remain with Amin through this night. Go, my friend. Soon Demetrius will return. He will need you."

Mary, always logical, agreed. "Yes. That is best." She glanced at the German girl, now pale and strangely quiet. "Christine, come with us my dear."

George nodded. "Demetrius will be shattered." George looked as though he was going to burst into tears. "How can I relay this painful message to my son?"

Without further conversation, the sad trio returned to the Antoun home.

As soon as they entered the house, George said in a shaky voice, "I will wake Pa and tell him the news."

Christine felt her face grow hot as she stood quietly and listened.

Mary agreed. "Yes. And, George, tell your father to dress and join us in the sitting room. I will make strong coffee."

Christine insisted on helping Mary in the kitchen. "I have to think of something besides this terrible night." Though she was horrified by Amin's death, Christine felt as though she was being eaten alive by the misery of not knowing Demetrius' relationship with the woman named Hala.

Normally, Mary would have refused the offer. Her small kitchen could not comfortably contain two people, but Christine had a quiet fire burning in her eyes and Mary's instinct suggested the girl's condition had a cause other than Amin's death.

Mary's mind was filled with unasked questions. Why had Christine returned from the safety of East Beirut to the danger of Shatila? Why was she not at the clinic with Demetrius where she would be normally? But Mary felt restrained in asking personal questions of the girl. She had purposely been cool to Christine from the moment she realized her son and the foreigner were involved in an intimate relationship. In spite of the fact that Christine shared their Christian faith, cultural differences between Europeans and Arabs were immense. Mary reasoned that her son would be happier with an Arab woman, a wife who would understand him. During the past year she had often told her son: "Demetrius, do not forget, there is a reason that black birds fly only with black birds."

Mary had not been unhappy to see the girl leave Shatila for Germany, though now that Christine had returned, she would show her every courtesy. Mary looked at Christine and gave a small smile while nodding, "Yes. I understand. Let's try and remove the image of Amin from our minds." She squeezed Christine's hand. "Life is so hard, Christine. I find I must continually remind myself that winter is always followed by spring."

Christine shivered as if she were hearing a voice from far away. Her own father had said that very thing to her on many occasions.

Unable to contain her intense desire to know about the woman named Hala, Christine stood close to Mary, not wanting George to hear from the other room, "Mary, do you know a woman by the name of Hala?" she whispered.

Mary involuntarily jerked, shocked by the one question she had not expected from Christine. *"Hala Kenaan?"*

Having brought up the subject, Christine could not stop. "I don't know. All I heard was the name Hala. A woman named Hala..." There was an audible change in her tone of voice. "A woman named Hala who is in love with Demetrius."

"What makes you ask such a question?" Mary responded shrilly.

Christine threw caution to the wind. Her earnest brown eyes sparkling with feeling, she explained. "Mary, Demetrius is still in love with Hala. I heard his words with my own ears."

Mary looked at the German girl in disbelief. Never once had she thought to connect Christine's somber mood with Hala Kenaan. She spoke rapidly, wanting to put the unpleasant topic behind them. "Child, that is impossible. My son and Hala Kenaan broke their engagement many years ago." Mary's face changed, and her jaw drooped as she quickly reflected on that turbulent time in her son's life.

George Antoun's head popped around the corner and he entered the kitchen. The three people were crowded within inches of each other. He gave his son's girlfriend a perplexed look before letting her know he had heard much of the conversation. "Christine, perhaps the Israeli bombs damaged your hearing?"

Christine gave a small moan, wondering how much Demetrius' father had overheard. From what she had observed, George shared everything with his son, and Christine knew Demetrius would be furious if he discovered her conversation with Mary. She clenched her jaw, thinking. After reminding herself Demetrius had just that evening told another woman he loved her, Christine felt renewed anger surge through her veins. She shook her head vigorously, her face set like granite. "I overheard Demetrius tell a woman named Hala he had never stopped loving her," she insisted.

George and Mary exchanged a long look.

"Well?" Christine touched Mary on the arm. Sensing Mary's vulnerability, she felt this was her only chance to learn something of this Hala. Soon Demetrius would be home, and she knew he would close like a clam, telling Christine nothing of what she had to know.

George pulled Christine by the arm, leading her into the small sitting area. "Come. Sit. Tell us what happened."

Forgetting the coffee, Mary followed. She, like her husband, knew Demetrius would never confide such a thing to them. He had been secretive for years now, since he returned from Karameh. Their only child was so different from most Arab children who generally revealed all of their personal life to their parents.

Christine felt the pull of her misgivings as her conscience pricked at her. She knew she should remain absolutely silent on this private topic, but her determination to learn all she could about her rival caused her to plunge ahead. Christine sank into one of the worn but still plump cushions and impatiently waited for the Antouns to find a comfortable spot.

George took his time getting settled, rearranging the cushions and lighting a cigarette before patting Christine on the hand. "Now. Tell us. What is this about our son and Hala Kenaan?"

Mary was silently staring into Christine's face. In the center of the tiny sitting room, their knees almost touched.

Christine's eyes teared as she told her story. "I couldn't leave Lebanon. Not after today's attack. I was afraid for Demetrius. When I went back to the clinic, Demetrius was treating a patient. I stood back, not wanting to interfere, and I overheard Demetrius and this woman named Hala speaking."

Mary thought for the first time about Hala's safety and quickly inquired, "Was Hala injured?"

"Yes. Demetrius was going to do surgery."

Mary made a sound with her tongue. "Serious?"

"I am not sure, but I believe so."

Mary looked at her husband and touched her lips with her fingers, looking worried.

"Demetrius will save her." George declared emphatically. George, like Mary, had always grieved that Demetrius and Hala had not wed. George wanted nothing more than to cradle in his arms the son of his son, and if Demetrius did not marry soon, George would not know that wonderful joy.

"Yes. Most likely she is already in recovery." Christine saw the worry on their faces, suddenly realizing that the woman named Hala had once meant something very special to George and Mary Antoun. "Anyway, while I was waiting, I overheard this woman tell Demetrius that she had always loved him and had waited for his return after her husband died. She begged Demetrius to forgive her and then asked if he still loved her."

Christine let out an anguished sigh and then sat still, staring into her lap, examining first one hand and then the other very carefully, wishing she had not returned to Shatila but instead was on her way to Germany.

"And, you say our son told Hala he still loved her?" Mary asked.

Christine nodded, tears flowing freely down her cheeks. "Yes. I will never forget! His exact words were: 'I have never stopped loving you, and you know it.'"

George looked stricken. He cleared his throat and rubbed his chin, wondering at the secrets in his son's life.

Christine put her head in her hands and sobbed with abandon. "Please, tell me about this woman. I *have* to know!"

Touched by the girl's pain, Mary jumped to bring a small towel, dabbing Christine's face. "You *must* stop this crying. You will make yourself sick." She added in an undertone, "I will tell you what you want to know."

Even though she felt heavy and sad at the idea of Demetrius and Hala's love story, Christine looked up expectantly.

George glanced at the front door. "Quickly, Mary. Before Demetrius returns."

Mary sat back down, curling her legs beneath her body and tucking the edges of her brightly flowered dress under her feet while going over in her mind what was long past. She stared at Christine wordlessly for a few long moments and spoke at last. "Christine, there is not much to tell. Demetrius and Hala were in love for many years. They became engaged before Demetrius started school at the American University of Beirut." Mary tossed her husband a sincere smile. "His father arranged his entrance to the school." She returned her attention to Christine. "Hala was hungry to get married, but she promised to wait for Demetrius for three years. While at school, our son discovered he had a great love for the medical profession. Demetrius was an excellent student and gained the support of the staff at the school. Even the Dean of the school told George that Demetrius was a natural physician."

"He was right, Mary. Demetrius is a marvelous doctor." From the first day she arrived at Shatila, Christine had been amazed at Demetrius' considerable medical skills. She had arrived in Lebanon with the idea that her training as a nurse would surpass the knowledge of physicians in that Arab country. She had been wrong. Demetrius Antoun was as good, or better, than any physician she had ever assisted in Germany. Christine, like many other Europeans in the small Levantine country, had discovered that the American University of Beirut Medical School graduated doctors the equal of doctors anywhere.

There was not the slightest sign of surprise on Mary's face. She had heard many other people speak of her son's great ability. She nodded toward George and then looked at Christine thoughtfully. "Demetrius was in a dilemma. We are poor refugees. He was forced to make a decision between marriage or school." The pain of her son's past agony was written on Mary's face. "Oh! How he dreaded telling Hala, for he had concluded they must postpone their wedding for an additional period."

"Demetrius was shaking when he went to tell Hala." George recalled. He looked at his wife. "Mary, do you remember how nervous he was?"

"Yes. Demetrius did not want to disappoint Hala. But, he knew that following the short and unhappy delay would come considerable rewards...for the rest of their lives. He only had to make Hala see his vision."

Christine was beginning to understand what had happened. All the unattached Arab women she had met had nothing on their minds but marriage.

"Hala was devastated and then angry. Hala told me she would not wait a second longer." Mary explained what Christine already knew. "In our culture if a girl is not wed at age twenty-two, people begin to gossip. And Hala wanted children. She said she would be too old by the time Demetrius became a doctor. In her frustration, Hala made a terrible mistake. To make our son jealous, she started a flirtation with Nicola Fayad." Mary looked at her husband for confirmation. "Hala was a beautiful girl and she could have had any man she wanted."

George grunted in agreement.

Christine fought a vicious pang of jealousy which shot throughout the length of her entire body at the thought of the unseen beauty of Demetrius' first love.

"Anyway, the flirtation got out of control. When Demetrius heard the rumor that Hala was seeing another man, he refused to come home, staying in an apartment at the college for two full months." Mary made a clucking sound in her throat. "When Demetrius did return, he was terribly excited. Our son had obtained a scholarship award from Americans who help support the University. This scholarship meant he could marry Hala and also attend medical school." Mary gave a sad half-smile. "But, by then, time had taken a toll. In her anger, Hala had continued seeing Nicola and he had proposed. I knew Hala Kenaan well. The girl did not mean for her plot to go so far. When Demetrius heard from his friends that Nicola had proposed, there was a terrible confrontation, and our son spat at Hala's feet, severing their relationship. His pride drove him away, and Demetrius refused to see Hala again."

"Arab men have too much pride!" George cried hotly, startling Christine.

Mary held up a protesting hand to her husband while she quickly finished the story. "Our son was heartbroken, but he never again spoke Hala's name in our presence, and he forbade us to mention the girl. It was as if every trace of their love was lost. After a short period, Hala and Nicola married and had two children before Nicola was killed in a freak accident in Beirut."

George interrupted, remembering. "It was only last year, a few weeks after you arrived in Shatila, Christine. Poor Nicola was washing the windows of a building in Beirut when one of the militia factions set off a car bomb in the middle of the city. Hala's husband fell three stories to his death."

"It is true Hala waited for Demetrius to come to her, but our son did not respond," Mary said, with a trace of sadness.

George interrupted. "And don't forget, the Lebanese Civil War was still raging. Instead of having a family, our son buried himself in his work, trying to save lives."

Christine had seen for herself the savage fighting which had engulfed the small country for so many years. War casualties had brought Christine to Lebanon. For the first time, Christine was thankful the Lebanese had been fighting one another all these years, if the war was a prime reason Demetrius had postponed marriage.

Christine wanted to marry Demetrius Antoun. Her heart skipped more than one beat as she had a horrible thought: perhaps Demetrius would now marry Hala Kenaan! Christine looked as though she was about to say something, but she could only whimper. She could not give voice to her pain as she remembered the tenderness shown by Demetrius when he confessed his undying love for the injured woman.

Mary gave the German girl a penetrating look, thinking to herself that all women, regardless of their nationality, were more alike than different. She was struck by the knowledge that the German girl truly loved her son and with that thought, Mary's impression of Christine became more agreeable. Before tonight, she had thought that Christine Kleist was just another Western girl needing supervision. Mary told herself she had been wrong. Feeling a touch of guilt, Mary comforted Christine, "Then, Christine, my son met you and left all that sadness behind."

George saw what his wife was doing and was glad. "Christine," he added, "I believe you are the only woman besides Hala Kenaan our son has loved. Other than Hala, you are the first woman Demetrius has brought into our home."

Christine was beyond consolation. Her face turned bright pink as she drew a painful conclusion from the night's events. Emphatically she said, "*That's* why Demetrius wanted me to leave Shatila. He had plans to go back to this Hala." She looked first at George and then at Mary, unable to suppress a violent shiver.

"No. That's not our son's way," George assured her. "Demetrius is not a man to spit and then lick that spit up. Once he was cut from Hala, he was truly finished." George had always liked the German girl, and for the first time, he thought perhaps she would make his son a good wife.

"George is right, Christine. Demetrius is too honest for such a scheme. Had that been the case, he would have told you." Over the course of the evening, Mary, too, had had a change of heart. Perhaps marrying Christine would be best for Demetrius. With a dead husband and two young children, Hala was burdened with a heavy load of baggage.

The lame attempts of Demetrius' parents to defend their son caused Christine to break into dreadful sobs once again.

Mary leaned over Christine and brushed back her dark hair with her hand, "Dear girl, never be sad for unknown things. You don't yet know what the night meant."

Just as Christine opened her mouth to respond, a red-eyed Demetrius burst through the door. Plainly astounded, his entire body suddenly tightened. Demetrius' eyes darted wildly from one person to the other, and the sound of his voice boomed like thunder. "Christine! What are you doing in Shatila?" His look alternated to his parents, "What has happened?"

Fearful of discovery, each of the three adults waited for the other to speak.

Grandpa Mitri saved the situation by entering the room. "Demetrius!" he blurted out. "Did you hear about Amin?"

Demetrius visibly shook. Knowing the news could not be good, his eyes suddenly grew large and anguished, all at once. "Amin? Has something happened to Amin?"

George leaped to his feet and went to his son, placing one short arm around Demetrius' waist. "Demetrius. Son, come and sit."

George's son stared down at him. "No, Pa. Tell me, now. What has happened?"

George rocked back and forth on his heels, wanting to postpone inflicting pain on his son. "First, we must sit."

Demetrius grabbed his father by the shoulder. "Pa. You *must* tell me."

George flushed and lowered his gaze. "Amin has been killed. By the Israelis."

Demetrius closed his eyes for a brief time. His body swayed. An expression of great pain slowly formed on his face. His voice was tormented as he finally whispered, "Not Amin, too, Pa. No…not Amin."

George led his grieving son to the sitting area.

Mary drew near her son, hugging his neck and whispering words only he could hear.

All eyes in the room were drawn to the tender scene.

Christine felt herself an intruder and forced herself to leave, going into the kitchen to prepare the coffee she knew everyone needed. Still, she overheard their conversation.

"I'm so sorry, son," Mary told Demetrius. "We all loved Amin."

Christine froze when she heard Demetrius reply. "Ma, that's not all." He took a long time before speaking. "Hala died tonight."

Mary was stunned. "Oh Lord! No!" she cried out.

George looked helplessly at his son.

Demetrius' brooding face belied the calm tone of his voice. "Yes. Hala and both her children. The children died instantly. Only Hala lived to receive medical attention, but…" He raised his hands, palms up, and then clapped them together in surrender. "There was nothing I could do to save her."

Christine stared at the second hand as it moved around the face of the clock on the kitchen wall. Hala Kenaan was dead! Dead! Dead! She would not lose Demetrius to the beautiful Lebanese woman after all! Christine had to brace herself against the sink to keep from dancing. She smiled before the horror of her reaction became clear to her. Christine reddened, feeling tremendous shame at her happiness. Christine shivered, fearing that she would be punished one day, and rightfully so, for her unspeakable emotion of relief at another woman's death.

Carrying coffee into the sitting room, Christine was quiet and remote, allowing Demetrius time to mourn with his family.

At evening's end, Christine's internal battle raged and guilt still whispered inside for her lingering joy; nevertheless, for the first time since returning to Shatila, Christine's mood of hopelessness lifted.

Chapter XVII
Christine Kleist

"Well?" Demetrius Antoun asked.

Taking a long time to answer, Christine Kleist dropped two cubes of sugar into the hot cup of tea, slowly stirring until the hard white cubes disappeared. Looking at Demetrius, Christine had an odd thought that a stranger's head had been attached to his body. The features of his face were tightly drawn and he looked nothing like himself.

"You are most welcome to come with us, Christine," Demetrius said. "I want you to know that."

"I know, darling." Christine took a sip of the hot drink and then gave Demetrius a dim smile. She could not deny the truth. "Hala Kenaan belonged to another time, a space in your life I did not share. I would not be comfortable at her funeral."

The conversation was becoming more and more strained, although Demetrius managed to conceal his relief when he added, "Are you sure?"

Christine slouched in her seat, running her finger along the rim of her cup. She nodded. "Yes. I am." She remembered the overworked nurses at Demetrius' medical clinic. "Besides, I think I had best work at the clinic this morning. I'll tell Majida to take the day off."

Demetrius paused and took a breath before agreeing. "Majida could use the rest. She hasn't taken a day off in over two months."

Christine's eyes were veiled as she looked beyond Demetrius' shoulder. Two months. Had it really been only two months since the Israelis attacked Lebanon? So much had happened since. Too much. Suddenly remembering there would be two funerals on this day, Christine's veiled look vanished and she turned back to Demetrius. "But come by for me afterward. I must go with you to Amin's funeral."

For a split second, Demetrius' eyes blazed with deadly hatred for his enemies, the first emotion he had shown since the night before. With a visible effort, he tried hard not to think, and harder still not to feel, as he put the Jews out of his mind and composed himself, "You must. Amin loved you."

At that thought, a terrible sadness came over Christine and she rapidly blinked her eyes two or three times in quick succession, trying to keep from crying. Her lips started to tremble, but she squeezed them together to stop the quivering. Christine missed Amin Darwish already. To the German girl, he had been Shatila's most interesting character.

Demetrius turned and faced the doorway when he heard the sounds of his parents and grandfather coming up the narrow hallway from their sleeping quarters. The room suddenly became full when George, along with Mary and Grandpa Mitri, joined Demetrius and Christine, circling the young couple as they sat at the small wooden table.

Christine gave them a small smile, even as her heart plunged. The Antoun family was frightfully poor. In better times and other cities, Demetrius would make a comfortable living as a physician, but in the poverty of Shatila Camp, he remained as poor as his patients. Christine had quickly seen that Demetrius did not have the heart to charge his impoverished patients. Often the doctor left his clinic at the end of a long tiring day with nothing more than a skinny chicken dangling from his hand.

She turned her gaze to George Antoun. Demetrius' father was wearing his only suit, a frayed brown affair clearly marking his status as a poor man. Mary wore her best black dress, a dress she had darned the night before. Her hair was covered with a dark blue scarf, a Christmas gift Christine had given her the year before. Grandpa Mitri's only suit had worn out years before, but he was wearing a clean white shirt and freshly pressed blue pants he claimed he owned from his youth. Earlier that morning, while pointedly staring at George's extended belly, Grandpa Mitri had proudly informed the family he was the same size at age seventy-nine he had been on the day of his wedding, nearly sixty years before.

Christine's smile grew wide, almost indulgent, thinking about the old man's visible pride in maintaining his slim figure. "Look at this." Christine waved her hand toward Demetrius' parents and grandfather. "Everyone looks so nice. And you look especially smart, Grandpa."

Grandpa Mitri rubbed his hand over his jaw, looking pleased with himself.

Mary gave Christine a congenial look, thinking to herself that the girl did have an agreeable manner, which was not the case with many Europeans she had met who seemed aloof and unfeeling in comparison to Mary's own hospitable Arab culture.

"Son, we are ready," George said.

Demetrius nodded. "All right, Pa."

Christine pushed her chair back and stood, following the family to the front door. As the Antouns walked away, Christine silently stood and kept a vigil as the four adults made their way down the narrow street. The Antouns were fortunate to be a close knit family. Christine felt certain that alone, none of the Antouns would find the courage to attend the funeral of Hala Kenaan and the funeral of their dear friend Amin, both on the same day.

Daunting questions came to her mind. Were all Palestinians doomed forever? She wondered, as she often had, whether the Antouns would ever return to their homeland, or if they were destined to drift endlessly without a single square foot of soil to call their own? Christine knew the snarled complications that lay in the path of peace for these people. They had always been ruled by others—Egyptians, Babylonians, Persians, Romans, the Crusaders, Turks, and British, before the Israelis, the latest occupation which had resulted in their present refugee status. Now, they were exiled in a country which had flamed into civil war, and, in the midst of that war, they suffered an invasion by their most determined enemies!

What lives Palestinians had lived!

Fearing there was no relief in sight for their special kind of empty agony, Christine shook her head in sympathy for all Palestinians before turning and going inside.

After eating an overripe apple, Christine rushed to prepare herself for clinic duty. Later, while taking a sponge bath, Christine held the tattered washcloth to her face and softly whispered, "I will make him forget her. I will."

Due to her uncommon beauty, Hala Kenaan had been a Shatila celebrity and her kind and generous nature had won her many true friends. So in spite of the apprehension that the Israelis might resume their bombing runs, several hundred citizens of the Shatila Camp wound their way out of the camp into the streets of Beirut toward the Martyrs Cemetery, a twenty-minute walk from Shatila Camp.

Even though the people of West Beirut were scampering about trying to replace supplies should the Jews resume their assault on their beleaguered city, they still stopped and stood in silent respect as the procession passed. People were watching from scarred storefronts and sidewalks, trying to catch a glimpse of the large photograph of Hala Kenaan and her two children displayed on the crude, oversized coffin. Excited whispers whipped through crowd...the coffin held the bodies of a beautiful young woman and her two children. Watchers closed their eyes and silently thanked their God they were not burying a member of their own family this day.

Had war not overtaken their lives, a church service would have been held for Hala and her children. Like Demetrius, Hala was of the Greek Orthodox faith. But families in war-torn West Beirut did not have such luxury, though a Priest had agreed to meet the family at the cemetery for a short service.

During the service, mourner's lips moved in silent prayer while fearful nervous eyes scanned the sky, hoping Israeli jets would not choose this moment to renew their attack.

The anguished cries and moans of Hala's mother, Rozette, Hala's surviving sisters, and her female cousins were terrible to hear. Almost out of her mind with grief from the loss of her first-born child and two grand-children, Rozette Kenaan beat her face, ripped out her hair and tore her clothes. Rozette finally fainted when Hala's youngest sister, sixteen-year-old Nadine, tried to throw herself into the freshly dug grave.

During the emotional scene, Demetrius stood quietly between his parents. Grandpa Mitri, Mustafa and Abeen Bader were near. While tears freely flowed down the faces of those around him, Demetrius' grief went beyond tears. Demetrius watched but did not see as Hala and her two children were buried in a common grave beside the grave of her deceased husband. Remembering that day so long ago when he had proposed, Demetrius strained with every nerve to understand how their youthful dreams had vanished.

As the last of the rocky dirt was pushed into a mound on Hala's wooden coffin, Demetrius told himself he should have been married to Hala, and that at her death she should have rested by his side, and not by the side of a man Hala still claimed was a stranger, even after years of marriage and two children. Now, he could only pray that his beloved Hala would find happiness beyond the grave.

The Muslim funeral service for Amin Darwish was less passionate, for he had not left a wife or children to mourn him. Besides, many who knew him felt joy that Amin had been reunited with his wife, Ratiba.

Demetrius was teary-eyed as he read a small poem Amin had written years before in honor of his bride Ratiba.

I have seen all the works done
by our great master,
and to know you, my wife Ratiba,
is to give my heart to his finest work,
and to praise Allah for his wisdom in
producing such beauty for a lowly creature
such as I.

With trembling fingers, Demetrius carefully placed the brown and creased page of the poem on Amin's shrouded form, along with three photographs of Ratiba and Amin taken long ago on a happy day.

At the close of Amin's funeral, Demetrius was in a somber frame of mind. Wishing to avoid the large congregation from Amin's funeral that was to meet at the Antoun home, he drew his father aside and said, "Christine and I will be at Amin's. I will pack away some of his things."

Earlier that morning, Mustafa had discovered a neatly written letter Amin had written years before, leaving all the little baker's earthly belongings to Demetrius Antoun, whom he claimed to love as dearly as if he had been his own flesh and blood.

"Son," George protested, "Your nerves are too frayed for such things. Your mother and I will help you tomorrow."

"No." Demetrius insisted. "I have to busy myself, Pa. Besides, I want to send a few of Amin's personal effects to his brother in Jordan."

A PLO official stationed in West Beirut had been successful in locating Amin's brother.

George thoughtfully pulled on his mustache. "Well. All right."

Demetrius leaned to his father and kissed him twice on both cheeks. "Don't worry, Pa. I will be all right."

George was silent as he leaned against the doorframe and followed the movements of his son and Christine as the couple made their way toward Amin Darwish's three-room house. His heart ached for his son. George's thoughts wandered, leading him back in time. An act was now coming back to haunt him, but he quickly told himself to forget the past. The past could not be changed. "Who could know what would pass our way?" George muttered under his breath.

Mustafa touched George's shoulder, wanting to draw him into a conversation about the latest news of the peace agreement.

George, his face red and the veins on his neck extended, shouted at his friend, "God Himself should forbid the horrible lives Palestinians have been forced to live!"

Mustafa opened his mouth in surprise and scratched his head as George marched angrily away.

Without once speaking, Demetrius and Christine ambled down the familiar path to Amin's home. While Demetrius was silently counting all the friends he had lost at the hands of the Jews, Christine was hoping they might find the opportunity to make love. They had not enjoyed a moment alone since the day the Israelis invaded Lebanon.

Entering Amin's house alone seemed familiar. There had been numerous occasions in the past when the couple had used the baker's home for a discreet rendezvous. Often Amin would purposefully drop by the clinic and inform Demetrius he would be gone for the entire day, selling his sweets door-to-door in the affluent neighborhoods of Beirut. Amin knew Demetrius and Christine would grab any precious moments of intimacy. Privacy was not a simple matter for an unmarried man and an unmarried woman in Shatila Camp. Most couples had to content themselves with a stolen kiss or a tender squeeze given in passing. The Arab community kept a close watch on their unmarried sons and daughters.

After locking the front door, Demetrius walked to the kitchen, picked up a bottle of cola, then found a small tin box filled with rice cake squares. Amin had made the rice cake squares especially for Demetrius the day before his death and Demetrius knew Amin would want him to savor the last of the precious sweets. He was touched by the thought that never again would he eat from Amin's table.

Christine voiced what Demetrius had felt from the first moment he had entered Amin's home. "Demetrius," she called, "I have the strangest feeling Amin didn't really die."

As a silent Demetrius returned to the sitting room, she handled the photographs of Ratiba which were scattered in front of the shrine, holding each one up and peering at the picture with interest. "It's more like he disappeared."

Demetrius knew what she meant. "We have been here so many times without him. It does seem Amin is due to arrive at any moment." Demetrius then collapsed on the floor, placing several cushions behind his back. He cradled the tin of cookies and the soda bottle in his lap. "God. If that were only true." Since Walid's death, Demetrius had felt safe by keeping his distance from his peers, and Amin was the last of his really good friends in the camp.

In truth, Demetrius Antoun had grown into a lonely man and often felt he did not belong in the Arab community he called home. Emotions tended to rule the Arabs, and Demetrius was too logical for his own people.

Once settled on the cushions, he motioned for Christine to sit. "Tonight, let's try and forget this day." He then startled her with a question he had never asked.

"Christine, do you hate the Jews?"

Christine stiffened, then opened her mouth to answer but could not speak. Finally, she said, "Don't ask a German such a question, Demetrius. I have no complaint against the Jews." Christine imagined that the question sprang from a world-wide notion that all Germans hated the Jewish race.

Keeping his eyes on her, Demetrius took a sip of soda, knowing there was more Christine wanted to say.

She was quiet for a minute before urgently adding. "Actually, I love the Jews, each and every one of them." Due to the Nazi legacy, Christine Kleist had a tendency to overcompensate in her admiration for the Jews, determined not to reinforce Jewish prejudices.

"Really? Not me. I hate them," Demetrius announced, while looking through the tin for a large rice cake to offer the girl.

"Demetrius! You don't mean that!" Slowly, over the past year, Christine had come to know Demetrius Antoun better than he knew himself. Though she often thought he avoided his emotions, Demetrius was a soft man, incapable of bitterness and hate. "Demetrius, I think you mean you hate the individuals who are responsible for the deaths of the ones you love." She took her finger and brushed the crumbs from his full mustache, wishing that Demetrius would pull her to him and tickle her on the neck with his mustache, the way he had done so many times before. The notion brought familiar chill bumps to her flesh. He didn't move, so she continued, "And, no one can blame you for that, darling. Certain Jews have killed people you love. You hate the individual who committed the act, not the entire race."

Smiling, he held out a rice cake. Stimulated by his liberating confession, he insisted, "Oh yes, I do. I hate the entire Jewish race."

Without speaking, Christine accepted the rice cake.

Demetrius' smile shut down. "It's too bad your father and his friends didn't finish them all off."

Christine dropped the rice cake in her lap and with eyes full of self-loathing, Christine covered her ears with both hands. "I won't hear such talk. I won't!"

Demetrius looked at her with mild surprise. "Well, Christine, don't forget, you are aiding and abetting enemies of the Jews."

"No. No. I never think of it like that."

Demetrius looked at the girl with renewed interest. "Mummm..." A new idea came to Demetrius as he wondered whether Christine was tormented by self-hatred for being the daughter of a Nazi, a man who had helped perpetrate one of the worse crimes known to humanity. And, if Christine indeed suffered guilt, then why was she volunteering her services to help the enemies of the Jews? That didn't make sense to him. Abruptly, Demetrius wanted to find the source of Christine's guilt. He turned his head to the side, puzzled. "Christine, tell me. Why are you in Beirut instead of Jerusalem?"

Christine's fingers plucked at her hair as she considered the question before making a surprising admission. "I did volunteer to work in Israel, but after a couple of months, I left." She smiled. "The Jews are experts at taking care of themselves."

Demetrius' eyes narrowed. Even though he and Christine had been involved in a sexual relationship for nearly a year, he knew very little about her. Since Christine was not an Arab, he had never taken the relationship seriously, even though Christine was pretty, intelligent, and highly respected in the Shatila community. Since his break-up with Hala Kenaan years before, Demetrius had gone through a number of short-lived love affairs with European nurses and various liberated Lebanese women he had met in Beirut. Once he was almost killed by an angry Lebanese man who had objected to his sister dating a Palestinian. Since the beginning of the Lebanese Civil War, most Lebanese had turned against the Palestinians, believing the refugees were the sole cause of their country's multi-faceted conflict.

Demetrius' thoughts returned to the moment. He stared at Christine. Suddenly and for the first time, he realized that even as Christine appeared calm, almost placid on the surface, underneath she was a swirling mass of conflict. Demetrius had a sudden passion to know this very complicated German woman much better.

Christine was staring intently into Demetrius' face, wishing she could know his thoughts.

Demetrius put the tin of cookies aside and finished the cola before sprawling across the floor. He propped himself on his elbow, cupped his face in his hand and then spoke, "Christine, tell me."

"Tell you what?"

"Everything."

Christine was secretly delighted. Since she first arrived at Shatila Camp, the Palestinian refugees had questioned her on every aspect of her life. That is, every refugee except Demetrius Antoun. He had accepted her explanation that she was nothing more than a nurse who wanted to travel the world, learning other cultures while helping the sick and injured. Now, today, as if seeing her for the first time, Demetrius was finally probing into her life.

She welcomed the long over-due inquiry!

During the past year, Christine had fallen deeply in love with Demetrius. She had explored every opportunity to know the man. But from the beginning he had been reticent and unwilling to share his past. Christine had learned a few unimportant facts from Demetrius' friends, but he remained an enigma. Now, finally, Demetrius at least seemed intrigued by her life story.

Christine needed only a moment's thought before deciding to tell him. She looked him full in the face. Demetrius' attention was so complete she felt strangely shy. She dropped her gaze and stared at her hands, her feet, the ceiling, anything to avoid Demetrius, whose eyes were riveted on her.

Christine spoke imperturbably. "There's not much to tell. My parents were Nazis. From Berlin. They bet on Hitler and lost the gamble. My father was an S.S. guard in the Warsaw Ghetto." Christine's voice became more animated. "My mother's father and only brother were taken prisoner by the Russians. Her mother was killed in the bombing of Berlin. Mother was alone when the Russians entered Berlin. She missed the last train West for the American and British sector and found herself stuck in Berlin, at the mercy of a very angry Russian Army." She paused to reflect. "Understandably so. I don't deny the Russians the right to hate Germans. Anyway, a unit of Mongolian soldiers abducted her when she came out of the shelter to find food. Mother was held captive by those soldiers for over a week. She was raped repeatedly."

Demetrius whispered, "Oh God, no."

"Yes. And they would have killed her, but a Russian officer learned what was happening and insisted they turn Mother over to him. Mother ran from her attackers, completely naked. The officer took off his coat and covered her before taking her to an undamaged apartment he had confiscated. Mother thought she had been saved, but this officer kept her locked up for three months, and even though he fed her good food and he didn't beat her, he did rape her every day of those three months." Christine's face had a far-away look. "That Russian officer was a strange man! He made mother pretend she was his wife, and had her prepare his meals and rub his feet and then told her if she didn't at least fake enjoyment of sex with him, he would kill her. He must have developed some feelings for her, for when she became pregnant, he arranged for an abortion and then let her go. He had found a younger German woman by then for his pleasure."

"Oh, Christine. I'm sorry."

"Yes. I know. Very few people know *that* side of the German story." Other incidents, equally horrible, told to her by friends of her mother flashed through Christine's mind. "There weren't many German women, or even young girls, in East Germany who escaped being raped by the Russians. Believe me, the German people paid a high price for their crimes." She paused, thinking to herself that that was another story—she didn't want to stray from her family history. "Anyway, a few months later, mother and father managed to find each other. They lived under the Russians until 1961. Right before the Berlin Wall was closed they made their escape from East Berlin to West Berlin. I was three years old."

Demetrius sat up, fascinated. "What about your father? You said he was in the S.S.?"

Christine nodded.

"What was his role in the Holocaust?"

Christine smiled. "You won't believe me if I tell you." The few times she had told others about her father's experiences in Poland, she had been faced with irritating disbelief.

"Tell me and see."

Christine hesitated, organizing her thoughts, wanting Demetrius to know that her father was not an evil person. "Well, believe it or not, my father was not the typical S.S. officer. Friedrich Kleist was, and is, a good man. He actually tried to save some Jews." Kind memories of her father, now an aged and broken man, caused a private inner pain. Christine looked at Demetrius, straightening her shoulders, as though she were bracing herself for his skepticism.

Trying to keep doubt from his voice, he asked, "How so?" Demetrius knew something about World War II, that some innocent Germans had been accused of war crimes; however, he had never read about good Samaritans disguised as S.S. officers.

Christine shook her head. “It’s a terrible story.”

“Christine. Don’t tempt me and then pull away. I want to know everything.” He rubbed Christine’s hand and then pulled it to his lips, nibbling and kissing her fingers.

“Well, you’ll have to stop that!”

Demetrius smiled and kissed her fingers one last time before placing her hand back in her lap, giving her a promise. “I’ve been missing you. Later, I’ll show you how much. But for now, go on with your father’s story.”

Christine returned his smile, thinking that no other man on earth possessed Demetrius Antoun’s sexual magnetism.

“Go on.”

“Well, as I said, father managed to survive the war without killing anyone. That was not an easy feat, not under the superior he served, a man named Karl Drexler.” Christine tugged on a strand of her dark hair, trying to recall everything her father had once told her. “Anyway, in 1942, this Colonel Drexler arrested some wealthy Polish Jew in the Ghetto. Father said that for some unexplainable reason, Colonel Drexler’s hatred for all Jews centered on this one man. The old Jew fled, but he left a large family, and Colonel Drexler took some children hostage. Anyway, when the Jew turned himself in, pleading for the release of the children, Colonel Drexler ordered father to torture the man. Father refused, expecting to be shot, but the Colonel just laughed and accused father of being a weakling, without the iron will for doing Hitler’s sacred work.”

Christine’s voice became hushed and Demetrius had to concentrate to hear her words. “Oh, Demetrius, that old Jew was tortured and killed right before my father…slowly strangled with piano wire.”

Demetrius took Christine’s hand again and held it tightly between his two hands. He shivered. “And the children?”

Christine’s eyes became wet. “I’m not sure what happened to

them. Father broke down, refusing to discuss that day any further. But my father did tell me that when he discovered Colonel Drexler's plan to send the entire family to Treblinka to be gassed, he took a chance and warned them." Christine took a breath of regret. "Except for one man, father never knew how many members of that family escaped, but he believed they ended up as smoke in the chimneys of Treblinka."

"Did your father tell those people what happened to the old man?"

She shrugged. "I don't know about that. But there's more. Father's kindly deed actually saved his own life. Near the end of the war, father had a shocking surprise. By chance he met one of the Jews he thought had perished at Treblinka. The man was a big, good-looking French Jew and father said he recognized the man immediately. He had escaped the gas chambers at Treblinka...God knows how...and was fighting in the Warsaw uprising against the Germans. Father said everything was chaos...Poles fighting the German army...Russians on the edge of the city.

Anyway, Father and Colonel Drexler were trying to get back to the Fatherland when they were captured by armed men. This Frenchman didn't recognize Father at first, but he instantly recognized Colonel Drexler. The Jew offered Colonel Drexler life in exchange for information...he wanted to know the whereabouts of the children. Colonel Drexler laughed, Father said. And then he told the Jew that he had sent those children to Germany for adoption...taunting the man that the Jew babies would grow up as good Nazis. The Jew beat the colonel to death. Father thought he was going to be killed, too, but when the man came to his senses, he remembered Father had warned his family and insisted to his comrades that Father be released to take his chances on escape."

Christine made a face. "That's the end of the story. Father ran away. He never knew what happened to that Jew, but for some reason, he's always been haunted by that one family."

"Whew!" Demetrius declared. "What an eventful life!"

"Whose?"

"Your father's." Demetrius quickly sat up. "Think about it."

Demetrius motioned with his hands. "He lived through the Nazi rise to power. He served in the S.S., an inherently vicious organization. Yet he didn't succumb to the moral philosophy of the S.S. Your father remained human, in the midst of those who had lost their own humanity, even risking his life to save people he was taught to hate and sometimes ordered to kill. He witnessed all of World War II, the most momentous happening in the 20th century. He lived under the Russians, for a time, and then escaped with his wife and child." Demetrius appraised Christine with a knowing eye. "After all that, instead of finding life revolting, he taught his child to care for others."

Christine raised a doubtful eyebrow. Was Demetrius teasing her?

His serious face told her no.

Without responding, Christine pondered Demetrius' words. Christine had always considered her heritage shameful. Once, after visiting the Auschwitz Death Camp in Poland, she had shrieked at her father, telling him of her disgust for his role in the massacre of the Jews. Friedrich Kleist had wept, admitting to his only child that the way he survived his guilt was to forget the greater part of his S.S. experiences.

Yet, when put in Demetrius' words, her father came across as a heroic man, rather than a Nazi criminal. Christine now regretted her harsh words to her doting parent. She gave Demetrius a grateful smile. "Demetrius, thank you for that."

Demetrius reached for her, and in spite of his enormous strength, he touched her with extraordinary gentleness. "One day, I'd love to meet your father, Christine. Not many people have the courage to do what he did."

Christine's heart leaped at that splendid idea. "Just name the date, darling," she murmured before surrendering to Demetrius' sudden urgent caress.

Chapter XVIII
The PLO

During the Israeli siege of West Beirut, a barrage of telephone calls and letters were exchanged between U.S. President Ronald Reagan and Israeli Prime Minister Menachem Begin. When President Reagan protested the continued Israeli assault on the beleaguered city, Begin retorted, "In a war whose purpose is to annihilate the leader of terrorists in West Beirut, I feel as though I have sent an army to Berlin to wipe out Hitler in the bunker."

When the U.S. President was unable to persuade Begin to stop the saturation bombings, and with Lebanese politicians appealing to Yasser Arafat to save Beirut, an isolated Arafat dropped the last of his demands and agreed to take his fighters out of Lebanon.

Demetrius and Christine returned to the Antoun home past ten o'clock in the evening. Hearing a melody of voices as they arrived at the front door, Demetrius grumbled irritably, "Company! Still?"

Christine didn't care. She had forgotten every bad experience of her life, even the embarrassing moment when Demetrius had called Hala's name as they made love. Christine had placed a finger on Demetrius' lips and soothed him, whispering "Shhhh." The incident had not been mentioned again.

For Christine, fear had been replaced by hope that the Lebanese woman would soon be forgotten.

Happily exhausted from an evening of love-making, Christine felt lingering sweetness of the last few hours. She placed her hand on Demetrius' arm and in a low voiced tremor, admonished softly, "Remember darling, you told me that even though life is filled with suffering, we should savor our blessings and leave behind our sorrows." She stared up at her lover, her eyes searching for a sign of affection.

Demetrius studied the German girl, wondering once again why women carried the glow of love for hours after the act of sex, while men instantly shifted to other matters. He smiled and gave her a sly wink, before lightly brushing her nose with his finger.

When Demetrius opened the door, the heat of the August night rushed past them and swirled through the room. He was relieved to see the blades on the small electric fan turning, even though the fan did little more than circulate hot air. Since the beginning of the Israeli invasion, the Israelis had tormented the hapless citizens of West Beirut by randomly cutting off their supply of electricity. For the first time in over a month, the electricity in Shatila was working.

The sound of voices grew louder. Christine peeked around Demetrius' broad back. Three men she didn't know were sitting on the floor, leaning against orange crate boxes. The strangers were talking all at once while George Antoun, Grandpa Mitri, and Mustafa Bader were silently drinking tea and listening intently.

Christine's mouth became dry when she saw that the uniformed men were heavily armed. She was routinely accustomed to seeing men carrying weapons in Shatila Camp and in the city of Beirut, but this was the first time she had known of weapons being allowed within the Antoun home.

George Antoun was a man who believed in compromise and peace, not violence and war, and he had made his home a sanctuary in Shatila. Christine had never known anyone to break George's ironclad rule of "no weapons allowed."

What had happened?

Before Christine could ask, the largest of the three strangers lunged forward and locked Demetrius in a fierce embrace. "Demetrius!" he shouted loudly. "I have missed you!"

Demetrius lifted the man and spun him around, peering closely into his face. "Ahmed! Is it really you?"

"Ah! You remember me, old friend?"

"Ahmed, you're a man who is hard to forget!"

Christine became rigid, staring at the emotional reunion. The man named Ahmed was nearly as tall as Demetrius but slimmer, almost skinny. He had an unkempt appearance, but if properly groomed, Christine concluded that he would be a very attractive man.

Ahmed tilted his head back and laughed uproariously, then held Demetrius at length with his arms and scrutinized his friend's face. Ahmed's brown eyes sparkled. "By God!" he said. "Look at this! Bigger and more handsome than ever. And, I hear you are a doctor, now! God has blessed you Demetrius! I knew he would!"

Ahmed then glanced at Christine with undisguised interest, and without warning, moved toward her. He grabbed Christine's right hand and pumped her arm up and down in greeting, while goading Demetrius. "Come now, Demetrius, are you too ashamed to introduce me to your lady friend?"

Unconsciously, Christine wrinkled her nose and pulled away. Ahmed *smelled.*

Demetrius patted Ahmed on his back, quickly retorting, "Christine, I'd like you to meet Ahmed Fayez, an old friend. Ahmed, Christine Kleist, one of our clinic nurses. Christine's from Germany."

Christine frowned. She was more than a nurse at the clinic! Christine loathed the way Arab men avoided the slightest mention of any personal relationship with the opposite sex. She touched Demetrius in a possessive way, putting her arm around his waist and drawing close, just to show the men she was more to Demetrius than he had acknowledged.

Ahmed lifted an eyebrow in surprise and grinned broadly at the couple.

A disconcerted Demetrius shifted his weight, causing Christine's hand to fall away. Then, arm in arm, he and Ahmed wrestled their way into the sitting room and dropped to the floor, cavorting like young boys.

The older men smiled and stared, as though recalling their own youth and carefree behavior.

Forgotten, Christine stood, feeling awkward and wondering what she should do. Perhaps Mary Antoun and Abeen Bader were together in the back room gossiping about the day's sad events while sewing; but Christine was not in a mood to join the women. She wanted to be with Demetrius for as long as possible. Unnoticed, she looked around the room. Mary had already covered most of the furnishings with black cotton cloth. The Antoun family was in mourning. Black cloth was draped over all pictures and windows and even across the large mirror that hung on the longest side of the sitting room wall. Christine knew the Antoun family must endure yet another hardship. When in mourning, an Arab family would not listen to radio, watch television, or even read books for pleasure. This would continue for one year. Christians found consolation from the Bible. Muslims sought comfort from the Koran.

The remains of the evening meal, which consisted of eggplant, sliced meat, yogurt, black olives and a small stack of round pita bread, lay in plastic bowls placed near the middle of the table. Christine's rumbling stomach was a reminder that she and Demetrius had missed lunch and dinner. After preparing two plates she carried one to Demetrius.

Without acknowledging her, Demetrius took the plate and began eating, still engaged in an enthusiastic conversation with Ahmed.

Christine had the feeling the two men felt alone in an occupied room. Feeling shut out, she sat quietly beside Demetrius and began to nibble on the food, listening carefully to the men's conversation. Christine quickly discovered that Ahmed and the other two visitors were fighters in the Palestinian Liberation Organization.

"Where were you when the Israeli's invaded Southern Lebanon?" Demetrius asked.

Before answering, Ahmed helped himself to a small piece of bread and a slice of meat from Demetrius' plate. He spoke while chewing. "Sidon."

"And, then?"

Ahmed's face grew more somber. "We were pushed back. We made our way into the city and rested in Sabra.

Grandpa Mitri made a rude remark. "Bah! You fighters are always marching in the wrong direction."

An embarrassed George Antoun cleared his throat.

The fighters gave George a sympathetic glance, letting him know that they took no offense.

Demetrius turned back to Ahmed. "Where were you during the siege?"

"We stayed in Sabra." Glancing from man to man, Ahmed gestured with his hands, turning his palms up, "Where else could we go?"

Located South of the city, the Sabra refugee camp nearly adjoined Shatila. Both camps had been relentlessly bombed.

The oldest of the fighters, a man named Ali, spoke. "For two months we lived in tunnels underneath the camp. We came out only to fight the Israelis."

Christine suddenly knew the source of the foul odors surrounding the men. But she also sensed their pride in having survived in a struggle against one of the world's best equipped and trained armies. They wear their dirt like badges, she thought. Smiling brightly at the men, she told herself these men were heroes, not terrorists. The Israelis were wrong to use such a word against them.

Mohammed, the youngest of the three fighters said, "Sleep and fight. Sleep and fight. This has been our life."

Ali grunted, "This time, they almost finished us off."

Ahmed gave a small laugh, trying to make light of one of the worst periods of his life. "Never! The Jews have had their hands on our throats for years. They can't finish us off but they are afraid to turn us loose!"

Everyone laughed.

Demetrius muttered, "We were all shut in like rats."

"Cornered, yes. But not locked in, thank God," Ahmed replied. Ahmed had a horror of confinement and had always vowed he would take his own life rather than submit to imprisonment.

"Nothing could stop the Jews," Mustafa remembered.

They all knew the light weapons of the PLO had no effect on Israeli jets. And, to make their lives even more miserable, the Israelis had shut off the water supply into West Beirut during the hot month of July.

Ahmed and Demetrius continued sharing the same plate of food. Christine's brow wrinkled with curiosity. While men of the PLO lived with their families in Shatila, and Demetrius had been quick to treat their wounds without questions or fees, Christine had never known Demetrius to share a close friendship with any member of the PLO. In the past, when she raised the topic of the fighters, Demetrius always changed the subject, saying only that he was better equipped to heal men than kill them.

Once, while in a rare talkative mood on the subject, Demetrius told Christine he understood the fighter's desire for revenge, but that the bloody ritual of exchanging Jewish lives for Arab lives was not the answer. In his opinion, solutions could only be found through peaceful means. Grimly, Demetrius had said, "The biblical verse of an eye for an eye blinds everyone."

Christine began to suspect Demetrius had withheld certain information about his past. Ahmed's comments reinforced her suspicions that the two men had shared some untold adventure in their youth.

Ahmed grinned and pounded Demetrius on the back again and again. "George, you should have seen your son in Karameh. I swear before Allah, Demetrius Antoun alone can destroy a hundred Jews! If he had remained a soldier instead of becoming a doctor, the Jews would not be in Beirut!"

Ali agreed. "It's true. I'd rather fight a Jewish tank with a stick than face Demetrius with a dozen men."

Ahmed grinned even wider and shrugged. "See? I am not a man who lies. Ali was there too!"

Mohammed looked at Demetrius with an expression of awe. "I have been told of your bravery," he said.

Demetrius was plainly embarrassed. He quickly changed the subject, and offhandedly asked, "Ahmed. Where is Yassin? And Hawad?"

Ahmed's grin vanished as he turned his head to one side sorrowfully. "We lost Hawad last year. And Yassin died in Sabra." A silent pause passed before he continued. "A phosphorous shell killed our friend. Yassin was turned into a torch." Ahmed's voice grew excited. "Demetrius, a day after Yassin died, his flesh still sizzled!"

Demetrius sat with his mouth open. He understood the horror of the man's death. During the worst of the Israeli attack, a young couple had brought their infant daughter to the clinic, a victim of a phosphorous shell. Demetrius had placed the baby in a basin filled with water, but nothing slowed the burning. Finally he spoke. "No! I cannot believe Yassin met such an end."

Ahmed shook his head slowly. There was no need for him to say what they all knew, that the Israelis had denied using phosphorus shells, even when the international news media confirmed many such horrific deaths.

Demetrius looked to his father. "Yassin saved my life. In Karameh."

Each of the men looked stricken, but no one said anything.

Finally Demetrius spoke, changing the subject. "Ahmed, let's be serious. Do you really have to leave the country?"

Each of them knew that a major stipulation of the Israeli demands was that all PLO fighters be exiled from Lebanon.

Ahmed exhaled noisily and his voice became shrill. "Can you believe it? We have been told to clean ourselves, cut our hair, trim our beards, and be ready to leave within the week." Ahmed's face took on a messianic stare. "We have been betrayed by all our Arab brothers. Now, this..." His arms began waving in angry frustration, his face contorted in disbelief. "The Lebanese want us out."

"What does Abu Amar say?" Mustafa asked.

Ahmed clenched his fingers into fists and spoke through closed teeth. "What can he do? One man against the combined forces of the Jews, the Americans and the Lebanese! If we do not agree to the peace terms, West Beirut will be leveled." His voice became low. "We must leave to spare the innocent women and children."

The six men began a spirited discussion about the likely fate of

Yasser Arafat and other members of the PLO. For weeks, there had been talk that PLO fighters, along with their leader, would be forced to evacuate Beirut. The agreement had been reached between powerful countries, all serving their own interests, and the Palestinians were the unlucky losers. No one could believe such betrayal. The PLO had been an important part of Beirut for many years.

The Israelis had won—on land and on paper. When they invaded Lebanon, the friendliest of Israel's Arab neighbors, one major goal was the expulsion of their deadly enemy, Abu Amar, known to the world as Yasser Arafat.

Ali looked as though he would weep. "Exiled again."

George took a ragged breath, "How can you exile a man already in exile?"

No one answered the question.

Mustafa spoke, "The Jews are like hungry tigers. They will end up swallowing everything." He shook his head in sorrow. "With this defeat, the road to Palestine has grown even longer."

The men were gloomily silent.

Ahmed's face showed great weariness, as though he knew the last battle had finally ended and he had been defeated. There were other worries: Ahmed feared he might never return to Lebanon or to Jordan. And how could the Palestinian civilians protect themselves from their enemies when their fighters were strewn across the Arab world. Yasser Arafat had selected Tunisia as his place of exile, and Tunisia was far away. But Ahmed brushed aside those thoughts for the moment and faced Demetrius. "My friends and I have been greatly honored. We have been chosen to depart with our leader. We will be leaving from Zarab on Monday, the 30th. Will you be there my friend?"

Demetrius didn't hesitate. "I will be there."

Ahmed nodded with satisfaction, before looking at Christine. "And bring your woman. This is a historic moment."

"She will be there, also."

Ahmed smiled and made a gallant gesture, bowing from the waist and kissing Christine's hand. He peered at his friend. "You are a lucky man, Demetrius." His expression changed, growing more serious. "Take care of her. The jackals await their chance."

Demetrius nodded but he didn't speak, thinking this was not the time to raise the topic of their vulnerability. Anyway, Demetrius thought the PLO fighters had exaggerated the dangers facing unarmed Palestinian civilians remaining in the refugee camps. And why wouldn't they exaggerate?

Standing at the door, Ahmed looked as though he could weep. When he raised his arms to give Demetrius a final hug, Christine was surprised to notice that Ahmed's smell was no longer offensive.

On August 30, 1982, Michel Gale crouched on the edge of an abandoned concrete emplacement at Zarab, Lebanon. As he smoked a cigarette, his thoughts returned to the letter he had received that day from his father containing news of Jordan's latest misadventure. Michel was furious with his sister for distressing their parents. He told himself that the moment his mission was accomplished, he would travel to New York, find his sister, and return her to Jerusalem. As a child, Jordan had frequently disrupted the tranquillity of the family. As an adult, her behavior was infuriating.

He took an angry breath before returning his attention to present matters. He looked around, wondering how much longer he would have to wait for his hated enemy.

Michel had chosen the observation spot with the same attention to detail that marked all his assignments. Located beside the harbor gate, his seat provided an ideal vantage point for observing the faces of men passing through the gate on their way to yet another exile. Michel's bad mood lifted at that thought. He almost laughed aloud. The Palestinian gangsters were finally getting what they deserved!

With field glasses in one hand and a small camera in the other, Michel waited. He used the field glasses to swat at a large fly that had landed on his cheek. Stone-faced, Michel stared into the mass of people gathered on the sides of the road. His upper lip dampened with perspiration from the August sun. His uniform smelled of stale cigarette smoke. "One more day," he muttered under his breath. "Only one more day."

After a summer of bitter fighting, known as *Operation Peace for Galilee* to the world and *Snowball* to the Israeli command, they had achieved the goals of Israel's Defense Minister, Ariel Sharon. The enemy was defeated, and their fighters were isolated and scattered across eight Arab countries. For nine days, Michel had watched the expulsion of the PLO guerrillas, taking photographs and committing to memory the faces of men he believed the Israelis might have to kill in some future action.

And, today, August 30, 1982, after ten years of semi-autonomy in Lebanon, one of Israel's most persistent opponents, Yasser Arafat, was leaving the country.

Michel continuously watched the street. The crowd was growing restless. Suddenly, families of the departing PLO fighters, along with a curious throng of Lebanese citizens which had gathered on the sides of the road, began to shout and cheer. In one smooth movement, Michel shifted the straps of the camera to his left shoulder, then lifted the binoculars to his eyes, watching the chaos of the scene unfolding below. A convoy of jeeps and trucks was making its way to the harbor. Men on the street began firing their rifles and hand-guns into the air.

Yasser Arafat was leaving the city. He was surrounded by diplomats, international camera crews, PLO guerrillas, and Palestinian supporters. The crowd became hysterical at the sight of the small scruffy man who wore his *kafeeyah* head-dress like a crown while sporting a pistol on his hip.

Trained to suppress his emotions while on active duty, Michel remained aloof from the emerging passions around him. His mirrored glasses screened the excitement which flickered in his eyes. Michel had been waiting for this day longer than he could remember. He only wished Stephen were alive to witness the humiliation of the Palestinians. Michel smiled ever so slightly as he reminded himself that Stephen would probably feel pity for their enemy. In spite of their disagreements, Michel was unable to remain angry with Stephen. Stephen Grossman was a man always ready to defend anyone he deemed mistreated. Perhaps the world needed such men.

Michel pushed the thought of Stephen out of his mind. A unit of French Foreign Legionnaires, wearing crisp khaki uniforms and identical sunglasses, held back the surging crowd. The Legionnaires had hard faces and muscled bodies. Michel respected the Legionnaires. Grim-faced American Marines surrounded the leader of the Palestinian people.

Michel was angry to see that Arafat's leave-taking had turned into a celebration. The little man was preceded and followed by cheering onlookers. Arafat was smiling and waving to the crowd, acting as though he were the victor and not the vanquished. Michel clamped his teeth together as his face twitched with anger. Arafat was a symbol of evil in Michel's eyes and he intensely hated the man and everything he stood for. Michel had to restrain a passionate desire to kill Arafat. Begin, Israeli's Prime Minister, had given the order not to shoot. He had promised the American President, Reagan, that Arafat would be allowed to leave Beirut alive. Yasser Arafat was fortunate that Michel Gale was a man who followed orders.

Michel studied Arafat's movements. He had a purposeful stride as he walked past a PLO honor guard. He paused to salute PLO banners lowered toward him. Then he was hurried into a black limousine by nervous guards and driven to the wharf. Soon, Arafat would board the Greek cruise liner *Atlantis* and be out of Lebanon forever.

A cold smile crossed Michel's lips as he turned his attention to the dispersing crowd. Michel thought Arafat had played the role of conquering hero very well, but he was now leaving a city which he had helped bring to ruin. Whether he admitted it or not, Arafat was being expelled by the enemy he had threatened to destroy.

After removing his sunglasses and tucking them in his pocket, Michel slowly moved the binoculars over the faces of the people, stopping suddenly when he saw the familiar face of a woman. She was framed in the sunlight...pretty... petite. Her skin was ivory pale. She was wearing a shapeless green dress, and Michel wondered if she was trying to disguise the busty figure Michel remembered so well. Her dark hair was pulled back from her face and tied with a yellow ribbon. Michel was looking at the woman who had shouted insults at him two weeks before, on the last day of the bombing. Michel might have known…the woman was a Palestinian sympathizer.

He was ready to resume his scan of faces when he noticed the man standing beside the woman. He was large and powerfully built. Good looking, too. Michel paused to blink his eyes. He felt a sense of uneasiness. There was something vaguely familiar about this man. He searched his memory, wondering perhaps if one of the PLO fighters had escaped detection, avoiding exile from Lebanon. Wondering what he should do, he squinted and returned his gaze to the couple just as the woman looked directly toward him.

Christine's eyes widened in recognition. She nudged Demetrius and pointed to the Israeli soldier. "Demetrius! Look! That's the soldier I told you about."

Michel Gale tensed as Demetrius Antoun looked toward him.

Their eyes met and locked in a steady stare.

Christine was suddenly frightened. "Demetrius, let's leave." She began to pull on Demetrius' hand, trying to make him turn away.

Demetrius pulled away from Christine and continued to glare boldly at the Jew. Although he uttered no words, Demetrius' expression was emphatic: Michel Gale was a hated enemy.

Christine frantically pulled on Demetrius' hand. The Jews now ruled Beirut and she did not want them to focus on Demetrius. "Demetrius. *Please.*"

Finally, Demetrius turned and slowly walked away. Not wanting the Jew to think he was afraid, Demetrius stopped on the crowded street and took a minute to adjust Christine's hair ribbon. Then he affectionately brushed Christine's cheek with his hand before guiding her through the crowd.

Michel jerked in surprise. The Arab's gesture was so human, so gentle, and so unexpected, that Michel was caught off-guard. Michel Gale had never thought of an Arab man as anything other than as a terrorist.

For some unknown reason, Michel Gale thought about the Arab couple for a long time.

Chapter XIX

Massacre

Saddened Palestinians from the Shatila Camp sat idle for fifteen days following the forced evacuation of the PLO fighters. Then they began putting their lives in order. Able-bodied men and teenage boys removed rubble and repaired shell-damaged homes. Debris was removed from the streets. The food markets reopened to brisk activity.

Demetrius Antoun, with the assistance of his staff, repaired gaping holes in the walls of his small clinic, replaced torn curtains, scrubbed bloodstained floors, restored electrical lines and replaced broken water pipes.

As their spirits lifted, hope returned to the Palestinians that their lives could return to normal. The PLO fighters were gone. The Israeli Government's pledge to the U.S. Government that there would be no further attacks on refugee camps seemed sincere. And the presence of the Israeli Army forced a halt to the Lebanese civil war.

Some saw the end of the civil war as a reward for enduring the Israeli invasion.

Then, an unfortunate event occurred which ultimately doomed many innocent Palestinians. At 4:10 PM on September 14, 1982, Bashir Gemayel, the dashing and newly elected Christian Maronite President of Lebanon, began delivering a lecture to a group of young women activists. Only minutes into his address, a remote control device ignited a bomb which reduced the three-story building he was in to rubble.

Though the bombing was carried out by a member of the Syrian National party, Palestinians were blamed.

Demetrius Antoun felt a sudden nervous spasm in his stomach when his father, George, stepped unannounced into the tiny cubicle which served as the Antoun Clinic office.

What now? Demetrius wondered, looking up from his desk.

George Antoun, looking older than his sixty-four-years, said wearily, "Son, a terrible calamity."

Demetrius immediately closed the medical reference book he had been reading. "What?" Demetrius stood up, his fears surging. Something must have happened to his mother or perhaps his grandfather. George had always avoided his son's clinic—to him, the sight of physical suffering required a stronger man than he professed to be.

"Very big trouble is coming," George announced.

Demetrius blinked his eyes a couple of times. "Pa! Please…you are killing me."

George spoke rapidly. "I heard the news from the radio. They fear Bashir Gemayel has been assassinated!"

Demetrius slapped his forehead with his hand. "No!"

"Yes." George paused. "And, I ask you, who will get the blame?"

Demetrius grasped the situation immediately. Bashir Gemayel, a Maronite Christian, was commander of the Phalangists, a Fascist fighting force formed in 1936 by Bashir's own father. Bashir believed the Palestinians were the cause of Lebanon's troubles, and he had never been reluctant to express his viewpoint. There had been many rumors that Bashir was a hand in Begin's glove and that he had promised the Israelis that if elected President, he would expel every Palestinian from his country. And, after years of unwelcome Palestinian interference in Lebanese affairs, Bashir's ideas were popular with the majority of Lebanese. Three weeks before, he had been elected Lebanon's President. As a result of his outspoken comments regarding Palestinians, the refugees saw the Maronite President as their dedicated enemy. If Bashir were harmed, blame would fall on the Palestinians.

Recalling the youth and vitality of the slain President, Demetrius edged toward his father and asked, "Was he shot?"

George shifted his feet. "No. A bomb. The Phalange headquarters in Ashrafiyeh was blown up. Hundreds of people had gathered to hear the President speak." He looked about quickly before adding, "Who knows how many are dead."

Demetrius lowered his head, trying to think. "Have they identified the body?"

"No. Not yet," George replied in a hushed voice. "But, if he were alive, would he not proclaim his life?"

Demetrius nodded and then glanced at the large wall-clock hanging behind his desk. He leaned over to pick up the thick medical book before taking off his white jacket. "It's nearly six o'clock." He patted his father on the back. "I'll get Christine. We'll be home shortly." Worried about his father's sallow color, Demetrius stooped to give him a hug. "Now, you go home. Try to relax."

"First I will see Mustafa to learn if he has heard the news," George said as he left the room.

Demetrius closed and bolted the clinic doors before setting out to find Christine. She had mentioned a house call to change the dressings on Nabil Badram, a three-year-old Palestinian boy who had lost both legs in the final days of the Israeli attacks. When moved, the child cried in pain, and Christine had been making daily visits to save Nabil the added trauma of coming to the clinic.

As he left the clinic, Demetrius could not stop thinking about Bashir Gemayel. As a Palestinian, he felt some relief from this man's death. Bashir Gemayel was the only man in Lebanon who had the power and charisma to accomplish the daunting task of Palestinian expulsion. But as a doctor and a humanitarian, Demetrius felt sympathy for the loss of any life and for the grief the dead man's family would suffer.

Demetrius worried about his father's predictions. The Palestinians would surely pay a price, but what price? The Israelis had already killed hundreds of Palestinians, and the PLO had been expelled. Besides, he told himself, Palestinians as the culprit was too predictable to be believable.

Demetrius met Christine as she was leaving the Badram dwelling. He explained the situation as they walked. Moving carefully, they avoided the craters and shell-holes which pitted the pathway. Neither talked much, and both noticed that people sharing the street moved purposely and carried an edge of tenseness in their manner.

The couple arrived at the Antoun home in time to witness a family squabble. George and Grandpa Mitri were listening to a radio broadcast, and Mary was protesting that such behavior was shameful during their period of mourning.

"Do you believe Amin Darwish can hear the radio from his grave?" Mary asked sternly. "If not, I beg you, do not commit this sin!"

No one was surprised when Grandpa again waved his hand, dismissing his daughter-in-law. Age had made Grandpa Mitri even more difficult.

George, too, was stubborn. "Mary, this is not a pleasure! For our own safety, we must know what is happening!"

Men were like children, Mary decided, always making excuses for doing the things they wanted to do. Determined to have the final word, she grumbled as she left the room, "Mourning is not a picnic!" She would prepare the evening meal and try to reconcile herself to the weak nature of men.

Since 1948, Mary Antoun had endured a series of catastrophes. Now, she could only accept the sorrow which she had decided came naturally to Palestinians. And, while Mary regretted the death of any young man, her real concerns went no further than the safety and happiness of her own son and husband. The fact that her family had escaped the Lebanese Civil War and the violent Israeli invasion without death or injury made Mary feel that God's Angels were protecting the ones she loved. During the worst shelling, Demetrius had been in the open, tending to the wounded fighters, paying no heed to his family's hysterical warnings. Grandpa had insisted upon staying above ground with his grandson, saying that if God were fair-minded, he would direct the Israeli bombs at an old man who had lived his life, rather than at a young man who had years of promise ahead of him. Neither George nor Mary could persuade either of them to take shelter. Mary had spent the three months in agony and terror. Now, with the war over, Mary was happier than she had been in years. Her beautiful son was alive and uninjured.

Without speaking, Demetrius sat beside his Grandfather and together they stared at the radio, listening intently to the announcer.

Christine gave a sigh. The man she loved was always worried with one crisis or another. She walked into the kitchen and stabbed some olives with a pointed stick and selected a piece of fresh pita bread.

Mary lightly tapped the German girl's hand. "Dinner will be ready soon!"

Christine smiled without answering.

The two women had become much closer since the night of Amin's death.

Mary watched as Christine peeked underneath the lid of each pot boiling over the gas flames.

Knowing the older woman would rather be alone in her kitchen, Christine grabbed another handful of olives and withdrew to the back bedroom. Once the door was closed she removed her blood-stained dress and slipped into some comfortable slacks. With the continuing tension and unrest in the city, Mary insisted that Christine remain in Shatila Camp, sleeping in Demetrius' room. Demetrius now shared Grandpa's bedroom, as he had done as a child. The arrangement delighted Christine, giving her more time to be with Demetrius.

After washing her face and hands, Christine joined the men in the sitting room, sliding onto a cushion near Demetrius.

George had tuned the radio to the Phalange-run Voice of Lebanon. They sat listening as the announcer insisted that Bashir Gemayel was alive, that he had walked out of the rubble of the Sasseen Street building unharmed.

Christine smiled. "He's alive?"

George furrowed his brow. "I don't think so," he replied.

"If that were true, Bashir Gemayel himself would be speaking," Demetrius explained.

A gloomy Grandpa Mitri shook his head before slapping a bony hand on his thigh. Grandpa had a troubled feeling about the entire matter, but he couldn't define that feeling, so he said nothing.

Mustafa and Abeen Bader arrived, entering the house without knocking. Abeen went into the kitchen while Mustafa seated himself. "I have heard from a good source that the Lebanese President was merely wounded," he declared. "He is in the hospital."

The news broadcast stopped. There was a moment of suspended silence, then funereal music began playing.

Demetrius slapped his palms together. "That's it. He is dead."

"So much for your good source, Mustafa," Grandpa chided.

No one dared predict the future, but Demetrius' words made Christine's stomach turn. "Bashir's men are known for their long memories. They will avenge their leader."

Mary interrupted them. "Come and serve yourselves."

All of Mary's large platters had been shattered by the bombing. The family had to serve their meals directly from the cooking pots into plastic bowls.

In spite of the delicious onion-garnished chicken served over rice and lentils, supper at the Antoun house was dismal. Looking at the sober faces around him, George wiped his mouth and said, "Even amid our tribulations, we must find the courage to be joyful."

Everyone listened stoically as Mary agreed. "George is right. We are alive. Thanks be to God."

There was more silence. No one was joyful. No doubt some were wondering if perhaps they had survived the Israelis only to be killed by their Lebanese brothers.

At 5:30 AM the following morning, Demetrius and his father were having an early coffee when they heard jet engines. The planes were flying far too low. The two men exchanged wary glances.

When Demetrius spoke, his voice was so low George could barely hear him. "Pa. There are strangers at the gate."

Never one to waver in a crisis, George rushed to wake his sleeping father and wife. "These are not strangers," he shouted. "The Israelis are back!"

Demetrius ran to Christine. "Dress! Quickly! You must go to the shelter!"

"What? Why?"

"The Israelis have returned!"

Christine simply could not believe the Israelis were resuming their attack. "Why?" she asked Demetrius through the closed door as she slipped out of her nightshirt and pulled a dress over her head.

Demetrius didn't answer. He was helping his mother gather a few valuables to place in the small bag she would carry with her to the shelter.

Christine came out, hopping on one foot and then the other, putting on her shoes and making her way down the narrow hallway. When she entered the living room, she saw Mary Antoun carefully placing a framed photograph of Demetrius in her black handbag.

By the time they were prepared to leave their home and enter the shelters, the screaming roar of the planes ceased.

Majida, the head nurse at Demetrius' clinic, arrived unexpectedly. "We just received a news bulletin," she reported. "The Israelis are claiming there are 3,000 terrorists still in the camps!" Mijida's brother was in East Beirut, spying on the Israelis.

"That's preposterous!" George exclaimed.

"There are no fighters here!" Christine shouted, looking first at Demetrius and then at Majida. She was furious! "I can confirm that!"

Majida shrugged. "That's not what the Jews think. The bulletin said the Israeli Army is invading West Beirut to complete its mission."

Christine's mouth dropped open.

Demetrius started for the door. "I'll open the clinic. We'll have casualties."

Christine ran after him. "I'm coming, too!"

Mary called after her son, "*Demetrius! Son!* Do be careful!" Mary remembered her relief at his safety only the day before. Had she brought the evil eye upon her son?

Demetrius turned at the door and gave his mother a quick smile. "Go to the shelters if you hear the planes return." He paused before adding, "And, don't worry…I will be fine. But, you can pray for me." Like most Arabs, whether Christian or Muslim, Demetrius truly believed that the moment of his death was already written. He would die when God decided he would die. Not one minute before, and not one minute after.

Demetrius, Christine, and Majida rushed to the clinic.

Once at the clinic, Demetrius helped Christine and Majida as they ripped white sheets, making neat piles of fresh bandages. They had already inventoried their supplies and knew they were dangerously low on everything except sulfa and cold medicine. Demetrius had planned to restock the following week. Never once had he thought the Israelis would resume their attack on the camps. Every person in Lebanon knew Begin had given Reagan a solemn promise that the attack on West Beirut would cease. So much for that promise!

They waited and waited. Nothing happened.

Three hours later they heard the first shelling. Loud explosions rumbled from West Beirut, only a few minutes from Shatila.

Two male nurses, Anwar and Nizar, reported to the clinic for duty. Anwar was the older and calmer of the two, but today his voice was shaking. "My cousin has just come from East Beirut. He said the Israelis are surrounding the camps."

"What do you think is happening?" Nizar asked Demetrius.

"Only God knows their plan, Nizar."

"The devil is more likely to know their plans, I would say," Christine added in a sharp tone, disgusted with the Israelis.

Several patients arrived at the clinic. Soon there were many more, most suffering from shrapnel wounds.

The staff worked through the lunch hour and into the afternoon. Patients became a blur of blood and bone. With each passing hour, the news and the wounds became grimmer.

After one patient said he had been chased into the camp by a tank, Anwar went to assess the situation. He returned panic stricken. "There are Israeli tanks all around the camp!" He tugged on Demetrius' arm,

"Doctor, what will we do?"

Demetrius continued stitching, closing a small hole in a woman's neck wound. "Keep working, Anwar," he replied.

Christine gasped when she heard the distinct rattle of machine-gun bursts. God! What's happening? she asked herself. Were the Israelis going to come into the camp fighting? The Palestinians would be defenseless. The expulsion of the PLO fighters left the civilians in the camps without protection. Christine felt their acute danger.

The clinic staff was quickly overwhelmed with gunshot victims. "Snipers," a victim mouthed to Demetrius when Demetrius began to examine the man's chest wound. "Snipers, everywhere." The man died before Demetrius could complete his examination.

Maha Fakharry, by now a woman over sixty, showed up at the clinic. Holding her arm, she reported she had been shot when she stepped outside her home. "Demetrius," she moaned, "armed intruders are inside Shatila. They are shooting women and children!"

Demetrius stood frozen to the spot. Finally, he called, "Nizar!"

Running, Nizar replied, "Yes, doctor."

Fear churned in Demetrius' belly. "Go! Check my family. If they are home, tell them to run, not walk, but *run,* to the shelters. Go quickly!"

Maha whispered to Demetrius, "The men who shot me were not Jews, they were Arabs. Arabs shot me."

Demetrius wondered if Maha was delirious.

The night hours passed, sometimes slowly, sometimes in a terrible rush. Demetrius saw the most serious cases. The nurses cared for minor wounds. Demetrius did not eat or drink for six hours. Finally, he allowed Christine to place pieces of meat and bread into his mouth while he performed surgery on a child's arm. The child's limb was missing below the elbow, and Demetrius had to cut away mangled tissue and bone before the flow of blood could be stopped.

Demetrius spoke to Christine. "He needs a transfusion."

"There is no more blood."

"I know." Demetrius' thoughts flashed to all the blood on the clinic floor...pooling...wasting...

Perspiration covered his face.

Christine wiped his face with a white bandage.

Demetrius had nearly completed his work on the child's arm when the tiny breaths stopped. The child had died.

Demetrius' shoulders sagged in despair. He looked at Christine for a long moment without speaking. "Oh, God!" He was near tears.

"Demetrius. What is happening?"

"I don't know. I just don't know." He suddenly remembered his parents. "Have you seen Nizar?"

"Yes. I forgot to tell you. He came back a long time ago. He asked that I tell you that your parents and Grandpa were not at home. They must have gone to the shelters."

"Thank God." Demetrius looked dazed. "Christine," he whispered, "don't tell anyone, but Maha Fakharry claimed the intruders are Arabs."

Before Christine could respond to that shocking piece of news, shouts of terror came from the front of the clinic. Demetrius ran to the front room and Christine followed closely.

The clinic waiting area was filled with armed soldiers.

Christine pulled on Demetrius' arm. "Jews!" she whispered loudly.

Demetrius quickly saw that the soldiers were definitely not Jews. They were wearing green military uniforms and were speaking perfect Arabic. A thin man with a mustache was obviously in command. The man stepped toward Demetrius and nudged him with his machine gun. "Who is in charge here?"

Demetrius pushed the barrel of the man's weapon toward the floor. Making no effort to conceal his fury, he spoke boldly, "I am the doctor. This is my clinic. What do you want?"

Christine's heartbeat jumped once again when she saw the determined look on Demetrius' face. He displayed no sign of respect, no hint of fear, only a murderous rage. These men would certainly kill him!

"We are here to take your staff for interrogation. We are flushing out the last of the terrorists."

"You stupid donkey, there are no terrorists here! Get out of my clinic." Demetrius stepped toward the officer. "Can't you see we are treating the injured? These people will die if we leave them."

The soldier paused and looked around the room at the miserable and wounded patients. "Are they all Palestinian?" A large number of Shite Muslim Lebanese lived on the fringe of Shatila. Those poor Lebanese citizens often utilized the services in the camp.

"They are all human," Demetrius replied.

"Point out the Palestinians!"

One of the nurses started to speak. "Do not answer that question!" Demetrius shouted.

Four of the female patients started to wail.

"We only want the Palestinians," the soldier repeated. "Lebanese are free to go."

"Go to hell," Demetrius shouted, then quickly asked, "exactly who are you?" Demetrius began to carefully examine the men's uniforms. All were green, but none had insignia. The men were definitely Lebanese, but he couldn't determine what faction or organization they represented.

"I ask the questions," the soldier barked. He turned toward his men. "Take all the medical personnel outside. Leave the patients." He looked at Demetrius. The doctor had an edge of fierceness about him. The soldier had no desire to have a confrontation within view of patients who might be Lebanese. He would return and interrogate the patients without the doctor's interference. He paused a moment more, then spoke in a conciliatory tone. "You and your staff will have to come. You won't be detained for more than an hour. Then you can return and treat your patients."

Demetrius considered his choices as he looked down at Christine. Her face was white, but whether from fear or rage, he could only guess. He made a decision to cooperate in the hopes the soldier was telling the truth. He exhaled. "All right." He looked at his patients. "Don't move anything. And don't worry, we'll be back in one hour."

Demetrius and Christine remained silent as the soldiers herded them from the clinic and through the streets, out of the camp.

Demetrius assessed their surroundings, searching for clues which might reveal the truth of the situation, but the camp was strangely silent. He saw smashed windows and broken doors, but no people, dead or alive. He concluded that the occupants of the camp must be in the shelters. At least he hoped that was the case. He also hoped that the intruders were from a renegade faction. Surely, the Israelis would sort them out once they discovered these men were shooting civilians.

Christine was shaking. Something was terribly wrong. Why didn't the soldiers interrogate them in the clinic? Why would they bother to go to this trouble? She was convinced they were going to be executed.

She looked up at Demetrius and he gave her a wink and an encouraging smile.

Nizar, Anwar, and Majida were walking behind Demetrius and Christine. Someone was sobbing. They could have turned to see, but that would have been rude. Probably Nizar, Demetrius thought. He was young, emotional, and easily frightened. And, also, during the past three months, he had lost four members of his family to Israeli air attacks.

After ten minutes of walking, they arrived at the entrance of Shatila. Dozens of armed soldiers milled about, smoking, eating, and drinking.

The soldier escorting the group told them to wait. He walked up the hill and went into a seven-story apartment building.

Demetrius stared after the man. As the soldier entered the building, Demetrius looked toward the upper levels of the building. Israeli soldiers were standing on the roof. Each soldier was staring through binoculars toward Shatila Camp. Demetrius was puzzled. It appeared as though the building was being used as a command post for the Israelis. Was he wrong? Did the Jews know what was happening inside the camp? Were these Arab soldiers reporting directly to the Jews? Confused, he looked back toward the camp. If the Jews were involved, Shatila residents were in serious danger.

Nizar, Anwar, and Majida kept their heads down and looked only at the ground. Any eye contact with the soldiers might be misinterpreted.

Christine felt protected by her German nationality and observed the soldiers guarding them. She was surprised to see that several of the soldiers were attractive women. She was even more surprised when two of the female soldiers spat at her, calling out, "Palestinian whore!"

Demetrius reacted as though he had been slapped. Lunging toward the women, he shouted, "Shut your filthy mouths!"

Christine screamed.

Demetrius began violently shaking one of the women soldiers, screaming, "*Shame!* You are a shame to your family! Go home to your father where you belong!"

Five male soldiers rushed to free the woman from Demetrius' grasp. As she was led away by a comrade, the woman looked over her shoulder to make certain her attacker had been subdued. She cursed loudly, calling Demetrius a mad-dog.

Demetrius was now surrounded by wild-eyed soldiers, all who were pointing guns at his chest. Demetrius taunted the men, motioning with his hand at the women soldiers. "Is that how you want your women? Tough and hard like Israeli women?"

The soldiers shifted their feet but kept their weapons pointed at Demetrius.

"I have had guns pointed at me before," Demetrius said defiantly.

Christine moved close to Demetrius. Speaking for the first time, she shouted in Arabic, "I am a German. This is my fiancé! Let him be!"

The new information produced an uneasiness in the Arab soldiers and they whispered among themselves for several minutes, looking first at Christine and then at Demetrius. They were obviously uncertain about what to do with a German prisoner.

One of them asked, "Is your fiancé German, too?"

"Yes!" she lied. "He is German!"

Demetrius brushed Christine aside with his hand, bellowing, "I am Palestinian, you swine!"

The armed men were itching to kill him, but they were too frightened of their commander to take such an action without his specific instruction.

When the soldier in command returned, he was told of Christine's nationality. The information made him distinctly uncomfortable. He frowned and paced as he tried to decide on the proper action. Finally, he pulled on Christine's arm. "Come with me. You will be released to your Embassy." He turned to his soldiers. "Take these four to the stadium for questioning."

When the soldiers tried to lead Demetrius and the others in the opposite direction, Christine sensed that if they were separated, she would never see Demetrius again. She reacted in the only way she could. She shouted, bit, kicked, and scratched. Her screams were so loud and long that several of the youngest soldiers held their hands to their ears.

The Arab commander tried to drag her away, but she managed to free herself. She flung herself on Demetrius, screaming, "No! No! No!"

Demetrius held her tight. "Christine!" he whispered, "Be calm…be calm…"

An Israeli soldier appeared, shouting at the men in Arabic, "What is going on here? This is just the sort of situation I warned you about!" He looked around uneasily. "Just a few moments ago foreign journalists were at this very spot!"

Plainly, the Arab soldiers were taking their orders from the Jews. The Arabs stared at the ground, uneasy with the Israeli's anger.

Christine's eyes widened. The Jew was the same soldier she had seen twice before: from the balcony in East Beirut on August 12th, and at Zarab, on the day of Arafat's evacuation.

The soldier didn't seem to recognize her, and even tried to pull her away from Demetrius.

Demetrius held Christine tightly with one hand. With the other hand he grabbed Michel Gale's arm and twisted.

The pain was intense; Michel thought his arm bone might snap, but he managed to keep his face free of expression.

Michel Gale was a large man and strong from years of military training; but Demetrius Antoun was bigger and heavily muscled. Michel was surprised when he realized that the Arab was not frightened: in fact he was strong enough to prevail in a physical test of wills. Challenged, Michel returned the Arab's stare.

The Arab, Demetrius Antoun, and the Jew, Michel Gale, continued to glare at one another—two men on opposite sides of a cruel conflict. The confrontation between the two men caused everyone to stand, speechless.

Demetrius tightened his grasp as he demanded, *"Let her go."*

Michel was astonished by the man's strength. He paled, then released the girl.

Demetrius loosened his grip, allowing his hand to drop to his side.

Michel shook his arm back and forth several times.

Showing no visible reaction to the scene he had just witnessed, the Arab commander informed Michel, "This woman says she is German. This Palestinian is her fiancé."

Christine, her face wet with tears and her voice angry and determined, issued a warning. "I won't let you take him away. If you do, there will be consequences you don't expect." She decided a lie might strengthen her position. "My father is a high official in the German government. If you take these people, any of them, all of Europe will hear about your brutality! My father will see to that!"

Michel gaped in amazement, suddenly remembering the couple. So he had been wrong—the woman was not Lebanese, or even Palestinian. She was German! "A German," he muttered, suddenly consumed by conflicting emotions. The woman was a member of the race he hated most, after the Arabs. He looked at Christine carefully as he thought about what he should do. Michel had been ordered by his superiors to keep the media away while the Lebanese were flushing out the terrorists. Now, this one girl could create serious difficulties. His decision made, he turned and gave the soldiers an order. "Take them," he made a circular movement with his hand, "All of them, to a safe place. Release them when your mission is completed." He wiped his mouth with the back of his hand, "Harm no one. That's an order." Giving the prisoners one last glance, Michel turned his back and started to walk away.

Demetrius was not satisfied. "I have to return to Shatila. I have patients to care for."

Another surprise. Michel turned, facing Demetrius once again. "You are a doctor?"

"Yes. And I have severely injured patients in my clinic."

Michel knew he could make no more concessions. "Your patients will have to do without you, doctor," he said sharply.

Sensing she had a strange hold on the Jew, Christine pleaded, "What about his family? Demetrius has elderly parents in the camp."

Michel smiled down at the small woman who tugged strangely at his heart. "Are they terrorists?"

Christine gave an exaggerated sigh. "Of course not."

"If they are not terrorists," Michel assured her, "then they have no reason to worry." Once again, Michel turned and walked away. His stomach was swirling with an unexplained emotion. He wanted to bring the German girl with him, to find out more about her, but he knew she would never leave without the Arab man, and that would be too risky. Thinking about the woman, Michel decided he liked her courage and determination. He was stunned to have to admit to himself he found the woman enormously attractive, in spite of the fact she was a German woman involved with a Palestinian. The worst of combinations!

Christine stared at Michel Gale's back. The Jew had saved Demetrius' life, she was certain of that. Since the Israeli invasion of Lebanon, she had imagined Israeli soldiers as mindless murderers—was that really the case?

The crisis over, Majida, Nizar and Anwar surrounded Christine.

Majida hugged her neck and whispered, "Christine, thank you…for life."

The soldiers led the group to a walled-compound, where they were all confined together. Demetrius, Christine, and the others could hear the clatter of gunfire and heavy explosions through most of the two days and nights they were held prisoner.

Unable to sleep, Demetrius paced, worrying about his patients, his parents, all the people he knew in Shatila Camp. He was certain something horrible was happening inside the camp.

Release came as a surprise. A Lebanese man in an unkempt khaki uniform unlocked the door. "You can return to hell now," he said matter-of-factly.

They jumped to their feet. Without waiting, Majida, Nizar and Anwar rushed through the open door. They were anxious to know the fate of their families.

Demetrius held out his hand to Christine. "Come on, let's get out of here." He began pulling her faster than she could walk. "First we'll check on my patients, then we'll go home."

"Your family will be sick with worry."

"Yes. I know."

They could hear the roar and clang of bulldozers long before they reached the camp.

Demetrius was almost running.

Christine barely managed to keep pace.

He ran and she ran.

When they entered the camp, what they saw caused them to stare as though in a daze. Shatila no longer looked like Shatila. Homes had been blown apart and piles of rubble lay where offices and stores once stood. Bulldozers continued the destruction.

When they arrived where the clinic had once stood, Christine recoiled in dismay. She watched as a pale Demetrius aimlessly milled about, kicking bits of metal and cement block, looking for some sign that the Antoun clinic had once existed. Nothing was left but shattered concrete.

Demetrius and Christine looked at one another but were too stunned to speak. What had happened to their patients?

Suddenly, remembering the most important thing of all, Demetrius grabbed Christine's hand, pulling her down the street toward the Antoun home.

Christine stumbled and fell but Demetrius yanked her to her feet.

They were gasping, insane with fear.

Demetrius was silently praying—God, let them be alive.

As they moved away from the area surrounding the clinic, most of the homes seemed intact. Demetrius began to have hope when he saw that the Darwish and Bader dwellings were undamaged.

Christine gave a small cry of joy when she spotted the wonderfully familiar gray blocks of Demetrius' home.

Demetrius' face was flushed with anxiety when he burst through the door. He called out, "Pa? Ma? Grandpa?"

The house was eerily silent.

Christine trailed behind, horrified as she glanced around. The place was a ruin! The interior of the house was wrecked—furniture overturned, mirrors broken, and food scattered. Disgusting messages were written in black paint on the walls. Christine's lips moved in a horrified but silent whisper as she read the horrible words of hate, "I will hump your sister! Death to all terrorists! Palestinian women don't give birth to babies, they give birth to terrorists!

Demetrius was in the back rooms, still searching, his voice straining. "Ma! It's Demetrius! Are you here?"

Looking around, Christine saw the black bag belonging to Mary Antoun—the very bag Mary and Demetrius had packed with the family valuables on the morning of the renewed attack. The bag was lying open, empty, obviously discarded by someone other than its owner. Christine gave a small sound of pain. Suddenly she was terribly afraid. Shakily she cried, "Demetrius!"

Demetrius stumbled through the narrow hallway. He stood, staring at the surrounding chaos.

Christine pointed, showing him his mother's bag.

Demetrius began to tremble.

Christine moved to his side, laying her head on his chest, longing for comfort, even as she sought to comfort him. "They must have been robbed before they could get to the shelters."

Demetrius tried but could not answer.

She felt his face with her hands. His skin was icy.

Finally, his voice low and sad, he said, "Christine, I fear something terrible has happened."

Christine's stomach knotted as she slumped against his chest. She was afraid to tell Demetrius her own feelings of dread.

Suffering inconceivable torment, Demetrius considered his options. He spoke rapidly. "We'll check the Bader's first, and then Amin's house. After that, we'll search the shelter." He blew out a breath before glumly saying, "If they are not in those places, we'll check the hospitals."

Retracing their earlier steps, they ran to Mustafa Bader's home.

The Bader home was undamaged, but no one was there.

Neither Demetrius nor Christine could believe what they saw when they arrived at Amin's home. Someone had defecated on Ratiba's photographs and on the cushions in the sitting room.

Demetrius shook his head, backing away, disgusted. "Were these men mad?"

They ran to the shelter nearest to the Antoun's house, which was now dark and unoccupied. Litter and spoiled bits of food were scattered about, suggesting the shelters had been recently used by a large number of Shatila residents. Demetrius stared blankly as he returned into the sunshine. "We will check Gaza Hospital first," he whispered.

They were on their way to Gaza Hospital when they saw the first group of bodies, stacked in the street like cords of firewood.

Christine could no longer mask her fear. "Demetrius. There's been a massacre." She put her hand to her forehead and staggered backwards.

Demetrius groaned as he walked among the bodies. A young man had his hands tied behind him. He had been stabbed. Some women and children had been shot. An elderly man's stomach had been sliced open. Demetrius stood in shock when he recognized several of the patients he had left in his clinic. The broken body of Maha Fakharry was draped over the body of a dead child. Maha must have fought for her life, for she had been brutally beaten.

The murderers had not overlooked the animals of Shatila. A cat and three kittens had been slaughtered. An injured horse lay on its side, barely alive but still twitching in its own blood. Demetrius wept as he struck the horse with a large stone, relieving the poor beast from its suffering.

The stench was unbelievable.

"Dear Lord," Christine repeated. "A massacre!"

After a careful examination of the corpses, Demetrius walked toward Christine, taking her hand and leading her away. "We can do nothing for them."

One street away from the awful scene, they found the site of a second massacre. Recognizing the pink-flowered-dress his mother had been wearing when he last saw her, Demetrius ran toward a pile of bodies that lay next to a wall. "Ma!" Mary Antoun's dress covered her head. Her underwear had been ripped from her body.

With tears streaming down his face, Demetrius yanked the dress from his mother's face and covered her naked body. Mary Antoun had been bayoneted in the back and side.

Christine was hysterically sobbing, rocking back and forth on her knees.

Grandpa Mitri lay on his stomach, directly beside his daughter-in-law. He had been shot in the ear.

Crazed with grief, Demetrius began to rush from one corpse to the next, shouting, "Pa!" Over and over he peered at the mangled bodies, looking at some of them four or five times. Finally, Demetrius looked at Christine and shaking his head in bewilderment, gave an impassioned cry, "Pa's not here, Christine."

"Oh, Demetrius!" Christine cried, then stood before stumbling over to Mary Antoun's body. She shuddered when she saw that the framed photograph of Demetrius was tightly clasped in his mother's hands. Even in death, Mary Antoun had been thinking only of her beloved son. Christine brushed bits of broken glass from the picture and held it to her chest before sinking once again to her knees. "God! Let this be a bad dream!"

Mustafa Bader came running down the street, yelling, *"Demetrius! Is that you?"*

Demetrius whirled around. *"Mustafa!"*

Mustafa was gasping violently. "Demetrius, you must come. *Quickly!* Your father is at the Gaza Hospital. He is still alive!"

Demetrius, utterly anguished, grabbed Mustafa by the shoulders and held him tightly. "Mustafa, does Pa know Ma and Grandpa are dead?"

Mustafa sobbed. "Yes. Yes. He was here. He witnessed everything!" Mustafa wept. "Your father could not save them, Demetrius."

The Gaza Hospital was filled beyond capacity with the wounded and dying. The single bed holding George Antoun was crammed into a small room meant for the storage of medicines. A drip was attached to his arm. George had been shot in the abdomen and left for dead. If his friend Mustafa hadn't found him, he would have died at the site of the massacre. George knew he was dying, but he forced himself to live...to live long enough to know the fate of his son.

George Antoun was a man living with a terrible secret, and he knew he must tell his son that secret before he died. George closed his eyes. He was saving his strength.

Abeen Bader fanned George with a bedpan. The doctor had told her husband that George had little time remaining, and she wanted to make that time as comfortable as possible. Abeen was devastated. Mustafa had told her the fate of Mary and of Grandpa Mitri. Now, Abeen was terrified that her husband would return with the information that Demetrius too had been slaughtered like a sheep. The intruders had killed many people, but their favorite targets were young men.

She heard quick footsteps. The door burst open and Abeen gave a small cry.

A blood-soaked Demetrius Antoun came into the room.

Mustafa and Christine crowded close by the death bed.

"Pa! It's Demetrius!" Demetrius hunched his large frame toward his father and lightly rubbed his hands across George's face. All the while his doctor's eyes were searching, trying to see the extent of his father's wounds. He winced when he spotted the blood seeping from the white bandages wrapped around George's mid-section.

George slowly opened his eyes. "Demetrius? Son, is your mother here?" George thought he might have died and was already in heaven with his wife and son.

"No Pa, it's just me, Demetrius."

George gave a little lurch forward, trying to close the short distance between himself and his son. "Demetrius... You are alive?"

"Yes, Pa. I am alive."

"Praise God. Praise God. You are alive." Tears filled his eyes. When their son hadn't returned from the clinic, George and Mary had spent hours of terror—frantic for his well-being.

"Pa. Don't upset yourself. You must recover."

George suddenly remembered the secret. His eyelids opened wide, and for a frightening moment Demetrius thought his father had died.

George bit his lower lip. "Son. I have to tell you something you won't like hearing."

Demetrius begged, "Pa. No. Later. Please, save your strength."

George slowly moved his head, looking around. He ran his tongue over his lips. "Is Mustafa here?"

"I'm here, George." Mustafa stuck his head around Demetrius shoulder. "I am here."

"Mustafa, can you take Abeen and wait outside?"

Mustafa's feelings were hurt. He was practically a member of the Antoun family. Still, he nodded in agreement. "If you say go, George, I will go."

Demetrius intervened. "Pa. Don't be silly. Mustafa can hear anything we have to say to each other."

George had no strength to argue. He nodded. He had to tell the secret before he died. If he didn't, he knew he would receive terrible punishment at the hand of God.

George stared directly into his son's eyes. "Demetrius, I know I am dying. Your mother is dead. Your grandfather is dead." His voice cracked. "You will be alone, now."

Abeen's lips trembled. "George, he will be our son."

Mustafa agreed. "He is our son, already."

George gave a faint smile, hoping that Demetrius would receive comfort from the Baders. Still, Demetrius had to know…every man deserved to know his heritage.

As a last act of tremendous love, George Antoun gathered all the strength in his dying body for his son. He clutched Demetrius' arm and tried to raise himself.

"Pa!"

George spoke sharply when Demetrius protested. "*Listen to me.* I have *one* thing to say before I die. Now, *let me be!*"

Demetrius fought back his tears. "Ok, Pa. I promise."

"Now, don't anybody interrupt me," George commanded. "Just listen to what I have to say!"

Demetrius nodded, his curiosity aroused.

George's voice grew stronger. "Demetrius, your mother never knew.

Your grandfather suspected, but he never asked me a single question."

Demetrius looked bewildered. "What is it, Pa?"

George's voice mellowed, "Son, your mother wanted a baby more than anything in the world. She suffered ten miscarriages during the first six years of our marriage."

Demetrius had heard that information many times, and he remembered his mother's words that he was a direct gift from God. He had always been made to feel he was the most special child ever to come into the world. "Yes, Pa. I know."

George sucked in a deep breath. "At the beginning of 1948, my father had three sons and one daughter. We suffered terribly during that time. When we escaped Palestine, I was his only surviving child," George explained. "Several months before we fled Haifa, we received word that a bomb had exploded at the Jaffa Gate in Jerusalem. That explosion killed my two brothers and my only sister, who were shopping in the city. Pa could not bear to bury three of his four children, so I went alone."

Taking his hand, Demetrius gently wiped the tears from his father's face.

George fumbled nervously. "When I left the cemetery, I wasn't myself." He looked at his son, his eyes pleading for forgiveness. "Son, remember that. Your Pa wasn't himself."

Demetrius was completely puzzled, wondering if his father was hallucinating. But Demetrius gave him a tender smile and promised, "Don't worry, Pa. I will understand."

A flash of doubt passed across George's face. He hoped that would be true. After sighing unevenly, he continued the story. "Well, I went to my youngest brother's home to visit and to help his widow pack a few things. He lived close to a Jewish neighborhood. While walking there, a group of Jews began to throw rocks at me and make rude remarks, telling me to get out of *their* city. Imagine that. *Their* city."

George's eyes turned dark, remembering that day so long ago. A day that changed more than one life forever. "I decided I had better turn back, or my father would not have a single surviving son to provide for him." His voice became ragged. "Son, I passed by a stranger's home and there I saw a woman in a courtyard. This woman was sitting alone, holding a small baby in her arms. She was singing. I stood there and watched that happy scene, knowing that Arabs were being killed, run out of our homes, pushed out of our own land, and I became crazy…I was not myself." George's face was filled with anguish. Ashamed of what he must confess, George's eyes fell from his son's face. "Son, your Pa hid behind the bushes, waiting. Some time passed. Then the woman put the baby in a small crib and went inside."

George's voice broke. "Son. I grabbed that baby and I ran."

Demetrius felt his body grow numb.

Abeen drew in a sharp breath and looked at her husband, her fingers over her lips.

Mustafa was staring dumbly at George's face.

Christine placed her hand on Demetrius' shoulder, not really sure of what she was hearing.

George straightened his back and looked his son full in the face. "Demetrius, you are the most wonderful son a man could ever have. Your mother and I have loved you more than God loves you." He touched his trembling lips with his fingers. His words rushed, as he wanted to finish the story before God claimed him. "My son, I stole you. You belonged to people whom I did not know." "When I die," he begged, "find those people. Find your rightful family. I have robbed you." His voice trailed away. "I have robbed you."

A chalky-faced Demetrius touched his father's hand. His voice was a whisper. "Where was this place, Pa?"

"Look through the documents at home. You will find the name of the street where your uncle lived in Jerusalem. The house where I found you was a few streets away. I know nothing more."

The room became quiet.

George Antoun closed his eyes, then quickly re-opened them. He started to speak once again. "I took you home to your mother. I told her an Arab family had perished in the same bombing that killed my own siblings. I told her that there was no one to care for you. Your mother was so happy she didn't ask questions. We raised you as our own."

There was movement behind Demetrius as Christine placed both her hands on his neck. Her hands were ice cold.

A strange thought came to Demetrius. He had to know his faith. Palestinians were either Sunni Muslim or Christian. Was he a Sunni Muslim who had been raised Christian?

Demetrius forced his voice to stay calm. "Was this a Christian neighborhood, Pa?"

With that dreaded question, George began to sob. He sobbed so hard the red circle on his bandage began to spread.

Demetrius smiled weakly. "Pa! It's all right. Don't worry. I don't care if I am Muslim or Christian."

Abeen comforted the young man. "Our God is the same."

George pulled his son to him and tried to whisper, but his voice was no longer under his control and there was no one in the room who did not hear. "Son. My son, the street I stole you from was inhabited by Jewish families."

The room was utterly silent.

Gasping, taking his last dying breath, George Antoun opened his eyes and cried out, "My son, my beloved son, you were born a Jew."

Part III

New York - Jerusalem: 1982-1983

Character Listing

Part III: New York–Jerusalem (1982-1983)

The Gale Family:
Joseph Gale *(father)*
Ester Gale *(mother)*
Michel Gale *(son)*
Jordan Gale *(daughter)*
Rachel Gale *(sister of Joseph)*

The Kleist Family:
Friedrich Kleist *(father)*
Eva Kleist *(mother)*
Christine Kleist *(daughter)*

Demetrius Antoun *(Palestinian physician)*
Anna Taylor *(American resident of Jerusalem)*
John Barrows *(British physician)*
Gilda Barrows *(wife of John Barrows)*
Tarek *(Arab porter working for Anna Taylor)*
Jihan *(Arab housemaid working for Anna Taylor)*

The deceased
Ari & Leah Jawor *(Holocaust survivors: friends of Joseph & Ester Gale)*
Helmet & Susanne Horst *(parents of Eva Horst)*
Heinrich Horst *(brother of Eva Horst)*
Karl Drexler *(former S.S. Commander of Shatila Camp)*
Miryam Gale *(daughter of Joseph & Ester Gale)*
Daniel Stein *(brother of Ester Gale)*
Jacques Gale *(brother of Joseph Gale)*
John & Margarete Taylor *(parents of Anna Taylor)*
George & Mary Antoun *(parents of Demetrius Antoun)*

Prologue: Part III

The New York Times, September 26, 1982
Article by Thomas Friedman, Times Correspondent

Beirut: U.S. Confirms the Killings

At 9 A.M. Saturday, a member of the United States Embassy staff entered Shatila, established that a massacre had taken place and informed his superiors.

Sometime between late Friday afternoon and Saturday morning, the militiamen in the camp appear to have made a concerted, but somewhat sloppy, attempt to cover at least some of their tracks.

Many buildings were bulldozed atop the bodies inside them. Some bodies were bulldozed into huge sandpiles, with arms and legs poking out in spots. In some areas the militiamen made neat piles of rubble and corrugated iron sheets to hide the corpses.

It is also possible, judging from the number of buildings that had their facades ripped off them, or huge bites taken out of them by bulldozers, that the militiamen were seeking to make many buildings uninhabitable so the surviving residents could not return...

Men, women, girls and young boys were all rounded up by the militiamen. Some 500 to 600 people, possibly even more, were then herded together and marched at gunpoint down to the main street of Shatila, where they were forced to sit along the road. Beside them were a number of corpses that had already begun to decay...

A number of men were taken off, their arms behind their heads. Some were taken behind piles of sand. Shots were heard. When the women began screaming, some of the men would be brought back to quiet them down...

According to a United Nations observer who saw more than 300 corpses discovered in Shatila so far, it was clear from the relative state of decomposition that some people had been slain as early as Thursday and others as late as Saturday morning.

Some bodies were found bloated and already decaying…

Chapter XX

Anna Taylor

Ester Gale lifted both hands above her head and proclaimed, "I am not a woman who argues with God!"

Anna Taylor sat opposite her friend at the small terrace table, smiling, listening and recalling other occasions when Ester's religious beliefs seemingly blocked the path of common sense.

"Anna, what can I do?" Ester leaned forward expectantly, her eyes focused on Anna's face.

Anna didn't waver when she said, "Don't be so dramatic, Ester. Hiring a private investigator to find your own daughter is hardly arguing with God. Jordan has been gone for over a month. You have every right to know her whereabouts."

Ester slumped back into her chair. "Jordan would be furious if she discovered she had been located by an investigator hired by her parents. She might even draw further away from us."

"I agree. That is a risk. But, can you continue as you are now, in agony?"

Lost in her own thoughts, Ester stared blankly past Anna. For nearly an hour they had been sitting at the round metal table on the flat-roofed terrace of Anna's Jerusalem home, drinking coffee and discussing Jordan. Still, nothing had been resolved.

Ester sipped her coffee, slowly, deliberately, and then returned the cup gently to the saucer. Her voice had a tinge of accusation. "You sound just like Joseph. He's determined to hire an investigator to find Jordan. I just don't approve of this crazy scheme."

"What does Michel think about hiring an investigator?"

"The same as his father. When Michel came back from Lebanon yesterday morning, Joseph and I planned to celebrate his safe return last night. Instead, the three of us spent the evening arguing about Jordan and what we should do." Ester paused and glanced at Anna with dread. "They both believe something terrible has happened to her."

Anna slowly shook her head while speaking. "On no, Ester, nothing has happened to Jordan. If that were so, the American authorities would have notified the Israeli Embassy. She just needed some time alone."

Anna adored both Michel and Jordan Gale, but she enjoyed a special relationship with Jordan…a relationship without secrets. Yet Jordan had left the country without ever mentioning her travel plans…so unlike her. The ache she felt when she first learned of Jordan's absence suddenly returned, and she hoped her voice wouldn't reveal her pain. "And where is Michel now?"

"At home packing. He says he cannot celebrate when he doesn't know if his sister is safe. Michel says if I do not agree to hire someone to find her, he will find her himself." Ester leaned forward. "Oh Anna, what should I do?"

After a short silence, Anna asked, "When is Michel leaving for New York?"

"Tomorrow evening." Ester looked skeptical. "Such wasted energy. Joseph and I have told him repeatedly we don't believe he will be able to find his sister in such a large city."

Anna's eyes brightened. She leaned over and placed her hand on Ester's arm. "Well, I do have one idea."

Ester blurted, "What? Tell me, please."

"If we do not hear from Jordan before Michel leaves tomorrow, I could arrange a discreet investigation. I have friends in New York who can be trusted in such matters. Jordan would never know."

The words caused Ester to suddenly sit up straight. "That's a wonderful idea!" Since the Gale family had arrived in Jerusalem nearly thirty-six years earlier, Anna Taylor had been a source of strength and support. Now, once again, she offered comfort when none seemed possible. Ester couldn't imagine what life in Jerusalem would have been like without the friendship of this American woman. "Would you do that?"

"Yes, I said I would, and yes, I will." Anna's voice was warmly reassuring as she re-filled Ester's cup. "The issue is settled. We'll wait one more day." She smiled mischievously. "If, by then, our little runaway does not contact us, we will begin our search!"

Ester stood abruptly. "I must go."

"No. Please, finish your coffee before you leave."

Ester blotted her lips with the white cotton napkin a final time and laughingly replied, "My husband is always telling me I should listen to your advice. He is right of course. So, I must find him right away and report that you have convinced me he was also right about what we should do." Ester's smile became wistful. "Joseph will be very pleased."

Anna stood, accepting Ester's need to leave immediately. She knew Ester wouldn't rest until the rift with Joseph had been repaired. Since the death of her own parents, Anna had never seen a couple more in love than Joseph and Ester Gale.

Anna placed her arm underneath Ester's and together the two women walked to the narrows steps leading down the side of the villa. "Please tell Michel he should not leave without stopping by for a short visit."

Ester nodded her head. "I will remind him." She paused and then added, "But Michel would never leave without seeing you." She leaned forward and kissed Anna first on one cheek and then the other. "I will telephone you later tonight."

Anna stood quietly watching as Ester crossed the cobbled street and began briskly walking toward the Gale home. Once again she recalled, as she often did following one of Ester's visits, the first time she saw Ester Gale, so many years before.

When World War II finally ended, thousands of European Jews who had managed to escape Hitler's death camps fled the continent in the hope of entering Palestine. Jews believed they would never find safety except in their own homeland...a homeland not yet recognized by the world, but promised to them in the Bible. When nervous Arab residents demanded that the British rulers of Palestine prevent the Jews from entering the country, the British responded by blockading entry into the small country by land or by sea. Still, many Jews, such as the Gales, eluded the British authorities. Leaving Cyprus at night in a small open boat, Joseph, Ester, and Rachel Gale had slipped past the British blockade.

When the Gale family finally arrived in Palestine, they were exhausted, hungry, and penniless. And although Joseph and Rachel's health was good, Ester's condition was so poor she was precariously near death.

Anna and her mother, Margarete, heard stories of the misery of the Jewish emigrants. They volunteered to nurse sick Jewish refugees, and Ester had been Anna's first patient.

When Anna first saw Ester she thought she was looking into the face of a starving, bald child. When she learned Ester was twenty-five years old, three years older than herself, she was stunned with disbelief. Suffering from severe malnutrition, Ester's entire body was hairless and covered with festering sores. Weak and dazed, she was haunted by the loss of her family and weakly called their names.

Despite the camp doctor's instruction not to waste time on refugees who seemed certain to die regardless of the care given, Anna adopted Ester as a cause. Determined to bring the Polish woman back to good health, she nursed Ester throughout long days and longer nights. Her efforts and prayers were rewarded. Slowly, imperceptibly at first, Ester regained her health and spirit. Within a few months, Ester changed from a stick-like figure who barely resembled a human being into a stunningly beautiful woman.

Anna knew her persistence had saved the Jewish woman's life. Ester knew this as well. Since those early days, the two women had been the closest of friends and the unmarried Anna was considered a member of the Gale family.

Anna turned and began slowly retracing her steps to the terrace. She returned to her chair and began to butter a piece of freshly baked bread, worrying about Jordan, hoping she was safe.

Jordan Gale had not been herself since the ghastly death of her fiancé, Stephen Grossman.

Anna sat staring at the empty chair across the table. A sudden, unpleasant idea filled her thoughts. The tragedy of others had defined her life. Yes, that was true. From the Johnstown, Pennsylvania, flood which orphaned her father, to the unremitting catastrophes visited upon the people of Palestine, tragedy had gripped the people she loved.

Unexpectedly, the memory of her mother and father filled her thoughts. Perhaps the idea of tragedy had summoned their faces, their voices, their laughter.

She returned the bread to the plate and rested her elbows on the table for a moment. A mist of perspiration had accumulated on her forehead. She wiped her face lightly with the napkin. The vision of her parents returned, flashing before her face, forcing her to recall the two most decent people she had ever known.

John and Margarete Taylor gravitated to Jerusalem after suffering terrible misfortune.

John Taylor was a ten-year-old child on May 31, 1889, the date of the disastrous Johnstown Pennsylvania flood. The child of a prosperous businessman, he and his family lived in a fashionable neighborhood of Pittsburgh, far above the man-made lake and dam wedged into the valley above Johnstown. He would have escaped the tragedy completely if his father had not been a wealthy man.

John's father, Horace Taylor, was a fisherman and avid outdoor sportsman. He and other like-minded wealthy Pittsburgh businessmen built summer cottages at the Southport Fishing and Hunting Club, which was located in the mountains North of Johnstown. The dam which created the lake used for recreation and sport at the club had been neglected. Ominous signs began to appear indicating that the dam was unreliable, but no repairs were made. No one ever considered what would happen to the small towns below the dam if there should ever be a break.

On that fateful Tuesday, Horace Taylor had an appointment to see a prominent businessman in Johnstown. Since the Taylor family was vacationing at their cottage at the Southport Fishing and Hunting Club, Horace decided to take his wife and three of his four children with him on the short trip. The child remaining at the vacation cottage was John Taylor, confined to his bed suffering from a mild flu.

The bodies of the Taylor family were never recovered, for when the dam broke, the Taylor family was somewhere in the path of a 40-foot wall of water that swept through the valley. Horace Taylor, his wife, Patricia, and their three youngest children, along with another 2,200 people, died in the Johnstown flood that day.

At the age of ten, John Taylor found himself alone in the world. His father's business manager accepted the boy into his home. John was too young to understand the implications of a man's greed, and even after reaching adulthood, he truly believed his father's business manager to be a trustworthy man quite capable of managing his father's business and thereby freeing him to complete his schooling.

But when John graduated from college he was confronted with a shocking discovery. John was penniless! Worse yet, he was heavily in debt.

The business manager swore on God's name that John's father had died leaving the Taylor business in a shambles of unpaid bills and empty warehouses. John was presented with a list of his newly discovered debts.

During this otherwise bleak period in his life, John met Margarete Frey. She and her widowed mother immigrated to America from a small village in the Eifel mountains of Germany. Destitute, they settled in Pittsburgh, having heard there were jobs there. They found work as maids, in the house of a wealthy banker.

John Taylor met Margarete Frey at a party the banker gave. Although John's debts were a great burden, he remained a young man of much promise among his father's friends and business acquaintances. He carried himself with an ease and grace of manner which one from the poorer classes can seldom learn. In the eyes of the banker, John was a likely candidate to marry his only daughter. But instead, John fell in love with the German maid!

When John proposed, he told Margarete, "I will consider myself to be the happiest man in the world if I can possess your heart, and if I cannot, I might not survive!"

John Taylor consecrated his life to Margarete Frey. He ended his social attachments to the circle of wealthy, disapproving upper-class friends of his father. Knowing that an immigrant servant girl would never be accepted into such a group, he took control of their destiny.

It was to be a magnificent love story.

Filled with religious conviction and disenchanted with America, the couple cast their lot as missionaries to the Holy Land. They booked passage aboard ship to Istanbul and from that sprawling Oriental city traveled overland through Turkey and Syria to Palestine.

The land journey became a seemingly endless ordeal. Riding donkeys across the bleak landscape, John and Margarete were forced to cling desperately to the poor animals as they searched for footing in the rocky, mountainous land of Palestine. Each day's travel brought the couple's spirits lower. Palestine appeared wild, forbidding, an almost uninhabitable land! When their paths crossed with that of a Bedouin caravan, John whispered to Margarete that, "the citizens resemble their country…as untamed as wild beasts!"

To summon the courage to continue the journey, John and Margarete frequently reminded themselves that their beloved Christ had walked these same narrow trails. The conviction that their feet were treading on the soil of an exalted land…a holy land which had been touched by heights the world had rarely known, steadied their resolve. Otherwise, they certainly would have abandoned their mission and returned straight away to America.

Happily, the sight of unforgettable Jerusalem calmed their fears and erased the pain and hardship of travel. The splendid walled city was even more beautiful than they had ever dreamed.

Jerusalem's history was one of agony and triumph, for the region was a place where religion was stronger than the state, creating an instability that brought forth a succession of conquerors.

In 1905, when John and Margarete Taylor arrived, Palestine was under Ottoman rule, as it had been since 1517. At the death of the first Sultan, a man who had ruled with a benevolent hand, the country had chaffed under harsh decrees issued from Istanbul by succeeding Sultans. The year John and Margarete made Jerusalem their home, the 400-year-rule by the Turks was on the verge of collapse. Partisan sentiments had begun to rumble under the thin veneer of Palestinian civilization.

After settling in the holiest of cities, John and Margarete devoted themselves to preaching, teaching, and nursing the poor, earning the respect of rich and poor throughout Palestine.

Over the years, Margarete bore three daughters. And, while John and Margarete spread hope and provided refuge from despair to any stranger in need, they fed their daughters' imaginations with tales of the Bible and provided their children with the warmth and peace of a happy family life. They taught their children to expect compensation in paradise, a consoling spiritual bonus which each child would carry for life.

John and Margarete's great love for each other remained intact through all tribulations, and their children never heard a hateful word pass between them.

Still, John and Margarete Taylor had their imperfections.

John's Sunday services were too long, resulting in a sleepy congregation of Arabs. Still, the assemblage of Christian Arabs admitted their own religious leaders were too argumentative to be eloquent, and until John Taylor died, they faithfully attended his Sunday services.

Margarete's strong character flouted the local tradition of secondary status for females, often dismaying the Arab males who looked askance at the boldness of the Western woman. Once, after Margarete had scolded a young Bedouin chief for forbidding his daughters an education, the chief took John aside, suggesting to the Reverend that his wife needed a firmer hand, that a beautiful woman should go unheard. John had quickly responded by stating his belief that a woman who was too obedient was simply not interesting, bringing to mind the chief's own wife, a timid woman who was too fearful to speak a single word in the presence of any man. Offended, the chief left and did not return to the Taylor home for several months.

Anna laughed aloud at the memory, her cheeks turning pink with pleasure as she recalled her father's enormous pride in his wife. Pushing back her chair, she stood and began to walk from one side of the flat-roofed terrace to the other, staring across the awe-inspiring city where she was born and had lived her entire life.

Jerusalem: a city which had touched its inhabitants with great sorrow since the first stone in the first dwelling was placed by a hopeful hand. Anna thought the man who had laid that stone beside the Gihon Spring must have imagined the surrounding hills would protect him and his family from roving marauders. Unfortunately, the land chosen lay in an exalted position and quickly became a busy market bustling with traders and caravans, creating fierce competition which repeatedly brought forth killing and unrelenting war.

Anna stopped pacing and stared, observing the beauty of the aged city. The Jerusalem before Anna's eyes was an enormous city, growing out of control, spreading in every direction. As she gazed through the thin morning light, she listened to the sounds of the city: the impatient burst of automobile horns, the howl of a lone dog, the harsh voices of men and women selling their cheap wares in the nearby bazaar. How the city had changed! When Anna was a child, few people lived outside the ancient city walls, but now the hills were burdened with stone dwellings, the immaculate, sprinkled gardens of the Jews giving way to the sand and scrub of the Arab lands. In the early days, long before the Zionist fervor of the late nineteenth century caused alarm in the Arab population, the Jews and the Arabs had lived side by side in peace, without loosening their fear and anger upon each other. But eventually, because of more and more Jewish immigration, the Arabs and the Jews began to see each other as threats until finally blood spilled onto the streets and dampened the soil of the hills. For a hundred years now, the Jews and Arabs had lashed out at one another, until their violence became familiar and felt almost necessary, as though the Jews and the Arabs were fulfilling some tremendous need in each other.

In fifty-eight years of living, Anna had survived three wars and lost more friends than she could count on her fingers. Each time peace was attempted, it always unraveled, and yet another round of mortars and exploding grenades would begin. Is there a curse on the city of God? She would ask herself. Even now, she did not know the answer to her question.

Footsteps interrupted Anna's thoughts. She turned her head to see who was coming. Tarek, the elderly Arab porter who had once served her parents, was walking toward her. "A letter just arrived from New York!" he shouted in his raspy voice.

She motioned with her fingers for Tarek to give her the letter.

A quick glance revealed that her name and address were written in Jordan Gale's distinctive handwriting. Anna grasped the letter and walked back to the table, sitting down and clearing a space on the table.

Tarek left her in privacy.

Anna smiled as she lightly touched the letter with her finger, feeling the roughness of the cheap paper, wondering what emotions the communication would unleash.

Opening the envelope with a breakfast knife, she took a deep breath as she slipped the letter from the envelope and unfolded the bulky document.

September 26, 1982

Dearest Anna:

Finally, I found the courage to flee my haunted country. Since the day of Stephen's funeral, I wavered about leaving. For me, Israel without Stephen is an Israel without life.

Anna, I would have come to say goodbye, but I feared my determination would vanish in the face of your calm voice and unique ability to apply sound judgment to what you affectionately term "purely emotional decisions."

I am glad I left the narrowness and monotony of Jerusalem. I had forgotten how wonderful it is to lose one's self in a city of millions. But New York was not my first stop. You'll be surprised to know that I took a detour to Paris and also traveled to Poland and Czechoslovakia.

For two weeks I tramped through the Polish villages and cities, seeing for myself the land that became the graveyard of my Gale and Stein ancestors. Imagine my surprise when I discovered the Poles still hate Jews! While searching for the Stein family home in Warsaw, I was actually met with hostile stares and menacing threats! One ghoulish man named Jan claimed he once worked as an errand boy for Grandfather Stein. He had the nerve to say, "it's too bad your mother escaped the gas!"

Poland is still a scary place for a Jew.

In spite of intense resistance, I discovered mother's old house. The large villa was rundown and in need of repair, but I could see that the Stein relatives had been quite wealthy before the war. The sight of the grand old home made me feel cheated, reminding me that Michel and I never had the opportunity to know the pleasure of doting grandparents.

From Poland I crossed the border into Czechoslovakia. Sadly, even with the friendly help of a large number of Prague natives, I could not find a trace of a Jawor or of a Rosner—it was as if Ari and Leah traveled to Jerusalem from nowhere!

After leaving Czechoslovakia, I came to New York. Since arriving, I have rented a brownstone apartment, been hired for a modeling job, and made two friends. As a matter of fact, I have just returned from a small party and for the first time in my life, had too much to drink. Perhaps that last drink loosened my tongue, for I feel the need to unburden my thoughts to someone, and who better than my dearest Anna? Since you are not here, I'll have to make do with this letter.

Anna, since the day I ran away from my parents, I have given a lot of thought to being Jewish, or perhaps I should say, Israeli, since we Israeli Jews completely differ from our American or European cousins. Being Israeli Jewish is a terrific problem, as you must know, since you have witnessed our upheavals from the first moment we swarmed into

Palestine, calling the land our rightful home and denying it to Palestinians. Following this train of thought, I have tried to reason why we have become what we are.

Bear with me, here goes!

To gentiles, Jews are a baffling race. Since the time of exile from Israel, over two-thousand years ago, Jews have scattered across the earth, living as unwelcome intruders wherever they might be. Discouraged from assimilating, Jews turned to each other and developed tight-knit family and community ties. Bound together as a people, Jews drew strength from anti-Semitism. In many countries, Jews were limited by law from becoming landowners. This discriminatory practice served one good purpose: Jews became professionals, developing a lasting tradition of higher learning for their children. Jews became doctors and lawyers, assuming high positions in universities and in legal systems. What the Jews never knew was that the very things they did made their situation worse. I realize now that Europeans hated Jews because Jews rose to the top of every profession they entered. Jews becoming teachers and doctors and musicians didn't please the Europeans, who liked to lock Jews in ghettos and pass laws to keep them poverty-stricken. When those laws failed to keep the Jews in their place, the Europeans killed them! Suffering pogrom after pogrom, Jews never fought their oppressors, instead, they patiently waited for the pogroms to end, telling their children that the tyranny always ended—to fight would only prolong the agony.

The Holocaust changed that way of thinking. Prior to the Holocaust, the Jews were thinkers, people of peace. After the Holocaust, these same gentle people who had preached non-violence turned into warriors, ready to fight the British Empire along with the entire Arab world if necessary, for a small strip of land to call their own.

I have asked myself a thousand times: was the Holocaust a good thing? To those six-million Jews who died, and to those who lived through it, the answer would be a definite 'no.' Still, without the Holocaust, there would be no homeland for Jews today. Jews would still be wandering the world, suffering great indignities in nation after nation. From horrific suffering came the fulfillment of God's word. Was the purpose of the Holocaust nothing more than God's grand plan to bring his children back to Israel? Certainly, without the death camps and the gas chambers, submissive European Jews would have never found the courage to fight their way back into Israel. The Holocaust paved the way for men such as my father to sire warrior sons such as Michel!

That thought brings to mind the first time mother ever saw me in military uniform. I had just graduated from high school and had been conscripted for my twenty-month's service. While father was nervous, uneasy with his rifle-carrying daughter, mother gazed at me with admiration. She squinted her eyes and looked off into the distance and I knew that mother was recalling some scene from her past which had nothing to do with the present. After thinking for a moment, she hugged me and then told me that of all things, she was most proud of her children's self-assurance.

I nodded, pretending to understand, knowing that her words had something to do with her tragic past, yet not wanting to turn her thoughts to a subject which always ended in profound sadness and depression. Even though mother and father rarely spoke of the Holocaust, I've always felt the weight of those dead relatives hanging around our necks.

Mother pointed out that Jews born in Israel acted as if they owned the space they walked around in, while many European Jews, survivors of prolonged discrimination and abuse, had a timid step about them, unsure of who they were or where they belonged. Mother said that the pogroms, the ghettos, and the Holocaust had a way of squeezing the confidence out of those Jews who managed to escape death in Europe, forever leaving them with a sense of fear. (Except for men like father, of course, men who swell with courage at the first sign of danger!)

I was caught quite off-guard by Mother's words, for while Father had always insisted that Michel and I show no fear to any person, mother has always been uneasy with the military atmosphere permeating Israel, fearing that such an environment would result in unfeel-

ing, heartless children. So for the first time ever, Mother was not put off by our warrior looks.

Anna, I was proud to wear the uniform of the Israeli military for only a short time. Then, I met a soldier named Ari Begin. (No relation to our current Prime Minister, mind you!)

Anna, I understand that everyone believes Stephen's death was the jolt that drove me to see the Arabs in a different light. Michel once complained that I should hate the Arabs who killed my lover, rather than make excuses for their murderous rages. When I told him the obvious, that Jewish injustice has reciprocal Arab injustice, my brother looked at me as though I had lost all reason. Michel Gale is not a man to let facts get in the way of his feelings.

Anyway, back to the reason I have come to want compromise with the Arabs. Stephen's death freed my once reluctant voice. But my dispute with the abuse of Jewish power began long before—the day I met Ari Begin.

I won't go into the details, but this Ari was a man imprisoned by hate. Hatred of the Arabs, of course. Ari Begin was a rather large man with a big puff of black hair that he proudly claimed stood on end at the sight of an Arab. He had an unusual claim—he kept a collection of severed Arab ears! This soldier purposely started fights with young Arab men so that in the process of fighting, he could bite off a part of their ears. Coming back from an army patrol, he would search through his pockets and then produce a bloodied ear lobe or two and gleefully pin those jagged ear parts onto a small board.

One day when I felt particularly courageous, I asked Ari why he collected Arab ears. He grinned and replied that he wanted every Arab bastard to know the fear and stigma of being a marked and hunted man, the same as Jews had been throughout history.

At that moment all I could see was a vision of cold-faced Nazis with bristling Alsatian dogs straining at their leashes, snarling at helpless Jewish women and children.

God forbid that our future is nothing more than a gang of Ari Begin's, torturing defenseless Arabs.

Anna, by producing such men, I fear we have already hardened our own souls.

I have just looked at the clock and I must be at work soon. I don't feel that I have succeeded in organizing my swirling thoughts and emotions clearly. The facts are quite simple: we Jews used to be the good guys. Now we are the bad guys.

In my opinion, our invasion of Lebanon proves we have lost our sense of right and wrong. Who can deny that Jewish egos have swelled along with Israeli borders?

Yesterday, I heard faint rumors of a massacre at the Shatila refugee camp in Beirut. Today there was a four-page article in The New York Times detailing the massacre. Anna, as I read the sickening details, all I could think was: Michel Gale is in Beirut. Michel Gale detests the Arabs.

I cannot believe that Joseph and Ester Gale were saved from one massacre only to bring forth a life that would inflict another massacre.

Anna, I was going to write mother and father, but that letter will have to wait for another day. Give them a call and let them know I am safe.

A kiss to all of you…

Yours,

Jordan

PS: Try not to fret about me. I have been working toward this moment for years. I remember you once told me that every end is followed by a beginning. I have a strong sense that New York is the start of a new beginning for Jordan Gale…

Anna's features were tightly drawn as she neatly folded and returned the letter to the envelope. Though greatly relieved to learn the girl was safe, Jordan's letter had wrenched her apart. Would Joseph and Ester's youngest child now live her life an ocean away from everyone who loved her?

Remembering Jordan Gale as an infant, Anna reminded herself

that from her first moment, Jordan had been determined to have her own way. She now asked herself: was Jordan's recent flight from Israel nothing more than a continuation of the mysterious fervor that had fueled the girl's heedless decisions throughout her life? If so, Anna feared Jordan would miserably fail in her quest for happiness.

Thinking of Jordan and recalling how the charming red-haired girl first came into their lives, Anna became lost in thought, telling herself that Jordan Gale was, in so many ways, like her father.

Anna stared thoughtfully across the balcony into the holy city, recalling Jordan Gale's biological father, the passionate and brave Ari Jawor.

Chapter XXI

New York: December, 1982

Christine Kleist pulled back and continued to stare into Demetrius Antoun's maddeningly unreadable face. Christine often thought that the more Demetrius knew, the less he told her. Still, her exasperation with him was overshadowed by her pleasure in what he had just told her. Her dark brown eyes sparkled with joy. "Darling! That's wonderful news!" A happy and unexpected gush of tears began making a path down her face. "When do you begin?"

Demetrius' eyes dropped away from Christine's stare. His reply was distracted. "Don't get so emotional, Christine. The position is low. The salary insignificant." He looked at her, smiling half-heartedly. "Don't forget, I'm nothing more than an assistant in a research laboratory."

Christine wanted Demetrius to be happy, but since those last dark days in Beirut, her lover was enveloped in gloom. In spite of the fact they were living together, she and Demetrius were as far apart as two people could be.

Christine fought back those dismal feelings and smiled broadly. She knew that a lot could go wrong with their future, but today was a good day! She had arranged the appointment at Bellevue, insisting to a reluctant Demetrius that the Bellevue Hospital Center was the best place for his medical talent. Bellevue was the oldest teaching hospital in the United States and the institution was well known for its international staff.

Demetrius shrugged and told her, almost as an afterthought, "The position opens next month, but..."

When Demetrius tried to speak, Christine refused to listen. "An assistant's position at Bellevue Hospital is only the beginning!" she interrupted. "Once you have the opportunity to display your knowledge, you'll be promoted. And, as soon as you pass your medical boards, you'll be allowed to treat patients." Her flushed face looked triumphant.

Irritation came easily to Demetrius these days. He placed his finger over Christine's lips. "Christine. Don't. Please."

Christine's cheerfulness vanished. Her expression looked remorseful and she spoke soothingly. "I'm sorry, Demetrius. I forgot." Just the day before, she had promised Demetrius that she would stop trying to control his life. Keeping that promise was proving to be difficult. Christine wanted nothing more than to organize their lives in such a way that Demetrius would be compelled to marry her. Was she pushing too hard? "It won't happen again," she said, miserable and apologetic.

Demetrius gave her a strained smile before turning away and dropping his keys into a small wicker basket on the dresser counter. His hands were shaking.

Demetrius was becoming increasingly uncomfortable with their relationship. Each day Christine found another way to hint that she expected marriage. Demetrius didn't want to hurt Christine, but marriage was the last thing on his mind. He consoled himself with the thought that never once had he misled her. Christine Kleist was a lovely, sweet woman, but he had never felt for her the intense passion that he had known with Hala Kenaan. Knowing that passionate kind of love, he would be satisfied with nothing less. Several times he had tried to explain his feelings to Christine, but she was not a woman to listen to what she didn't want to hear. Now, despite his honesty, Christine persisted in her efforts to make the relationship something it never could be.

Their eyes met in the mirror as he began to unbutton his shirt, and they stared at one another for a few seconds.

Christine's fears burned in her like an unwelcome revelation. Nothing was developing as she had hoped.

Demetrius decided that tomorrow would be a good day to tell Christine that although he loved her, he was not in love with her. Instead of gathering in intensity, their relationship had faltered, then fallen apart. He broke the uneasy silence, forcing a jocular tone to his voice. "Oh I forgot to tell you. We've been invited to a party tonight."

"A party?" Christine's face registered surprise. They didn't know anyone in New York.

"The physician who hired me, John Barrows, said he and his wife were having a small gathering with some of their neighbors. When he learned we had been in the country for only three weeks, he insisted we come."

Christine's color faded. She raised her voice, then rushed and stood in front of the mirror, staring at her own reflection. "Demetrius! Look at me!" Christine began to turn from side to side, pulling at her hair. "I can't go out like this!"

Demetrius blinked and stared for a few seconds before understanding she was worried about her appearance. Moving beside her, he turned Christine around by her shoulders and lifted her chin with his fingers. With an amused smile, he said, "What are you worried about? You'll be the best-looking woman there." Christine Kleist *was* an uncommonly pretty woman.

Christine gave a noncommittal grunt. In Shatila Camp she had had little time to concern herself with appearances. If she managed to keep her face scrubbed and her hair washed, she felt lucky. But since they had arrived in New York, Christine was acutely aware that every place they went, admiring female eyes locked onto her lover. She had become quite conscious of trying to look her best.

Demetrius leaned forward and gave her a quick kiss on her head. "Now, I'm going to have a shower." He glanced at the clock on the bedside stand. "You have plenty of time. We don't have to be there for another two hours."

Christine walked toward the small bedroom closet. "All right. I'll find something nice to wear." As she slid hangers back and forth, she began to hum, rocking forwards and backwards on the balls of her feet, trying to make a decision.

Demetrius removed his clothes, wadding them into a ball and tossing them into a wooden clothes hamper. He draped a blue towel over his shoulder and walked into the bathroom. Pulling back the shower curtains, he sat on the edge of the tub, turning the water on and adjusting the temperature. Remembering something John Barrows had told him, he raised his voice above the sound of the running water. "Hon, John Barrows said casual dress!"

Christine shouted, "Good!"

Demetrius gave a deep and noisy sigh as he stepped over the tub and into the shower. With his eyes closed, he stood quietly. He soaped his body and stood motionless for a long time, trying hard not to think. Demetrius Antoun was a wretchedly unhappy man, more now than he had ever been, in a life that had been crowded with unhappiness. Possessed by a great rage at the untimely deaths of his family, along with the image of his father's dying face and the memory of his shocking proclamation, Demetrius had ample cause for despair.

Moments after confessing that his son had been born a Jew, George Antoun stared blankly at the ceiling and then gasped twice before crying out for his wife, Mary. Shortly afterward, George died a gurgling, bloody, and painful death.

The days following his father's death were a blur of misery. With every member of his family dead and buried and his clinic destroyed, Demetrius had sought comfort from Mustafa and Abeen Bader. Whether the subtle change in their devotion was real or nothing more than Demetrius' imagination, the Bader's had seemed ill-at-ease, stilted in their affections with the man they had once claimed they loved as their own son. Their once close relationship was suddenly filled with unsaid things, and conversation no longer flowed with the ease and familiarity of refugees who were bonded by love, exile, war and death. More than once Demetrius had sensed Mustafa's accusing eyes on his back, as though overnight, Demetrius had shed his Arab skin and was suddenly a hated Jew. Though the Baders were never openly hostile and on several occasions had even advised Demetrius to forget his father's dying words, cautioning him not to confide to anyone in the camp the truth of his birth, they could not dismiss George Antoun's confession: Demetrius Antoun was a Jew. Neither could they forget that years before, during the dispute with his father, Mustafa, and Amin regarding his future, Demetrius had refused to fight their enemy, claiming he "had made a separate peace with the Jews." Those hasty words returned to haunt the young man. One late evening, when they believed Demetrius was sleeping, Demetrius had overheard Mustafa reminding Abeen of those words, asking his wife if she thought it possible for a man to be mysteriously drawn to his own blood, even without knowledge of familial connection.

Demetrius felt bitter when he recalled that the couple had shown visible relief the following morning when he informed them that he was leaving Beirut. Christine's father had obtained a visit-visa for Demetrius to travel with Christine to Germany. Demetrius had intended to take a short trip, feeling that he needed time away from the violence of Lebanon, but Demetrius would never forget that Mustafa and Abeen treated him as though he had already gone, even before he had left. He had mailed them several postcards and sent them his address in Germany and in New York, but the couple had not responded. Their silence made Demetrius understand that he could never return to the only home he had ever known.

The visit to Germany had not been an improvement. Christine's parents seemed to be a mild, inoffensive couple who fiercely loved their only child. Clearly, the Kleists wanted their daughter to have whatever would make her happy, but they appeared apprehensive and morose in the presence of her Arab suitor. Friedrich Kleist tried to make Demetrius feel more welcome by criticizing Jewish policy in Palestine; however, Christine informed Demetrius that over the years her father's Nazi guilt had festered and flourished into a great admiration for the Jewish state. With Christine's words, Demetrius knew her father was misrepresenting his true opinion of the Jews, believing an Arab would embrace any criticism of their Jewish enemies. Such deception, however well-intended, made Demetrius feel even more uneasy.

After only a week of awkward attempts at conversation, a wise Christine asked her father to pay a visit to one of his friends, a man prominent in the German government and a close friend of the American Consular in Germany. A few days later, Demetrius' passport was stamped with a coveted work-visa for the United States.

America had been a disappointment. Living in the refugee camps, reading about the appealing, democratic land of America, Demetrius had developed the idea that America was the empire of the future: the country where truth and freedom were not mere words and citizens welcomed their immigrants with affection. Now, after living for only a few weeks in the United States, he had discovered that while some citizens were warm and friendly, life in America was not as he had imagined. The American people seemed consumed by a lust for personal wealth which interfered with having close families and friendships.

Years before, when Demetrius had spoken of his fantasy of making a new life in America and forsaking the violent heritage of his own land, George Antoun had smiled faintly before saying, "Remember only one thing my son, God does not bestow all his gifts upon one man or upon one country." Demetrius had not understood at the time, but now he knew the meaning of his father's words. As there were no perfect men, there were no perfect countries.

Now, he agonized over questions which seemed unanswerable: where is my home? Where do I belong?

Intruding upon his thoughts, Christine peeked around the door, "Darling, shall I send in a rescue team?"

A startled Demetrius stood blankly for a minute. "Give me but a moment!"

Christine's voice was impossibly cheerful. "Just checking!"

Demetrius reached for the shampoo. While washing and rinsing his hair, he was struck with a vision of brown hillsides and green valleys. The picture he saw in his mind was of Palestine, the land he had briefly visited so many years before. With that haunting mirage, he understood he had received a sobering answer to his own question: Demetrius Antoun could not escape the land of his birth. Even though he had fled that place, the land he abandoned was still attached to him. As a Palestinian, he had been successful in pulling himself away from Palestine. As a Jew, he was being drawn back into the crevasse.

Suddenly, he was overwhelmed with the possibilities of a new life. He reminded himself that somewhere in the land of his birth there was a couple who had lost a son. Somehow, someday, he promised, Demetrius Antoun would find a way to be reunited with the man and woman who had given him life.

Not knowing what else to do, Demetrius prayed. "God, help me—help me go where my destiny lies."

A short time later, Demetrius and Christine left their apartment on 16th Street and took a cab to John Barrows' brownstone apartment on 22nd Street.

Even as they climbed the steps to the Barrows' home, they could hear the sounds of music combined with noisy gossiping and arguing. An exotically beautiful woman wearing a smashing red sari answered Demetrius' knock, welcoming them effusively. She identified herself as John Barrows' wife, Gilda, and instructed the couple to join the party while she continued with her hostess duties.

The apartment was decorated in the theme of India. There were wisps of diaphanous fabric draped over the furnishings, with Hindu murals hanging on the walls. Brass trays and pots were set around on the tables. Indian classical music was flowing from the stereo.

Demetrius and Christine exchanged gleeful smiles, anxious for the warmth and energy of the Barrows' party to restore them to the rhythm of life. Neither of them could remember the last time they felt joyful.

Demetrius saw John Barrows across the crowded room, who gave them a welcoming nod. The British physician was holding a fat green stone Budda in his hands and telling an outrageous story about it. A burst of laughter rounded the circle of listeners.

Demetrius took Christine's tiny hand into his larger hand, giving it a slight squeeze. "I forgot to tell you, in addition to being brilliant, John Barrows seems to be quite a character."

"I'll say," Christine agreed absently. Mesmerized by their surroundings, Christine was staring at a dark-skinned man wearing a jeweled Sikh turban and seated behind a straw basket. The man was passionately blowing a long, slim musical instrument. Christine was horrified to see an angry looking cobra snake balanced on the Persian carpet. She shivered and stared. After satisfying herself that the snake was nothing more than a rubber fake, her eyes strayed from the cobra to the faces of the Barrows' guests. Bits of conversation and laughter drifted throughout the room.

Several young men were moving about the room, handing out glasses of wine and offering snacks. Demetrius easily reached out and lifted a glass from one of the moving trays, offering the glass to Christine, "A drink?"

"Not now. Later."

Demetrius smiled and took a tiny sip. "Delicious." He gave Christine's hand another squeeze.

Christine gave Demetrius a questioning look, wondering what had happened to change his dour mood. For the first time in months, Demetrius seemed serene. What transformation had occurred during the short period Demetrius was in the shower? Christine was grappling with those thoughts when she felt a probing stare. She turned her head slightly and saw a large man standing in the corner of the room. The man's face was imperturbable, but she recognized him instantly. Christine gasped and clutched Demetrius' arm so tightly that her fingers turned white.

Demetrius peeled her fingers away from his arm. He gave her a dark, almost angry look. "Christine! Please!"

Thinking that she must be mistaken, Christine glanced toward the man's face once again and then quickly away. No, she was not mistaken. She closed her eyes and swallowed.

The man responded to her fearful reaction with a deep throated laugh which rose above the sounds of the party.

She attempted to pull Demetrius close, to tell him about the man, but at that instant John Barrows appeared. After introducing himself to Christine, John whisked Demetrius away to look at a piece of furniture he had recently purchased in Yemen, gaily telling Christine to make herself at home.

Glancing over his shoulder, Demetrius gave Christine an amused smile as he walked away with his host.

Christine wanted to follow Demetrius but she couldn't move.

The man moved quickly for someone of his size. He smiled, regarding her affectionately. His voice was smooth and cultured. "Well, hello, again."

Christine stared at him dumbly before a glint of anger came into her eyes. She burst out, almost snarling, "You!"

The man looked at her with a mocking smile. "You know, I'm glad to see that you are safe."

Christine was so surprised she could do nothing but repeat herself. "You!"

Michel Gale gave a hearty laugh. "Come," he said, steering Christine with his hand to a corner of the room.

Christine acquiesced, but not without trepidation. She looked around, desperate to find Demetrius, to tell him the unbelievable news that the Israeli soldier they had seen the day of the massacre was at the party.

Michel took a glass from a tray and thrust the drink at her. "Here." His fingers lightly brushed Christine's hand as she accepted the glass he offered. "You look like you need a drink." He looked at her in a kindly way. "Don't worry. I won't bite."

Thinking the alcohol might clear her thoughts, Christine gulped the liquid and gave a loud swallow before looking Michel full in the face. *"Who are you?"*

The man drew on his cigarette, gazing straight at her. "Let's see. My name is Michel Gale. I'm on leave from the Israeli Defense Force, visiting my dear sister in New York." He glanced at his watch and then toward the front door, "Who, I might add, is unusually late." He paused, appraising her. "And, you?"

Christine refused to tell him anything. Her voice tinged with accusation when she whispered, "Are you following us?"

Michel laughed loudly. "No. I'm not following you. When did you leave Beirut?"

Christine was speechless, struck with a sense of unreality. She stood, undecided, not knowing what she should do. They exchanged stares for several moments before she said anything. The pause allowed her to remember that the man had saved Demetrius' life. Had Demetrius been sent to the stadium as the soldier had originally ordered, Demetrius would have died along with the other Arabs taken there. Christine later learned those Arabs had been brutally murdered by their captors. "If Demetrius recognizes you, he'll kill you," she warned.

Michel's eyebrows shot up in surprise. "Oh?" Still, he didn't seemed overly concerned, and his mouth widened in a slow, sensuous smile.

"Yes. He will!" She glanced around the room, "Listen, Demetrius Antoun is not a man who concerns himself with consequences."

Michel was obviously delighted with her, and nothing Christine could say would dim his enthusiasm. He had often thought of this German girl, and with this fateful meeting, he felt that destiny was pushing them together. "Don't worry about me," he told her. "I can take care of myself."

"I'm *not* worried about you! I'm worried about Demetrius. He'll go to prison if he kills you." There was an edge to Christine's voice. "Listen to me. Everyone Demetrius loved was murdered during the massacre." Her voice lowered to a whisper. "He blames the Israelis for their deaths."

In a flash, the botched assault at Shatila passed through Michel's mind. He stared back steadily. "Oh?" he said sarcastically. "Arabs kill Arabs and the world blames the Jews!" He quickly asked, "You tell me, why should the Israeli Army take the blame for the insatiable Lebanese lust for revenge?"

Recalling the Jewish soldiers surrounding Shatila, confining and dooming the innocent Palestinians, Christine swelled with anger. "You are of the same odor!"

"I'm sorry to hear you say that," he told her, his voice tinged with annoyance. Michel didn't have a shred of remorse for the dead Palestinians. For too long, his blind hatred of the Palestinians had been harnessed to the cause of a safe Jewish homeland. Still, not wanting to end the possibility of a relationship with the German girl, he decided to be conciliatory. "I admit, the mission went terribly wrong."

Christine's face was fiery but she said nothing.

Without turning his eyes from her, Michel finished his drink, admitting to himself that the German girl had a mysterious quality that drew him strongly. Once again, he smiled. The scent of her lightly flowered perfume drifted between them. Michel involuntarily touched Christine's arm. He thought her skin felt like velvet.

With a swift nervous gesture, Christine pulled away. She opened her mouth to alert him again to the danger of an enraged Demetrius, then closed it without speaking. Michel Gale was beyond warning. Christine smiled tightly as she spoke. "When you're nursing a broken skull, don't say I didn't warn you!" With a thump, Christine put her wine glass down on a brass tray and straightened her shoulders before walking away, moving as quickly as possible through the crowded room.

As Michel stared at Christine's rigid back, warm affection radiated from his face and a small smile played at the corner of his mouth. Never had he been so attracted to any woman! Michel felt a rush of relief over his recent break-up with Dinah.

John Barrows' distinctive British accent drew Christine toward the balcony of the brownstone. Looking over and around the guests, she was relieved to see Demetrius leaning against the iron railing of the balcony, peering with interest at the British doctor who was running his hands over a wooden bench.

Desperate to tell Demetrius they had to leave the party, Christine failed to look where she was going. Colliding with a small man carrying a plate of boiled shrimp, red sauce, and warm butter, Christine was dismayed to see that her dress was badly stained, but she quickly realized she now had an excuse to take Demetrius away from the party.

Gilda Barrows immediately appeared and saw what had happened.

"Oh, no! Disaster! Christine, come with me."

Christine shook her head. "No. No. I'll get Demetrius. He can take me home."

Gilda waved dismissively. "Nonsense. You just arrived." After giving Christine a scrutinizing glance, she said, "We're about the same size. Come." Taking her hand, Gilda pulled a reluctant Christine up the stairs toward the master bedroom.

From the top of the stairs, Christine looked down and noticed a striking beauty with flowing red hair walk into the room. She was staring intently, as though she were searching for someone.

Although she looked nothing like Michel Gale, an unexplained flash of intuition told Christine that the woman was the Jewish soldier's sister.

Upon her arrival in New York, Jordan Gale had rented the apartment directly below the Barrow's, and Gilda was the first neighbor she had met. They immediately liked one another and quickly became close friends.

Jordan smiled brightly at no one in particular. While Jordan Gale was a woman who had recently denied the possibility of happiness, she quickly learned to cover her gloomy philosophy with a cheerful demeanor. While looking for her brother, Jordan worked her way through the crowded room, hugging and kissing many of John and Gilda's guests. Even though she had lived in New York for less than four months, Jordan was well known. The week she arrived in the city, while leaving the Elizabeth Arden Salon on Fifth Avenue, she had been discovered by one of New York's preeminent photographers. The man was fascinated by Jordan's distinctive beauty and teased her about her name, asking if she had been named for a country. Jordan responded by calling him a dolt for not knowing that Jordan was a common Jewish name which had nothing to do with the country of Jordan, but rather was the English form of Yarden. The man was even more drawn to a woman who had no desire to charm him, for he had become jaded—bored with women willing to do most anything for a chance at fame. The Israeli woman was a refreshing change. Anyway, the man was smitten and Jordan's career as a cover girl soared when the influential photographer pressed two leading fashion magazines to select her face for their covers.

With her lavish red hair, enormous green eyes, and flawless complexion, Jordan Gale was a beautiful woman. Her figure was too voluptuous for runway modeling. However, it would have been perfect for her social calendar, had she been so inclined.

For a short time after arriving in New York, Jordan had acquired and dropped lovers with obscene abandon, but she quickly arrived at the conclusion that every man she bedded seemed interchangeable with the man before him. Merciless with her suitors, Jordan left a line of broken-hearted men. Quickly tiring of the complications resulting from the large number of eager admirers, and after confiding to Gilda Barrows that her passion was turning into bitterness, she wickedly asked Gilda to start a rumor that Jordan had fallen hopelessly in love with a married man, a political figure in Jordan's home country of Israel. After a time, the rumor anchored, and Jordan's telephone stopped ringing.

Jordan settled back into mourning the death of Stephen, the one thing she claimed that bound her to life. Other than her closest friend in the city, Gilda Barrows, and her brother, Michel, no one in New York knew the truth of her lonely, miserable life.

An attractive girl named Clara, who was so desperate to date Michel Gale that she watched his every move, mentioned to Jordan that her brother had just stepped onto the balcony. Jordan hurried to tell Michel the reason she was late. Knowing that Michel would be gruff and irritated by her tardiness, Jordan's lips curled into a teasing smile. Jordan thought her brother was too rigid, and she loved to nettle him. She pushed her way through the crowd, passing through the sliding glass door out into the crisp December air. Michel was standing with a group of six or seven men engaged in an animated conversation, and for a short time Jordan went unnoticed.

She paused, patiently waiting for the right moment to draw her brother away from the group.

Then she saw him.

Jordan's eyes grew large as she stared at the most handsome man she had ever seen. He was tall, broad-chested, and slim, with dark brown hair that had a slight curl. She thought the stranger's handsome face was almost femininely beautiful, but he was saved from that fate by a strong, chiseled bone structure. He had wide-set eyes and sensuous lips…lips that were only partially covered by a full mustache. Completely entranced, Jordan followed the sculpted line of the stranger's jaw down to his solid square chin. Jordan clenched both her fists in suppressed excitement.

John Barrows saw her before she said anything. "Jordan! We've been waiting on you!" John threw his arms around her neck and pulled her into his circle.

Jordan peered around John's shoulder, unable to stop looking at the stranger.

A spark of curiosity crossed Demetrius' face. He thought the woman was exquisite.

After exchanging greetings with the men she knew, Jordan found herself standing directly in front of the delectable stranger, who was even taller than she'd first thought. Jordan was a tall woman, and until now, only her father could make her feel small. One glance from Demetrius' gray eyes, and Jordan was enthralled. She stared openly at the man. When introduced, she gave a small pleasant laugh, trying to muffle the tension in her voice. "So nice to meet you, Demetrius Antoun." She liked saying his name, not hinting that she knew, or cared, that the object of her attention was quite obviously an Arab.

Demetrius' dimpled smile came slowly. His voice was deep and lightly accented. "Miss Gale. My pleasure." Demetrius bowed his head, ever so slightly. Demetrius felt Jordan's presence from his head to his toe, but he gave no outward sign of his sudden and unexpected attraction.

That was not the case with Jordan, whose face was a clear confession of her feelings.

The situation quickly became awkward, and several of the men vacillated between staying and leaving. Finally they began to drift away, leaving only John and Michel with the bewitched couple.

Slowly Jordan grew calm, but she and Demetrius continued to stare at one another.

Michel narrowed his eyes, looking first at Demetrius and then at Jordan. Michel didn't like what he was seeing. Jordan was making herself too obviously available. Michel thought he might laugh at the transparent expression on her face. If Jordan were anyone but his sister, he surely would. Normally, Michel took little interest in the men his sister dated, but Demetrius Antoun was an Arab, and in Michel's mind, it was the only nationality strictly forbidden to an Israeli Jew.

Michel had purposely sought out the Palestinian, unafraid of the reaction Christine had feared. Michel wanted to find out about the girl, to see for himself if Christine and the Arab were married. He had not been surprised that the Arab showed little reaction to him when introduced. Michel knew he looked vastly different in civilian clothing and in a civilian surrounding, and that women, more so than men, tended to remember personal details. Demetrius Antoun had given him a brief questioning look, but otherwise, he had been perfectly polite.

Absorbed, Jordan and Demetrius began to talk.

Discovering that he was a Palestinian refugee, Jordan felt a surge of joy, delighted that this gorgeous man was from her own country. Unable to keep the pleasure out of her voice, she inquired, "And what part of Palestine are you from?"

Demetrius felt a sudden and wild yearning to lean over and kiss this beautiful woman passionately on the mouth. His voice became thick and strained. "My parents lived in Haifa. Until 1948."

She smiled at him, ignoring the implications of the year. "Haifa. That's my favorite city." She purposely touched his arm. "My parents live in Jerusalem." The purr of her voice was soft. "Have you been there?"

Michel began to glare. Seeing his sister flirt with an Arab brought to mind all the old hatreds which had built in his mind for years.

Keenly perceptive, John insisted that Michel give his opinion of the carved Yemeni bench which he had pushed into a corner of the balcony.

Michel refused to move, trying to think of a tactic to get his sister away from the Arab, without creating a scene. From past experience, Michel knew that Jordan could not be pushed. To do so now would be a mistake; it would accomplish nothing. His sister was a strong stubborn woman who delighted in scandalizing her family.

Clearly uncomfortable at the swirl of emotions around him, John dragged the bench from the corner, raising his voice and saying, "A little Yemeni man made this bench. He hand carved the wood with a small pocket knife." He patted the bench with his hand. "Jordan, come and have a seat."

Jordan and Demetrius smiled at each other.

Jordan stepped toward the bench, accidentally catching the heel of her shoe between an open space in the wooden flooring.

Jordan tripped.

Demetrius caught her in his arms.

Jordan's action came unbidden. Ever so lightly, she touched Demetrius' face with her hand.

At that very moment, Gilda and Christine came outside looking for John and Demetrius.

Seeing Demetrius and Jordan locked in an embrace, Christine looked as stunned as if she had been unexpectedly threatened with a flame-thrower. She rocked backward from the emotional pain.

The situation quickly deteriorated.

Overwhelmed by jealousy, Christine cried out, "Demetrius! What are you doing?" Not giving Demetrius time to respond, she turned her attention to Jordan. "And, who is this woman?"

Demetrius released Jordan from his grasp and stared at Christine.

Seeing this exceptionally pretty woman, sensing immediately she must be with Demetrius Antoun, Jordan could only hope that her face didn't show the disappointment she felt. Jordan looked up at Demetrius, who showed no emotion.

Determined to avoid an embarrassing scene, Demetrius held out his hand. He spoke softly, yet his words sounded like a command.

"Christine, I want you to meet Jordan Gale."

Even as he spoke, Demetrius had a rush of thoughts. He knew that by meeting Jordan Gale, he had arrived at a turning point in his life. Nevertheless, he was a fiercely private man and had no intention of exposing personal matters before people he barely knew. He and Christine would settle their differences in private. Then, unattached, he would approach Jordan Gale.

Only God knew what would happen as a result of the events of this night.

There was a horrid silence as Christine and Demetrius stared at one another.

Christine grew increasingly uneasy, wishing with all her heart she could take back her words.

For an instant Jordan thought the woman was being melodramatic, but then she changed her mind, telling herself that if Demetrius Antoun was her man, she might react in the same manner.

Gilda put her hand around Christine's waist. "Christine, come on. What's going on here?"

Michel fought the urge to take Christine into his arms. A strange thought flashed through his mind. He wished he were the man Christine Kleist loved to the point of uncontrolled jealousy.

Christine's breath was shallow and fitful. She was anxiously wavering between hope and fear, hope that she was wrong about what she had seen and fear that she was not. Yet, she knew she was not wrong. Christine had known Demetrius for too long to take the situation lightly. He was not a man that lied. *About anything.* And he was not a man who flirted with other women. *Everything* was serious for Demetrius. That knowledge terrified Christine, for she knew that something very important had happened in Demetrius' life during the brief time she had been away.

Four horrifying words kept running through her mind: I have lost him! I have lost him! Giving Demetrius a look of love and grief, mixed with anger and betrayal, Christine uttered a strangled cry before breaking away from Gilda's grasp and fleeing.

There was an awkward, shocked silence. Everyone was still for a long moment, looking at each other and then back at Demetrius, wondering if anyone understood what had happened.

Demetrius put down his drink on the balcony railing. He was terribly embarrassed. "I apologize. Christine is not herself." He looked regretfully at Jordan Gale before he began to walk away.

Torn between protecting his sister and going after Christine, Michel made a quick decision. Jordan was a big girl, she could take care of herself. Michel tapped Demetrius on his shoulder. "Let me go," he said. "Christine and I know each other...from another time..." His voice trailed off. "Another place..." Michel stared knowingly into Demetrius' face. "Why don't you stay here?" He then glanced at Jordan. "With my sister."

Michel was gone before Demetrius could protest.

Chapter XXII

The Lovers

Shaking with emotion, Christine fled the Barrow's brownstone apartment. She ran from the building and out into the quiet street, not knowing where to go or what to do. After telling herself that Demetrius had every right to be angry, and knowing there would be no greater agony than facing him, she reverted to a long-forgotten childhood habit: rather than face an unpleasant scene, Christine hid. Spotting a row of tall shrubs in the small park located directly in front of the row of brownstone buildings, Christine ran to take cover in those bushes. Breathing heavily, she sat on the ground with her eyes closed.

"Christine," cried a man's voice from the street.

Christine peered through the thin branches of the shrubbery and saw that the caller was Michel Gale. She held her breath.

"Christine!"

"Go away," she whispered, "*go away.*"

Christine recoiled in horror when she heard an unknown voice shout to Michel, "Are you looking for a little bitty woman with long dark hair?"

Christine's eyes followed the sound of the voice and she saw for the first time a homeless woman sitting on a park bench no more than three feet away. She gasped. Was that woman now going to tell Michel where she was hiding?

"I am. Have you seen her?"

"She crawled under them bushes right there." The woman made a gesture toward Christine's location.

Michel blinked once and then looked in Christine's direction. Perfectly composed, he began to walk toward the bushes.

Christine looked around wildly, searching for a way to escape. There was a block wall directly behind the shrubs.

"You kids have a fight?" asked the woman.

"Sort of," Michel replied dryly.

Knowing she was about to be caught in a ridiculous situation, Christine placed her fingers over her lips and whimpered, "Oh no."

Michel squatted down on the ground, facing her. His face suddenly appeared through a break in the bushes. "Hi."

Blushing, Christine fought to keep her composure. "Oh. Hello."

"Shall I join you? Or would you rather come with me?"

"Oh. I don't know." She glanced around. "It's nice here."

Michel nodded. "Looks comfortable."

"Yes." She smoothed her skirt. "It is."

Michel sat quietly for a minute before holding out his hand. "Christine," he said, "come with me."

Christine stared into his eyes, trying to make up her mind whether she should trust him.

Then he smiled. "Come on, honey. Come with me."

She took his hand.

After pulling her out from behind the bushes, Michel brushed the dirt off her dress.

Christine listened in silence when he suggested, "Let's go to your place and get your things. You can leave a note." He added, "In fact, I've been thinking about taking a trip to Florida."

A sad Christine nodded. She knew that her relationship with Demetrius was over. She stared at Michel Gale, stirred by a new emotion. Suddenly, Michel made her feel safe. "A trip to Florida sounds nice," she replied.

Michel hailed a taxicab. They said little during the ride across town, but Michel held tightly to her hand, as though he were willing her the strength she would need.

After packing her bags, Christine took one last look around the apartment. She felt like she was in a bad dream, one minute wishing Demetrius would walk through the door and stop her from leaving, and the next minute reminding herself that her relationship with Demetrius had always been one-sided. It had left her as unfulfilled as it must have left Demetrius.

"You should leave a note."

"No. Demetrius will understand," she replied with a choking sadness that broke Michel's heart.

During the first few days of her broken romance, Christine could think of nothing but Demetrius, still feeling his appeal from afar.

Michel was unbelievably patient, listening to Christine's intermittent outbursts of sorrow.

As the days passed, Christine became aware of Michel Gale's own special charm. Michel was a good-looking, well-traveled man who had a wonderful sense of humor. After Demetrius' dark nature, she began to appreciate and even enjoy Michel's lighter disposition. She was having fun for a change.

One evening, while dining at Joe's Stone Crab, one of Miami's famous landmark restaurants, Christine admitted to herself that her infatuation for Demetrius was beginning to fade, replaced by a strong attraction for Michel.

Michel seemed to sense the change. "Let's go dancing," he suggested, "slow dancing."

Lightly touching his face with her fingers, Christine replied, "No. I have a better idea. Let's go back to the hotel."

He gave her a long look and then paid the check.

Returning to the hotel, Michel was like a man who was hungry. Once in the room, standing face to face with Christine, he pulled his hands through her hair and down her neck and across her back. "God, Christine."

She began unbuttoning his shirt. "Michel."

He kissed her neck and shoulders. "I've wanted you since the first day I saw you."

She laughed softly. "I detested you."

"I adored you from the first minute." He kissed her on the lips, slowly at first, then with an urgency that caused them both to gasp for breath.

Michel gripped her shoulders and stared into her face, saying, "I love you, Christine Kleist."

"How can a Jew love a German?" she teased.

Between kisses, Michel whispered, "Christine, can you love a Jew? This Jew?"

Christine drew back and gazed up at him, looking completely lost. Finally she spoke disbelieving, "God, Michel. I can't believe it, but I think I'm falling in love with you."

Michel looked at her with intense pleasure, kissing her nose, her cheeks, her lips. He lifted her off the floor and carried her to the bed, pulling her down, kissing her again and again, reaching for her body with both hands.

Two weeks later when the time came for Michel to return to Israel, he took Christine with him, introducing her to his parents. He announced that Christine was the girl he intended to marry.

Christine was astonished to discover that her affection for Demetrius Antoun had become a dim memory, and her relationship with Michel Gale was becoming all that she had ever wanted.

April, 1983 in Jerusalem

A chill radiated across the room when Joseph Gale confirmed Christine Kleist's story. "Yes, child. I will never forget the name." His voice shook with anger as he emphasized each word, *"Colonel Karl Drexler."*

Joseph's expression turned fierce as he looked Christine squarely in the eye. "Only the dead have forgotten Colonel Drexler."

Christine leaned back in her chair, her body limp. She lowered her eyes from embarrassment and shame. A terrible sadness was reflected on her face as she whispered, "Oh, no. I hoped it wasn't true." She put her head in her hands and swayed back and forth.

Ester Gale was leaning forward. Her face was ashen and pasty and her eyes looked startled. Ester was restraining herself with a great effort. The German girl's words were past belief!

Michel slouched low in his chair. His voice was hoarse and disbelieving. "This is too weird, too weird." He looked at Christine and asked resentfully, "Christine, why didn't you tell me?"

Christine was silent. She wanted to tell Michel she had been careful not to reveal her suspicions until she was absolutely certain, but witnessing the irritable look on his face, she said nothing.

Anna Taylor watched the scene with alarm, bracing herself for a difficult evening. She glanced at Christine, feeling cross with the German visitor. Anna's mother often said that disaster came by the way of mouth, and this night was ample proof of Margarete Taylor's wisdom. The simple fact that Michel was engaged to the daughter of a Nazi was burdensome enough, but now this latest connection was just too unsettling!

Several seconds passed. Finally, Christine lifted her head and turned to Joseph and Ester. She spoke in a small, shaky voice. "I'm so sorry. Can you ever forgive me?"

Joseph's angry expression softened. Looking at the girl's stricken face, he was reminded of war's widening circle, affecting generations yet unborn. "Forgive *you*? My dear, there's nothing to forgive *you* for."

Christine felt the older man's sympathy for her circumstances. Tears of shame filled her eyes as the far-reaching deeds of the Nazis once again returned to haunt her. Looking into Joseph's handsome, kindly face, she wondered how the German citizens of her parent's generation had ever justified exterminating such a man.

Ester's shock worsened, leading to laborious breathing. The gray color, the dark rhythm of those days, the stench of death, all rushed back to her at the mere mention of the Warsaw Ghetto and the S.S. soldiers.

Joseph was observing his wife intently. He rushed to Ester's side, and placing his hands on her face asked, "Darling, are you all right?"

Ester didn't speak, but she clasped her husband's hand and then nodded that she was fine.

Anna walked to Ester's side, giving her friend a reassuring touch on the shoulder. Underneath Ester's strong exterior was the fragile core of a long-grieving mother. No one knew this better than Anna.

Joseph gave Christine a perplexed look. "Are you absolutely certain of what you are saying?"

Christine swallowed hard before responding. She knew the information she had divulged was accurate, but she now wondered if she had been wrong to tell the Gales that she was the daughter of Friedrich Kleist, a S.S. guard at the Warsaw Ghetto. Had her relationship with the Gales now been irrevocably altered by the revelation of who she was? Christine didn't want to become a source of pain to Michel, a reminder of events that had greatly wounded his parents. If that happened, would he go his own way, forgetting all they had become to each other? Christine felt bumps rise on her flesh, as though she had just read her own epitaph.

Feeling four sets of piercing eyes on her face, Christine blundered ahead, dully answering Joseph's question. "Yes, I know I am right. My father repeated the story to me many times. Earlier today, when Michel told me how his mother's family perished, I knew the details even before he spoke." She looked to Michel for confirmation.

"She's right," Michel responded, "Christine told me things I'd never heard about the Warsaw Ghetto." After a silence he said, "But I had no idea she was speaking about my own family."

Like the vast majority of Jews who escaped Hitler, Joseph and Ester had told their children little more than the basics: that their families had perished during the Holocaust. Growing up in Israel, consumed with the survival of the young country, Israeli children were too far removed from the gas chambers and the death pits to feel the full horror of European Jewry's final fate.

For the first time in his life, Michel felt a keen loss. He also felt slightly chagrined knowing that a German child born of Nazis knew more of the Holocaust than a Jewish son of survivors.

Christine gave Michel a small apologetic smile, hoping he still loved her.

Michel smiled back. Everything was all right.

Christine cleared her throat as she returned her attention to Joseph. She was sifting through her memories, making sure she had her facts straight. "As I told you, my father was a S.S. guard at the Warsaw Ghetto. He witnessed the unspeakable crimes committed against your family." Her voice lowered, "Father said he had never seen a man fight with Joseph's ferocity. He said eight S.S. guards were required to defeat you before they were able to get to your wife and child." Christine's voice choked. "He has never forgotten that horrible night!"

Friedrich Kleist's words told in his daughter's voice swept the room like a frightening avalanche.

Michel stared at his father with new insight, thinking with pride that Joseph Gale's courage equaled his kindness.

Joseph took a deep breath as he closed his eyes and placed his middle finger over his lips. Joseph forced repressed memories to the surface, reliving the most bitter night of his life…a night he had spent the last forty-years trying to forget. Buried images of German faces, looking all the same, flooded his mind.

"My father said you saved his life," Christine added. "At the end of the war. Do you remember that?"

Joseph grunted and stood upright. His memory was suddenly nudged by this girl's words, bringing to mind a certain German face. From that slight recollection, Joseph's consciousness moved at a dizzying pace. He recalled the man and his action. An individual deed which lifted that particular man above the coarser undertakings of the S.S. guards. He spoke slowly, unable to believe the amazing coincidence. "Friedrich Kleist. *That S.S. guard is your father?*"

Christine's voice rang with excitement. "Yes! Yes! You remember him?"

Joseph dropped heavily into his armchair and stared directly at

Michel. For the first time, Joseph wanted his son to know everything. His face wore a tortured expression, though his words were slow and deliberate. "Michel, this happened at the end of the war. A year or more after Daniel and I escaped the transport train to Treblinka. We had been living in the Polish forests with the partisans, fighting with them for all of that year, blowing up trains, truck transports... Your mother was still living with a Polish farming family—it was too dangerous to remove her from that place.

Then one day Daniel and I slipped into Warsaw to gather information about a convoy of weapons. While we were there, the Russian Army suddenly started beating back the Germans. Daniel and I stayed in Warsaw, knowing the end of German occupation was near. We heard the Russian cannons for days. With the Russians so close, all of Warsaw rose up in a fury against the German bastards." Joseph Gale glanced at Christine. "Uh, sorry."

Christine waved her hand. "Never mind. I understand."

"The Poles miscalculated. They thought the Russians would join our battle. Instead, the Russians abandoned the Poles." Joseph's lips tightened in anger. "Russian tanks sat on the other side of the Wisla River, not making a move." Joseph looked thoughtful for a moment. "Only after Warsaw was leveled and a quarter of a million Polish fighters and civilians perished, did the Russians enter the city."

A dim memory came to Michel. He asked, "Is that when Uncle Daniel was killed?"

Joseph frowned. In his mind, his life had always seemed an unforgivable reminder of Daniel Stein's death. His voice became flat. "Yes. That's when Daniel died. After surviving the death transports, the resistance assaults, and the Polish Uprising, a Russian soldier executed Daniel. He covered his mistake by reporting to his superior that Daniel was a German soldier disguised in civilian clothing."

The room was very quiet.

In a restrained tone, Anna said. "We all need a drink." She went into the kitchen.

Joseph continued, "The survivors of the Polish resistance tracked the fleeing German soldiers, who were making a fast retreat to their

Fatherland. I don't remember the exact details, but I did recognize your father. And I spared his life." Joseph turned his head and gazed lovingly at his wife. "I spared his life for one reason, and one reason only. Friedrich Kleist saved Ester's life." He looked back at Christine. "Your father warned Daniel. Told him that Colonel Drexler had ordered Friedrich to load the Stein family onto the next train to Treblinka." He paused before adding, "for gassing." Joseph inhaled deeply. "We had so little time to prepare. Only Ester was saved. She was sent out of the Ghetto in the garbage wagon and spent the remainder of the war living with a Polish family in the countryside." Joseph thought the unthinkable. "Without Friedrich Kleist, Ester would not be here today." He paused before looking at his son with obvious affection, adding, "nor would Michel."

While digesting the shocking information, Christine saw an image of Friedrich Kleist's face flash before her. In Christine's mind, by risking his own life to save the life of one Jew, her father was redeemed and for the first time, absolved of his Nazi past.

Just as Anna was walking from the kitchen with drinks, a strangled scream burst from Ester.

Everyone looked at her in astonishment.

Until that moment, Ester had been quiet, but Joseph's testimony had been too much to bear. Ester jumped to her feet and rushed to Christine's side, clinging to her arm.

Ester's eyes horrified Christine.

Ester's voice sounded like a primal cry. "Did your father tell you what happened to my baby?"

Christine's color turned pale as she observed Ester's suffering face.

With outstretched arms, Joseph went to his wife and held her close. "Ester, don't. Don't do this to yourself, darling."

Unleashing the silent bereavement of forty-years, Ester struggled to free herself from her husband's grasp. She threw herself on the floor at Christine's feet, her hands in Christine's lap, her words spilling out one over the other, beseeching the German girl to remember. "Miryam was just a baby...not yet three-years-old...blonde...and blue-eyed...Joseph was told our baby was sent to Germany for adoption.

The Germans abducted many fair-skinned Polish babies...did your father tell you that?"

Christine, frantic, began to tremble, casting about in her mind for some good news with which to console Ester Gale. Christine didn't know what to do, so she lied, hoping that her father could unravel the mystery of the missing child. "My father didn't say, but I'm sure he must know." Her voice trailed off. "Surely he will know...but he didn't tell me."

Ester put her head in Christine's lap and wept bitter tears. "Miryam... my baby."

Awed by the depth of his mother's pain, Michel jumped to his feet. "Mother, don't cry." He pulled at his mother's shoulders. "Mother...please..."

Anna was enraged. No part of a war on civilians was crueler than the separation of a mother from her child. Why had the German girl brought up the past? Anna no longer cared about Christine's feelings. Her lips curled cynically when she said, "Do you make a habit of reminding people of forgotten things?"

Christine's entire body was shaking.

Michel defended her. "Anna. There's no need to speak to Christine in that way. She is only trying to help."

Ester gave Anna a penetrating, almost accusing look, "Forgotten? Anna, the memory of my baby hits me like a bullet, every second...every minute..." Ester looked back at Christine. "Christine, you *must* telephone your father." She turned her head and stared at Joseph. "We will invite Christine's family for a visit." Her voice rose in excitement. "He will tell us where to search for Miryam!"

Joseph reached out and lifted his wife to her feet. "Ester. Ester. Darling, too many years have gone by."

Ester's tears flowed. She shook her head, her pleading voice barely audible, "Just to see her Joseph...to touch her...to know my baby didn't suffer...to know my baby is alive."

Joseph sighed deeply, staring regretfully into Ester's eyes. He, like his wife, wanted nothing more than to see their precious baby one more time. But Joseph knew the odds that Miryam had survived were very small. In spite of what Colonel Drexler had claimed, more than likely the man had sent Miryam and her blind cousin, David, to be gassed. But even if Miryam had been sent to Germany and adopted, thousands of German civilians died during the last year of the war. In Joseph's mind, Miryam was lost to them forever.

Ester couldn't stop. "I know what you are thinking. Miryam has a German mother…our child won't remember us… But, Joseph! Joseph! *We have to try*!"

Joseph begged his wife, "Don't build this hope, Ester. Not again."

For years after the war, Ester had written letter after letter to German authorities and various agencies assigned the task of locating blonde Jewish babies who had been shipped from occupied countries into Germany for adoption. Ester's efforts had come to nothing. There was no trace of Miryam Gale or of the blind boy, David Stein.

After twenty years of searching, Ester put away her pen. But, she had never missed a day praying for her child…praying that little Miryam had not been too frightened…praying that Miryam had found a kind home…praying that Miryam had survived the war…praying that Miryam was now a grown woman with children of her own.

Ester shouted at Christine. "Call your father! Call him!"

Overcome by the power of Ester's emotions, Christine stood up. "Michel?"

Michel looked at his watch. "What time is it in Germany?"

"Time?" Ester screamed, "What does time matter? *Wake him!"*

Christine ran to the telephone.

Michel followed.

New York City

Jordan inhaled deeply. She loved the musty smell of old books. The New York City Public Library had miles and miles of bookshelves housing millions of books. Jordan ran her fingers across a plated glass case displaying several priceless manuscripts. She had been raised to appreciate books and had once been told of the extensive library stolen from her mother's family during the Holocaust. She briefly closed her eyes and visualized the old family home in Warsaw, trying to imagine the richness of her mother's life before everything was lost.

Jordan now wondered what had happened to those books. Had Moses Stein's treasured library been destroyed in the Warsaw Uprising, or were those old books now in the possession of Nazi's descendants? If so, what a pity, she thought to herself.

After spending an enjoyable hour in the huge building, Jordan walked outside, carefully positioning herself to make certain she could easily see Demetrius when he exited one of the three main doors of the building. Demetrius had been in the library for hours.

A bit sleepy, she soon found herself yawning. Covering her mouth, she thought what a wonderful afternoon to laze around. The weather was perfect...bright sunshine, a cloudless blue sky, warm April breezes. Even the birds seemed to be singing their mating songs more resolutely today.

Jordan smiled as she watched a happy couple lounging on one of the expansive terraces. The young man and woman were locked in a passionate embrace, reminding Jordan that birds weren't the only creatures with mating on their minds.

Sighing loudly, Jordan engaged in her favorite distraction...thinking of Demetrius Antoun. From the very beginning of their sizzling love affair, Jordan recognized that Demetrius was not an ordinary man and that such a man and such a relationship seldom came more than once in a lifetime. Demetrius had the same quality of goodness and integrity which had drawn her to Stephen, but there was a delectable flavor of passion and shrouded mystery surrounding Demetrius that had been missing with her first love. Jordan had never been happier, not even in her happiest days with Stephen.

She remembered the letter in her purse, and the thought absorbed her for a short time. Just that morning she had received a communication from her parents in Jerusalem. The letter concerned Christine Kleist, Demetrius' former girlfriend, and reported news which Jordan did not want to share with Demetrius. Christine was engaged to her brother! How that would fit into Jordan's plans with Demetrius was a troubling thought. Jordan did console herself with the idea that the news was not just bad, but also good, according to how one perceived the information. Now she no longer had to concern herself with Demetrius' palpable guilt for hurting Christine.

The letter was not the only secret Jordan was keeping from Demetrius. Jordan had not yet told Demetrius that she was adopted. In the beginning of their relationship, she had simply forgotten to tell him. Jordan considered Joseph and Ester Gale her true parents. She rarely gave Ari Jawor or Leah Rosner a thought. Once she almost blurted the news out to Demetrius, but then she remembered the Arab attitude toward adoption. All the Israeli Arabs Jordan knew were suspicious of anyone who had no known blood family, believing that without full knowledge of parents and grandparents, you could not truly know or trust the child. Jordan quickly decided she would first let Demetrius come to know Joseph and Ester Gale. Later she would tell him about Ari and Leah Jawor.

Jordan seldom questioned Joseph or Ester about the long-dead couple who had given her life. Closing her eyes, Jordan leaned her head against her raised knees as she thought about what she had been told.

Ari Jawor and Leah Rosner had lost everyone to the gas chambers. They were the only survivors of two large Czechoslovakian Jewish families. They had met while on the Auschwitz death march. After the war was over, they made their way into Palestine, fought side by side, and between battles, said their marriage vows. Years passed before Leah became pregnant. In 1955, when Leah proudly announced she was expecting a baby, the couple anticipated the birth of their child with enormous happiness.

Three months before Jordan was born, Ari was killed while on a secret mission into Syria. When Ari died, Leah simply gave up, losing her taste for life. When Leah realized she might die during childbirth, she pleaded with Ester Gale—her closest friend—to raise the baby as her own. Hours after giving birth, Leah *had* died, and Jordan belonged to Joseph and Ester. The Gales had raised her as their own, and were the best parents any child could ever have.

Shrugging, Jordan forced herself to put all thoughts of her birth parents aside, reminding herself that she *had* told Demetrius every other thing about her family—the good and the bad—from the pre-war happiness of the European Gales and Steins, to the tragic deaths of an older sister and brother.

Jordan quickly recouped her blissful state of mind.

Earlier in the day, Jordan, along with several other models, had been hired to display the latest summer fashions for a local publication. Jordan had spent much of the morning cavorting between the sculptured lions and Corinthian columns of the lavishly ornate marble building. A few days before, Jordan had pleaded until Demetrius agreed to visit her at the photo-shoot. She wanted to share everything with the man she loved.

Jordan smiled again, gaining more than one appreciative glance from several young men who were sunning, reading, or just killing time during their lunch break. She took no notice, instead remembering that when Demetrius had made his appearance at the shoot, everyone reacted exactly as Jordan had silently predicted. The excited photographer had taken one glance at Demetrius' face and told Jordan he could guarantee her new lover a lucrative modeling career. The three other models on the shoot had flirted outrageously with the newcomer, insensitive to Jordan's presence and Demetrius' lack of response. Quickly bored with what he plainly considered a frivolous manner of earning a living, as well as the endless photo retakes and the numerous catcalls from passing young men to the beautiful models, Demetrius had given Jordan an apologetic grimace before taking refuge inside the library.

Demetrius was still in the building, although he had returned once during the shoot, to inform Jordan he planned to spend whatever time it took to read some compelling text on Jewish history which he had discovered. Jordan had not complained. She was thrilled

Demetrius was making an effort to learn about her Jewish heritage. She told herself his curiosity was an auspicious sign that he was as sincere about their relationship as she was.

She began to hum a haunting love melody.

A few more minutes passed, and then Demetrius came sauntering through the middle entrance of the building into the sunlight.

Waiting for Demetrius to notice her, Jordan's heart raced with excitement.

Demetrius' mind was elsewhere. He had taken the first step toward finding his Jewish family by spending time in the library researching Jerusalem neighborhoods. In his hand he held a listing of locations and streets which had been jointly occupied by Arabs and Jews during the turbulent 1940's. The documents he had found at George Antoun's Shatila home were difficult to decipher. Demetrius knew the neighborhood but not the street where his uncle had lived. He would have to keep searching.

When he saw that Jordan was watching him, a small and imprecise expression of surprise crossed his face. He had been certain Jordan had returned to her apartment. Not yet prepared to share the truth of his birth, Demetrius was uncertain what to do with the documents in his hand. He abruptly stopped and took the time to fold several sheets of paper before carefully placing them in his pants pocket.

A curious Jordan stared pointedly at the papers but didn't ask questions. She had learned that Demetrius was an extremely private man.

Demetrius' unsettled look dissipated. He smiled in greeting. "Here you are!"

When Jordan stood up, Demetrius took both her hands in one of his. "Sorry! I didn't know you were waiting!" He squeezed her hand. "Forgive me?"

Reveling in the sensations his touch created, Jordan forgot everything. Her face flushed with happiness when she gave him a dazzling smile. "I didn't mind, sweetheart. After the shoot finished, I waited inside for a while." She told him something he didn't know. "Did I tell you that I once worked as a librarian. I was only sixteen...I ran away from home and got a job in a library in Tel Aviv. It took Pops a week to find me." Jordan threw her head back and laughed.

Demetrius laughed with her. "You? A librarian?" That's what he liked about Jordan Gale. She was completely unpredictable in a zany, fun kind of way, and filled with surprises. The power of their attraction had been so overwhelming, and the ensuing relationship so fulfilling, that Demetrius felt he had known Jordan a very long time. He often reminded himself that they had met only four short months before.

Jordan's eyes swept the crowded area. "Then I came out and sat in the sun. It was nice to loll around and do nothing for a change."

"Lolling does sound nice," Demetrius teased.

Jordan pulled Demetrius close to her, rubbing her body against his in a suggestive manner. She looked directly into his eyes. "Make a wish." Her lips parted in a seductive smile.

Demetrius closed his eyes and placed his lips on Jordan's cheek, lingering for a time to breathe in her scent. His voice brimming with promise, he said, "Take me to your place and I'll show you what I wish."

Jordan rubbed his chest with her open hand before pulling his head down to the level of her lips. She lightly touched his ear with her tongue before whispering, "Wish granted."

His voice husky with desire, Demetrius confided his thoughts. "Jordan Gale, you are the most sensuous woman alive."

Jordan was impatient. "Let's go!"

Hand in hand, they ran down the steps two at a time.

"Let's take a taxi," Jordan suggested. She gave her lover a sly smile, "I can't wait."

Demetrius grinned, then looked right and left. "All right." Soon, a rather worn looking yellow taxicab came bouncing and scraping up to the curb. Jordan gave a low laugh when Demetrius told the driver, "As fast as you can… without breaking the law." With Jordan's head snuggled against his shoulder, the driver took them careening through the streets to Jordan's brownstone apartment on 22nd street.

They ran up the stairs, giggling like two children.

While unlocking the door, Jordan dropped her keys three times.

Once they were in the apartment, they struggled to remove their clothing, stopping every now and then to exchange feverish kisses.

Someone knocked at the door.

"Damn! I'll bet Gilda heard us come in," Jordan whispered. Jordan lived on the floor below the Barrows' unit, and the two women often took tea together at the end of the day.

His voice thick, Demetrius said, "Leave it." Then he grasped Jordan tightly, kissing her with a deep throated kiss that seemed to go on forever.

The persistent knocking continued.

Jordan's hands curled around his neck and then into his hair.

The door went unanswered.

Hours later, Jordan was sleeping soundly.

Demetrius approached her sleeping figure quietly before leaning over and lightly touched her lips with his lips. Jordan didn't awaken but her lips curled into a small smile. Demetrius stared at her for a minute, then pulled the coverlet under her chin and left the room, climbing down the spiral staircase to the sitting room on the lower level of Jordan's apartment. Through the cracks between the curtains, Demetrius saw it was still dark. He began to search for Jordan's cigarettes. Since meeting Jordan, Demetrius had begun to smoke. He looked around in the dining room and on the kitchen counters, finally spotting the edge of the cigarette packet sticking out from underneath Jordan's crumpled blouse on the floor.

Soundlessly, he slipped on his pants, and with cigarettes and lighter in hand, he walked out on the balcony. Leaning against the railing, he lit a cigarette. Demetrius closed his eyes and inhaled deeply, holding the smoke in his lungs until it started to burn. He exhaled, then looked unseeing toward the large apartment building that faced Jordan's brownstone.

The night had an uneasy stillness which matched his mood. Demetrius had known for some time that he was deeply in love with Jordan Gale. And with this relationship, he knew he had finally come into adulthood: loving Jordan for her kindly, generous nature, bright mind, and keen wit, yet aware that this bewitching girl could be unpleasantly self-centered and stubborn and on more than one occasion, deliberately rude to people she did not like. Knowing all this, he still loved her.

Demetrius had an important decision facing him, and he knew he had to make that decision alone, without the tantalizing presence of the woman he loved. More than anything in the world, Demetrius wanted to ask Jordan to marry him. Yet before he took that step, he had to look into himself, to make certain his intense desire to know his past had not propelled him into the relationship. Demetrius had guilt enough about Christine. He did not wish to hurt Jordan, too.

And, if he wed her, could he hold her? There had never been a good time to confess the truth: that the Arab man Jordan loved was really a Jew. How would Jordan react when she learned Demetrius was not who she thought he was?

Demetrius cursed silently, wishing he did not know the truth of his birth. How would he ever reconcile the Arab life he had lived with the Jewish life he now had to learn to live?

The oppressive weight of that secret weighed heavily on their relationship. He had to tell her the truth, for even now, Jordan often mentioned that she was affected by his changing moods—moods she must know came from the unspoken circumstances of his life.

If he told her he was really two men inside the same body, an Arab and a Jew, would she ever believe him again?

Demetrius was suddenly struck with the absurdity of his situation. He began to laugh. He laughed so hard he thought he might wake Jordan's neighbors. He bent over and muffled his mouth with his hands, making the laughter sound like sobs.

Jordan stepped onto the balcony. "Demetrius? Are you all right?" she asked, alarmed.

His emotions churning, Demetrius bunched his eyebrows together and stared at Jordan, smiling and frowning at the same time. His unexpected words offered proof that common sense is blind when confronted by passion. Calming himself, Demetrius blurted the question he had wanted to ask for weeks. He didn't dare give himself another minute to think, shocking himself as much as he surprised Jordan. "Darling. I was just wondering, will you marry me?"

Jordan stared at Demetrius, speechless.

Demetrius was scarcely breathing, waiting for her answer.

Jordan was strangely paralyzed. She had daydreamed about this moment since the very beginning of their relationship. A million thoughts raced through her mind: if she married Demetrius Antoun, her family would be torn apart. Jordan knew a man like Michel, who was loath to unite with the Arabs in friendship, would never accept an Arab for a brother-in-law. Still, Jordan refused to forfeit the future she desired because of Michel. Her brother would have to adjust. But, nationalities and family difficulties aside, she and Demetrius were completely opposite in every way. She was emotional...Demetrius was analytical...she was open...Demetrius was secretive...she enjoyed large parties...Demetrius like quiet evenings with a few friends...she relished telling and playing jokes...Demetrius was too serious a man to recognize a joke when he heard one... Still, in spite of these differences, each of them drew strength from the other, and Jordan knew that Demetrius loved her with the same desperate intensity with which she loved him.

Jordan looked into his waiting face, knowing that regardless of every solid argument against the relationship, she simply couldn't live without him. An inner voice nudged her, telling Jordan that for all their distinctive differences, their marriage would be happy.

Demetrius sounded worried. "Well... Will you marry me, or not?"

Jordan's smoldering green eyes told Demetrius her answer even before she spoke. "Of course I'll marry you, darling." She tilted her head to one side and smiled wickedly. "Actually, I was going to ask you to marry me if you had waited much longer."

Demetrius remembered to extinguish his cigarette on the balcony railing. He held out his arms. "Come here."

Jordan went to him, and they held each other very tight.

Demetrius picked her up in his arms and carried her into the bedroom.

While making love, Demetrius lifted her face in his hands and whispered, "My wife?"

"Yes, my darling, yes!"

Chapter XXIII

Visit to Jerusalem

After the 1967 War, when the Israeli government assumed the role of occupier, political differences dividing the country became more visible. Although Menachem Begin's Likud Party Government took an uncompromising stand on the question of a Greater Israel, refusing to return occupied territories, many Israeli citizens became uncomfortable with their government as conqueror and denounced the Likud Party as being extreme. The unpopular 1982 invasion of Lebanon added to the political divisions within Israel. After the massacre in Shatila and Sabra refugee camps, hundreds of Israeli citizens marched through the streets of Jerusalem to demonstrate their opposition to the government's actions.

Responding to public pressure, Prime Minister Begin formed the Kahan Commission to investigate the massacre in Beirut. The Commission concluded that the Begin Government should have anticipated the possibility of violence when the assassinated Bashir Gemayel's Phalangist troops were allowed into the Palestinian camps. The Commission recommended the Minister of Defense, Ariel Sharon, be removed from office. In the face of such harsh criticism, Begin grew increasingly hostile, declaring he was being persecuted.

Begin's opponents claimed the Prime Minister had a "Holocaust Complex" and predicted Begin's fanatical hatred of Arabs would lead their country into ruin.

This was the mood of Israelis when the former S.S. Warsaw Ghetto Guard, Friedrich Kleist, and his wife, Eva, arrived in Israel on June 6, 1983. Later that same day, Jordan Gale and her Arab fiancé, Demetrius Antoun, arrived in the country to inform Jordan's family of their engagement.

Friedrich Kleist

Friedrich and Eva Kleist were now regretting their decision to save funds by traveling from Frankfurt to London in order to travel to Israel. The British Airways flight from Heathrow Airport in London to the Ben Gurion airport in Lod, Israel was filled with American tourists. The tourists were seated near Friedrich and Eva Kleist. The typical sounds of suppressed laughter and animated conversation bubbled from the excited vacationers, but one woman in particular had a loud grating, cackle of a laugh, and she had kept up a steady stream of laughter since the plane left Heathrow Airport.

Every time the woman laughed, Friedrich grew more irritated. He made an impatient move with his head and told his wife, "This really is intolerable!" His words were drowned in the general uproar.

Eva gave an exaggerated sigh. Friedrich was not himself.

In truth, Friedrich had been thrown into utter confusion the moment his daughter telephoned with the shocking news she was in the home of the Jewish couple whose memory had haunted Friedrich for the past forty years. The call had come over five weeks earlier, but to Friedrich the news felt as fresh as a raw wound.

Eva looked at her husband in silence. Eva had discouraged the trip, but once she understood that Friedrich was determined to face the Jewish couple and would go to Jerusalem alone if necessary, she had packed her bags. Now she was worried about her husband, believing it entirely possible for Friedrich to suffer a nervous collapse. Everything about Friedrich's behavior suggested immense agitation. He was taking sudden deep breaths. He was shifting nervously in his seat. When he wasn't flipping through the pages of one magazine after another, he was looking at the group of Americans with impatient defiance.

Eva patted Friedrich's hand. "Calm yourself."

Friedrich looked at his wife with grim intensity. He took two or three deep breaths and gave his wife an awkward sort of wry smile. "Sorry." Still, there was something anxious about his expression.

A calm face concealing desperate thoughts, Eva said to herself. "Friedrich, you don't have to do this," she told him disapprovingly.

Friedrich hunched up his shoulders, looking at her with piercing eyes. "Oh, Eva, but I do…I do…"

Eva nodded. The time for talk was past, she told herself. Nothing had been completely right with Friedrich since 1945, the year he returned from Poland.

When Friedrich left his seat to go to the lavatory, Eva leaned her forehead against the window pane and stared gloomily into the clouds below, looking without seeing, remembering the last time she had known complete happiness. Scenes from the past appeared in her mind, sharp and clear. The youthful face of a pretty girl arose dreamlike from the depths of her memory.

In 1940, Eva Horst was nineteen-years-old. Like many Berliners, the Horsts were a musical family who reveled in the cultural richness of their city. Susanne Horst played the piano and Helmet Horst was an enthusiastic violinist. While a young Eva took lessons on both instruments, she was more comfortable with the violin, and soon put all her energies into matching her father's expertise. Eva's younger brother, Heinrich, preferred the trumpet.

In April, 1940, when Eva received confirmation from Wilhelm Furtwangler that she had been hired to play violin for The Berlin Philharmonic, a proud Helmet took the family on a special outing to a popular café on *Unter den Linden.* Friedrich had not yet enlisted in the S.S., and he joined his fiancée and her family in the celebration.

Looking forward to a bright future with the Philharmonic, and flushed with anticipation over her upcoming marriage, Eva anticipated a golden time awaiting her.

How could she have guessed the devastation that loomed?

In the beginning, everything seemed so right...the Nazis appeared to have Germany's best interests in mind. After their humiliating surrender in 1918, Germany's economy collapsed and inflation raged, making most Germans destitute. Once Hitler was elected, their lives began to improve. Hitler gave Germans jobs...public works...respect for Germany. Their pride in being German returned.

During the summer of 1939, the Nazi propaganda machine succeeded in convincing Germans that Poles were committing atrocities against Germans living in Danzig. Germans truly believed Polish citizens were torching German homes and killing innocent Germans. In the face of such outrages, Germany mobilized. What else could be done? When Germans protected Germans by attacking Poland, England and France came into the war, interfering in an internal matter the Nazis claimed had nothing to do the British and the French.

In December of 1941, Eva and Friedrich married. After a short honeymoon in the Hotel Adlon, Berlin's most exclusive hotel, Friedrich was sent to the Eastern Front as a guard in the Warsaw Ghetto.

From that time on, their lives went downhill.

In response to the air war over London, the British had begun retaliatory air raids over Berlin, but in the beginning they were unable to inflict serious damage. The German government cleverly disguised the great city, building dummy towns around the city edges and covering buildings with painted netting which portrayed those buildings as open parks. Until 1943, the bombings were little more than inconveniences, but that situation changed abruptly when British planes were re-equipped with larger engines, making them capable of carrying larger bombs. Berlin reeled from the 1943 attacks which threatened to destroy the city.

Eva was fortunate to play for the Berlin Philharmonic, since musicians in the great orchestra were exempted from any kind of military or state service. While her parents and brother cleared rubble, Eva played the violin. The Nazis knew Berliners would endure most inconveniences but would rebel at giving up their cultural activities.

Eva rarely saw Friedrich during the war. During brief furloughs he would appear unannounced at their apartment in Berlin. Once, when a troubled Friedrich confided to Eva what was happening to the Jews, Eva didn't believe it was true. How could it be true? Germans were a civilized people! Friedrich was mistaken! The Jews were being used as workers, nothing more! After Friedrich returned to Poland, rumors continued to circulate about the "final solution" for Jews, but Eva remained unconvinced.

In 1945, fifteen-year-old Heinrich, and fifty-year-old Helmet were summoned for full military service. Eva first realized their world was collapsing when Helmet and Heinrich, along with other young boys and old men, marched through the streets past somber citizens and out of the city to protect Germany's Eastern front from the advancing Russian Army. The memory of that day still caused Eva's eyes to brim with emotion. The sight of a young Heinrich carrying his bright yellow leather school case packed with extra underwear and food supplies, a case which the year before had held his schoolbooks, was a pathetic picture forever etched in Eva's memory.

The dreadful end to twelve years of what had begun as glorious Nazi rule came quickly. Berlin lay in a rubble of ruins with 80,000 Berliners dead. In the last battle for Berlin 30,000 civilians were killed. Susanne Horst was one of the 30,000. Heinrich and Helmet Horst never returned from the Eastern Front. Years later, Eva learned from a former prisoner of the Russians that her father and brother had been taken to Siberia Russia. Both Helmet and Heinrich Horst perished after years of being brutally worked in Russian coal mines.

Alone, living in a hole in the ground that once was the Horst basement, Eva was captured by the victorious Russian soldiers and brutally raped...time and again. Although hers was only one of thousands of similar horrible experiences, the memory of her shame and suffering would be with her forever.

After weeks of searching the destroyed city, an emaciated Friedrich finally found Eva. Friedrich had long ago discarded his uniform and Eva had difficulty reconciling the stranger in the dirty and torn civilian clothes with the image of the smartly uniformed S.S. soldier she had married. The man who returned from Poland was greatly changed from the man she had wed. Friedrich was no longer a proud German. Instead, he was bitterly ashamed of his German heritage. Eva and Friedrich quickly grew at odds over their differing opinions of German war guilt. Unlike Friedrich, Eva believed the war had not been entirely Germany's fault. Like other Germans who refused to admit the truth, she blamed the Allies for Germany's current problems, conveniently forgetting why Germany had been attacked and destroyed.

Even after the ghastly truth of the death camps was revealed, Eva made excuses for the Germans. How could they have known the truth? German news was nothing but Nazi propaganda. From the very beginning of the war, citizens were forbidden by sentence of death to listen to outside news sources. The Horst family were "good Germans" and they obeyed the Nazi laws. Those who did listen never told others for fear of being reported to the authorities. What could the individual German do? One person against the entire system? How could they have stopped the killing of Jews, even if they had known? As far as Friedrich, he was in the military. A military man must follow orders. How could he be a German soldier and not obey?

Eva Kleist dulled her mind to the past. Like most German women, she tried to forget the war and instead, carried on with the business of life. With so many men dead, Germany had to be saved by its female population. Eva's strength overpowered Friedrich and he became quiet and subdued. During one of their frequent arguments, Eva once accused him of being already dead.

After Christine's birth, Eva and Friedrich's thoughts were centered on protecting their child. Chaffing under the increasingly harsh rule of their Russian conquerors, they made a successful escape into West Berlin just two months before the construction of the Berlin Wall in 1961.

The years since had not been easy. Friedrich was eventually able to find employment but only with the assistance of his former S.S. associates. In the American sector of Berlin, former members of the S.S. had risen to high administrative positions in the local government. Friedrich was rewarded with a good job in the city government of West Berlin.

Although Eva had struggled to raise Christine to take pride in her German birthright, to understand that other nationalities had always been jealous of German organization and abilities, the girl was more like her father than her mother. Wanting to understand the complications in her parents' relationship, and the secrets they kept from her, Christine had sought out the truth of their Nazi past, then turned against everything German. The girl had fled to a foreign land, taking up the cause of a swarthy race of people Eva could never understand. First she became romantically involved with an Arab, and now they had learned Christine was engaged to marry a Jew! Was there no longer a way to reach their only child?

Eva made a clicking sound with her tongue. They should have had more children. She accepted the blame for that mistake. After being raped, she cringed at the thought of being touched by any man, even by Friedrich. Friedrich had been understanding, too understanding. Their sex life had sputtered and finally died completely with Friedrich claiming he would rather forgo his pleasure if it left his wife in tears. Eva had never given her feelings away, never told Friedrich that she needed him to continue to try and reach her…that healing would come in time…if he had only tried. Friedrich never knew her feelings and so they grew further and further apart. After the birth of Christine, she and Friedrich had lived together as chastely as brother and sister, with nothing between them but the love of their daughter.

The airline stewardess startled Eva when she tapped her on the shoulder. "The Captain is preparing to land. Please fasten your seat belt."

Friedrich's features were tightly drawn. Seeing his wife's worried look, he made a surprising remark. "Eva, once this is past, you and I must try to renew our lives."

Eva stiffened, then smiled as a pleasant thought came to her. Perhaps with this journey Friedrich might overcome the mysterious sorrow that had fueled their differences throughout the past forty years. After this ordeal ended, would they finally find peace? Eva smiled again at her husband. If only that were so...

Friedrich leaned over and gave her a brief and wholly unexpected kiss on the cheek as the wheels of the plane touched the runway.

The bright glow in Demetrius Antoun's eyes faded when Jordan whispered, "Wait until Michel learns his niece or nephew is going to be half-Arab!" She chuckled with glee.

Demetrius looked apprehensively at the woman he loved, never knowing what to expect from Jordan.

Three weeks before, Demetrius had been unprepared, even startled, when Jordan discovered she was pregnant. Except for one careless lapse, they had been careful to use birth control.

After thinking about their predicament for a few hours, Jordan told her fiancé how joyful she was. They were in love...their plans were to marry, anyway. The pregnancy did nothing more than push forward the date of their wedding.

Demetrius was less pleased, for two reasons. His financial situation was troubling. Although John Barrows had been understanding and volunteered to hold Demetrius' position at Bellevue Hospital in New York until he returned, Demetrius keenly felt that Jordan's camaraderie with Gilda Barrows was the reason for John's decision. Demetrius recoiled at the thought of receiving special treatment because of friendship, but Jordan was brazen, willing to use any and all contacts to get what she wanted. The second reason for his displeasure was his Arab background. Although he wanted nothing more than to have children with Jordan, Demetrius' conservative Arab views still influenced him...pregnancy should come after marriage.

Nevertheless, God had decided for him. They would marry as quickly as possible.

Deciding she must tell her parents about her pregnancy in person, and marry Demetrius in Israel, Jordan had insisted Demetrius accompany her to Jerusalem. Obtaining a visa had been surprisingly easy. Jordan's best friend from her school days was in charge of issuing visit visas at the Israeli Embassy in Washington. Although disapproving of Jordan's fiancé, the woman had relented to Jordan's pleas. She hoped the reality of marrying an Arab would come to Jordan once she returned to a country that frowned on such involvements.

Events moved so quickly Demetrius had difficulty believing he was jetting across the Atlantic on his way to Palestine. Although he told himself that he was setting out toward new uncertainties, this trip would be vastly unlike his past visit with Ahmed Fayez and other PLO fighters. Demetrius would now be a legitimate visitor to the lost land of his father, Mustafa Bader, and Amin Darwish.

While Jordan appeared unconcerned by the possible reaction of her family to her upcoming marriage to an Arab, Demetrius was uneasy. Also, he had a second concern. He had not found the courage to tell Jordan he had been born a Jew, and now he wondered if he had waited too long...if the secret should now go with him to the grave. And Christine... During the taxi ride to the airport Jordan disclosed the shocking information that Christine and Michel Gale were engaged. Christine was in Jerusalem with the Gale family! Had Christine disclosed the confidences she knew about his life? That terrible possibility caused Demetrius' stomach to churn. In an effort to get his mind on other matters, Demetrius forced himself to open a book. But with numerous thoughts of his past and future swirling through his mind, Demetrius could comprehend nothing of the words he read.

In the beginning stages of her pregnancy, Jordan felt sleepy. In spite of her rising excitement over the turn her life had taken, she placed her head on Demetrius' shoulder and slept most of the ten-hour flight from New York to Paris.

In Paris, Demetrius' Palestinian documents created a lengthy delay as he underwent a thorough security check by suspicious El Al agents, employees of the Israeli airline. Finally, after an hour of questioning and a full body search from three agents, Demetrius was allowed to board the El Al plane.

Jordan was incensed. Surely the agents could see that Demetrius was nothing more than what he professed to be, an Arab man traveling with his Jewish fiancée. Or perhaps that was the real problem! The agents had looked positively enraged when Jordan verified she was going to marry an Arab. Demetrius had said nothing to the agent's objections and cruel remarks, but for a tense moment his eyes had narrowed. Demetrius Antoun was the proudest man Jordan had ever known. She knew he would not accept the belittlement Israeli Jews in positions of authority often inflicted on Arabs. But most importantly, Jordan wanted nothing to happen that would cause Demetrius to rethink his decision to marry a Jew.

She stared into his face, but as usual, Demetrius' expression was unreadable, and Jordan had no idea of his true feelings. Without thinking, she embraced and kissed him, not caring what anyone thought.

Receiving disapproving looks from all directions, Jordan glared haughtily at everyone as they boarded the plane.

The hours passed like minutes. After landing at the Ben-Gurion Airport and enduring a second interrogation concerning Demetrius' business in the country, Jordan arranged for a private taxi to take them the thirty-mile distance from Lod to Jerusalem.

Unexpectedly happy to be back in Israel, an excited Jordan chatted amicably, pointing out various biblical sites to her lover.

Although he tried to appear interested, Demetrius was in a bit of a daze. This thought kept running through his mind: that after thirty-five years of exile, Demetrius Antoun had finally come home.

Ester Gale looked intently and searchingly at Friedrich Kleist, trying to place this particular man in the sea of stern Nazi faces she recalled from that dreadful night in the Stein's Warsaw apartment so long ago. Nothing of Friedrich Kleist was familiar, though she was struck by his size. In Ester's memory, the S.S. troops who had guarded Jews were as big as giants. In spite of his sturdy build, the German man in her parlor was only slightly above medium height. His gray hair was thin, his cheeks hollow and his chin rounded. Ester tried hard not to reveal her amazement that the former S.S. guard was astonishingly average in appearance, although she admitted to herself that Friedrich Kleist's face was pleasant and sensitive looking.

Joseph Gale remained motionless, deep in thought as he scrutinized the German. Age had altered the man's appearance, but there was something vaguely recognizable about Christine's father. After a full five minutes, Joseph decided Friedrich Kleist was the man he said he was. Joseph cloaked his feelings of bitter anger with a welcoming smile. He held out his hand courteously to his former enemy, reminding himself that by saving Ester, Friedrich Kleist had saved them all.

Friedrich's face was distraught and his hands fluttered. At first glance, he recognized Joseph Gale. Here was the French Jew Friedrich remembered so well! Friedrich hesitantly stepped forward and grasped Joseph's hand, holding on as though he feared he might fall.

Standing slightly behind and to the side of her husband, Eva Kleist looked at the Gale Jews with a special curiosity. Admittedly, through no fault of their own, these people had altered her own life in an unpleasant way. She wanted to be friendly but her smile was forced.

With his arm wrapped around Christine's waist, Michel glanced anxiously at his mother. Despite the spots of pink on her cheeks, Ester looked frightfully pale. Michel knew his mother's emotions were at a peak and she was struggling not to blurt out the only question that really mattered. Where is baby Miryam?

Christine's eyes filled with tears. Her father's wish had finally come true. After this meeting, perhaps Friedrich Kleist could find the peace he had sought for so long.

With Friedrich still clinging to Joseph's hand, the two men stared at each other.

Ester's eyes were locked onto the former S.S. guard.

Eva shifted uncomfortably.

No one spoke.

A woman's voice came from another room, offering them an escape from the awkward silence. "Joseph, we'll only be a moment!"

Joseph explained to their guests, "My sister, Rachel, and our friend, Anna, are preparing refreshments."

"Yes. You must be exhausted. Come and sit." Ester's voice had a catch but she maintained her composure as she pointed out the most comfortable of the easy chairs.

Christine sat close to her father. "We went into Jaffa for a bite to eat," she said to Joseph and Ester.

"Oh dear," Ester said reproachfully. "Rachel and Anna have been cooking for most of the day."

"We only had a snack," Michel quickly assured his mother.

Michel and Christine had met the Kleist couple at the airport alone, agreeing that it was best for their respective parents to meet privately in the Gale home. Who could guess what emotions the meeting might arouse? While waiting for Christine's parents to clear Israeli customs, they had decided that a quick stop might refresh Friedrich and Eva, who were certain to be exhausted after their journey from Germany through England to Israel. The ancient port city of Jaffa was only ten miles from the airport and they had detoured there to take Friedrich and Eva to one of Christine's favorite restaurants, the Aladin in Old Jaffa.

Within minutes of arriving at Jaffa, they knew they had made a mistake. While Eva Kleist feigned an interest in the quaint beauty of the small domed building which had been a bathhouse during the days of Roman rule in Palestine, Friedrich had sat like a stone, barely sampling the food ordered by his daughter. Although he was pleased to see his only child and made several gestures of affection toward her, Friedrich made it clear that his main business was with Joseph and Ester Gale.

After a short and strained conversation, Michel suggested they leave the restaurant and start the drive to Jerusalem. Once in the automobile, the Kleists had stared silently out the car windows, barely responding to Michel's and Christine's feeble attempts at conversation. After the first few miles, the foursome made the trip in silence.

Now that he was in the presence of the Gales, Friedrich had forgotten everything he'd planned to say. He stared down at his lap.

"Jaffa is a lovely city," Ester said, trying to put the man at ease.

Eva agreed. "Yes. Christine told me the town was settled before Noah's flood and was named after one of Noah's sons." She paused. "It's difficult to imagine that such biblical tales were true."

Everyone nodded.

A cranky voice came from the kitchen. "Anna, I *told* you not to add so much sugar!"

Joseph looked uneasily toward the doorway. With each passing year, his sister became more testy. He wished Rachel had not come at this time, but when she heard about the Kleists' visit, she had insisted on making the trip from the Degania Alef Kibbutz. The only four people Rachel genuinely loved were Joseph, Ester, Michel, and Jordan Gale, and any opportunity Rachel saw to interfere in their lives, she took.

Rachel had not lived in Joseph's house since 1948. A family tragedy had occurred that fateful year, resulting in a bitter argument between Joseph and his sister. Rachel had moved out in a huff and settled at Degania Alef, the first of all Kibbutzim, which was located on the shores of the Sea of Galilee. For three years Rachel did not see her brother and his family, but after she apologized for her harsh words, she once again participated in family gatherings. In their youth, Michel and Jordan spent summers with Rachel, who was in charge of the Kibbutz accounting office.

Rachel had never had a suitor. Unfortunately for everyone who knew her, Rachel Gale had not settled comfortably into the role of old maid.

A bustling Rachel came out of the kitchen. She was balancing a tray loaded with glasses of freshly squeezed lemonade. Rachel had changed little since the day she had arrived in Palestine. She was still squat and plain.

Anna Taylor followed her, bringing a tray of freshly baked cookies.

Both women wore scowls on their faces. Rachel had never liked Anna, feeling that the American woman had usurped Rachel's position in her own family. Most importantly, she blamed Anna for the 1948 family tragedy which had brought about the estrangement between sister and brother. But the source of that argument was a topic forbidden by Joseph, and so Rachel could never say exactly what was on her mind. Still, Rachel never missed the chance to pick a quarrel with the American woman; like a sore that couldn't be left alone.

Their stiff backs and rigid faces were clear signals the two women had been arguing.

Michel tried unsuccessfully to suppress a grin. Since childhood, he had witnessed their constant squabbling.

After serving the Gale guests, Anna and Rachel sat on opposite sides of the room.

Joseph leaned forward, still looking at Friedrich. Without saying a word, his expression demanded an account from the German.

Nibbling on one of the cookies, Friedrich built up his courage. After placing his glass of lemonade on a small table, he cleared his throat and looked at Joseph. His voice sounded low and hoarse, but as he spoke his tone gathered in strength and intensity. "When Christine called to say she had found you, I was so relieved. I have thought of your family many times." He nodded at Ester. "I was comforted to hear you were reunited with your wife although I was told she suffered terribly." He grimaced.

The hard intensity of Joseph's look wavered slightly. "Yes. Ester's survival is a miracle. I don't know if Christine told you, but after you warned Daniel Stein that the family was going to be deported to Treblinka, my wife was hidden by a Polish farmer. For nearly three years Ester spent her days in an underground shelter, going out only at night. Unfortunately, only four days before the Germans retreated from Poland, the Gestapo received a tip that the farmer was hiding Jews. Gestapo agents tortured the man's wife until the farmer revealed the hiding place of the Jews. Then the agents raked the shelter with machine gun fire. Of the nine Jews in hiding, only Ester survived."

Joseph glanced at his wife. "Ester was left unconscious from her wounds. The Gestapo left her for dead." His eyes half-shut, Joseph added, "The farmer, his wife, and their three sons were then executed, leaving Ester alone, wounded and without food except for a bag of rotten potatoes." A look of affection mingled with remembered fear crossed Joseph's features as he gazed at his wife. "When I found Ester, she was nearly dead. I don't know how she held on, but she did." Joseph shook his head in an effort to shake off the image of Ester's condition the day he pulled her limp figure from the crudely dug shelter. "If I had come a day later, I would have lost her." He paused before explaining, "The moment the Germans left the city, I went searching for that farmhouse. My brother-in-law was a shrewd man, or I would have never known where to look." Joseph gazed thoughtfully at his hands. "The night Daniel struck the deal, before we gave the farmer his payment in diamonds and before we took Ester out of the ghetto, Daniel forced the man to draw a map showing the location of his small farm. The farmer was uncomfortable with anyone knowing the location of his home, but Daniel was insistent." Joseph looked away. "Daniel and I memorized that document, then burned it, knowing that if either of us were ever captured with the map in our possession that Ester would be doomed." Joseph's face looked drawn. "Ester left the ghetto in a garbage wagon. The wagon driver was bribed to slow down at a pre-arranged location." He paused. "Of course, everyone else in the Stein family perished. When Daniel and I returned from the rendezvous with the farmer, the Stein apartment had been emptied. Everyone had been taken." Joseph made a twirling motion with the index finger of his right hand, indicating the loved ones who had gone up as smoke from the chimneys of Treblinka. "The following week, when Daniel and I were put on a transport, we managed to escape from the train."

Friedrich's eyes were red-rimmed. "I suffer terrible nightmares about the Stein family." He gave his wife a quick look. "I've told Eva many times that the spirits of those unlived lives visit me every night."

Not wanting anyone to think that Friedrich was begging forgiveness, Eva bristled. "I've told Friedrich that every single person who lived during that dark time has nightmares." She waved one hand in the air. "It's only natural."

Everyone in the room looked at Eva with startled expressions.

Christine was plainly embarrassed, wondering to herself why her mother wanted to diminish Jewish suffering. She was relieved and grateful that the Gales were too polite to rebuke her mother. She smiled at Joseph Gale.

Michel glanced at his mother, worried about how the troubling conversation might be affecting her, but he quickly saw that nothing existed for Ester Gale but Friedrich Kleist.

Friedrich cleared his throat. "I came to tell you that I regret deeply what happened that night in the ghetto." Tears came to his eyes as he said very quietly, but with an air of utmost fervor, "I am not seeking forgiveness. The sins committed against your family are unforgivable. You have every right to hate all Germans..." He faltered slightly. "I only wanted to say that I am sorry for the unspeakable crimes Germans committed against you, and against all Jews." Friedrich felt that the task of explaining the inconceivable acts perpetrated by ordinary Germans was impossible, and he added in a sinking voice, "I know now that the crime of silence was the beginning of Germany's downfall."

Joseph's expression was mournful, yet his gaze remained penetrating. Was Friedrich Kleist here for himself, or for them? He decided not to make the man's confession easy. Joseph did not respond.

Friedrich silently held out a shaking hand and pointed to three trunks sitting by the front entrance. "I am returning something that belongs to you."

Ester inhaled loudly as she stared at the trunks. Thinking only of Miryam, she asked herself, was the German returning her baby's bones and ashes?

Joseph was thunderstruck. "What do you have that belongs to us?" he asked loudly.

Friedrich stood and walked toward the largest of the trunks. As everyone gaped in amazement, he opened the trunk and began to pile books into stacks on the floor.

Perplexed, Rachel looked at her brother. *"Books?"*

Astonished, Joseph didn't answer. He hadn't a clue about the German's purpose.

"After Colonel Drexler sent me for your library," Friedrich explained, "he had all the books transported to his home in Berlin. After the war ended, I searched for his wife..." He looked knowingly into Joseph's face. "I told Mrs. Drexler that her husband had perished in the battle for Warsaw, and that a shell fell directly on him, killing him instantly."

A flash of appreciation crossed Joseph's face. Joseph had never confided to anyone that he had beaten the S.S. officer to death. Not even to Ester. Some things were best left unsaid.

"Anyway, while at the Drexler home, I recognized a stack of boxes. I knew the boxes well, for I had done the packing. I told the Colonel's wife what was in the boxes and questioned her on what she planned to do with the books. She saw that I wanted those books. As a reward for notifying her of the circumstances of the Colonel's death, she gave the books to me." He lovingly ran his hands over one of the books. "Anyway, I kept the collection in good condition, hoping that one day I'd have the opportunity to return them to the owner." For the first time since entering the Gale household, Friedrich looked almost happy. "I brought a selection of books with me." He looked around the room, undeniable pride on his face. I wanted to show you that I had taken good care of your library. When Eva and I return home, we will send the remainder of the collection to you.

Joseph and Michel quickly gathered around the books, kneeling to the floor and examining pieces of the lost library of Moses Stein.

Joseph looked at his son. "Michel, these are your grandfather's books."

Michel was very pensive. He picked the books up, one by one, reading the titles aloud. "*The Decameron...Charlemagne...Montaigne...Rollin's Ancient History...The Republic...Rousseau's Confessions...*" Michel opened the pages of

Rousseau's Confessions and read, "To my beautiful and brilliant daughter, Ester." Michel seemed to choke on his next words. "Your loving father, Moses Stein. April 2, 1937."

Ester looked on, sad and silent.

Friedrich didn't utter another word, but he was unable to pull himself away from the books. He had waited so long for this moment and now he felt as proud as if he had restored the Gale's lost heritage.

But Friedrich's satisfaction was not long lived.

Ester's burning eyes stared at him. Unable to control herself any longer, Ester vehemently cried out, "I *must* know about my baby!"

Friedrich flinched in surprise.

Ester stood up, and was staring with fixed, almost frightened eyes.

Joseph seized his wife by the shoulders. "Ester…in good time…sit down, darling."

Before the German couple had arrived, Ester had promised Joseph she would let him approach the topic of Miryam. She had been unable to keep that promise.

Ester was watching every movement of Friedrich's face, trying to guess the news she would soon hear.

Joseph coaxed Ester to sit down before turning to Friedrich. "Do you have any information on our child? Colonel Drexler said she was deported to Germany…for adoption. Perhaps you remember where she was sent in Germany…a city…an area perhaps?"

Friedrich raised his eyes toward heaven, crossed himself, and uttered a silent prayer. His face became completely transformed as an overpowering inner loathing came over him. He grew terribly pale and his lips trembled.

By Friedrich's actions, Joseph grasped the truth. His voice flat, he stated what he suddenly knew. "Miryam is dead."

Friedrich made the slightest movement of his head, acknowledging Joseph was correct.

Ester moaned. "No."

Joseph's eyes were heavy and sad. He quietly asked, "How? When?"

An agonizing vision passed through Friedrich's mind. The unbearable memories, accompanied by a feeling of deep shame, caused Friedrich to begin weeping.

Everyone stared, unable to speak.

Friedrich cried convulsively and gasped for breath.

Christine ran to him. "Poppa…"

Friedrich shook his head, no. He had a tormenting need to tell the Gales everything, but he knew the truth would be equivalent to the event …cruel…horrible…unspeakable. He brushed his daughter aside, his tone of voice pleading. "Don't ask me that question. Please…just take comfort from the fact your child is free from suffering."

Joseph's eyes glittered and a frenzied look of pain contorted his face. His tone of voice became more urgent. "You will have to tell us. Nothing is worse than not knowing. We must know how our precious child died."

When Friedrich didn't respond, Joseph pleaded, "For God's sake man, have pity!"

Christine's eyes met Friedrich's own. "Poppa…you must."

Friedrich tried to regain control of his emotions. He wiped his face and blew his nose before muttering, almost as to himself, hardly realizing what he was saying, "All right. I'll tell you. After we left the apartment that night, I tried to comfort the babies as best as I could. But after leaving you, the two children cried themselves to sleep." Friedrich addressed himself directly to Joseph Gale. "I never harmed those children. I want you to know that."

"I believe you," Joseph answered. "Now, go on."

"No one harmed them, at first… The following morning Moses Stein came to Pawiak Prison. He turned himself in and announced we must return the children to his family." Friedrich slowly shook his head. "That old man truly believed the children would be released. I tried to reason with the Colonel to let the babies go, but no… The Colonel hated Moses Stein…he said something like the old Jew had lived a life of luxury, and had stolen everything he had from Aryan victims."

Friedrich looked at Joseph, anxious for a sign that he had revealed enough.

"Go on." Joseph told him.

Friedrich sighed. "Anyway, along with your babies, Colonel Drexler had at least four or five other Jewish children imprisoned. Children who were scheduled for extermination." His words became rushed. "Colonel Drexler was insane. I always thought so. After that day, I had no doubt." Friedrich wiped his glistening brow with a trembling hand, looking at Joseph for confirmation.

Joseph agreed but encouraged him to continue. "Yes. I know. Totally insane. Along with many other Germans. But, go on."

"He ordered us to bring all the children into a room next to Moses Stein. The two rooms were divided by a glass window." Friedrich looked down, clearly choking on words he did not wish to speak. "Colonel Drexler went into a killing frenzy…he turned the most vicious dogs on the children…" Friedrich reluctantly glanced at Ester. "Your father was forced to watch as the dogs…"

A terrible scream broke from Ester Gale. In her primal scream, every human tone was gone. Her scream seemed to have no end, and the ones listening were filled with absolute horror at the unbearable pain behind it.

Joseph tried to hold his wife in his arms.

Anna and Rachel rushed to Ester's side.

Michel was frozen in despair at his mother's grief.

The front door burst open. Jordan Gale came running into the room. Demetrius Antoun followed.

Jordan pushed everyone aside, struggling to reach her mother. *"Mother! What's happening? Mother!"*

Ester continued to scream, and she waved her arms about.

Jordan shook her. *"Mother! It's Jordan!"*

When she regained her senses enough to recognize Jordan, drops of saliva flew from Ester's mouth as she shouted, "Daughter! Daughter! Miryam is dead…Miryam is dead…" Ester sobbed inconsolably, the pain of her loss as acute as on the day Miryam was taken.

Joseph gathered his wife in his arms and carried her into their bedroom.

Jordan grabbed Demetrius by the hand and they followed Joseph, shutting the door behind them.

Every person remaining in the room was reduced to tears.

Friedrich's entire body was jerking from his convulsive sobs. Holding his face in his hands, Friedrich seemed to strangle on his word. "Since that day, I have hated being German!"

Eva wiped the tears from her eyes. The image was horrible. Still, feeling the need for German suffering to be recognized, she spoke a second time. "We Germans suffered, too."

Hearing those words, a hostile Rachel Gale examined Eva Kleist from head to toe, too shocked for a short moment to reply. This German woman was carrying German suffering too far!

Feeling she had become the center of attention, the focus of Jewish resentment, Eva tried to explain. "I lost my entire family…our home was destroyed…our cities lay in ruins…and…"

"Don't compare!" Rachel interrupted in an angry voice. *"You can't compare!"*

Michel signaled to his aunt to be quiet.

"Don't tell me what I can say, Michel!" Rachel shouted at her nephew as she recalled her own grief…grief she had kept bottled inside for years. She glared at Eva Kleist. "You want to know about suffering? I'll tell you about suffering! Of our family, only Joseph and I survived. We lost our mother …father…two brothers… Our parents were gassed at Auschwitz! Michel? Only God knows how Michel died. We *never* found a trace of that gentle man. And, Jacques! Only God in heaven can forgive you for what your people did to Jacques!" Rachel's words began to spill out, one over the other. "My brother was a resistance hero, the bravest man I've ever known. Do you know what the Gestapo did to my beautiful, brave brother?" Rachel was actually screaming, the veins in her neck distended. "Jacques' cell-mate survived. He told us the nightmare my brother lived. The Gestapo tortured Jacques for weeks…ripped out his nails…burned his body…but, *my brother told them nothing*! When Jacques revealed nothing, they decided perhaps he was innocent, and they promised him life." Rachel's voice lowered. "Oh! How my brother wanted to live. Wanted to live to see his brother, Joseph...wanted to celebrate the defeat of evil... They promised Jacques he would live!" she shouted. "They kept him imprisoned for years...then they shot him the day they fled France...made Jacques dig his own grave...taunting him as he dug...then shot him in the head. *Don't you dare tell me about German suffering!"*

Eva stood to her feet, her voice tired and weary yet tinged with irritation. "Friedrich, let's go. I told you what would come from your kindness."

But Friedrich Kleist was firm. "No. Eva, these people need to say these things." He paused briefly. "And also, I need to hear them." He looked kindly at Rachel. "Whatever you wish to say, you certainly have the right."

Looking into Friedrich's contrite face, seeing that her hated enemy had punished himself more than any court or tribunal could dictate, Rachel felt years of bitter anger evaporate all at once, giving way to crushing sorrow. She dropped to the floor, mumbling and sobbing. "If only Jacques had lived. Only Jacques..."

Anna knelt beside her old enemy. Cradling Rachel's head in her lap, she cried, "Oh Rachel, I'm so sorry...so sorry."

"Only Jacques..."

Tears flowed down Anna's cheeks, glistening, then falling away.

Chapter XXIV
The Mystery of Baby Daniel

Demetrius sat quietly at the table on Anna Taylor's rooftop balcony. As he waited for his hostess to join him for morning coffee, the shocking events of the previous evening filled his mind. Even in the calm light of a new day, Demetrius still could not believe they had arrived in Jerusalem at such an inopportune moment.

Demetrius knew few details of the terrible calamity which had visited the now sorrow-stricken Gale home. He had been told nothing more than that Christine's father had finally resolved the mystery of Joseph and Ester Gale's missing child, Miryam, from the days of World War II, and that the information had been unspeakably ghastly.

Moments after they'd reached the Gale residence, Jordan summoned their family physician, who arrived within minutes, bringing a strong sedative for a hysterical Ester Gale. After Ester fell into a deep sleep, Jordan and Demetrius left her side, leaving Joseph alone with his wife.

Stepping into the living room, they confronted further bedlam which had developed during the time they had been cloistered with Jordan's mother. Rachel was weeping and calling out for her dead brother, Jacques. Anna Taylor was fanning Rachel with the pages of an open magazine. Christine was sitting on the floor cradling her sobbing father, while Michel circled them. Eva Kleist was nowhere to be seen.

Once the physician saw Rachel and Friedrich's condition, he decided to sedate them too. Michel carried Rachel into his bedroom, while Demetrius lifted Friedrich and followed Jordan into her bedroom. With Christine clinging to her father's hand, Demetrius placed the former S.S. guard on Jordan's bed. Once satisfied that none of the three patients were any longer in danger, Demetrius and Jordan joined Anna, Michel and Christine in the sitting room.

Demetrius found himself facing Christine, and the former lovers exchanged one short glance of confusion and dread. Michel and Jordan observed this glance uneasily, but Demetrius and Christine quickly resumed their awkward manner with each other—silent as strangers.

Each of the five people in the room wanted to escape the painful emotions that lay hidden in their hearts, and so with all three bedrooms in the Gale residence occupied, there had been a flurry of questions and suggestions relating to sleeping arrangements.

After the doctor examined each of his patients, he informed a worried Christine that Friedrich Kleist would sleep for the next twelve hours. Christine expressed a desire to return to the hotel where her parents were registered, telling Michel that she must see about her mother, who had fled the Gale home with suppressed anger smoldering in her eyes.

Michel nodded in agreement, and without speaking to Jordan and Demetrius, or even confirming their presence, he took Christine's hand and led her from the house.

"Michel, are you going to sleep in the street?" Jordan called out.

Michel begrudgingly paused at the doorway, then turned. "Don't concern your-self with my whereabouts, Jordan," Michel said coldly, slamming the door as he left.

"Jerk!" Jordan shouted at the closed door.

Demetrius didn't know what to say. He was visibly uncomfortable with Jordan's outburst with her brother. An Arab would just as soon renounce God than attack a family member. And Arab families did not resort to name calling, regardless of the circumstances.

Anna glared at Jordan. "Stop it! You're acting like a child!"

Jordan wasn't offended in the slightest. "Well, he is a jerk," she insisted, grinning mischievously at Anna.

Demetrius believed that Jordan should stay with her mother. "I can stay at the hotel, also," he offered. "Tell me where it is located."

"No! I won't have it!" Jordan exclaimed. "Your first night in Jerusalem? We must think of something else!" Jordan was worried that Christine might try to slip into Demetrius' hotel room hoping to rekindle their love affair. Knowing little of Michel and Christine's relationship, Jordan assumed the German girl was still in love with Demetrius.

"Demetrius, you will stay in my home," Anna said. "I have plenty of space."

Demetrius reluctantly agreed when he saw that Jordan was more comfortable with that arrangement. He looked at Jordan with a hint of dismay. Could she possibly still be jealous of Christine? Even though they were expecting a child and planning their wedding? Unwilling to argue with Jordan about where he would sleep, Demetrius lightly shrugged his shoulders and concluded that no man would ever understand the mind of a woman.

"I will sleep on a spare cot at mother's side," Jordan announced, pacified.

After kissing Jordan good night and gathering his belongings, Demetrius accompanied Anna to her home.

Not understanding the intricacies of Jordan's relationship with the Arab man, Anna said little during the fifteen-minute walk to her villa. She knew nothing more than what Michel had told her, that Jordan had taken her rebellion against everything Jewish to an irrational extreme by becoming involved with a Palestinian Arab. In Michel's opinion, Jordan's affair with the Arab was nothing more than a way of rebelling against her family. Anna had to bite her lip to restrain herself from asking Michel if his engagement to the daughter of a Nazi held some similar meaning.

Anna took a deep satisfying breath, congratulating herself for not having married. And for not having children. As much as she loved Michel and Jordan there were times they exasperated her beyond belief!

What a night! They had all been surprised by Jordan's and Demetrius' unexpected appearance. The only good thing about the terrible evening was that the pandemonium had kept Michel and Jordan from engaging in one of their all-consuming verbal battles. Anna had never known siblings who disagreed on as many subjects as Michel and Jordan did, yet she knew their love for each other was genuine. One thing Anna did not doubt was that Michel and Jordan's meeting would have been painfully unpleasant had Jordan and Demetrius arrived at any other time.

Glancing sideways at Demetrius, Anna saw he was in deep thought. They continued to walk in silence.

After showing her guest his quarters, Anna retired, thinking to herself that the morning would be a better time to become acquainted with Demetrius Antoun.

Demetrius did not immediately go to bed. Instead, he opened the room's French doors and stepped onto a small balcony adjoining the guest suite. The balcony was unlit, and Demetrius turned in surprise when he heard the chirp of a bird. He squinted his eyes and peered into the dark. A bright yellow songbird was sitting motionless in a small cage. Watching the tiny creature with sympathetic interest, Demetrius was suddenly engulfed by a long-forgotten memory.

From the time he learned to speak, a young Demetrius had pleaded with his parents for a pet. For his sixth birthday, his father proudly presented him with a yellow songbird. A laughing Demetrius tried to hug the cage. "I'll name this bird Melody," he announced, "she's sure to sing!"

Weeks later, the bird had not produced a single note. Melody was a cheerless creature. She sat forlornly in her cage hour after hour, watching the blue sky with tiny eyes seemingly filled with longing. Even after Demetrius plied Melody with seeds coated in honey, the dejected bird sat silent.

A perplexed Demetrius asked his Grandpa Mitri a question he had been pondering for days. "Grandpa, why do you think Melody is sad?"

"Who knows the mind of a bird?" Grandpa replied.

Demetrius bent down on one knee and stared intently at Melody. "Is she sad because she is trapped in a cage?"

Grandpa stared at the bird for a long time before replying. "Maybe, Demetrius. Birds are meant to fly."

"Should I set her free, Grandpa?"

Grandpa carefully scrutinized his grandson. "If you set her free, you won't have a pet. Don't forget, it took you three years to convince your Pa to buy this yellow bird."

"Yes. I know." Demetrius pushed his finger through the cage and tried to touch Melody. The bird turned its back. Sighing, Demetrius opened the cage door. "Fly, Melody, fly away," he said softly.

When the confused bird simply sat and stared, Grandpa pointed to a small stick laying on the ground. "She needs encouragement."

Demetrius picked up the stick and gently prodded the tiny bird, pushing Melody from her cage. Melody flew, landing on the roof of the neighbor's house. She gave an excited chirp.

Hearing the bird's voice for the first time, Demetrius laughed with delight.

"You were right to set her free," Grandpa told him.

Immediately sorry that he no longer had a pet, Demetrius craved reassurance. "Did I really, Grandpa?"

Grandpa didn't answer for a moment. When he finally spoke, he did so hesitantly and looked troubled. His words were confusing to his young grandson. "Demetrius, your own Grandpa is living in a cage."

"You're not in a cage, Grandpa!" Demetrius protested.

Grandpa Mitri paused before explaining in a somber tone. "Living in Lebanon might mean freedom to some, boy, but to a man exiled from his home, any place is as confining as a cage."

Demetrius was silent.

After taking the time to light his pipe, Grandpa spoke again. "Remember one thing, Demetrius, never believe you can improve upon nature. None of God's creatures should be caged."

The bird on the balcony chirped once again and the distant memory faded. The thought of Melody rankled Demetrius' conscience. Without giving himself a moment to think, his decision clouded by passion, Demetrius opened the cage door. His heart gave a heave as he whispered softly, "Fly, little bird, fly." The caged bird immediately flew from the cage. While watching the excited bird leaping from limb to limb in a nearby tree, Demetrius whispered, "That was for you, Grandpa." A happy gleam crossed Demetrius' face.

Demetrius smoked a cigarette before returning to his room and preparing for bed. Before going to sleep he remembered that he was nothing more than an exhausted survivor. He was without the family who had loved and raised him, but he quickly reminded himself that he had escaped the caged life of exile so bitterly endured by thousands of fellow Palestinian refugees. Not only had he escaped, but some unnamed force had opened a door for the return of the prodigal son. Tomorrow he would begin the search for his true parents.

Demetrius slipped contentedly into a sound and untroubled sleep.

The chatter of Anna's maids and the smell of fresh bread woke him early the following morning. While he was showering, a note was placed by his bedside, requesting him to join Anna Taylor at eight o'clock on the balcony for coffee and rolls. Reading the note, Demetrius was struck to the heart. In his youth, Mary Antoun had made a habit of leaving bedside notes for her son, reminding him of one thing or another. Not wishing to dwell on thoughts of his loving mother, Demetrius rubbed the expensive paper with his fingertips and wondered about the Taylor woman. Jordan's friend seemed like a refined lady. And she certainly had a feel for true decorum. He hurried to get dressed.

Although no one was in sight, the table was already set when Demetrius walked onto the balcony. After sitting alone for what seemed a long time, Demetrius peered at his watch. The time was exactly eight o'clock. At that moment, he heard the crunch of quiet footsteps on the terrace. He followed the sound with his eyes. Demetrius quickly stood when he saw Anna briskly walking toward him.

"Demetrius," Anna said. "Good morning."

Demetrius nodded his head. "And good morning to you, Miss Taylor." Demetrius pulled back a chair for Anna to sit beside him.

Taking her first good look at the young man, Anna smiled brightly. "I hope I haven't kept you." During last evening's traumatic events, Anna had barely noticed Demetrius Antoun.

Demetrius leaned toward her, carefully pushing her chair toward the table. "No, do not worry," he replied. "I have been enjoying the magnificent view." He waved his hand in the direction of the city before looking closely into Anna's face. He hoped he had not inconvenienced the woman with his unexpected presence.

Anna saw his look of kindly concern.

"Did you sleep well?" Demetrius inquired.

"Hardly," Anna replied. The dark circles underneath her eyes magnified the previous night's misfortune. She smiled at Demetrius once again. Anna quickly decided she liked the looks of Jordan's latest boyfriend. Demetrius had a gentle aura about him, a charming quality glaringly absent in Israel's toughened youngsters. "Coffee is on the way," she said.

"Wonderful," Demetrius remarked, sitting down. A quiet man with people he did not know, he said nothing more and instead stared into the city of Jerusalem.

Anna was relieved. There was nothing which annoyed her more than idle chatter. Anna gazed penetratingly at Demetrius' features, thinking to herself Jordan's young man was unbelievably handsome. Anna had always said that the two Gale men were the most attractive men she had ever known, but she had to admit that Demetrius was even more handsome than Joseph or Michel. She could easily understand Jordan's physical attraction to Demetrius, despite the fact he was an Arab.

Unlike her Jewish neighbors and friends who were struggling to secure Israel, Anna had no prejudice against Arabs. She had grown up with Arab playmates and throughout her entire life the Taylor home had been filled with Arab servants. Although she had never stated her feelings, and her closest friends were Jews, Anna generally felt more comfortable with Arabs than she did with Jews. Her own father had often stated that Arab adults were, in many ways, like children. The Arabs Anna had known were of a benevolent nature and would rather drink tea and gossip than organize armies and fight. Anna felt that this characteristic explained why, in military matters, the Jews always seemed to prevail over the Arabs in Palestine. Zionist Jews from war-torn Europe had a hard edge about them and were willing to build their future on the annihilation of another people. Palestinian Arabs were soft and not so purposeful as their Jewish neighbors.

Anna wondered about Demetrius. She recalled a bit of information shared by Michel. Demetrius' family had been part of the tragic Palestinian Arab exodus which occurred during the 1948 war. After so many years of exile in Lebanon, had he grown bitter? And, if so, how would he ever overcome that bitterness to form a union with a Jew?

Demetrius was very pensive, almost abstracted, as he looked past Anna's face and toward the various sights of Jerusalem. He felt irrevocably drawn to the shimmering city and sensed that Jordan's world was now his world. Demetrius finally spoke, his voice wistful, "I never dreamed Jerusalem would be this beautiful."

Anna threw a quick glance toward the city and was about to reply when they were interrupted by the appearance of Tarek and Jihan. Tarek was carrying a large pot of coffee and Jihan followed with a tray loaded with freshly baked pastries and breakfast rolls.

"Ah! Tarek and Jihan! Finally!" Anna spoke gaily, clearing a small space in the center of the round table.

With a curious detachment Demetrius watched the couple. Both were walking with slow caution. Step by step, Jihan was following Tarek like a shadow. When Demetrius looked into Jihan's eyes he flinched, but quickly recovered. The woman's eyes were colored milky brown and Demetrius knew without asking that Jihan was blind. He stood to assist her.

"Don't!" Anna said, clearly offended.

Demetrius immediately sat down. He flushed crimson. "I am sorry."

Anna patted his hand, her way of telling him not to worry.

After greeting Anna, Tarek looked at Demetrius with undisguised interest. Then he placed the coffee pot on the table and left.

As skillfully as any sighted person, Jihan began to pour coffee into the two small cups. Demetrius watched closely. Not a drop was spilled.

Anna turned to Demetrius. "Other than the two days of the week when she goes to visit friends in Bethlehem, Jihan always serves me." Anna didn't add that the ritual was a great source of pride to the blind woman.

Then something odd and unexpected occurred. As Jihan walked past Demetrius, she paled and stopped. She made an inaudible sound in the back of her throat.

Demetrius and Anna exchanged puzzled glances before turning in surprise to look at Jihan.

"Jihan? Are you unwell?" Anna asked, perturbed.

Demetrius felt uneasy. Jihan's unseeing eyes were fixed steadily on his face. She laughed a strange little laugh and began to move her feet in a circle. For a moment he thought the woman was going to dance.

"Jihan! What on earth?" Anna called out in a high voice. "Tarek! Come quickly!"

Tarek arrived so rapidly that Demetrius realized the man must have been sitting concealed behind the stairs.

By this time Jihan was rubbing her hands together and laughing loudly, still staring in Demetrius' direction. Just as she started to lunge with outstretched hands toward Demetrius, Tarek grabbed her from behind and the two began to struggle.

With Anna shouting instructions for Tarek to give Jihan a sedative and put her to bed, Tarek forcefully pulled the blind woman away. Jihan began to speak breathlessly and incoherently to Tarek. Neither Demetrius nor Anna could understand a word she was saying.

Anna stood with her mouth open, shaking her head. "What on earth?"

Demetrius believed that Jihan must be insane, and he was relieved the woman had not become violent. "What a strange woman," Demetrius finally said.

Anna continued to shake her head, baffled. "I must confess I have no idea what was going on."

Demetrius tried to shake his feeling of uneasiness. "How long has she been blind?" he asked. Perhaps, he thought, Jihan's blindness was recent, and possibly her depression over the condition was leading to a nervous collapse.

His question struck Anna forcibly. She fell back into her chair and then looked at Demetrius with so much remorse that Demetrius regretted asking the question.

Anna bowed her head. "No. When Jihan came to live with our family, she had her sight. That was many years ago."

"What happened?"

Anna didn't speak for such a long time that Demetrius thought she was not going to answer him. When she finally spoke, her voice was very low, as though she was speaking to herself. "I'm afraid I have to accept the blame for Jihan's blindness." Anna trembled, remembering the disaster of years past. "I was only a child at the time, and I unwittingly played a role in the dark impulses which brought about Jihan's blindness."

Demetrius was unable to suppress a strange and queasy curiosity. "Whatever do you mean?"

Anna scanned his face eagerly but said nothing. Her entire body was tingling. For a reason she could not define, Anna felt compelled to tell the young man the horrifying story, yet she knew she should restrain herself. Only four people knew the truth of Jihan's blindness, and those four people were Jihan, Anna, and Joseph and Ester Gale.

Demetrius waited silently, his heart full of vague forebodings. After the past evening, he had little desire to learn of other sorrows, yet he sensed Anna's need to confide a powerful memory.

An instinctive feeling overtook Anna. She clutched at Demetrius' hands. "I don't know why, but I feel strongly that I must tell you Jihan's story."

Demetrius did not reply, but he nodded. People always seemed to seek his confidence. Perhaps the reason lay somewhere in his medical training, which had taught him to highly value every individual. He sighed and sat back in his chair, listening carefully.

Anna looked steadily and intently at Demetrius as she spoke. As she summoned up past memories, the expression on Anna's face became almost childlike. Her voice became light, as though she were speaking of happy, carefree times, rather than of a terrible tragedy that had darkened many lives.

"I remember the day as if it were yesterday! I had just turned eleven-years-old and was playing in the back courtyard. After hearing shouts and screams I ran to the front of the house and saw a young Bedouin girl clinging to my mother's skirts. I stood transfixed by the sight of the young girl dressed in the colorful garments. She had long black hair and olive skin, and to be honest, I thought she had arrived straight from the pages of the Bible.

My attention shifted when I noticed a crowd of men, pushing, trying to get past my father. One of the men was Jihan's father." Anna blew out a noisy breath. "And, to this day I have not forgotten the leathery face of that particular man. He was shouting with such intensity that the creases in his face were accentuated by his anger. He was calling for his daughter to depart the nest of non-believers and accept her fate as ordained by Allah. The men of Jihan's family were seeking vengeance on the poor girl, threatening to throw her into a well. They claimed Jihan had been caught in a compromising position with a male cousin. And, they meant to kill her. "Honor killings," they called them. The murder of females in order to restore family honor. Well! Thank God Father had lived in Palestine long enough to know that in the mind of an Arab man, a compromising position might mean nothing more than a harmless conversation. So he protected Jihan.

Jihan's father finally left, but not before shouting to his daughter that in his eyes, she was dead. Jihan was forbidden to return to her father's tribe."

Anna took a swallow of cold coffee before continuing.

Demetrius saw that Anna's hands were trembling. He was mesmerized by the story, and he found himself hoping that Jihan's father had not returned and maimed his own daughter.

Anna wiped her upper lip with a tissue. "Well, from that time, Jihan lived with our family." She looked at Demetrius, greatly agitated. "Then an incident occurred which brought about Jihan's blindness. And I was to blame."

Demetrius leaned forward, resting his elbows on the table.

"A few months later I was playing a silly game with an Arab girlfriend, a game I called "Jihan." I designated my small friend as Jihan while I re-enacted the part of Jihan's father coming to punish his daughter. Without understanding the possible damaging effect of my words, I shouted that Jihan had sinned and that a righteous God insisted upon retribution." Anna affirmed gravely, "Don't forget, I was raised in a devoutly Christian home. Everything had to do with God. Anyway, I told my young actress friend that her sin would be punishment on earth, or everlasting burning fire in hell! I was so realistic that my small friend cringed in fear and rushed past me to hide in the house."

Anna stirred anxiously. "I truly did not know Jihan was napping close by underneath a tree. She made her presence known with cries of terror at my harsh words. Nothing I could say or do would comfort Jihan, who was now convinced she was going to burn in hell.

I barely noticed Jihan again until the following Sunday church service. Father was especially passionate that day when he read the words, "If thy right eye offend thee, pluck it out, and cast if from thee, for it is profitable for thee that one of thy members should perish, and not that thy whole body should be cast into hell." Many Arabs in the congregation wept with terror, Jihan among them."

Demetrius knew instantly what Anna was going to tell him. He crossed himself devoutly.

Anna shook her head in sorrow. "I should have remembered the earlier incident!"

Demetrius quietly reminded her, "You were only a child."

Anna smiled weakly. "After the service, none of us noticed Jihan's absence from the noon-day meal. Later that afternoon I slipped from the house and went into the storage building to look for a box of toys mother had received from a church in England. The toys had been sent for mother to give to the children of the poor. I wanted one certain toy and thought if I took it from the box, no one would notice.

As I walked toward the building, I was surprised to hear a strange whimpering noise coming from inside. After listening for a moment, I decided the noise must be from an injured animal." She paused before explaining, "In those days it was not uncommon for Arabs to bring their old or wounded beasts to empty areas of the city and leave them to starve. My sisters and I sometimes saved the poor beasts. So I cautiously searched throughout the darkened building hoping to find the animal. I discovered Jihan instead. I was momentarily relieved, but I quickly realized that Jihan was terribly upset. And, I saw that she was holding something behind her back."

A small shiver ran the length of Anna's body. "I demanded that Jihan show me what was in her hands. She didn't say a word. When I moved toward her, Jihan jabbed first at one eye and then the other. She had sharpened a stick!"

The image was appalling. Demetrius cringed. "Great God!"

"Neither eye could be saved. Father blamed himself for the tragedy, repeating over and over that he should have recognized Jihan was unstable and susceptible to religious fervor. Father stated many times that if he had learned nothing else during his thirty years in Jerusalem, he knew that Arabs take everything literally."

Anna suddenly remembered that her guest was an Arab. "Oh, forgive me, Demetrius."

Demetrius gave her a quick smile. He acknowledged, "Don't worry. What you are saying is true." He smiled even broader. "Every Arab I have ever known does take each word spoken, literally."

Anna patted his hand before continuing with her story. "None of us ever recovered from the incident, but over time, Jihan grew into her blindness. I tell you Demetrius, it was as if Jihan's blindness freed her.

No longer shy, she began to sing Bedouin folk songs. She even performed a few times. She exchanged gossip with the other women. Jihan began to have special affection for young children and became a favorite babysitter for mother's friends." Anna was very quiet before she said, "Jihan was absolutely wonderful with children."

"How horrible for you," said Demetrius, looking kindly at Anna.

"Yes. Jihan's presence never lets the painful memory fade. Yet, I am responsible for her well-being and could never send her away."

After sitting quietly for a few minutes, Demetrius felt there was nothing more to say. Remembering the former evening's business, Demetrius changed the subject. "I hope Jordan's mother is feeling better."

Anna brought out her words with an effort. "I fear not. To be told that dogs ripped her child to pieces! That image will haunt Ester every remaining minute of her life."

Remembering Jordan's pregnancy, Demetrius said, "I cannot fathom the pain of losing a child."

"And, what if you lost two babies?" Anna said.

Demetrius remembered. "That's right. Jordan told me that an older brother died, also."

Anna's lips tightened as she selected a roll from the pastry tray.

"How unlucky," Demetrius murmured.

Anna could just bring herself to say, "Yes." She remained quiet for so long Demetrius realized she was finding it difficult to continue. "And Rachel Gale blames me."

"You?"

Anna stared at Demetrius, her face white with grief. "If Jordan never told you the details, don't blame her. She knows little of the incident, other than that an older brother died years before she was born. The subject is absolutely forbidden."

Anxious to understand why his host was blamed for the death of Jordan's brother, Demetrius touched Anna's arm, "Would you tell me, please," he asked.

Anna felt a twinge of regret in her heart for raising the topic. She gazed pleadingly into Demetrius' eyes. "Please understand. You must not discuss this matter with anyone in the Gale family. This news about baby Miryam has broken all their hearts." After reflecting a moment, Anna added, "They don't need a reminder of baby Daniel."

"Daniel." Demetrius repeated softly.

Anna's voice grew flat. "The boy was going to be named Daniel after one of Ester's brothers. Six days after he was born and two days before the Brit Ceremony when he would have been circumcised and named, they lost him."

Demetrius urged Anna to continue. "Was it a childhood disease?"

Anna was momentarily confused, forgetting for a moment that Jordan would have told only what she knew. She waved one hand at Demetrius, wanting to drop the subject. Anna was plainly upset. The features of her face became distorted as she said, "What do the details matter? The baby was lost, that's all."

The thought flashed through Demetrius' mind that he was being terribly rude. "I am very sorry. Please forgive me." He would question Jordan some other time. He started to stand. "I must check on Jordan." He smiled reassuringly at Anna. "Do not worry, nothing of what you have confided will ever be told."

"Thank you for that." She paused, then insisted, "You must have a decent cup of coffee before you leave."

Demetrius refused. "No, thank you. I will have coffee with Jordan. And if Jordan's mother is feeling better, I will ask Jordan to take me to the neighborhood where my father's brother once lived. I wish to see that place."

Anna's flagging spirits lifted slightly. "And, where was that?" she asked.

"I don't know the exact street address yet. I will ask around in the neighborhood. But my uncle lived in the Musrara area."

Anna gazed at him awkwardly. "Musrara? Your family lived there?"

"Yes. My father's brother. He was killed in 1948." Demetrius squinted before looking away from Anna's face. "There was a bombing at the Jaffa Gate. My father lost both brothers and his only sister in the explosion."

Anna gave Demetrius a very odd look.

Mildly curious, Demetrius inquired, "Why do you ask?"

Anna was evidently stirred up with emotion. "Please don't take Jordan there," she said uneasily. "And don't raise the subject of the Musrara neighborhood with the Gales."

"Why do you say that?"

Anna remained motionless for a full minute, deep in thought. Finally she raised her head and told Demetrius, "All right. I'll tell you. Musrara is the neighborhood Joseph and Ester first lived in when they came to Palestine. It was there that baby Daniel was taken."

Demetrius began to listen incredulously. "The baby was *taken?* he asked. "From their home in Musrara?"

Close to tears, Anna nodded.

Demetrius surprised her when he clutched at her arms and spoke in a horrified whisper. "You *must* tell me, *everything!*"

Anna winced, but her words came rapidly, "I told you already. The baby was taken. And I was blamed by Rachel."

"Why were you blamed?"

"I wanted to help. That's all. I pressed Ester to allow Jihan into her home. Jihan was wonderful with babies. Ester was weak, not yet fully recovered from the war years. With two small sons she needed help to care for them. Rachel was so difficult and Ester was unwilling to stand up to her sister-in-law..." Anna paused, then raised her voice. "I was only trying to help, but don't you understand? If only I had not pressed Jihan upon Ester! Don't you understand?" Placing her head in her hands, Anna's voice cracked. "Little Michel was suffering from a bad cough, and Ester had taken him to the doctor, leaving Jihan sitting on the terrace with the baby. The sniping had stopped and Ester felt safe leaving Jihan with Daniel. Jihan left the baby alone for a moment, only a moment. Someone must have been watching and waiting. But how could a blind maid see an intruder? Jihan placed little Daniel in his crib while she went inside for his bottle. When Jihan returned, someone had stolen the baby from his crib!"

Anna looked into Demetrius' face. "The mystery of what happened to that baby has haunted us all, for every moment we have lived since that day. With war in the air, Jerusalem was in chaos, yet every available man and woman searched every inch of this city. There was never a trace of that baby. It was as though he disappeared into thin air." She shook her head slowly. "Ester Gale nearly died from grief."

Demetrius had turned ghostly white. He could hear nothing but his dying father's words. "Son, your Pa hid behind the bushes, waiting. Some time passed. Then the woman put the baby in a small crib and went inside. Son, I grabbed that baby and I ran."

The implications of what he had learned caused Demetrius to stagger backwards.

Anna quieted, staring intently at Demetrius. She saw something in Demetrius' eyes that had not been there before. He had the anguished look of a trapped and wounded animal.

Just as Anna stood to reach for Demetrius, loud shrieks came from within the villa. Tarek came from the stairwell toward Anna. "Mistress! Jihan is having a fit."

Anna hesitated, looking from Tarek to Demetrius and back again.

Tarek waved his arms in the air, calling out, "She is foaming like a mad dog!"

Torn between leaving and staying, Anna continued to look at Tarek and then back at Demetrius.

Demetrius stood looking at her with a frightened, fixed stare.

Tarek called to her again. "You must come! Quickly!"

"Demetrius!" Anna exclaimed, "wait here! I'll return shortly!"

Demetrius did not response. He was too horrified to speak.

Chapter XXV

Resolution

All conversation stopped instantly when Anna rushed breathlessly into the Gale home. Her eyes anxiously searched the room, "Is Demetrius here?" Anna asked loudly.

There was a general exchange of puzzled looks before a perplexed Jordan answered. "No, Anna. Didn't Demetrius stay the night in your home?"

Anna's voice was shrill. "Yes! Of course he did! And we shared morning coffee. Then there was a small emergency with Jihan, and I had to leave Demetrius for a short time. When I returned, Demetrius was gone!" She paused. "And he took his belongings with him." Anna briefly closed her eyes and took a deep breath. "I prayed he was here."

"He's an adult, Anna," Rachel snapped, "don't get so excited."

"He probably went for a walk," Joseph suggested.

Jordan didn't agree. "With his suitcase?"

Michel listened with narrowed eyes and compressed lips. He said nothing, although his thoughts were racing. What mischief was Demetrius Antoun up to? Was he a terrorist? Had he used Jordan to gain entry into Israel? Michel had never trusted the Arab.

"Did you look everywhere?" Christine asked. "In the villa? On the grounds?"

"Yes, of course!" Anna said stridently. "We searched every possible place. When we couldn't find him, I immediately came here."

Worried, Jordan looked at her father and stammered, "It's not like Demetrius to walk away like this."

Joseph turned to Anna. "Did he appear upset?" Although he had lived in Israel for nearly forty years, Joseph would never understand the mind of an Arab. Just the week before, an elderly Arab merchant in the old city Souq had taunted Ester, telling her he wished the Jews would return to Germany so that the Germans could complete their divine mission. Had the previous night's dis-cord between Germans and Jews affected Demetrius in some strange manner?

Anna seemed lost in thought and didn't respond.

Jordan repeated her father's question. "Well? Was Demetrius upset about anything, Anna?"

"He was rather emotional, Jordan," Anna finally said. She looked troubled. Knowing the mention of baby Daniel would further agitate the Gale household, Anna did not confess the subject of her conversation with Demetrius. Instead she said, "And, truly, I don't understand why our conversation upset Demetrius so, since the matter had nothing to do with him." Anna wanted to add more but stopped herself.

Jordan's frightened eyes rested on Anna's face. Just as Jordan opened her mouth to ask Anna to repeat the exact exchange between her and Demetrius, Michel impatiently interrupted. "Jordan, for God's sake! Don't you see? Your Arab lover has intentionally disappeared!"

"Michel, what are you talking about?" Jordan asked, perplexed.

The overpowering loathing Michel felt for Jordan's lover burst forth. "Demetrius Antoun got what he wanted, and then he vanished." Michel punctuated his remark with an unpleasant smile.

Jordan visibly shuddered. Still trembling, her voice almost failing, she murmured, "Don't say such a mean thing, Michel. It's not true. Demetrius would never do such a thing." She moved her hands in a gesture of bewilderment, and her voice was filled with fear. "Papa, this makes no sense. I know something has happened to Demetrius."

Deep in thought, Christine's brow was wrinkled. Christine believed she understood Demetrius better than anyone, and she suspected that his sudden disappearance had something to do with George Antoun and the secret of Demetrius' birth. Christine asked herself whether, once in Israel, Demetrius may have discovered he was unable to face his Jewish past. Perhaps he had fled across the border and into Lebanon.

Crouched on the edge of her seat, Rachel looked from Anna to Jordan to Joseph and then back to Anna. Rachel remained uncharacteristically quiet, not interfering in the crisis, but she grasped that something very strange was happening and listened carefully.

Increasingly agitated, Jordan turned imploringly to her father. "Papa, we must search for him! Please believe me! Demetrius would never leave without an explanation. Something is wrong!"

Looking at Jordan's anguished face, Christine stared in surprise, realizing for the first time that Jordan knew nothing of George Antoun's deathbed confession. Christine stirred uneasily.

Michel was choking with anger, disgusted and indignant. "What a little fool you are, Jordan," he sputtered. "Don't you see? Your Arab used you only long enough to gain entry into Israel, nothing more."

Jordan had heard quite enough from her brother! Her fear and confusion turned into anger. Her green eyes sparking in fury, she turned quickly toward her brother. "Take that back, Michel! I mean it!"

Michel was glad the Arab was out of their lives and wanted him gone forever. He thought Jordan should see the man for what he was. "The man's a user, Jordan," Michel snarled. "He took advantage of his relationship with Christine to obtain a visa for America and then he used you to enter Israel!"

A shocked Christine protested. "Michel! Where did you get such an idea? That's simply not true." The Demetrius Antoun Christine knew was too honorable for such a scheme. She pulled lightly on his arm. "Michel, believe me when I say you are wrong about Demetrius."

For the first time since they met, Michel glared at the woman he loved. "If you believe otherwise, Christine, then you're as big a fool as my sister." Michel was acutely conscious of the fact that his own sister, along with the woman he intended to marry, were blinded by affection for a man Michel was beginning to hate bitterly.

Jordan's heart was throbbing so violently she could not speak. Something dreadful had happened to Demetrius and instead of helping her, Michel was so filled with hate for Arabs that he was attacking an innocent man. Her brother knew nothing of the truth, yet had anointed himself accuser and judge.

Michel was overcome by a tormenting need to make Jordan and Christine see Demetrius Antoun for what he really was. "Who cares if he is gone?" Michel muttered, sneering, "He's nothing but a filthy Arab!"

"Michel!" Anna shouted.

Infuriated by her brother's words, Jordan lost her composure. Her face contorted, she rushed at her brother, and uttering little screams, she began pounding on Michel's chest with both fists.

Michel remained motionless for several seconds, then seized Jordan's hands, roughly pushing her away.

For a horrifying minute Christine thought the pair were going to exchange blows! She jumped to her feet. "Michel!" she screamed. "Stop it!"

"Enough!" Joseph shouted, shoving his son backward with one hand while lifting Jordan off her feet with his other. Joseph pulled his daughter across the room and away from her brother.

Although they had not fought physically since childhood, Michel looked fierce and defiant, as though he might strike Jordan.

Rachel pulled her nephew's ear. "Michel! Shame!" she shouted.

Her hands over her mouth, a dismayed Anna watched the drama unfold. Everyone's emotions were clearly out of control! She dreaded reintroducing the topic of her conversation with Demetrius, but knew she had to tell something of what they had discussed. With that information, perhaps someone present could resolve the mystery of Demetrius' disappearance. Anna simply didn't know how to word the incident without casting the memory of baby Daniel into motion all over again.

Jordan was crying in terrible agony. "Papa! We have to find him! Please, Papa!"

"What is going on?" cried Ester Gale, who, after hearing the commotion had rushed straight from her bed.

Sobbing bitterly, Jordan flung herself into her mother's arms. "Mother! Demetrius has disappeared!"

Ester loved her two surviving children with the intensity of a woman who had lost two babies in monstrous, unspeakable circumstances. Nothing aroused Ester's temper more than seeing Jordan or Michel hurt in any way. Although Ester had not been pleased to learn that her son was planning to marry the child of a Nazi, or that her daughter was dating an Arab, she would never forbid her children what they claimed brought them happiness. Ester laboriously examined Jordan's face. "Daughter, stop crying," she said gently. "Tell me what has happened to your young man?"

Jordan couldn't speak for sobbing.

After tenderly wrapping her arms around Jordan and settling her on the sofa, Ester quieted Jordan's cries, then looked indignantly around the room. "Will someone please tell me what is going on with my child?"

Joseph quickly spoke. "Anna was about to tell us, darling." He looked toward Anna. "Now, Anna, please continue. What was it that so upset Demetrius?"

Jordan's sagging frame shifted upright.

Everyone turned to Anna, completely attentive.

Anna sighed heavily. "Of course, I'll tell you what I know," Anna agreed, while seating herself close to Ester and Jordan. With an indescribable mix of emotions, Anna told about the morning's incident regarding Jihan. She reluctantly mentioned Demetrius' plans to visit his dead uncle's home. Gloom overshadowed Anna's face when she said, "I told Demetrius not to take Jordan to the Musrara area. Then he inquired, wanting to know my reason." She glanced at Joseph. "I am sorry, but I had to tell him something of your lost son. I told Demetrius about the mystery of Daniel. That your baby was stolen from your home, and was never found." Anna grimaced. "Demetrius became overwrought about your lost son. I admit, Joseph, I am completely baffled by his behavior."

Rachel was extraordinarily moved by the memories Anna's story evoked, but she tried to keep her mind on the matter at hand. "Is Demetrius an overly emotional man?" Rachel asked her niece. Most Arabs keenly felt another person's pain and were quick to weep, but that tendency alone didn't explain the level of the young man's reaction to a sad story. After all, Demetrius Antoun was a doctor and was surely accustomed to all sorts of tragedies.

"Well, yes." Jordan murmured. "Demetrius is very tender-hearted, but not to such an extreme." Jordan's lower lip began to tremble and she was near tears once again. She looked at her mother, confused. This was the first Jordan had heard of a kidnapped brother! "I just don't understand! I thought baby Daniel *died.* He was *stolen?"*

Ester patted Jordan's hand. "Later. I will tell you later, darling. Just know your father and I were unable to fully discuss the tragedy." Jordan nodded then laid her head on her mother's shoulder and began to sniffle.

Though Anna's words reawakened the memory of their lost son, neither Joseph nor Ester gave any indication of their feelings. They, too, were perplexed by Demetrius' reaction to their infant son's disappearance. The couple exchanged a brief but mystified glance.

Knowing his father would rebuke him harshly if he spoke another word, Michel folded his arms and said nothing.

Trying to analyze what she had just heard, Christine shivered. The impact of Anna's words began building. Unable to prevent her thoughts from escaping, Christine became the center of attention when she clutched her head and began to mutter, "Oh my God! Oh my God!"

Joseph was the first to speak. "What?"

Jordan straightened her back and stared. "Do you know something about this, Christine?" Jordan asked accusingly.

Still holding her head in her hands, Christine looked around at her listeners. "Oh my God!"

Jordan felt the blood pumping through her heart.

"Oh my God, Michel!" Christine said, trembling. "Demetrius has learned who he really is!"

All the Gales, as well as Anna, were overcome with confusion.

Joseph tried to calm her. "Dear girl, get a grip on yourself and tell us what you are talking about."

Christine was shaking all over. She looked around in bewilderment. "Oh God! This can't be true!"

Michel pulled Christine close to him and gave her a little shake. "Christine, you are not making any sense! Now! Tell us what you are talking about!"

Christine swallowed hard before addressing Joseph Gale. "Did you have a baby boy stolen in 1948?"

Fighting his emotions, Joseph made his voice firm. "Yes, Christine. You heard what Anna said."

"Was this baby less than a week old?"

Joseph slightly nodded, his confusion growing.

"And was he stolen only a few days after the Jaffa Gate explosion?"

Joseph gasped and drew back. "How did you know that?"

Christine's words cut through the room. "Was there a woman with this baby, a woman who was singing?"

When Joseph didn't answer, Ester shouted, "Yes!"

"And did this woman place the baby into a crib and leave him alone on a small terrace?"

Anna answered in a whisper, "Jihan."

Joseph stood rigid and open-mouthed, knowing what he was about to hear, yet still disbelieving.

Michel was utterly disorientated. How was it that Christine knew *everything* about his family?

Ester was leaning forward.

Sitting with her mouth open, Rachel was breathing heavily.

Wild with impatience, Jordan urged Christine to tell them more.

"What has this got to do with Demetrius, Christine?"

Christine now knew for certain that Demetrius was Joseph and Ester Gale's lost son. She could tell from the trapped expression in Joseph's eyes that he too understood. Christine gently placed her hand on Joseph's shoulder and spoke without raising her voice. "I will tell you what I know. Although raised by Palestinian Arabs, Demetrius Antoun was born to Jewish parents."

Jordan gasped loudly.

After a short pause, Christine continued. "I was present when George Antoun, Demetrius' Arab father, confessed on his deathbed in Shatila that Demetrius was stolen from a Jewish home in Jerusalem. This happened the same week as the Jaffa Gate bombing. George came to Jerusalem to bury two brothers and one sister who were killed in that bombing. One of his brothers lived in the Musrara area. When George tried to go to that place, he was attacked by a Jewish gang. Overcome with grief, angry at the political situation in Palestine, and hating all Jews, George temporarily lost his mind and stole a Jewish baby, a male child, who was only a few days old. He took that baby and fled to Haifa. When the Antouns were forced to run to Lebanon, they took the child there and raised him as their own son. They had no other children." Tears trickled down Christine's cheeks as she looked first at Joseph and then at Ester. "This morning, Demetrius made the discovery that he is your lost son." Her voice became very low. "And that is why Demetrius has run away."

"Shut up! Shut up! Shut up!" Jordan broke away from her mother and ran to her father. "It's not true, it's not true! Tell me its not true, Papa!"

A multitude of thoughts were rushing into Joseph's mind. He was recalling the tension-filled but joyful day so long ago when their second son had been born. He clearly remembered Ari's visit and the news of the terrorists bombing that had taken Arab life. He found himself reliving those moments of fear that Jerusalem's Jews would pay dearly for the Irgun gang's irrational act. He sighed noisily. It was now certain that he and Ester had paid the ultimate price for the Jaffa Gate bombing. They had lost a precious son. He glanced at Michel. Arab revenge had robbed them all. Michel had lost a brother...Rachel a nephew...But worst of all, baby Daniel had been robbed of his family and his heritage...an innocent Jewish baby, raised to believe he was an Arab.

Joseph slowly turned to look at his wife. Ester was sitting with both hands clasped to her bosom. She was staring sorrowfully at her husband. Ester had always believed her infant son was kidnapped to be murdered. Was the male child born to her thirty-five years before truly alive? Had baby Daniel been raised by Arabs? Was her son now within her reach?

Michel stood up, his mind in turmoil. A long-forgotten memory stirred...the sounds of a crying baby that had come and gone too quickly. Suddenly the clear vision of an empty crib and distraught adults came to him. He said pensively, his voice almost childlike, "Someone stole the baby?"

Ester jerked backward and stared up at Michel. Those were the exact words a young Michel had spoken on that day so long ago when Joseph had informed Michel that his baby brother was gone.

Anna was looking toward Michel but didn't see him. She was recalling the words spoken earlier in the day by Jihan just before the medication took effect, words that Anna thought were the rantings of a woman losing her mind. Anna muttered aloud, "Jihan told me Demetrius was Daniel. She kept repeating, the baby is alive...the baby has returned. The mystery of baby Daniel is solved!" Anna spoke in wonderment. "The other servants have always claimed that Jihan has psychic powers. I never believed them, before now." She turned toward Joseph Gale, "For certain, Joseph, somehow Jihan recognized him...somehow she knew Demetrius was baby Daniel." Anna shook her head vigorously, as though attempting to clear her thoughts. She looked at Ester and whispered, "Dear God! Jihan was right!"

Ester nodded, then holding out her hand she beckoned to her husband, her voice oddly calm. "Joseph, watch your daughter. She's about to faint."

Jordan's eyes were rolling back into her head.

Joseph and Michel reached for Jordan at the same time. Michel placed her on the sofa and briskly patted her cheeks with his hands. "Jordan!"

Christine ran into the kitchen to get a cold cloth.

With tears streaming down their faces, Anna and Rachel held tightly to each other. The last twenty-four hours had been unbelievably hard for both women.

When Jordan opened her eyes, she mumbled, "Mommy! This can't be true."

Ester knelt beside her. "Shhhh, darling." Ester scrutinized Jordan attentively. She had never seen such an expression on any human face. Her daughter was utterly incapacitated by pain.

Jordan sobbed quietly. "Mommy, you don't understand. You can't understand. We are in love." Her voice cracked. "Mommy, I'm going to have Demetrius' child."

With her hands resting lightly on her daughter's face, Ester stared up at her husband. "Did you hear that, Joseph? Our daughter is going to have a baby."

Joseph knelt beside Ester and took his daughter's hands into his hands. "It's going to be all right, sweetheart."

A terrible expression passed over Jordan's face as she cried out, "Demetrius doesn't know I am adopted! He has run away and now we'll never find him!"

"Hush…hush… No, no, don't worry. Your father will find him."

"We have to find Demetrius…we have to find him! Demetrius must believe I am his blood sister!"

Joseph agreed. "Yes. The boy must be in a terrible state."

Michel was staring uncertainly toward his father. "Do you believe Demetrius Antoun is your son?"

Joseph spoke in an unnatural sounding voice. "Yes, Michel. As unbelievable as this sounds, I feel that Demetrius Antoun is my son." Without taking his eyes off his eldest child, Joseph paused before adding, "And, Michel, Demetrius is your brother."

Michel was in a terrible emotional ferment and his face was twitching, but he spoke with a calm voice. "If that is what you believe, then I'll find him. I'll ask everyone in my unit to help if I have to. One way or another, I'll find him."

Joseph stood up and seized his son's arm, and looking at him with his wide gray eyes, said, "Yes, Michel, go and find him."

Ester stood, staring at Joseph, hope flickering in her eyes. "Can it be true, Joseph?"

Jordan raised herself on her elbows before putting her feet to the floor and standing. Ester took her hand and together the two women gathered around Joseph and Michel.

Jordan wrapped her arms around Michel's neck. "Please, find him, Michel, please," she pleaded softly. "I can't bear to live if you don't."

The shock of the news that her long lost son was now found caused Ester to cling tightly to her husband. With glittering eyes, Ester looked past her husband's broad shoulders into her son's face. "Find your brother, Michel. Find your brother and bring him home," she said.

Michel Gale never even noticed his own tears.

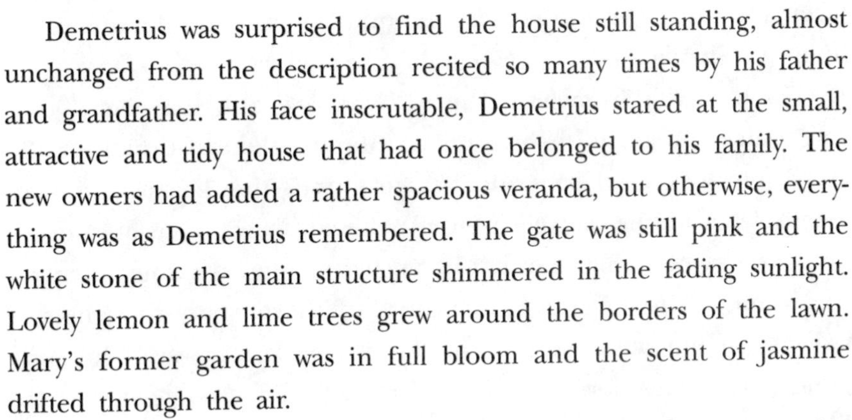

Demetrius was surprised to find the house still standing, almost unchanged from the description recited so many times by his father and grandfather. His face inscrutable, Demetrius stared at the small, attractive and tidy house that had once belonged to his family. The new owners had added a rather spacious veranda, but otherwise, everything was as Demetrius remembered. The gate was still pink and the white stone of the main structure shimmered in the fading sunlight. Lovely lemon and lime trees grew around the borders of the lawn. Mary's former garden was in full bloom and the scent of jasmine drifted through the air.

Demetrius' fingers caressed the large house key in his pants pocket as he mentally conjured up in his mind the interior of the house. George's study was on the left side of the hall entry and the family room was to the right. His parent's bedroom was adjacent to the study and Grandpa's small room was situated between the kitchen and back entry. Demetrius clasped the key tightly between his fingers, wondering if the key would still unlock the door. He almost smiled as he thought about the new occupants of his father's home and how they might react if he sauntered in like an invited guest.

Demetrius' thoughts were born of desperation. After discovering he was the lost son of Joseph and Ester Gale, and most painfully, the brother of Jordan, Demetrius had been a man consumed by the blackest despair. With no thought of where to go or what to do, he had aimlessly walked the streets of Jerusalem, alternating between cursing God and accusing God of coordinating dreadful catastrophes from the moment he gave him life. Knowing he must leave Jerusalem, that he could not face Jordan with the information he now possessed, Demetrius took a taxi to the train station and purchased a ticket for the next train leaving the city. As if by fate, the train was bound for Haifa. When the shock of the train's destination eased, he became exhilarated by the idea that he was traveling to the city of his Arab parents. Once settled onboard the train, Demetrius searched through his suitcase and retrieved the treasured land deed and door key to the Antoun home in Haifa. He was now grateful that he had taken the time to retrieve these important items from his destroyed home in Shatila.

The train ride from Jerusalem to Haifa was torturously slow, but it gave Demetrius ample time to reflect. More frightened than he could ever remember, Demetrius admitted to himself that he was tired and weary of the life he had been given. With this latest piece of information, he was now truly a man without a family or a country. Tears of fury came to his eyes and he suffered a short, angry thought that George Antoun was to blame for this dilemma. Because of his Arab father, everything normal had been denied him. George had raised him as an Arab, and then destroyed any possibility of him living an Arab life by disclosing the truth of his birth. George's deathbed confession had set the stage for two irreconcilable opponents, an Arab and a

Jew, to possess the soul of his stolen son.

Demetrius sat quietly, thinking about his Arab father. Remembering the good and kind man who had raised him, Demetrius' anger was short-lived. He reminded himself not to condemn his father, but instead to place the responsibility for his predicament on the violence and insanity which swept up an entire country. That madness created a fatal chain of circumstances which drove a frightened and enraged man beyond the limits of civilized behavior. By taking a child who belonged to another, George committed a terrible crime which had haunted him throughout the remainder of his life. But, if he valued his freedom and the welfare of his wife and father, once he had kidnapped the Jewish infant, there was no turning back.

Demetrius decided not to indict George Antoun.

His thoughts turned to Jordan. Demetrius wilted anew in despair. Dreading the horror and loneliness which he knew would begin the moment he accepted reality, Demetrius fought to regain control of his emotions. He knew he must forever close his mind and heart to the love he had shared with Jordan. For now, any thought of their ill-fated relationship was intolerable. He could not allow himself to even daydream about Jordan without becoming uncontrollably agitated.

Smoking one cigarette after another, he stared out the window at the changing and picturesque views of the rocky hills of Jerusalem and the green valleys of the countryside. He saw Arab Bedouin herders tending their flocks and in his mind he contrasted the sight with the modern buildings in Israel's cities. The drastic changes a group of determined European Jews had brought to the ancient land were marvels to be noted.

When the conductor announced the train was pulling into Gallim, Haifa's central railway station, Demetrius' eyes flashed with excitement. He had finally arrived in the beloved city of his Arab parents, George and Mary Antoun.

From his first glance, memories of Beirut were rekindled. The city of Haifa bore an uncanny physical resemblance to the Lebanese capital. Haifa was etched into the wooded mountainside of Mount Carmel.

Homes and businesses clung from the top of Mount Carmel all the way down to the Mediterranean Sea. From what he could see, the beaches appeared to be white and sandy.

When Demetrius gave the taxi driver the name of his father's neighborhood, the old man responded in a rush of words worthy of a tour guide that Haifa was built on three levels and that the neighborhood of his destination was called Hadar Hacarmel. It was located in Haifa's midtown district. If the taxi driver was surprised later that his passenger wanted to exit at a small park directly in front of the address given, he gave no indication of his feelings.

For three hours, Demetrius sat in the park and studied the home he felt was still a part of his life. Not wanting to frighten the women and children sitting in the garden, Demetrius patiently waited for the man of the house to return.

Late in the afternoon, a middle-aged Jewish man entered the front door of the house without knocking. Never considering the possible consequences, Demetrius lifted his bag and walked away from the park, across the street, through the gate and to the front door of the house. With feverish expectation, Demetrius looked around. What he saw felt so familiar that his spirits began to brighten. After setting his bag on the cobbled walkway, Demetrius took the door key in his hand, and lightly knocked on the front door.

A small boy about five-years-old answered the knock.

Demetrius nervously smiled. "Is your father home?"

The child squirmed, then turned and ran, shouting, "Papa, there's a man to see you." The boy left the door standing open.

Although burning with curiosity to take a quick look inside the house, Demetrius stood quietly, taking deep breaths to strengthen his courage. He desperately longed for a friendly face.

A small thin man with a haggard appearance walked down the short hallway toward Demetrius. Standing apart at some distance, he stared at the visitor coldly and calmly. "Yes?" He asked, "What do you want?"

Demetrius smiled hopefully and declared, "My parents once lived here. I wondered if I could come inside and see their home." Wanting to prove who he was, Demetrius held out the house key, swinging the key by the worn black velvet ribbon. "Here is the key." He fumbled in his shirt pocket. "And I have the deed."

Not expecting such a request, the man was momentarily confused and uncertain. He gazed intently at Demetrius without speaking. What was the Arab's motive? Did he believe he could reclaim his father's house?

Desperately wanting to see the study where his father had worked, and the rose garden his mother had tended, Demetrius tried to put the man at ease, "Sir, please know that I do not harbor dishonorable intentions. My parents recently died," he stammered. "I desire nothing more than to see inside the home where they lived and to walk in the garden my mother cherished."

The man's complexion had paled, but he did make a slight movement with his head which Demetrius interpreted as a positive sign.

Encouraged, Demetrius continued. "George and Mary Antoun lived in this house. The family left Haifa in 1948 when I was an infant. My parents spoke about their family home many times." Demetrius edged forward. "May I come in, please? For only a few moments?"

The Jewish owner made a hesitant movement with his hands. For a short minute, he considered permitting the Arab to enter. The man was neatly dressed and behaved in a courteous manner. Suddenly reminding himself not to be foolish, that the man could be a terrorist, his positive reaction alternated. He lurched forward to close the door before the Arab could enter. "Leave now, or I'll call the police!" he threatened.

The door closed, making a loud cracking noise.

Demetrius blinked in surprise. Completely deflated, he stood with the key dangling from his hand. He thought of knocking once again, but then he overheard the sounds of several excited voices. A woman peeked from a front window and screamed, "He's still here!" The voices grew ever more alarmed. He heard a woman shouting into a telephone for the police, "Come! Quickly!" she said. "A large man, an

Arab, is trying to break into our home!"

Realizing he was nothing more than an intruder in his father's home, Demetrius carefully placed the large key over the handle of the door, picked up his bag, and slowly walked away.

Epilogue

Tuesday June 10, 1983

Dearest Jordan:

Is there a more incomparable drama in the records of mankind than the Jewish baby stolen and raised in Arab lands? Believing himself Arab, living for the defeat of his hated Jewish enemy, only to make the momentous discovery he is in fact what he has hated most? I believe not...

Please apologize to Anna for my unexplained departure. She must have thought Demetrius Antoun a most uncivilized guest. How could the poor woman have known that her tragic tale of the unsolved mystery of Daniel Gale wielded thunder and lightning in my soul?

Jordan, many were the times I yearned to share my oppressive secret. I rolled the words over in my brain and practiced them on my tongue, but time after time, a thousand terrors limited my will. Fearing my story would not seem credible and would win me nothing but your hatred, I succumbed to temptation and postponed the tortuous subject. As a last resort, I promised myself I would confide the damnable secret while in Israel, after our wedding, but thanks be to God, fate intervened and saved us from a most disastrous marriage.

Jordan, this is the most difficult sentence I have ever written. You must abort our child. Quickly!

I wish I could leave you with the magic of consoling words, but all I can think is this, I would give my own life for one more moment with you if only we were not who we are.

And now, goodbye...goodbye... And, never forget I

Overwrought, Demetrius quickly put his pen down, unable to finish writing. For a long moment he stared at the tightly drawn drapes covering the full-length windows of his suite in the American Colony Hotel in East Jerusalem. He listened for a moment without breathing. The distant sound of an automobile faintly penetrated the room. Yet he sensed the presence of a person close by. He listened again. He began to wonder if he had become hypersensitive. Since checking into the hotel the night before, he had spent his time drinking coffee, smoking cigarettes, and thinking. He lifted the half-empty coffee cup for another small swallow, then lightly placed the cup on the copper serving tray.

His imagination was out of control, he told himself. Clamping his teeth together, he pressed his fingers against his eyelids, losing himself in thought. Tomorrow he would cross the Allenby Bridge and travel to Jordan. From Jordan he would make his way into Lebanon. Then he would try to travel to Tunis, to find Ahmed Fayez. His old friend Ahmed would never turn him out, especially at his moment of greatest need, no matter if Jewish blood did fill his veins.

Taking a deep uneven breath, Demetrius cupped his chin in his hands and sat staring at the words he had written, wondering how Jordan was faring. He decided she would be fine. She had her family. And perhaps the knowledge that Demetrius was a lost son of the Gales would serve as a unifying medium between her and Michel. Perhaps now Michel would see Arabs differently.

He picked up the pages of the unfinished letter and read over the words. As he read, his face sagged into a great weariness, giving him the appearance of a man who was eating himself away from the inside.

Another noise, a thump against the room door, interrupted his thoughts. This sound was real and had nothing to do with his earlier imagined fears. Demetrius slowly eased his large body up from the desk chair without making a sound. He walked quietly toward the door but stopped in surprise when he saw the door handle move slightly.

On the other side, Michel Gale turned the key which he had confiscated from the frightened hotel clerk. Opening the door, he walked into the room. He was wearing his military uniform.

"Michel!" With shock radiating throughout his body, Demetrius' jaw slackened and his mouth opened.

Michel said nothing, but his eyes burned with emotion. He had succeeded in finding his brother! Michel's army friends had painstakingly checked every hotel in Jerusalem, East and West, until they discovered that an unusually tall and powerfully built Arab was a guest at the American Colony Hotel on the Nablus Road. The men had surrounded the hotel and placed a guard at Demetrius' door until Michel arrived.

For a small imprecise moment, Demetrius wondered if Michel was there to assault him. As Demetrius braced for an attack, the unexpected happened. Michel smiled. A most wonderful warm and gentle smile. Then he quoted from the Bible. "'And you shall know the truth, and the truth shall make you free.'"

Demetrius took a long swallow. He knew the verse well, John 8:32. But what on earth was a Jew doing quoting from the New Testament?

Michel's smile grew even wider, as he explained, "Our resident Christian, Anna, told me to tell you that."

Demetrius nodded, still utterly confused.

"But, I believe you only need to hear one thing, Demetrius."

Demetrius found his voice. "And, what is that?" he croaked.

"That Jordan was adopted. She's not your blood sister."

"What did you say?"

Michel spoke rapidly. "After you were kidnapped, something happened to mother. Maybe it was physical, perhaps it was mental, but she was never able to conceive again. I was destined to be an only child. Then, Leah Jawor, a close family friend, died during childbirth. The woman had no remaining family so she bequeathed her baby to us." Thinking of his sister, Michel smiled affectionately. "Not that she did us any favor!" He paused before adding with a burst of laughter, "Jordan's birth mother was a terror, as is Jordan." He laughed. "But never mind. Jordan keeps the Gale family humble."

Demetrius' face became completely transformed. His lips trembled, and his eyes began to tear. He wanted to hear Michel's encouraging words a second time. "Then Jordan is not my sister?" he asked breathlessly.

A smile lingered on Michel's face at the sight of his newly-found brother. "No, Demetrius. She is not your sister." He paused, then smiled once again. "But I am your brother."

Demetrius was unable to speak.

With extraordinary energy, Michel lunged at Demetrius and grasped him tightly. "Now. I've come to take you home," he whispered.

Two of Michel's army friends notified the Gale family that Demetrius had been found and that very soon the two Gale boys would be home. Suggesting that the family needed privacy, Christine forced Anna and Rachel to wait with Christine and her parents inside the house. Joseph, Ester, and Jordan sat stiffly on straight-back chairs in the front garden. While Demetrius' parents and Jordan sat quietly with their eyes focused on the road, Rachel and Anna were whispering with excitement and taking turns peeking out the sitting room windows. Although they could not participate in the family reunion, they would observe. Christine sat quietly between her parents, who were quite overcome by the emotional household they were visiting.

Suddenly, the sounds of an approaching vehicle could be heard.

Ester's face was taut as she leaned forward and stared. "Is that a military vehicle?"

Joseph stood. "Yes."

Jordan tightly clasped her hands. Her heart was beating so violently she could see the collar of her blouse jump with the same rhythm as her heartbeat.

The jeep came to a quick stop. Michel stepped out of the driver's seat and walked around to the side of the vehicle. He opened the door and took his brother by the arm. The two men then stood side by side, staring at their parents and Jordan.

Jordan began walking toward the men, then running. "Demetrius!" she cried. Leaping into his arms, she buried her face in his shoulder, whispering, "Demetrius. Demetrius."

Michel stepped aside.

Too emotional to speak, Demetrius gripped Jordan, hard.

Inside, Rachel and Anna were hysterical with joy. Even Rachel was actually kissing Anna. "Without you, we would have never found the boy!" she muttered.

"It was Jihan, I swear!" Anna replied.

An excited Christine couldn't restrain herself one minute longer. Grabbing her parents by their hands, she led them to the window. Weeping, the Kleist family held each other closely as they stared at the moving reunion.

Unable to hold back for even a second, Joseph and Ester rushed forward. While stroking Demetrius' face, Ester saw her husband's eyes in her son's face. In a faltering, hoarse voice, she said, "Joseph, our son has your beautiful gray eyes."

Looking at his newfound son's smooth olive skin and sensitive face, the past came flowing back. Remembering the unvarying appearance of Ester's brothers, and at their first meeting how he had remarked that each of the Stein men looked as sensitive as a scholar, Joseph was struck by the reality that Demetrius had inherited much from uncles he was fated never to meet. He looked at Ester and smiled. "I think our son looks more like your side of the family, my darling."

It was then that Michel's tears spilled forth. Joining his family, Michel wrapped his arms around his brother, his sister, and his parents, pulling everyone into a small clustered circle, standing together, as one.

Unbidden, words of joy and celebration came to Joseph, who gazed toward the heavens and exclaimed, "Blessed are You, Lord our God, Ruler of the universe Who is good and does good."

Like a splendid dream, the Gale family of Israel stood as a symbol of what the Gale family of France and the Stein family of Poland, had once been.

The End